RUTHLESS *Desire*

EVE L. MITCHELL

Eve L. Mitchell
Ruthless Desire

www.evelmitchell.com

Editorial services provided by Helayna Trask with Polished Perfection.

Cover design provided by JJ's Design & Creations; jjsdesigncreations.wixsite.com/mysite/services-pricing

Cover Photo provided by Wander Aguiar Photography: www.wanderbookclub.com

Cover model: Ben Selleck

RUTHLESS *Desire*

For those that have lost and felt alone, you are never alone.

Note from the Author

This is a book of fiction, general landmarks, places, cities etc are referenced, but my knowledge of them is from maps, wikipedia and my imagination.

Please note that the deviations that there may be from the cities or places mentioned in this book or surrounding area are to fit in with the story.

I am a British author and although I try to make my story as universal as I can, there are British spellings, phraseology, and terminology that I refuse to eradicate from my writing. I'm perfectly okay with that. I am after all, the author ;)

Ruthless Desire

She is his past. He is her future.

Since childhood, Quinn has been surrounded by three great guys: a best friend, an ex, and the one she holds forbidden feelings for. She knows they will go to any lengths to avenge her. After all, who better to have at your side than a Devil?

But what will happen when her darkest secret is finally revealed?

For what she wants, she cannot have. What she desires, she cannot take. And what she loves, she lost the right to claim. It's too late for her battered heart, because she knows without a shadow of a doubt that Gray Santo doesn't believe in second chances.

Gray took Quinn's presence in his life for granted. After all, she's always been there. He believed she was the one girl he could always have—until she chose another. Although almost two years have passed since she walked away from him, he will do anything to help Quinn get retribution for a grievous wrong.

Tired of living in his twin brother's shadow and after being cast aside for his cousin, Gray isn't interested in coming in last place again. The days of looking back are over.

Or so he thought.

Quinn's making it impossible for him to ignore her. She needs Gray to remember he once loved her. Because this time around, the stakes are too high for him to forget.

The odds are against them, but the only way to win…is to play the game.

Three guys, three girls, one game. The Devils are back. Are you ready?

Ruthless Desire is book 2 of 3 in the Ruthless Devils Series. It* ***cannot *be read as a standalone and needs to be read after Book 1. This is a college sports romance, and may contain triggers for sensitive readers. Due to mature content, it is recommended for readers 17+ only.***

Playlist

'Someone You Loved' - *Lewis Capaldi*
'Angel' - *Theory of a Deadman*
'Undisclosed Desires' - *Muse*
'I'm On Fire' - *Chromatics*
'Stone' - *Whiskey Myers*
'Red Run Cold' - *World's First Cinema*
'In Chains' - *Shaman's Harvest*
'Skin' - *Rag'n'Bone Man*
'Say Something' - *A Great Big World, Christina Aguilera*
'Silent Voice' - *Shamen's Harvest'*
'Talking to Myself' - *Linkin Park*
'Love Me Or Leave Me' - *Three Days Grace*
'Try' - *Pink*
'Broken Pieces' - *Andy Black*
'Closer to the Edge' - *Thirty Seconds to Mars*
'Get Up' - *Shinedown*
'Something to Believe In' - *Young the Giant*
'Heroes' - *Zayde Wolf*

Honesty is a weapon
Be careful how you wield it
When you're tired of running
Stop. It's time to play the game.

EVE L. MITCHELL

Prologue

QUINN, AGE TEN

"We can't move her again; it's the middle of the school year."

Mommy was arguing with daddy again, and I closed my eyes tiredly as I listened to their raised voices. They always seemed to be angry these days. Sitting on my bed, I looked at my shoes, black patent Mary Janes, and white socks with a frilled edge. I glared at my shoes and socks. I hated socks, and these shiny black shoes were for another girl. I liked my feet bare. My feet needed to breathe. Like the rest of me.

I flinched when I heard the door bang, and a few minutes later, the sound of the car engine and then silence. Daddy was gone, no doubt returning to base. To the navy yard where he got to yell at people all day long and order them around.

I waited patiently, and then there was a soft knock on the door.

"Hey, little girl, want to go for ice cream?"

Looking up at my mommy, I nodded once. Her face looked tired, the dark circles under her eyes were getting blacker, and the sparkle in her warm chocolate brown eyes was gone. Something was wrong with my mommy. Daddy didn't see it, or if he did, he wasn't talking about it.

"Is daddy coming?" I asked as I stood and straightened my white dress.

"No, baby, he's got to work."

The two of us headed to the front door, and I reached for mommy's hand. "Are we moving again?"

I felt the soft squeeze of her hand as mommy opened the front door, letting me through it before she turned to lock it. "Yeah, baby, I think so."

"I don't like it here anyway," I said to her as I skipped to mom's car. It was true, I didn't like this base. There were hardly any girls to play with, only boys. Boys were dirty.

Mom waited until my seat belt was on before she pressed a quick kiss to my head. As she started the car, she looked at me over her shoulder. "You sure you don't mind moving, Quinn?"

"No, mommy, if we have to move, we have to move. Daddy's work's important." I grinned at her as I pulled my pigtails. "He protects us all."

My mom turned to face forward, but I saw her sad smile as we drove away from the house. "He does, my sweet girl, he does."

Quinn, age eleven

"You're a girl?"

I looked at the dark-haired boy staring at me with confusion. His hair was long, *hippie long* as daddy called it. His blue eyes stood out against his tanned, golden skin. He had skinny shoulders, but his hands were large. Glancing at his feet, I saw he had big feet too. When I was five or six, we had a dog called Buster. When he was a puppy, he had huge paws, and daddy said he would grow into them. That's what this boy reminded me of, Buster. Waiting to grow into his paws.

"You're a boy," I sassed back at him.

"Where's your brother?" he asked me as he walked towards me, looking over my shoulder as if expecting someone else.

"It's just me."

His face scrunched up, and he looked back towards the big house that sat beside ours. "But they said there was a boy…a new student."

"What's his name?" I asked as I stepped towards him. Maybe he was lost, he looked lost.

"Quinn."

"That's me," I told him with a happy smile. He wasn't lost, he was confused. People always thought my name meant I was a boy.

"But you're a girl."

Maybe he was dumb? "Well, what's your name?" I asked him impatiently.

"Jett."

I laughed. "Like the plane?"

"No. Like the colour."

"What colour?"

"Black."

"You're named after the colour black?" That was even worse than my name. He nodded. "Oh. Well, it could be worse, you could be called purple."

"Or puce."

"What's puce?" I asked him curiously.

"Pink...I think." He grinned at me, and I started to giggle.

"I think Jett suits you."

He scratched his head and looked back towards his house. "We're playing in the pool. Do you want to come?"

"I can't swim."

His eyes rounded in shock. "My brother and cousin are there; we will help keep you up." A large hand extended towards me. "Come on, I won't let them drown you."

"Are there girls?" I asked cautiously as I stepped closer to him.

"No!" Jett looked horrified. "Girls suck."

"But *I'm* a girl."

Jett looked me over before he grinned again. "Nah, you have a boy's name," he said as he grabbed my arm. "Come on, Quinn, let's teach you how to swim."

"I need a bathing suit!" I protested as he pulled me along behind him as I looked down at my shorts and T-shirt.

"You're fine."

When we got to the big house that sat back from ours, half surrounded by trees, I stared up at it as he pulled me along the fence until we were in a back courtyard with decking, chairs and a large pool. Tearing my attention from the grand house, I saw two boys playing in the water. One looked so much like Jett he had to be his brother, and the other one was bigger but looked like them too. Both stopped playing and stared at me.

"Where's her brother?" the one who looked like Jett asked.

"This is Quinn," Jett said before he jumped into the water. When he surfaced, he shook his wet hair out of his face. "She can't swim."

"Then why is she here?" the other boy asked.

"So we can teach her how to swim." Jett swam over to the end of the pool and got out. His shorts and T-shirt stuck to him, and as he looked down at his clothes, he looked back up at me and smiled. "See, you don't need a swimsuit," he told me confidently.

"I don't want to teach her to swim," the boy who looked like Jett said.

"Okay. Ash and I can do it," he told him as he walked towards me before adding, "you can sit and sulk like a girl."

I watched the boy glare at his brother as the other boy, Ash, laughed.

"You're called Ash?" I asked him. He nodded. "What's your name?" I asked the other boy.

"That's my twin, Gray," Jett told me. "I'm older."

"You all have strange names."

"They all mean dark or black," Jett said as he reached me. "Our older brother is Onyx."

"Oh, my name doesn't mean anything like that."

"How old are you?" Ash asked curiously.

"I'm eleven," I told them. I saw Ash and Gray exchange looks. "What is it?"

"Are you stupid?" Gray asked. "That why you're older but in our class?"

"No! My dad's in the navy, we move around a lot." The boys exchanged looks again, and I knew they didn't believe me. "I'm not stupid!" I almost stamped my foot in temper.

"Want to come into the water?" Jett asked me as he waited patiently.

Shaking my head, I took a step backwards. "No."

"She's stupid *and* chicken."

I glared at Gray as he bobbed in the water, smirking at me. "Am not."

"Then get in," he said as he nodded at the pool edge.

"I can't swim," I repeated his brother's earlier words.

"Not going to learn standing on the deck though, are you?"

"I don't want to learn."

"See? Stupid." He laughed as he looked over at his cousin. "She's nothing but a chicken."

Ash started to laugh, and Gray made clucking sounds like a chicken. Jett tried to hide his smile, but his brother was now flapping his hands about like wings. His challenging glare was making me angry, and to show him I wasn't a chicken, I jumped into the water.

And I sank like a stone.

My arms scrambled frantically, and I took a huge breath as the water rushed into my mouth, and I screamed, which only caused me to swallow more.

Hands grabbed my arms, and then my head was out of the water. Clumsily and painfully, the boys dragged me to the end of the pool where I coughed and choked out the water that I'd swallowed. I was crying, but I didn't care that they were going to make fun of me.

A big white towel was wrapped around me as a hand rubbed my back, and I looked up at Gray as he watched me with concern.

"Didn't say drink the pool," he said softly. "Thought you said you weren't stupid?"

"You okay?" Ash asked me as he watched me with wide eyes.

"I think so." Scrubbing my nose, I looked at all three of them. "That was a bit stu…silly," I admitted.

"I think you were brave."

Looking at Gray, I felt a flutter in my tummy. He thought that I was brave? "Really?"

"You can't swim, and you jumped into the water anyway," he said as he nodded. "You're a daredevil. Like us."

"Reckless," Jett murmured in agreement as he sat beside me. "You want to try again?"

No, but as I looked at the three of them, I found myself nodding. "Maybe in the shallow end?"

The three boys laughed and were soon hauling me up to my feet and throwing the towel onto the lounge chair.

"C'mon, we're going to teach you how to be a *real* Devil."

QUINN, AGE TWELVE

"Hi," I greeted as I walked around the side of the pool towards the three of them.

Jett stood and came over to me, grabbing my hand. "We thought you would want to be alone."

"Why? You never let me be alone any other time."

"Mom said you'd want to sleep," Gray told me as he watched me.

"I close my eyes, and all I see is her in the coffin."

"Want to play Call of Duty?" Ash asked as he came to stand beside Jett and me.

"Okay," I agreed and followed the three Santo boys into the house, away from my home, where the people were crowding our front room and eating small plates of finger food as they watched me with sad faces.

"Quinn, sweetheart, why are you here?" Sable Santo rushed over to me and wrapped her arms around me.

"Dad's got people to look after. No one will be looking for me," I assured her. I met Gray's eyes, and he nodded once in understanding as he walked over to his mom and took my arm.

"She's with us, mom, she's fine," he told his mom as he pulled me away.

"But…" Sable looked at all of us as she watched the boys form a semi-circle around me. "Okay, I'll tell your dad. I was going back over anyway."

We went to the den, and we played video games, and we never spoke about the fact that I buried my mom today.

They were my best friends.

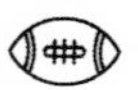

QUINN, AGE FIFTEEN

As I walked around the pool in the dark, I could see the darker shadow as he lay out on the lounge chair. Gray ignored me as I approached and remained silent as I lay down on the lounge chair beside his.

"Thought you were on a date?" he asked me softly.

"I was." I stared up at the star-filled sky. "He asked her to marry him."

Gray grunted but said nothing.

"It's only been three years since mom died."

"You think it's too soon?" he asked.

"Don't you?"

"Dunno." I heard him move slightly, and then he was on his

side, facing me. "It will always be too soon for you; she was your mom."

Shifting, I faced him. "He said he loved my mom more than life itself."

"Why do you think that's changed?"

"Because he's *marrying* someone else."

"So? You think he should be alone? And unhappy?"

"I'm not saying that!" I argued back.

"What are you saying?"

I turned so I was on my back again. "You turn everything into an argument."

"You just don't like hearing the truth." I said nothing. We lay in silence for a while longer until Gray spoke again. "So…the date?"

"He kissed me." My heart was racing as I waited for his reaction.

"Where?"

Despite myself, I laughed. "On the lips."

"Which ones?"

"Gray!"

I heard him snigger as he turned to lie on his back again.

"He wants to go out again."

"Tell him you're busy."

"Why?" The silence stretched, and I was sure he wouldn't answer before I heard him move as he was sitting up.

"Because I told you to." Gray stood and walked away from me. At the edge of the pool, I saw him looking back at me. "Just do it." He couldn't see me clearly in the shadows, but that didn't mean he wasn't waiting.

"Okay." My voice floated across the decking, no more than a whisper, but he heard it. I saw his head jerk in a nod once before he disappeared into his house. Staring up at the night sky, I wondered why I agreed before I closed my eyes, too afraid to question myself further, knowing that unlike the stars, the answer wasn't that far out of reach.

Quinn, age sixteen

"Jett, I need to talk to you." I watched him finish his push-ups, his toned golden skin on display—he never cared that he walked around shirtless in front of me. To Jett, I was no more than another member of his family. I liked that about him. Actually, I loved that about him.

"So, talk." He grunted as he started doing sit-ups.

"Didn't you do all of this already?" I demanded as I watched him effortlessly go through his exercises.

"Yeah, but I need to be fitter."

"You're going to burn out," I chided as I slipped down onto the floor and held his feet. "What?" I asked when I saw his raised eyebrows. "I always help."

"You do always help, Queeny." He grinned as he resumed his workout. "What's going on under that mass of black hair?" he teased me.

My hair had always been wild and untamed, but when we hit high school, I knew I had to put more effort into my appearance. The boys were easy—they grew into their looks—but I needed to exfoliate, buff, wax and straighten my hair to look as effortless as they did. "Ash kissed me."

Jett stopped his sit-ups and leaned back on his hands as he considered my words. "You kiss him back?"

"Yes."

"Why?"

I stared at him. I didn't have an answer. Ash kissed me, and I kissed him back. "I dunno. 'Cause I thought he wanted me to?"

"Don't be stupid, Quinn. A guy kisses you, does *anything* with you that you don't want, you knee his balls, kick his face in and then tell *us*, and we'll beat the fuck out of him."

"You going to beat Ash up?" I asked him mockingly.

"Do I need to?" Jett stood and wiped his neck with a towel and waited until I shook my head. "So, you wanted him to kiss you?"

I bit my lip. Ash had started paying more and more attention to me. I couldn't say that I didn't like it. I saw the way they were with girls, and had been envious. They weren't like that with me, of course—I was their friend—but it stung when I heard them say pretty things to girls who didn't deserve it. *I* deserved it. Jett had already had sex with two different girls, and Ash almost had sex with Carlie at a party the other week, but she chickened out and only gave him a hand job. Is that why he kissed me? He thought I was more of a sure thing than Carlie?

"I don't know," I admitted.

Jett stared at me and then rolled his eyes. "Queeny, I can't tell you who to suck face with—just make sure whoever it is, you *want* to be doing it."

"What about us?" I asked him in a whisper. "The Devils?"

"The group?" Jett shrugged. "We're friends, it'll be weird, but it won't change anything between me and you, at least."

"You'll still be my bestie?" I asked playfully, hoping he didn't see the need I had to make sure he would never leave me.

"Always. There isn't anything you could do to change it. C'mon, I'm starving." Jett punched my shoulder as he passed me, and I grinned as I followed him to the kitchen.

Quinn, age sixteen

"How much longer you going to string him along?" Gray asked me, his hard stare boring into mine.

"I'm not stringing him along," I snapped back at him. Why did he have to be so close to me? All I could smell was *him*.

"Yes, you are, you're being a prick tease. He wants to fuck you; do you want him to fuck you?"

"I'm not being a prick tease!" I shoved at his chest to get him to stand back. "Fuck you, Gray. What happens between *me* and Ash is between me and Ash."

"What happens between you and my cousin happens to *all* of us. Why the fuck are you playing with him?" Gray moved back into my space, and I stared up at him. I was almost five eight now, but Gray was still taller.

"I'm not *playing*, I like him," I told him defensively even as my heart raced as he stepped closer to me.

"Yeah, you *like* him?" Gray's eyes narrowed as he smirked at me. "That why you let him stick his fingers in your cunt last week?"

Gasping at his vulgarity, I stepped back and hit the wall behind me. "Don't be such a dick," I hissed at him as my eyes filled with tears.

"Gonna spread your legs for Ash, *Queeny*?" Gray pushed his chest into mine as he glared down at me. "That what you want, so desperate to be a *Devil* you'll let him fuck you?"

My hand stung, and I realised it was because I slapped him. Slowly his head turned back to face me, revealing my handprint on his face, and I chewed my inner cheek as my body stilled, waiting for the eruption.

Jett was fiery but fair. Ash was lighthearted and laid-back with a temper that rarely let loose. Gray…Gray was *fury*. He always seemed to be moving, as if he could barely contain the wild energy inside him. The smallest thing would set him off, and usually Jett or Ash needed to haul him back.

"That was stupid," Gray murmured as he dipped his head. "Always knew you were stupid."

"I'm not stupid, you fucking dick, I just don't fucking like you when you're being a prick."

"Liar."

My retort was swallowed when he kissed me. Not soft and gentle like Ash had kissed me. Gray was unrestrained, his mouth dominated mine, his kiss was savage like him, and his tongue tasted every inch inside my mouth. Hazily, I realised I was kissing him back just as eagerly. His hand was tight in my hair, his other hand already cupping my sex as he ground his palm against the small bundle of nerves that throbbed for him.

As quickly as it began, it was over. Gray pushed me away from him as he wiped his mouth with the back of his hand. "Fucking make up your mind, but stop being a fucking liar," he snarled at me before he turned and walked away from me.

I was still crying when Jett found me, and then *he* got pissed off when I refused to tell him why I was crying, which only made me cry more.

Quinn, age seventeen

"I don't want to go to the movie," I snapped angrily as I looked at Ash. He'd had his another growth spurt over the summer and now was standing proud at six four. My own height had stopped at five ten, much to my disgust. I'd been hoping to be closer to six feet so I didn't have to always look up to the Devils, but my DNA had other ideas, and instead of filling me upwards, I had filled outwards. Last summer, my boobs became more generous than they had been before, a fact my boyfriend, Ash, was very grateful for. My once stick thin legs now had shape to them, and my hips were intent on keeping any morsel of food that I put in my mouth straight on them.

I watched the guys devour any food in front of them like a

swarm of locusts and still look like needles. I looked at the amount of carbs they ate, and I could feel my stomach bloating. But I ran with them in the morning, I worked out with them in the evening, and I kept myself fit and healthy, at first so I could keep up with them and then because I genuinely enjoyed it.

"I don't mind staying in, if you want," Ash said with a grin as he lay back on my bed, his hands tucked beneath his head as he watched me with expectation.

"I'm not in the mood," I told him as I pulled on a long sweater over my T-shirt, covering me completely and sitting mid-thigh over my leggings.

"Ugh, you're never in the fucking mood," he grumbled as he got off the bed and headed to my bedroom door. "I don't know what's wrong, and you won't talk to me, so tell Jett, he'll tell me, and we can move on. Okay?"

He was an idiot. Jett would never tell him, and *that's* why Jett was my best friend. I heard the front door bang and knew he was gone. I counted in my head, and then my stepmom poked her head around the door.

"Trouble in paradise?"

"No, Anne, all good here," I lied as I forced the smile. She was a nice enough lady, she just wasn't my mom, and although our relationship was a good one, I knew she wanted it to be more.

"We can talk about it if you want?" she said as she took a step further into the room.

"No, honestly, it's just Ash. He gets riled up during the season."

"Okay, sweetie, but I'm downstairs if you want to talk."

I nodded and she left me alone. Hours later, I was in the den, in the dark, with only the light of the TV illuminating the room. Ash had sent a few texts, and I'd replied. He was with Gray and Jett hanging out at the stadium. Probably doing the stupid shit that they did when they were bored and idle. I knew they wouldn't be alone—girls *and* guys hung off them like bad smells. I had no fear he would cheat on me, though sometimes I wished he would.

"Why you in the dark?"

I yelped in fright as I turned to look at Gray as he closed the den door firmly behind him.

"Watching TV, why you freaking me the fuck out?" I snapped at him as I flicked the lamp on. I watched as he dropped his body onto the couch and gasped when he turned to look at me.

"What happened?" I was on my feet, crossing the room and leaning over him, inspecting his bruised cheek and blackening eye.

"Dick pissed me off."

"The world pisses you off," I told him dryly.

Gray huffed out a laugh as he turned his face away from me and my probing fingers. "Can see down your top," he muttered as he leaned over and turned the lamp off.

I felt the familiar swoosh in my tummy when he glanced at me quickly before he straightened in his seat.

"I don't mind you looking." The words were low and husky and scared the shit out of me that I said them out loud.

Gray's eyes met mine. He had only ever kissed me once, before I started dating Ash, and I still remembered his lips on mine. "Don't." His voice was soft, almost too quiet, but I heard the plea in it.

I wished that I had been drinking so I could blame my next actions on alcohol, but I had no excuse. My hands trembled as I pulled the sweater and T-shirt over my head, revealing my plain white bra to him. Gray's eyes widened, but he said nothing. His eyes travelled down my body as I pushed my leggings down, and then I was in front of him in only my panties and bra.

With hands shaking, I reached for him as I moved closer, picking up his hand and placing it on my breast. Gray licked his lips but said nothing as his hand rested there, not even squeezing.

"Touch me," I whispered as I lowered myself over his legs and straddled him.

"Quinn, I…" His words stopped when I picked up his other hand and pulled it high onto my thigh.

"Do it," I encouraged him. His hand moved slightly, and I inhaled sharply. Slowly his thumb made a circle on my bare leg. "I need you to touch me," I whispered in the quiet of the room, the light from the TV casting shadows over his face.

"If I touch you, I may not stop."

I had never heard Gray unsure about anything in his life. His eyes never left mine, and his hands didn't stray from where I had placed them. "Then don't stop."

I watched as his eyes closed, and I saw him clench his jaw as he tipped his head back, and I felt the shiver that ran through his body. When he looked at me again, his eyes were alive and wild, and my body erupted in goose bumps at the intensity of his stare. Firm solid hands circled my waist, and he lifted me off of him and onto the couch. Swiftly Gray stood, and then he was bending over me.

"I would fuck you, Quinn, I would fuck you so hard you would never remember having another man's dick in you, but I won't fuck you for two reasons."

My heart was racing so fast I was scared I was going to pass out. "What reasons?"

"You're not mine." He straightened, and I grabbed for my sweater to cover myself, my embarrassment suddenly washing over me. Sobering me. Gray snatched the sweater and tossed it behind him. "I like seeing you laid out like this before me. Isn't *this* what you wanted?" His words were cruel, mocking. "Don't get shy now. Why don't you spread those legs for me so I can see what I'm passing up on?"

"Don't," I whispered back his earlier plea as I stared up at him, feeling completely exposed, and his mouth twisted into a sneer.

"Break it off with Ash, it's time to end the charade. Once and for all." Gray strode to the door in anger.

"Gray!" I called him back, and he stilled, his head half turning as he waited. "What's the other reason?"

I heard his grunt as he opened the door. "I don't fucking want you."

Quinn, age eighteen (two weeks later)

The tears spilled over as I watched Ash throw the chair across the room. His rage was real, and I felt miserable as I watched him rip his hurt out as he destroyed the classroom.

Gray was silent in the corner, watching me, with narrowed eyes. He hadn't spoken a word. Jett was torn between Ash and me. He kept looking at me, the question in his eyes, but he hadn't asked.

"Who the fuck was it?" Ash demanded as he crossed the room and grabbed me. Jett was beside him, his hands on his to stop him from shaking me. "Get off me, I won't fucking hurt her," Ash growled at him. Dark blue angry eyes glared at me with hate. "Who the fuck did you let fuck you?"

I said nothing as he pushed me back, away from him. Jett grabbed my arm to stop my stumble. I flinched when Ash kicked the table and sent it crashing into a wall.

"You fucking *bitch*, I *trusted* you."

"I know." I wiped my eyes as he turned to look at me. "I'm sorry."

"Sorry?" Ash looked at me as he gave a startled laugh. "You're *sorry*?" He glanced at Gray, who remained silent. "I don't give a shit if you're sorry, tell me who you let fuck you."

I said nothing, and then he was in front of me again. All the anger seemed to drain out of him. "Why?" he asked me, and I wished he had hit me rather than look so broken.

Ash's head dropped into his hands as he yelled out his frustration at my silence. My eyes once again flicked to Gray's, and I felt my heart rip in two as he merely watched, cold and distant.

"Please, Quinn, tell me why?" Ash asked me softly as he looked up at me, and I fought back the words that would destroy us all.

"It was either going to be me or you," I told him instead, wiping my eyes quickly as I pulled myself up straighter. "We both know we didn't really work; I just made the first move to end it."

"Quinn," Jett's voice was quiet, but I heard his surprise at my words.

"What?" I looked them all over, one too pained to look at me, one who wasn't sure he was hearing my words properly, and one who saw right through me. "We're Devils. We fuck who we want, when we want. That doesn't change just because I'm a girl."

"You're a bitch."

I looked at Ash, and I inclined my head. "I didn't think you would be this upset," I told him as I swallowed past the lump in my throat. "I didn't mean to hurt you."

I turned and left the classroom, hurrying past the students who took the chance to see into the devastation of the classroom as I ran to the girls' bathroom to get away from the stares and the whispers. Inside, I washed my face and let out a few tears as I screamed internally at the damage I'd done.

As I wiped my face with coarse paper towels, I looked up and jumped when I saw Gray leaning against the door, his hand on the lock.

"You happy now?" I asked him angrily. "Is that what you wanted?"

Idly, he flipped the lock and advanced towards me. A large hand wrapped around my throat as he brought his lips down almost on mine.

"No." His lips crushed mine, and I opened for him as his hands tugged at my shirt and his cold hands travelled over my skin. Gray pushed me until I was almost sitting on a sink, and then his hand was under my skirt, his fingers pushing my panties aside before sliding two inside me. "Open wider."

I spread my legs, not caring he was so rough, not caring I had just broken his cousin's heart, not caring he was going to fuck me in the school bathrooms. I bit his shoulder when he pushed inside me to stop my scream, and then he was slamming into me. Angry eyes glared at me as one hand dug into my thigh and the other squeezed my throat. My hands clutched at his shoulders as he pushed inside over and over until I was falling over the edge, and I heard his answering grunt as he emptied himself inside me. As his breathing returned to normal, he pulled out of me and fixed his pants.

Without a word, he turned away from me, but as he stopped to check his phone, he turned back to me. "This didn't happen."

"Because you don't *want* me?" I mocked him as he unlocked the door. His cold laughter echoed in the bathroom as the door closed behind him.

Quinn, age eighteen

The party was boring. A few months had passed since Ash and I had broken up, and I was still adjusting to life as a non-Devil. They'd shut me out. I expected it of two of them, but Jett's silence stung. He told me that he wouldn't let it interfere with our friendship, but I guess me saying I'd cheated on his cousin was a line that even Jett Santo wouldn't cross.

The students at our rival high school didn't care I was no longer a Devil; they didn't care that I had once been the *queen* of

Cardinal Saints High School. Well, they had, until they saw that *I* no longer cared; maybe I never had.

One of the basketball team had sucked my neck earlier as I gave him a half-hearted hand job, and now he was drunk, and I was bored and fed up with fighting off his clumsy hands. I couldn't remember whose party this was, but I was on the balcony, which was accessed from their parents' bedroom. Parents who weren't here.

Parents were never there when they were needed.

Curling my legs under me, I stared down at the pool and to the party still going strong. Some girls had opted to lose their bikini tops as they played and teased in the pool. Guys were either drooling over them or were playing a drunken game of basketball. Others were shacked up in dark corners where low moans could be heard over the noise, even from where I was.

I watched Elise and her bitch friends cross the lawn like they were something. *Sluts.* Ash had fucked all of them in one night, one after the other, not realising it was a different girl, and not one of them had any self-respect to point out his mistake.

Ash had slept with almost every girl in school now to let me know he didn't care about me. It hurt. It hurt because he was going to realise one day, he really didn't care that way about me, and he was going to feel like shit. I knew this because I was already there.

Suddenly, I saw the three of them in the shadows, black bandanas over their faces, hoodies up. It made me sit up and pay attention. This was a rival school; they were going to get their asses kicked if they were caught. Like shadows, they melted into the darkness, but I knew them, I knew what they were doing.

Mayhem.

The lights went out. The music cut off. Screams and splashes came from the pool, and then I heard the whisper racing through the darkness.

Run.

I was leaning over the balcony now, looking for any telltale signs of them, but it was too dark. I felt the wide smile, and I realised I hadn't grinned like this in weeks. Hearing the door to the bedroom open, I spun quickly. He was in front of me. Tall, broad, the bandana covering his face, the hood drawn low. He tossed something to me, and I caught it deftly.

"Let them know who was here," Gray whispered, and then he turned and was gone again.

With a smile and lighter step, I left the bedroom, the spray can of paint in my hand. This party needed to know the Devils had been here.

I had been fooling myself. I would *always* be a Devil. I just needed to remind *them* of that. *All* of them.

CHAPTER 1

Quinn

Present

Staring around the kitchen with my mask of indifference on, I willed my insides to stop shaking as I stirred the ingredients together. I had been here only a few times since we started college, usually when Ash or Gray weren't. Ash, I think, was truly clueless as to how close Jett had kept me during our "estranged" times. Gray knew, he just chose not to acknowledge it.

There were a lot of things that Gray Santo chose not to acknowledge.

As I added the chilli flakes to the mix, I felt myself smirk at my inner thoughts. Gray was not alone in his *selective* recollections. There was a lot of shit that had happened between us that I didn't acknowledge either.

He was no innocent, but then, neither was I.

Ash sat to the left of the breakfast bar as Gray lingered like a wraith behind me, with four or five of the team scattered around the kitchen dining area as I explained the nutrition of the dish I was making.

Sometimes, I hated the fact that I was best friends with the Devils. They took a lot of shit, and therefore I took a lot of shit. They also caused a lot of trouble; therefore, I caused a lot of trouble. On a more personal level, I had been on both sides of their *rule*. I had stood with them as they caused mayhem, and I had trembled when their anger was pointed at me. I was currently back beside them, which is why it was "natural" for my assignment in my nutrition course to be allocated to the Cardinal Saints football team.

And because I was an extension of the Devils, ten of the football team had all volunteered to help with my assignment. I was to make them meal plans, check their food intake, see when and what food worked best with them. Record every meticulous detail as if they were actually under my care and I were responsible for them.

Coach Bowers had signed off on it, and his daughter, Dr Sanchez, was overseeing my work. The assignment was for two months and was fifty-five percent of my grade, so I could not afford to fuck this up. I could not afford for *them* to fuck this up for me.

I had met the Santo boys when I was eleven and they were ten. Twins and a cousin who may as well have been their triplet. There were four days between them. *Four* days. Ash was due to be born the month before, but the stubborn bastard had refused to leave the womb until he was ready. His poor mom, Charlotte, was the slightest female I had ever met. Everything about her was petite, and she had not only birthed the monster, but he had also been three weeks overdue, ensuring her pregnancy was sheer hell.

I caught him staring at me as I spoke and started basting the chicken breasts with the marinade I had made. All low fat, all calorie counted, all fresh.

I offered him a small smile. It had been so ugly between us for so long. I was tired of it all. His face remained stoic, but he hadn't cursed me out and he hadn't thrown me out. I was taking the olive branch, even if he didn't know he was offering it.

The front door banged open, and I heard them before I saw them.

"Are you *insane*? You're insane, aren't you?" Ava's voice was raised, and I exchanged a quick glance with Ash, who was grinning as we all listened.

"I'm not insane. You're fucking delusional if you think that fucking dick doesn't want to bend you over and fuck you." Jett's snarl was loud, and I could hear him marching towards the kitchen.

"You're *impossible*!" Ava yelled at him, and all of us waited for Jett to come into the kitchen.

"*I'm* impossible?" We all heard Jett stop. "Are you fucking kidding me? You *gave him your number!*"

I winced and I saw Ash open his mouth in an O before he slipped off his stool. Gray had also moved from his corner towards the door, whether to hear better or intervene, I wasn't sure. Hoping it would be the latter, I looked over at him at his side profile and saw the smirk playing about his lips. Maybe I gave him too much credit.

"Giving a guy my number does not mean I'm going to have sex with him, you complete fuckhead. Why would I do that when I'm with you?"

Good question, I thought as I heard the silence. I stopped basting and put my hands on the counter. Gray looked my way, and I saw the amusement dancing in his eyes.

Silence meant either Jett was about to explode or they were already half undressed in the hallway.

"How many guys have your number?" Jett sounded calm. Collected.

The occupants of the kitchen all held their breath, and I knew I wasn't the only one who was screaming internally for Ava not to answer, or at the very least we were getting prepared to run if the answer was not what he wanted to hear.

"You're being ridiculous. If you must know, lots of guys have my number."

Oh, Ava. I heard several like-minded groans.

"Lots?" I heard my best friend's low tone, and Ash was already halfway to the door as was Gray.

The squeal of surprise caused me to jump, and I was hurrying to the hallway with everyone else.

Ava was flat against the wall, her legs wrapped around Jett as he kissed her, his hands buried in her hair, and her hands were already tugging up his T-shirt. Several of the guys were chuckling as they headed back to their seats.

Gray coughed loudly, and Jett slowly and leisurely broke off the kiss before he turned to look at the three of us. His grin was wicked as Ava dropped her head onto his shoulder in embarrassment at the audience.

"Am I late, Queeny?" Jett asked me casually as his hands slipped under his girlfriend's top, and he chuckled as she hit his shoulder to stop.

"You're late, and the in-lesson entertainment wasn't needed," I answered him lightly.

"Sorry, Quinn," Ava called out as she lifted her head to see the three of us standing there. "He's a caveman," she said as she looked down at Jett with a small smile.

"Caveman, huh?" he asked her before he lowered her from the wall. With a quick move, Ava was over his shoulder. "I'm taking Wilma upstairs," Jett told me with a cocky smirk. "Play nice with the boys, Quinn. Send me what I need, and I'll check in with you later."

Gray snorted and was already heading back into the kitchen, while Ash lingered for a moment, and we both heard Ava question why Jett was such a complete alphahole. Ash and I exchanged a grin before we both realised it, and then he was striding back into the kitchen.

I heard the door close on the upper level, and like a good friend, I closed the kitchen door firmly so we didn't have to listen to either Jett or Ava as I finished my food prep lesson.

"Right, where were we?" I asked lightly as I crossed the room. Weirdly, the craziness that was the relationship of Jett and Ava had calmed me down, and I felt more confident as I finished the meal prep and told the guys how they were to record their food intake for me.

When I was finished and clearing the work counters, I was left with only two Devils.

"Are you sure this won't mess up my training regime?" Ash asked me quietly.

"I have your training schedule from Coach Bowers and the sheet you filled in for me already. Every single plan I have created is catered to each individual. It's not a one-size-fits-all. I know what I'm doing."

Dark blue eyes met mine, and he said nothing. As the silence stretched, I wasn't sure if I should speak. Our truce was tentative, but that didn't mean it would hold. He looked over my shoulder, and whatever he saw in his cousin's face, he gave me a slight nod before he was on his feet and left us in the kitchen.

My time alone with Gray was limited at the best of times, and I felt my palms get clammy. Turning, I forced the smile as I piled the cleaning cloths onto the counter.

"You good with yours?" I asked him.

His light blue eyes were cold and distant as he watched me, with his arms crossed against his chest. "You know I hate fish."

"You should eat at least one oily fish per week." I could hear the boredom in my own voice; this was not the first time we had this conversation. I opted for sports therapy when I was fourteen, and from then until now, every week, it seemed I was arguing with these guys about my food recommendations. Even when I hadn't been "in" with them, I'd still kept an eye on them.

Jett hated any green vegetable but would eat it if forced, and he needed to be forced.

Ash watched every calorie like it was an enemy. His dad played defence, and Ash was determined to play tight end. He refused to put more weight on, his fear that the draft would see him, know his father, and a team would select him and change him from a tight end to a defensive lineman.

Gray hated fish. Hated it. He would force it down quicker than

Jett would his greens. Put chicken in front of Gray, and he would eat it every day and night until the end of time. I would not get a good pass if I fed the running back of the Cardinal Saints variations of chicken, salad and pasta every day.

I had been outside of their friendship for a short time, but even then, six years—*six* years—of telling these stubborn, bullheaded men what to eat was still a battle. Why would they never listen to me?

"I should also fuck a different girl every night to keep it entertaining, but I don't."

Pulling my hair out of the makeshift bun I had created for the lesson, I fluffed my hair out as I reached over for my purse, my hands wanting to wrap around his throat and squeeze tight. "You say such *charming* things it's a wonder your bed is ever empty." My smile was saccharine sweet, and as I left the asshole standing in his kitchen, I heard his low chuckle as I left the house.

Prick.

Our relationship was rocky, everyone knew it. Ash believed his cousin took his side when I broke it off with him. Gray had never spoken up in my defence. And why would he? It wasn't like he told them he was the one who told me to end it. It wasn't like he was going to turn around to his family and tell them he had fucked me in the girls' bathroom not fifteen minutes after I confessed to Ash I'd cheated on him.

He knew I would never tell them either. I was already public enemy number one at that point, no need to drag him down with me.

Because for all the resentment I held for Gray Santo, the truth was simple. I had been a willing participant. I had crawled onto his lap half-naked and begged him to touch me. He hadn't, but had he shown less restraint that night, I *would* have cheated on my boyfriend. I would have, and the fact that I had the intent to cheat made me just as guilty as if I had actually had sex with someone else.

Not someone else.

Gray.

As I walked back to my dorm, my mind was on the past. There had always been something between Gray and me, a pull, a...bond? No, not a bond; that was too...*binding*. An attraction?

The very first day I met him, he called me stupid and a chicken. No, attraction was definitely not the right term. Yes, he was gorgeous, but they all were. It was more of a...challenge? Yes. He tested me and questioned me on every goddamn thing. Always pushing me. Always fighting back.

He argued over every single thing. Even when the fucker agreed with me, he would twist it so he looked like he didn't. It was frustrating. *He* was frustrating. It was a constant fight, a struggle, a seemingly never-ending wrestling match. One where I would not be beaten and he would not give in.

Gray was exhausting, it was true, but he was addictive. I craved him like he was a drug. When he turned away from me, I had never felt so empty. So alone.

Jett had stepped back for a few months to give Ash time to accept the breakup, which meant he watched his cousin sleep with anything in a skirt. Gray, to the best of my knowledge, kept his thoughts to himself. Was it guilt that stilled his tongue? Or his usual indifference to human emotion?

I laughed lightly as I climbed the stairs to my dorm suite, my harshness towards him lightening my mood. I had a reasonable sized one-bedroom apartment with an adjoining bathroom and a separate living space. I shared a kitchen and larger common area with three other girls, but they were clean and tidy, and I hardly ever saw them. I knew they were all friends and hung out, but the offer was never extended to me.

Why would they?

I was Quinn Lawrence. I was friends with the Devils, and I was not known for being overly friendly with anyone else. Yes, I had female acquaintances, and there were lots of people I talked to, but I rarely spent time with them outside of campus hours.

Ava was the closest thing I had to a girlfriend, and she was wary of me, as well she should be. I hadn't given her a warm welcoming. True, I'd thought she was a conniving snake trying to ruin my best friend's career, but even though I was the *cheating bitch* in our group, I was still one hundred percent loyal. You did not mess with my boys.

I thought Ava was playing Jett, so welcoming I was not. When I found out what had actually happened and knowing Jett would blame himself, I had made it my personal mission to befriend Ava. In truth, as I got to know her, I liked her. She was funny, open and so genuinely honest I wanted to wrap her in cotton wool so she always stayed so guilelessly innocent.

Ava took everything at face value, and I truly wondered if her naivety was what drew Jett to her. Even though she had a sharp tongue and she spoke without thought, she wasn't malicious. She wasn't insincere. She wasn't fake.

She and Jett were perfect together. Her wholesomeness was exactly what he needed to keep him centred. Adding on to that, she was almost as obsessed with football as he was; she was the perfect partner. It had been a few weeks since the incident with Derrick, and I think we had all accepted pretty quickly that Ava wasn't going anywhere.

Slipping off my sneakers, I put them in the bedroom where I dropped my book bag. Walking back into the living area, I dropped ungraciously onto the couch, and as I closed my eyes, I heard the ping. I could ignore it. A minute later, it pinged again as a reminder I had a message.

With a low groan, I pushed myself off of the couch and went to the bedroom. I was pretty sure I knew who it was.

Gray: **You back?**

I contemplated ignoring him, but he would just message again. Control freak bastard.

Me: **Yes**

Tossing the phone onto my desk, I lay back down on the couch again. He wouldn't text again. Knowing I was back home would be enough.

How did we ever become this? All those years ago, when I met them the very first day, how did we become four awkward kids to this...*mess* that we were now?

Onyx, the twins' older *psychotic* brother, had told them when the three of them were twelve that I would either break them or make them. I hadn't understood what he meant then, and I wish I didn't know now.

My actions had only made them stronger. Lonely and unsure and so pathetically desperate to be *seen* by them, that I was a girl just like the girls they were chasing, I had let Ash kiss me. It was a mistake that should never have been repeated. But repeat it, I had.

To Jett, I would always be a sister. He saw me as nothing more, and weirdly, I had absolutely no desire for him to see me any other way. He was attractive, he was funny, he had a mean streak, and he was a shit hot quarterback, but all I ever wanted from him was his friendship.

Ash had been almost the same, but Ash said pretty things to girls to get kisses. I knew he didn't mean them, but Ash never looked at me the way he did the other girls, and it pissed me off. When I told him that it did, he had laughed, and then he started to whisper pretty things in my ear, and his quiet words had made me blush. Jett hadn't paid attention, but it wasn't Jett's reaction I was looking for.

Gray had noticed, and it thrilled me that he did. Where Jett could be mean, Gray was cruel. Where Jett had a quick temper,

Gray was explosive. Where Jett would be confused and would ask, his brother would become still and silent. And patient.

As Gray waited silently, watching and waiting for me to fuck it up, I made a mistake, because I'd forgotten.

Forgotten that he was the most dangerous one of them all.

CHAPTER 2

Quinn

I LOVED OCTOBER WHEN THE AIR TURNED COOLER AT NIGHT BUT WAS still pleasant in the daytime. The autumnal colours of orange, brown and black dominated, and the aroma of pumpkin spice drifted lazily over the air. Leggings and mid-thigh sweaters were calling to me, and I could use my long hair like a scarf to protect me from unwanted prying eyes and the chill that was creeping in.

Sitting on a wooden bench between the cafeteria and the stadium, I had a textbook open on my lap as I stared out over the campus, sipping my coffee. Students bustled to and from classes, and I relished people-watching as I made up little stories in my head about the people as they passed.

"Hi," Ava said to me as she approached.

Was she cautious? I made my smile brighter to appear more welcoming. "Hey."

"Can I join you?"

"Of course." My hand patted the bench, and she sat down beside me. "How's your day been?"

"So far?" Ava gave a small laugh. "The professor from hell roasted me, once again. The professor who thinks I'm a jersey chaser pities me, and I had too much chocolate at lunchtime and feel sick."

"Just a normal Monday then?" I asked her with a smile, and she laughed along with me.

"Yeah, although on the bright side, Ash protects me mostly from Leitch, and Jett just grins at Professor Matson every time she looks like she wants to save me from myself."

"Ash protects you," I murmured as I picked invisible lint from my leggings.

"Yeah." Ava shifted uncomfortably. "How has your day been?"

"I had a two-hour practical this morning. I massaged and rubbed down two volunteers, although I think I may have dug *too* deep into my second guy's calf." I grinned at Ava as she listened. "He started getting a hard-on when I was doing his legs, so a little bit of pain is the best fix."

Ava barked out a laugh as she looked over the campus. "Does that happen often?" she asked me with a wide smile.

"More than I would like to admit," I told her as I shrugged. "I mean, it's natural, and I will always have to accept it as part of the job, I guess, but the guy was so busy eye fucking me, I had to remind him who I was."

"Pain will help with that." Ava's eyes danced with laughter, and I nodded.

"Yeah, I find it does. My consolation is that proper athletes are going to be too exhausted to get junior up or will have an actual sports injury they need me to fix." I sipped my lukewarm coffee. "Horny college guys, or girls, are not what I'm going to be dealing with on a daily basis."

"Girls?" Ava asked me as she turned towards me curiously. "I never even thought of the girls," she said with a bemused smile. "I mean, wow, how sexist am I?"

"Meh, it happens. My hands are enough to turn anyone horny," I told her with a wink, and she laughed out loud, drawing several pairs of eyes our way.

"Mia and I are going into Cardinal tonight. Atticus Dawn is playing, and Wade likes support." Ava tugged her ponytail. "Mia was kind of dating the lead singer, and it's a bit awkward, but Wade *is* our friend, and I wondered if you wanted to come with us?"

I had nothing to say. I was sure my face showed my surprise, which irritated me, as I was used to being a blank mask. "Um." I swallowed. "You're asking me to go with you?"

Ava didn't even notice my hesitation, or she chose to ignore it.

"Yeah, I think you'd enjoy a night with the girls, no lurking Devils, and I want to get to know you better."

She did?

"Why?" *Subtle, Quinn.*

"You're important to Jett, you're his best friend, Jett's important to me, and I think you and I, well, we got off on the wrong foot, and despite that, you still went out of your way to smack our heads together." Ava nudged me gently with her shoulder. "I think you'd be a good friend to have. And plus, I think you need a night out listening to country rock and letting loose."

"You think *I* would be a good friend to have?"

"Maybe?" Ava grinned at me impishly. "And I'm legit awesome to have as a friend. I don't judge, I forget secrets, and I punched Gray Santo and lived to tell the tale."

My giggle was so ridiculously girly, if I had been an observer, I would have rolled my eyes. "Jett told me," I said as I regained my composure. "I would have given anything to have seen it."

"They had me pressed between them like I was the meat to their sandwich." Ava scowled. "Cocky bastards."

"They are," I agreed. "They have to be."

"Because they're Devils?" Ava asked me curiously as she rubbed her hands up and down her arms as if she were cold, despite her lightweight jacket and the warmth still in the air.

"No, because they're athletes. Their mindset is already switched on to being the best and winning. Sometimes they forget they can fail." My smile dimmed, and realising I had sobered the mood, I closed my textbook. "So," I said with bright cheeriness, "country rock, not my first choice, but I like live music. I'm in."

Ava's worried frown at my earlier words cleared as she beamed at me. "Really? Yay!"

With a slight tilt of my head, I searched her face. "You thought I would say no?"

Ava pulled her sleeve nervously before lifting her shoulder in a half shrug. "Honestly? I wasn't sure." Standing quickly, she picked up her book bag. "But I hoped you would say yes. We'll pick you up? At seven?"

"Sounds good." I nodded in acceptance, and with a wave, she said goodbye and was heading to her last class of the day. Picking up my own stuff, I headed to the Phys Ed building. I had time to work on my spreadsheets and notes for my assignment. Doubting myself was not new to me, but I still felt self-conscious when I texted Jett.

Me: **Ava asked me to go see her friends band tonight**

Jett: **She never told me, where?**

I hesitated. Did I tell him, or did I just ask if he had a hand in it?

Me: **Did you ask her to ask me?**

Jett: **Why the fuck would I?**

Jett: **Did you say no?**

Jett: **Queeny?**

"Jesus, calm down," I muttered as I replied.

Me: **You're right, why would you? Sorry, guess I'm not used to your hook ups being friendly**

Jett: **Get used to her, she isn't going anywhere**

Me: **Good**

Pushing my phone back into my purse, I headed into the study rooms. I settled into a secluded booth before setting my work on the desk and getting headphones. Selecting Shaman's Harvest, I put their albums on shuffle and concentrated on my work.

Two hours later, I was packing back up and contemplating dinner. Checking my phone, I had a message waiting.

Gray: **Girls night?**

It was unlike him to text like this. Debating whether I should reply or ignore him, I opted for the easier option.

Me: **Seems so**

He didn't reply, and I didn't expect him to. I thought things would be easier now, but who was I kidding? It would never be easier. I broke any chance of easy we had when I was eighteen, and then whatever salvation may have been there for us, was taken from me.

Pushing the ugly memories back into the box I kept them in, I did allow myself a small smile. Our bridges may be rubble between us, but he still cared. The simple two-word text message was Gray's way of knowing where I was and who I would be with, and I knew that when I went home tonight after being out, I would have a text message ensuring I was home.

Now, I just needed to know what to wear. What did you even wear to a country rock gig? Were they country or were they rock? I remembered the night that Jett and the others went to check out the band to see if Wade was shady, and then I saw them at the party later.

Ava had on a skirt, and her friend was in jeans. Scowling at my wardrobe, I decided that jeans were an "all occasion" item. Nights were cool now, so I opted for a long sweater and dark blue jeans. Knee high boots and a loose silk scarf gave me casual but enough for an "evening" vibe. They sometimes found a party later, and even if it was a Monday, I needed to be armed and able for anything.

Ava was nothing if not punctual, and at seven, I got a text saying that she was outside. Why did I feel nervous? I was almost twenty-one years old for fuck's sake. Squaring my shoulders, I headed down to meet them and was delighted that Ava was in skinny jeans, a loose sweater and a light jacket. A battered pair of Chucks were on her feet, but then I noticed with Ava, she usually had them on.

As I got into the cab, I nodded at Mia in recognition. She smiled. We weren't friends, and I didn't think we ever would be. She looked at Ash with more interest than I liked, which was completely fucking hypocritical, but I had made enquiries and discovered Mia was a frequent flyer in the dating pool of Cardinal

Saints. Although I didn't think she was loose sexually, she was well-known for moving from one guy to another with not much time between them. There were girls like that, afraid to be alone, and she had that look.

Her long auburn hair and pale skin tone made her stand out. She was gorgeous, and I had seen Ash spend too long looking at her too, but he had taken in the dynamic of the friendship of the girls, and knowing Ava was with Jett, he hadn't done anything more.

I guess one really fucking awkward ex relationship in the "group" was enough.

"I haven't seen you much since the football game." Mia smiled at me, and I realised she was trying to break the uncomfortable silence.

"I didn't realise that so much time had passed," I lied with a smile.

"Time flies when your bestie has abandoned you for hot abs and a killer throwing arm." Mia tried to make her tone light, but I saw the flash of guilt on Ava's face and the sadness on her best friend's face.

"Young love," I murmured with a pitying smile. "Are you seeing anyone?"

Well, now I just looked like I was propositioning her.

"No, I was but I, eh, broke it off." Mia rubbed her hands over her jeans. "I mean, it wasn't much, just a few hookups, nothing serious."

"Why'd you break it off?" I asked.

"We all want to know that," Ava spoke up. "And just as a heads-up, did I tell you that he's the lead singer of the band?"

She had, plus I already knew, but I played dumb anyway. "Oh. Alex?"

Mia blushed and Ava grinned at her but answered me, "Oh

yeah, the night you were evil to me at the party, he said you were nice."

"Evil?" Mia questioned.

Awkward. "I think evil may be a stretch," I said quietly.

"You told me Jett was going to ruin me and you would enjoy watching." Ava laughed good-naturedly, and I realised she wasn't being a bitch, she was genuinely laughing at the memory.

"He has ruined you though, hasn't he?" I teased her slightly. "And I'm pretty sure he's ruined you for any other."

Ava lost her smile and looked serious for a moment. "Yeah, probably." She sighed loudly before she grinned again. "Dick."

"So things are good?" I asked her. It probably was uber personal and in some form of overstepping, but he was my best friend, and she was his first proper girlfriend. I had the right to be protective.

"Yes." Ava's beam would have lit the darkest corner of the night. "He's...wonderful."

I caught Mia's eye roll, but I also saw her genuine happiness for her friend. "You know she hated him all through high school, and now she's all Lil' Miss Saint."

"He is a colossal dickhead," Ava protested with a playful swipe at her friend. "But he's my dickhead," she said proudly as she looked at me shyly. "Sorry, is this weird for you?"

I blinked. "Um, no, why?"

"Well, you said he's like your brother, doesn't it freak you out?" Ava asked me as the cab reached Cardinal.

"Oh, no, trust me, there is nothing you can tell me about any of them that I don't already know!" I gave a genuine laugh, and she laughed with me.

"So, you're like the extended sister?" Mia asked me curiously.

"In a way." I nodded.

"You have more willpower than me," Mia said with a grin to Ava. "I would have climbed at least one of them like a monkey up a tree."

I felt my face freeze my smile in place.

"You've never hooked up with any of them?" Mia asked me curiously.

"Ash is my ex," I told her bluntly and took a perverse delight in how quickly she lost her playful smile. I saw her eyes flick to Ava, who didn't look like this was news to her.

"I didn't know that." Mia's hard stare was for her friend, who was avoiding eye contact.

"Why would you?" I gave a careless shrug. "Ex means in the past."

"Yeah, um, sure."

"That's us here," Ava broke the uneasy silence. She handed the cab driver a twenty and then we were on the sidewalk outside a bar, all of us avoiding looking at one another.

"Is this an issue?" I asked them both. "I can easily go."

"What?" Ava looked alarmed. "No! I want you to stay, this doesn't have to be weird."

"And it really isn't weird," Mia piped up. "He's hot, he's bound to have a hotter ex, and I can still look, right?" She looked at me with an almost dare in her eyes.

"Honey, you can touch for all I care."

She didn't look convinced, but there was fuck all I could do about that. "We going in?" I asked.

"Yeah, um, just to let you know, and avoid any other awkwardness... Mia wasn't the only one who has a history with the band. It was friendly and nothing actually happened with Shane, but he and Alex, well, they kind of aren't friendly to us anymore."

"Then why are you here?" I asked.

"Wade's my friend, and it's his band," Ava said easily as if telling me snow was white.

"Loyal," I said with narrowed eyes to both of them. "You too?" I asked Mia.

"Heck yeah, Wade's been our friend since the beginning of last year."

"I like loyal." I opened the door to the bar, and we went in. I hadn't been in here before. There was an awful lot of wooden furnishings, and it looked more hunting cabin than bar. However, the atmosphere was light and I could see it was clean. The Devils had taken me to worse places.

As we walked in further, I felt the tug of my sleeve, and glancing back, I looked at Ava in question. Mia had walked around us and was heading straight to a blonde who I recognised from social media as Wade's girlfriend.

"You okay?" Ava asked me as she shifted from foot to foot nervously.

"Ava, your friend isn't the first girl that's liked Ash openly. The main difference is that at least we're no longer together. When I was with him, that was different, but now we're...friends."

"That's nice though," Ava said to me, completely clueless.

"Yeah, it's peachy."

"I'm missing something?" Ava asked me with a tilt of her head.

"Jett's told you nothing?"

"He said if I needed to know, you would tell me," she confessed. "He mentioned you and Ash used to be a couple, but he didn't say anything else. And honestly..." Ava hesitated as she looked past me. "I forgot." She shrugged. "Your relationships with each other are tight, I can see that. I also know I'm still on the outside, and that's okay, because I'm there for Jett. If I make friends with any of you, that's a bonus."

"It's refreshing, your honesty."

"I don't do subtle very well," she said with a grimace. "I didn't bullshit earlier; I think you would be a good friend. You take no bullshit, and I respect that." I watched as she tugged her sweater. "Mia's a flirt. She isn't the easy girl people think she is. I know she has a reputation for being a 'love them and leave them' type, but she doesn't sleep with most of them. She just likes company."

"I have no judgment of your friend; I know what gossips can be like. Her business isn't mine and mine isn't hers. Or yours for that matter. You and Jett are a couple—I respect that—but he is my best friend, and he will tell me things, and I can't stop that...and I won't."

"He talks to you about me?"

Ava looked too delighted for me to keep a straight face. "Yes, he does," I said as we resumed walking to her friends. "He's happy."

"Oh." I watched her look at her feet as she tried to hide her wide happy smile. "I think that just made me stupidly delirious," she whispered to me.

I couldn't help it—she was irresistible, and the pull to her genuine openness made me feel very protective of her.

"I'm glad, but now I need you to do me a favour," I said to her quietly as the band stopped their preparations and was looking at us. "Lie for me when I tell them I know their music."

Linking her arm through mine, Ava smiled at me as we reached them. "Quinn, I got you, girl."

Alex smiled at me in welcome, and I was quickly introduced to the others. Mia caught my eye once and smiled at me, and throwing my usual caution to the wind, I returned the smile.

I had this.

CHAPTER 3

Gray

"WHY SHOULD WE GO?" ASH WAS LOOKING AT ME WITH A RAISED eyebrow. "Country rock is not my thing. Any of our things. It's gonna suck balls."

"Have you seen him?" I asked my cousin casually as I jerked my thumb over my shoulder at Jett, who was searching through a drawer in his closet for fuck only knows what.

"So…we're going so he can keep an eye on his girlfriend?" Ash asked with a groan. He was lying sprawled over the couch in Jett's room and was still only half-dressed since his shower after practice. He had a large purpling bruise on his back and side where he took an extra heavy hit from the defensive lineman earlier today.

"He's trying to be cool," I said quietly to my cousin as I watched my brother quietly freak out. It was funny. "But it's eating him up inside, knowing she is in the same place as the guy who liked her and she almost hooked up with."

"Will the redhead be there?" Ash asked with interest as he sat up. "I wanted to get some shut eye before tonight, but you know, I wouldn't want to let my cousin down."

"And the redhead is a bonus?" I asked him dryly.

"We all need perks, Gray." Ash winked at me as he stood. "I need ten minutes." I watched him walk out of the room when Jett turned to me.

"Ten minutes for what? I thought he showered?"

I barked out a laugh and then held my hands up innocently. "He thinks we should go to the bar," I told him.

Jett started to grin and then lost it. "I can't."

I hadn't been expecting that. "Why?"

"She'll think I'm a clinger or something."

"So?"

My twin genuinely looked stumped, and then I saw his eyes gleam. "You're right, I don't have to apologise or feel guilty, she's my girlfriend."

"Exactly." I nodded even as I wanted to shake him. He really was a fucking caveman.

"And it will do the guy good to remember who her boyfriend is."

"Absolutely," I agreed while fighting back my laugh at his wholly predictable behaviour. "You tell them," I added with a smirk, which unfortunately the dumb shit noticed.

"You're pulling my chain?"

"Of course I am, don't be a Neanderthal." My brother folded his arms across his chest as he lifted an eyebrow in question. "You can't go in and throw your weight about. Ava will kick you in the balls. Again."

Jett grinned with pride as he rubbed his crotch. "But she treats them so well."

Shaking my head, I gave my brother a playful shove as I walked past him. "You have five minutes to remember you're a Devil and not a pussy-whipped dick."

"You know I'm not stupid," his quiet voice halted my exit. "She'll be okay."

"I know." I didn't turn to look at him and waited for a moment before he spoke again.

"I need to check on her too sometimes," Jett said softly. "Even Ash does."

I swallowed past the lump in my throat. "I know."

"As long as you do."

Looking over my shoulder at my brother, I nodded once. "I have it handled."

"I know, brother." He watched me, his serious face so like my own. "You have to loosen the hold though."

Rolling my neck on my shoulders, I tried to ease the tension.

"I'm trying." I walked out of the room before he could say anything else.

In my own room, I went to my bathroom and washed my hands and face. With hands clenched tightly onto the sink, I looked at myself in my mirror. My hair was longer than it normally was. I preferred it close cut, but I had let it get too long on top. My skin, like any athlete who played his sport outside, was tanned. Jett and Ash were both taller than me, but I was broader over the shoulders. I wasn't overly vain; I knew I was decent looking, and I had enough women throw themselves at me to prove it.

Quinn never threw herself at me. Not really. Jett nicknamed her Queeny early on; she just had a regal presence about her. Her head was always high, her back straight, and she had the "get the fuck away from me" vibe down even when she was eleven.

I didn't need to be going to the bar to make sure she was okay. I had put the walls up, and she had respected them. But I could see her struggling. When Jett texted me a few weeks ago to say she was hurting, I didn't even ask him how he knew she needed *me*. Not *him*.

I had dropped everything and ran to her. She had sobbed in my arms for what she lost, and I had held her and promised to those above I would find out who hurt her, and I wouldn't sleep until I had fulfilled that promise and buried their carcasses.

Quinn deserved pain in her life. She caused me enough, and she deserved to feel what I felt. But she didn't deserve what she had gone through. She didn't deserve anything close to that. None of the girls did. We had three films now, each a different girl, each a different heartbreak.

Selfishly, I was glad Quinn wasn't on any of the film. I was barely holding on as it was, and if I had seen her on that table... I closed my eyes against the fury. The rage burned inside me, and I didn't know how to put the fire out.

Rubbing my hands over my face, I pulled my T-shirt off, and

putting on an identical black one, I grabbed my hoodie and my bandana. We would go from the bar to the next house. The plan wouldn't change despite the small detour to the bar. I just needed to know she was okay, and I knew just putting my eyes on her, even for a brief moment, would calm my inner beast so I could be right for tonight.

We couldn't fuck up. We couldn't get caught either. I didn't want to go to jail, but I would. For her.

With a disgusted grunt at my foolishness, I went out of my room to get the others. We'd check on her, she'd be fine, and we could move on to tonight's job.

Ash grinned as he held up his bandana. "Great minds."

"Easier," Jett said distractedly as he checked his room for anything he might miss. "We go straight there after an hour in the bar, okay?"

"An hour?" I asked him as we descended the stairs of the dorm house.

"Problem?" Jett asked casually as he looked over his shoulder at me.

"No. Just thinking it's a long night," I replied. "Got an assignment due at nine."

"Fuck, bro, why you never better prepared?" Ash chided.

"'Cause I do my best work on a tight deadline half asleep."

"He really does," Jett agreed as we got into my car. I didn't have an R8 like my brother. I had a nice, black, sleek Mercedes. It didn't stand out as much as Jett's car, and it wasn't the environment killer SUV that Ash had. I had a hybrid, and I didn't give a flying fuck if they called me a hippie, one day my kids would inherit the world I left behind.

"So...how do we play this?" Ash asked as pulled the seat belt on. "Do we just tell them Jett's a needy fuck, or...?"

"How about we play to your horndog rep and say you're needing some red in your life?" Jett snapped at him with a glare.

"Or," I interrupted their argument, "we just say fuck all and remember we're Devils, not fucktards."

Jett snorted and Ash grinned.

"Seriously, you both know better. How the fuck can you both be letting pussy distract you so much?" I asked them, the scorn heavy in my tone.

"Aww, we'll find you someone, cousin, we'll get a little psycho you can call your own, who will match your little psycho soul." Ash reached over and patted my shoulder in a consoling manner as my brother gave me a tight smile, a smile that didn't meet his eyes, I noted. Turning my attention back to the road, I ignored them both.

When we got to the bar, I parked the car around the back, out of sight, and as one, we entered the bar. I saw her before I was even fully through the door. She was laughing at something Ava was saying, and Ava was doing wild hand actions as she told her story. How Quinn could hear her was beyond me, the music was so loud, I could feel my ribs vibrating from the speakers.

Jett's hand on my arm surprised me, and as I looked at him in question, I saw the softness in his eyes as he watched them both. "Look at them," he said to me softly.

Turning my head, I saw what he did. Quinn's guard was lowered, her laugh was genuine, and her smile was wide. She looked...she looked like she used to. Before all the shit. Before the Devils fucked her life up.

Ava was laughing so hard; one hand was on her side, and the other was on Quinn's arm. They looked so relaxed together that I took a step back. "We shouldn't have come."

"We don't need to go over," Jett told me as he grabbed Ash's arm and shook his head. Ash looked over at the girls, and then I saw him scan the room for the redhead. When he saw her coming back from the bathrooms, alone, he nodded.

We stayed at the back of the bar, and not one of them turned to check out their surroundings. They were enjoying the music and more importantly each other's company. Far too many guys for my liking, for any of our liking, approached them, and they were all sent away with a smile but a firm no.

The band broke for a break, and that's when Jett stood from his stool. As one, we moved through the crowd, and then like he had all those weeks ago, his arm encircled Ava, pulling her back into his chest as his head dipped and he whispered in her ear. Her cry of delight alerted Quinn and the redhead, and I watched as Quinn's easy manner vanished and the mask dropped back in place.

"Hey," I greeted them as Jett greeted Ava a whole different way.

"What brings you here?" Quinn asked us casually, and both Ash and I looked at Jett. Despite herself, she smiled as she shook her head in despair, her eyes rolling as she looked away with a grin. "Obviously."

"Did you just get here?" the redhead asked as she watched us all. I saw her hesitance, and I paid more attention to her. Her body seemed to angle towards Ash, but I noticed she kept her attention on me.

"Yeah," I lied. "Just passing by."

"You were passing by last time too," she reminded me as her eyes ran over me. I could see she liked what she saw at the same time that I saw Quinn notice.

"That a crime?" I asked her as my hand slipped into my back pocket. "What's your name again?"

"Mia," Ava said as she pulled away from Jett. "Have you all met? I forget if we've done proper introductions."

"We met the night of the party when 'Bama showed up," I answered Ava as I watched Mia. "You were friendly with their wide receiver. You know Dust?"

I watched her eyes shift nervously to Ash, and I pocketed that look for later. "Yeah, met him a few times."

"Hmm." I smiled at her, and I saw her already pale skin whiten.

"So we need to convince you that the Saints are who you should cheer for and not the Lions." Ash's friendly smile fooled so many fucking people.

"I don't know much about football." Mia visibly relaxed as he spoke to her, and I saw Quinn's face ease as she watched them.

"How can you be friends with Ava and know nothing?" Ash asked in disbelief as Jett chuckled while he buried his head in Ava's neck.

"It's a skill," Mia told him with a light laugh as she smiled at her friend, and I saw the genuine affection they had for each other.

I needed to warn Ash off this one. He fucked with her, and he would fuck us all. We weren't over the last balls up, never mind adding another one into the mix.

"I need to go to the little gals room," Ava said as she disentangled herself from Jett.

"I need a drink," I said to my brother. "Coke?" I asked him and Ash, who both nodded.

"Oooh me, please," Ava said to me as she pulled out her wallet. "If that's okay?" She looked at me nervously, and I fought the urge to bare my teeth at her. I knew I made her nervous, but I hadn't made the effort yet to make her comfortable.

I refused her money as I turned to the bar. Did she remember I knew she risked her full scholarship for extra money because she was so hard up? Like I would take money off her. As I rested on the bar counter, I felt the body press into the small space between me and the next customer.

"You scare her," Quinn told me as she gathered her hair over her shoulder. The faint smell of lavender and vanilla drifted over to me as she ran her hands through her hair, patting it in place.

"Scare her? Bit dramatic, no?"

"You're a scary ass prick, and you know it."

I grimaced as I held my hand up to the bartender. "Six Cokes." I met Quinn's look. "I assume you're here to help me carry them?" I mocked her gently.

A rueful smile skimmed her lips quickly. "You know me so well," she said softly.

The bartender put six sodas in front of me, and I gave her a twenty. Grabbing a tray, I placed some on it and put two into Quinn's hands as I gave her the same look I gave Ava. "Don't ever forget it, Queeny." Moving past her, I stopped when I heard her quiet rebuke.

"As if you would let me."

Quinn manoeuvred past me and headed back to the others, and I watched her go. Why did I come here? She was fine. I was a fool to think she would be out of her depth. I was ready to leave.

Twenty minutes later, the band was playing again, and both Ash and I had heard enough country rock to last a lifetime. "We need to go," I reminded my brother. With a tap on my arm to let me know he heard me, he pulled his girl into him and told her goodbye.

"I need to piss." Ash clapped my shoulder as he headed to the back of the bar.

With a nudge to Jett, I gestured to the door and made my way out of the bar. The cool air was a welcome reprieve, and I walked around the back of the bar to the car.

I heard her approach before she knew, that I knew, she was there. "Stalking?" I asked as I opened the car door.

"You're going to do something stupid."

In the dark of the evening, I watched the streetlight illuminate her face. She was so fucking beautiful; I felt a surge of anger as I looked her over. Her legs were long and slender, her stomach flat because she kept herself fit and toned. Her tits were shown off nicely under that sweater, but the scarf covered the slender column of her throat, which was a pity. I remembered only too well how good my hand looked wrapped around it. Her straight white teeth pulled at her lower lip in uncertainty as she looked at me with wide eyes. Eyes the colour of dark chocolate, the expensive kind that ruined you for all other chocolate.

"Am I?"

"I told Jett to tell you all to stop. I told *you* to stop." Her eyes dropped to her boots. "Why do you never listen to me?"

"It's not all about you, Queeny."

"I hate that fucking nickname."

My smirk let her know I knew that and I didn't give a shit. Jett called her that all the time, why couldn't I? "Go back inside," I told her instead.

"Tell me where you're going."

"Home."

"Liar."

"Then why ask?" Crossing my arms, I watched her closely, reading the body language, knowing she was unsure.

"You used to be honest with me," Quinn told me as she wrapped her arms around her waist. "Brutally so."

I heard Jett and Ash approach, and I dipped my head at her as I got in the car, closing the door, keeping her out. As she spoke to Jett, I watched her try to plead her case to him. He gave her a kiss on the side of her head, effectively ignoring her, and then he and Ash were in the car with me.

"Ready?" Jett asked me, and I nodded as I put my phone in my pocket, the text sent.

As I slowly drove past her, I saw her reach into her back pocket and pull her phone out, and as I turned onto the road, one final glance in the rearview showed me her standing staring at the car, her face showing her anguish.

Clenching my jaw, I thought about the text I just sent her. Fuck it. I had no regrets. Not anymore.

CHAPTER 4

Quinn

STANDING WATCHING THE CAR DRIVE AWAY, I LOOKED DOWN AT HIS text.

Gray: **I hear you, I've always heard you...I'm just done listening**

Unexpectedly I felt tears, and hastily I wiped one away as it had the audacity to spill over. I wasn't used to crying; my emotions were under control. Tight control. I had cried so much for so long I was done letting my emotions rule me. Wrapping my arms around myself, I made my way slowly back to the bar, but as I rounded the corner, I was surprised to see Ava standing there, waiting for me. Her hesitant smile made my feet falter, but I plastered my smile on my face and tried to loosen my arms from the fake comfort they were giving me.

"Hey." I looked at her as she literally hopped from foot to foot in uncertainty, and I braced myself for the question that I knew was coming.

"Where do they go?" Ava's eyes showed her anxiety, and I cursed my Devils for leaving me with this to deal with.

"They have practice tomorrow, early."

The *that's bullshit* look she gave me was merited, but it wasn't my job to soothe her concerns. I felt a pang of...guilt? *Was* it my job? Ugh, this friendship thing sucked.

"I'm not stupid." Her whisper was worse than the stab of guilt I had felt.

We stood for a moment longer, and I knew that the fleeting feeling of belonging I had felt earlier was disappearing as quickly as it had come.

"I don't know where they're going." I surprised myself with my own words, and I saw Ava mirror my shock, but she speedily overcame it as she took a step forward. "I don't know, they don't tell me either," I added quickly.

"But you know why?" Ava's eyes were shrewd as she watched me. My resolve must have been clear on my face as I saw her slowly nod in acceptance. "I understand, if it was Mia...I wouldn't be saying shit either." Her hands ran through her ponytail as she looked away from me. "Is it bad?"

"Ava," I began.

"Don't tell me. I know that it is. He's been out twice when he thought I was sleeping."

Twice? Pushing my alarm down, I curbed my tongue.

"He comes back and it's late and he feels...off." Troubled green eyes met mine, and I saw her harden herself for the reply to the next question. "Is he seeing someone else?"

"No."

The speed of my reply caused her to smile with relief. "Really? I know we're new and we started off, well, wrong, but I..." Ava's troubled look eased as I placed a hand on her arm.

"He will never cheat, I promise you. He isn't and he wouldn't."

She startled me when she gave me a hug, and I awkwardly patted her shoulder. "He makes me crazy," she admitted with a self-deprecating roll of her eyes. "I'm *that* girl. The crazy clingy girl that knows her boyfriend is insanely hot and women will throw themselves at him."

"Of course they will." I wasn't dissuaded by her frown at my honesty. "He's a nineteen-year-old good-looking guy with a very big future ahead of him; people will want their hooks in him, in all of them, very early on. He knows that. They all do. It's one of the reasons they're so fucking arrogant."

"Just one?" Ava teased as she shook off her melancholy.

"Yeah, they're also all overbearing, trust me." I nudged her shoulder with mine. "They're also disgustingly stubborn, and I swear Ash was in that womb with the twins—they're more like triplets sometimes. When they set their mind on something, they do not let go." Watching her secret smile, I nodded in agreement. "You know that better than anyone."

"He is persistent."

"Bah!" I laughed. "He cares about you so much, trust me." Watching Ava question herself and then give herself an inner shake was a nice distraction from my own problems.

"Sorry," she mumbled.

"Don't worry about it, they're a lot to take."

As she concentrated on the sidewalk, I felt her lingering uncertainty and was ready when she raised her head to me one more time. "Is it illegal?"

"You need to talk to Jett," I deflected like a pro. I saw the understanding, and I appreciated it, more than I realised that I would.

"You did tell me you were the fourth Devil." Ava placed her hand on my arm. "I shouldn't have asked, it was a bitch move, and I would have smacked me down if I were you, so thank you for being kind."

Kind? Me? Well, that was a first.

"And of course it's shady shit," Ava carried on. "I fear for the opposition."

"Opposition?"

"The other team."

"Of course." Gesturing to the door to the bar, I asked if she wanted to go back in, and as she turned to walk back into the bar, I marvelled at her naivete to think they were merely out causing mayhem with their upcoming competitors. However, as I followed her inside, it didn't make me feel much better in that I didn't know what they were doing either, but I knew it sure as shit wasn't college pranks.

I noticed that Ava's friend Mia, who seemed like a nice enough girl, didn't seem concerned that Ava and I had been gone. She was dancing with some other girls, and it was another five minutes before she turned, looking for her best friend. I understood now how Ava had wandered drunk out of a party alone. My mom used to say you shouldn't judge a book by its cover, but I already had Mia whatever-her-name-was in the book bargain bin. The cover looked good, but the story within had no depth. She was shallow and self-centred, and I was by no means a saint, but I didn't abandon my friends. No matter how much they wished I did.

"Does she always leave you?" I asked Ava as the band announced they were wrapping up their set.

"Hmm?" She looked over at Mia and smiled fondly. "She's sociable. Literally can talk to anyone."

Except you. "What's next?" I asked instead of airing my thoughts.

"Party probably." Ava gave me a smile, but I saw the tiredness in her eyes.

"Or we could get food?" I suggested as I watched Mia laugh with the bass guitarist's girlfriend.

"Food?" Ava's eyes lit up in anticipation before she was looking at Mia. "Mia won't want to eat, but she might want to go with Bea and the others." She patted my arm, which I assumed was a command to *stay here*, and then she was crossing the floor to her friend.

"You look lonely."

I fought the eye roll and looked at the guy who had sidled up beside me. "If you've been watching, you'll know I'm here with people."

"Saw your guy leave you."

How long had he been watching? "Aren't you observant," I snarked at him. Tall but not too much taller than me, dark hair in a low fade, stubble that looked more unkept than designer, grey T-shirt pulled too tight over his shoulders, and instead of looking fit and formed, he should just have gone the next size up.

"You're gorgeous, how could I not notice?" He smiled and I was sure he thought it was a sexy smirk. Instead, he looked sleazy.

"You said you saw me with my guy, right?" I asked him with a smile.

"Yeah, he left you. I wouldn't leave you, baby."

Ugh, kill me now. "Aren't you a catch," I murmured and saw the idiot ignore my tone and think I'd complimented him. "My guy's coming back."

"We could split now?"

Was he serious? Oh, he was, I realised as he stepped closer.

"Want to?"

"Want to? What? Split, with you?" I shook my head as I gave him my best pity smile. "No."

His whole demeanour changed, and I looked over to make sure Ava was out of the way. "Too good for me, *Queen*?"

He now had my full attention, and I looked him over again. He was older than me—I would say mid-twenties—and his brown eyes were hard, while his earlier flirty tone was gone. "Yes, I am."

His hand snapped out and held my arm tight, and I was ready to punch him when I heard Ava call for me.

"Let go of me, now, before I rip your balls off," I warned him, my voice low.

"Your Devils aren't here now, bitch." His arm tightened, and I didn't let him see he was hurting me.

Stepping into his space, I met his glare with my own. "Who said I needed them?" My hand shot out, jabbing him in the throat, and I felt immense satisfaction as he dropped my arm and covered his neck as he coughed. Stepping back, I smiled at him. "Touch me again, it won't be my hand in your throat, understand?"

"You okay?" Ava was beside me, and as I turned to reassure her, I saw her glare at the guy and realised she was here to back me up in case I needed it. "Did he hurt you?"

"I'm good." This girl just kept on earning my respect, and I liked it.

Ava looked to the bar and the few onlookers I had attracted, but she raised her hand to the older woman at the bar. The woman turned to the bouncers, and soon they were on either side of him and escorting him out.

"You have friends in high places," I teased her, and she gave me a tight smile.

"We'll be careful when we leave. I don't want the scumbag waiting for you." Ava squeezed my hand before she pulled me after her to her friends and asked them to wait outside with us until our cab was here.

I didn't want to tell her I was perfectly capable of kicking the guy's ass myself, and truthfully, it was entertaining watching her bossing the guys around. She was protecting me, and I decided I would personally castrate Jett if he fucked this up with her.

"I'll come with you," I heard Mia tell Ava. "Sleazy douches have taken me out of my social mood."

"So you want to come have some food and be Debbie Downer with us?" Ava baited. "You're not ruining my pizza fest with your sour mood."

"No, I won't." Mia stuck her tongue out at Ava, and I watched as they giggled. "I'm not eating pizza though."

"Eating on Monday gives you all week to work it off." It was how I justified slices of cheese pizza on a Monday night anyway.

"Exercise?" Ava looked horrified.

"Yeah, running, Pilates, light weightlifting."

"Like actual exercise?"

"And look at that, you're already running with me on Wednesday and Friday morning," I told her with a grin.

"You look like you seem pleased." Ava's voice was high-pitched, and I realised I was her worst nightmare.

"Healthy body, healthy mind." The mantra I repeated every day to myself.

"Cab's here," Mia said as she pulled Ava to the car and they called their goodbyes to their friends. Mia looked at me with a grin. "You've just become her kryptonite."

"Yeah, well, sex with a Devil is all well and orgasmic, but you need more than that to be in shape," I said with a smirk as I got into the car. "Exercise builds stamina. Trust me, Ava, he'll thank you. Or me," I mused. "Semantics."

"Where you heading?" the cab driver asked, and we paused awkwardly as we exchanged looks.

"You can come to ours," Ava offered. "It's not much, but it's clean and it's home."

"Sounds good."

It *was* small. It was tiny, but they looked so at home I kind of envied them.

We sat and shared a cheese pizza, with music playing in the background, and I learned more about Ava and Mia. I realised the dynamic I had missed before, they were as close as sisters. They were in the same class at school, and both having one parent families, their moms had realised early on that when money was tight, you pooled your resources. So instead of paying for two sitters, they paid for one who watched two girls. Ava joked that it was a good thing they got on so well, or maybe it wouldn't have been so successful.

"What about you?" Ava asked me as she rubbed her tummy after finishing her slice. "Siblings?"

"No. Just me."

"But you have three brothers, kind of." Ava reached for her glass when Mia snorted.

"Awkward. She slept with her brother, remember?"

Ava looked at me and then started to laugh. "Sorry, I never thought."

"It's fine, what's a little incest between friends?"

Both girls froze before they collapsed in laughter, and I laughed along with them. "So, Mia, music major?"

"Yeah, afraid so."

"What do you play?" I asked her, even though I knew. I just wanted the conversation off of me and the Santos.

"My voice." Mia gave me a mock bow. "I play the chords I was born with."

Wow.

Ava was also speechless before she cracked up again and gave her friend a playful swat. "What bullshit was that?" Ava cried. "You play the chords you were born with? That's...that's just..."

"Dickish," I spoke.

Ava nodded and Mia was scarlet. "I made it up in class today. We have to write bios for the upcoming arts show, and I wrote it down and hated it, but the prof was all gushing about it, and I thought I would try it out. Sounded bad?"

"A little pretentious," I murmured as Ava was already sitting back down with a notepad and pen.

"For someone who hates to sing in front of an audience, you cannot say you play the chords you were born with." She gave me an exasperated look as she turned back to Mia. "We'll brainstorm; I'm fuelled by cheese."

My snort of laughter earned me a grin from both girls. "Okay, what do you sing?" I asked her. "Soprano, mezzo or alto?"

Mia looked impressed as she looked at me. "I range between mezzo and alto."

"You must be good to get in here with just your chords," I told her honestly. "Okay, lay it on me."

"Lay what on you?"

"Sing."

"Oh."

I watched the girl I had thought shallow and self-centred become a complete introvert in the space of seconds. I knew I must look as shocked as I felt. "You're *shy*?"

"Horrifically so," Ava answered as she leaned into her friend in a show of support. "Stage fright is real, hey, Mee?"

"It's cracking hell."

She also didn't swear, and I thought that was peculiar. What was the point of a good rant if you didn't drop the f-bomb a few times? Where was the satisfaction in that? "What if I turn my back?" I asked curiously.

"You're still *you*."

Ouch. "That is true."

"I don't mean it that way," Mia apologised. "I mean you're *Quinn Lawrence*, you're intimidating."

"Oh."

"Don't be silly," Ava scolded her. "This is Quinn, she's perfectly normal."

Perfectly normal? Was that more of an insult? I wasn't sure.

"Keep them coming, ladies, I'm here for a while longer," I dead-panned. My phone buzzing with a new text alerted me to the fact that that may not be the case. Ava also grabbed her phone, and I realised the Devils were heading home.

Gray: **You home?**

Me: **No.**

Gray: **?**

I remembered his earlier text and his attitude and decided to fuck with him.

Me: **With company**

I waited as I saw the three dots come and go, and my heart stuttered when I received the thumbs up emoji. Tossing my phone on the floor face down, I looked up to see Mia watching me, and I slapped a smile on my face. Her look was thoughtful as she broke the stare and reached for the empty pizza box to tidy up.

I had maybe been too hasty in my assessment of Mia Davis.

CHAPTER 5

Gray

She had company? Was she fucking kidding me? Glancing at my watch, I checked the time. It had been three hours. Three fucking hours, and she had company?

"Gray!" Jett's tone was sharp, and my head jerked up to look at him.

"What?" I snapped as I pulled my hoodie off, tossing it on my bed as I kicked my sneakers off.

"Why are you getting undressed?" Jett asked me curiously. "You're not listening to me," he sighed, and I thought about the last few minutes. Nope, I'd heard nothing.

"What?" I asked him again, my impatience seeping through.

Jett raised his arms in front of him in a dismissive gesture. "Forget it, I'll go myself."

"Go where?"

"To Ava's."

"Okay." Why the fuck did I need to go with him? He was a big boy. Heading to my bathroom, I stopped at his next words.

"I'll take her home first."

She was with company... I huffed out a rueful chuckle. My hands on the side of the doorframe, I turned and looked at my brother. "Quinn at Ava's?"

"Yes," he answered, exasperation bleeding into his tone. "I told you this."

"Was thinking of my assignment," I lied easily. "You taking Ava back here?"

"Yeah, see if she goes for it."

"You're falling deep." He didn't have time for this. I mean, his girl was nice enough, but personally, I didn't see the appeal. She did like football though, so that was something. I didn't particularly like his loss of focus though. "Can you stall hot and heavy until after the season?"

"No." My bedroom door had been opened, and Jett closed it behind him as he stepped further into the room. "You want to say something to me?"

"Pretty sure I just did."

"I'm not fucking up the season, I know what I'm doing with football, with Ava *and* with Quinn." Jett shoved his hands in his front pockets, and I knew it was to stop him from clenching his fists.

"Two of those three things are time sensitive," I reminded him. The season was short, the window of opportunity that we had on scumbag central was small, and the only thing that didn't matter at this moment in time was Ava.

"You think my girlfriend doesn't matter?" Jett asked me with narrowed eyes.

"Not at the moment. If she cares, she'll hang around, but you have other things to be doing. Other than her."

"The fact we're related blows my mind sometimes." He turned and yanked the door open, closing the door hard behind him.

I knew my brother better than anyone, and I knew I should have handled that better. We were eight games into the season, we were undefeated, we could not fuck this up, and we had four games left. Grabbing my hoodie, casting a defeated look at my desk where my workbooks were, I headed out of my room to find my asshole brother.

He was already halfway down the block, and I set out in a light jog until I was pulling up alongside him. Jett's hood was pulled low, and his shoulders were slumped as he walked, straightening when I fell into step beside him. We walked the few blocks to Ava's dorm in silence until he turned to me.

"I'm not going to let you down on any of it," he spoke quietly.

"I know."

"Then what was the shit for?"

"I'm tired, I have an assignment due, we have a lot going on." None of this was a lie.

"At least tonight's video wasn't as bad," Jett said to me quietly.

"Wasn't it?" My hands curled into fists in my hoodie as I stared straight ahead. "I see her on that table every damn time."

He was quiet as we neared the steps for Ava's place. "I know, maybe you shouldn't watch."

"Maybe you should go fuck yourself."

Jett grinned at me. "Subtle." With a hand on my shoulder, he stopped me from climbing the stairs. "Gray, we'll bring them down," he promised.

Meeting his stare, I shook my head slightly as I looked over my shoulder to make sure there were no ears nearby. "You don't understand. I don't want to make them *pay*, I want to cut them open, pull their insides out and fucking feed their intestines to them."

Jett watched me and then he smiled widely. "Well then, when you paint such a pretty picture, who am I to deny you?" He ascended the few stairs, and I decided to hang back. The place looked shit small; I felt claustrophobic looking at it.

Leaning against the wall in the dark, I started to think about my assignment. It was half-done, and as I saw the time was after midnight, I was in for a night of no sleep. We had practice at six before class and then practice at three for three hours. I could already feel the weariness drag me down.

The door opened, and I heard Ava call out to her roommate as they left. It made no sense he was taking her from here to ours—he'd have been better staying here. Quinn came down first.

She hesitated at the foot of the stairs, her senses on alert before she turned and saw me standing there. Kicking off from the wall, I walked over to the three of them.

"Why are you here?" she asked me.

"Hi to you too," I snarked. "C'mon, I'm walking you home."

"I'll manage." Quinn's shoulders were tense, and I saw her look towards Jett, who was pretending he wasn't listening.

"*Manage* a hell of a lot more quickly so we can move it along," I told her as I gestured at Jett to move along so we could get this over with.

"See you tomorrow," he called to me, and I flicked him the finger as I started walking without Quinn. I hid my smile as I heard her curse and then hurry to catch up with me.

"Why is your brother always so pissed off?" Ava asked Jett, and I didn't think she knew she could be heard, or maybe she just didn't care.

I ignored Jett's reply, no doubt it would be something he thought would be funny. Asshole.

"You don't need to do this," Quinn said, breaking our silence as we walked, and I stayed silent. "Gray, you can go."

"Or you can be quiet, and we can enjoy a quiet walk to your apartment."

I heard her teeth grind, and I knew she was biting her tongue from whatever heated reply she was going to give me. Instead, she surprised me with her next words.

"Was tonight a success for you?"

"It will never be a success until my hands are wrapped around one of the motherfuckers' throats." Out of the corner of my eye, I saw her head dip, and I hated that the usual fearless Quinn was timid.

"You know most people would say I deserved it."

"I'm not most people," I bit out. "And these *people* ever say that shit to you, you send them my way."

Quinn said nothing, but I knew her back straightened a little. My phone buzzed in my pocket, and I pulled it out.

Jett: **Quinn had trouble at the bar, some douche hit on her and got nasty...Ava thinks he hurt her, but Quinn wouldn't say**

anything.

My hand snatched her elbow to stop her from walking so I could read the text again. He knew better than to think Quinn would speak to anyone who wasn't us.

"Booty call?" she asked me as she tried to keep her voice indifferent.

"Sure." I resumed walking as I put my phone away. "Come on."

At her apartment door, I didn't walk away but waited expectantly. It was quite clearly not what Quinn was expecting as she looked at me pointedly and then the stairs back outside.

"I need to piss."

"Ever the eloquent gentleman," she muttered as she led me inside, and I headed to the bathroom. I knew her well: she would have the boots off in seconds, and then she would take off the scarf and, depending on her state of tiredness, her sweater.

Giving her a few more minutes, I flushed the toilet and then exited to find her exactly as I predicted. Bootless, socks off and in the middle of taking her sweater off. I saw the dark bruises on her upper arm before she had the sense to hide them from me.

"What happened?" I asked her casually as I leaned against the door, watching her face.

"When?" Her look of confusion cleared when she saw me look at her arm, and she immediately tried to hide it.

"Horse has already bolted, bit late to lock the stable door." My voice was calm, which was unlike me. "Who was it?"

Giving up any pretence, Quinn dropped her hand and shrugged as she sat on her bed. "Not sure. I thought he was hitting on me, and I told him to fuck off."

"I'm sure you handled him with care and compassion."

"He called me Queen and said that my Devils weren't there to save me."

Pushing off the doorframe, I crossed the room to her, and

crouching down to be eye level, I reached out and traced the bruises. "You don't know him?"

"No. Older than me, sleazy looking, but I guess some people would think he was good looking," she said as her eyes tracked my fingers as I gently caressed her skin.

"And you wanted to walk home alone?" I snarled as I stood. "You've lost your mind."

"I can handle myself, Gray." Quinn looked up at me, her gentleness gone. "I throat punched the asshole, and the bouncers threw him out."

"Well, that was stupid, now you're even more on his radar."

"I'm fine." Angrily she stood, her hands on her hips. "You can leave now." Quinn's eyes closed for a brief moment as she tried to calm her temper. "Thank you for taking me home, but it wasn't necessary."

"Yet again, we agree to disagree."

"Gray..." Quinn tipped her head back before she looked at me. "Let's just call it a night."

"Sure."

I was out the door without another word, but I did wait until I heard the door lock. The walk home was quick, and I took the stairs two at a time to the top landing where our rooms were. Hesitating at my brother's door, I listened for signs of him and Ava going at it. Hearing nothing, I tapped the wood lightly. He must have been waiting for me, as the door opened quickly and he followed me into my own room.

"She okay?"

Quickly I told him what she told me and about the bruises.

"You know what this means?" Jett said to me thoughtfully.

"She needs watched at all times." I felt the heaviness settle on my shoulders.

"It could be nothing," Jett tried to reason.

"Yeah, or it could be a whole lot of something."

"She's going to resist," Jett warned me as if I hadn't known her as long as he had.

"So? What else is new?" I pulled my own hoodie off. "Isn't that what you told me recently?"

Jett grinned, but it faded as he walked over to my desk. "You have a long night ahead."

"Don't sleep much anymore anyway."

His look told me he knew, and he headed to the door. "We're getting closer to a breakthrough. I know we are."

"Or, you could let me go back to Harry's and kick the shit out of him until he tells me what I need to know."

Jett hesitated. "Work on your assignment. I'll talk to you tomorrow."

Fifteen minutes later, I was dressed for bed, knowing if I passed out at my desk, I would at least be comfortable. Checking my alarm on my phone, I realised I had a text.

Quinn: **Why did you come tonight?**

Me: **Jett**

Quinn: **He ask you to walk me home too?**

I struggled with my answer because if I said yes, she would know it was a lie. Grunting, I put the phone down. I wasn't getting into it with her over text message. With a wide yawn, I picked up my notes. I needed to concentrate, and she was the biggest distraction I'd ever met. I was deep into my notes when the phone went again a while later.

Quinn: **Why do you keep doing this? It's giving me whiplash**

Ignore her. Leaning back in my chair, I stared at the ceiling as I thought about it. She was probably right, but I couldn't afford to let her under my skin. Not again. Jett had kept his friendship with her after the showdown with Ash, and I hadn't exactly been distant either. I knew I should have taken some of the blame that day in school, but I hadn't done anything. I *had* walked away the night she crawled onto my lap in only her underwear.

Quinn had never wanted Ash. Sure, she cared about him—a blind man could see that—but she didn't *like* him. Not like he thought. Not like she pretended.

That was my fault too. I knew she had been trying to make me jealous. It had amused me. Using my cousin to get a reaction out of me? Stupid. I genuinely thought Ash would let it go, but he didn't. It turned out he'd been interested. More than interested.

I'd been so sure of him turning her down, I'd said nothing. Until it was too late. He made a move, and she let him. She let him kiss her, and then she ran to Jett and told him, and he hadn't done what he should have done, which was tell her not to be rash.

When he told me later that same day, I thought I was going to punch him. It wouldn't be the first time I hit my brother, but it would be the first time I hit him over a girl. Then Ash told me he'd fingered her, and my rage had been so real I envisaged murdering him right there and then.

She let him touch her? Had I been wrong? Had I read her wrong, the whole situation wrong, was it Ash she actually wanted?

So I cornered her, and I'd kissed her. A dick move, I knew. He was my cousin and I loved him as much as I loved my brother, but Quinn had always been mine. I needed to know I was right, that it wasn't Ash she wanted, and I *had* been right. The eagerness with which she kissed me back soothed all my worries. I'd even put my hand on her pussy—he had, why shouldn't I? Quinn hadn't pushed me away, she'd moaned, and that moan had brought me back to earth.

Certain I had stopped them both from making a mistake, I'd walked away from her after telling her to stop being a liar. It wasn't *him* she wanted, it was *me*. I knew it, and she just proved it.

I was so confident in myself I'd been speechless a few days later when Ash told us all that they were now officially dating. I'd watched her as he told us and she hadn't been able to look me in the eyes. *Chicken*. She was a chicken when she was ten, and she was a chicken when she was seventeen. I'd had enough of her and her stupid indecision.

Their relationship was a rocky one, which I knew it would be. They didn't fit well. As friends, they were perfect, and it probably shouldn't have brought me as much amusement as it did when I watched them try to be a couple and fail. Quinn needed someone to challenge her, and Ash needed someone to *need* him. Instead, he let her do what she wanted, and she was so goddamn independent she never asked him for anything.

Months later when she crawled half naked onto my lap and begged me to touch her, I had almost given in and fucked her right then, but I couldn't. She was with Ash, and I couldn't do that to him even though he did it to me. He'd taken what was mine and tried to make it his own, and every time they were in front of me, I wanted to scream in fury.

Jett said nothing, just observed silently as he always did. I think he suspected, but he never raised it with me, and I never volunteered.

The day she broke it off with Ash, the whole time she spoke to him, she looked to me for reassurance, and I gave her none. I could see she was in pain; I could see she was scared, and I didn't care. I wanted her to *feel* it, feel it as I had felt it for five months. Five fucking months of seeing them together. Five months of watching him touch what was mine and watching her try to ignore the fact she was with the wrong Devil.

When she ran from the room, Jett told me to check on her while he calmed Ash down. And I did, I followed her and saw her run to the bathrooms, and that had pissed me off even more. She was open and vulnerable—had she forgotten who she was in this school? How many people there were who would want to *watch* her break. My temper was riding high, and when I saw her look so wrecked, my inner turmoil was warring with itself. Comfort her or rebuke her? I never meant to kiss her. I never meant to lose control. I certainly had no intention of fucking her in the girls' bathroom. But that was how much Quinn affected me. She made me impulsive, and that made me act without thought of consequences.

Rereading her text, I threw the phone behind me onto my bed. I needed to concentrate on my classes and my career; there was no room in my life anymore for Quinn. We'd right the wrong that was done to her, to those other girls, and it would be over. I'd given her chances, and at every opportunity, she'd fucked me over.

Picking up my pen, I concentrated on my assignment. My focus was on school and on the draft. Playing ball professionally was all that mattered, and there was no room in my life for distractions.

The days of looking back were over.

CHAPTER 6

Quinn

He never answered. I didn't expect him to. He was about as communicative as roadkill. Despite the late night and the restless sleep, the fact that I ate two slices of pizza just before midnight had me tightening the laces on my sneakers for my morning run.

Doing my stretches and warm-up, I left my dorm room and set off at a reasonable pace, keeping to the main walkways. I passed a few people, either like-minded running enthusiasts or students eager to get to the library.

As I approached the stadium, I was focused on my pace and the music playing in my ears. That didn't stop me from being aware of him as he drew alongside me, and with a quick glance, I took in his side profile. His hair was damp from practice, strands clung to his forehead, and he was still in his practice jersey and loose shorts. Gray didn't acknowledge me, just ran alongside me, keeping pace and not pushing for me to go faster until the last stretch as we came full circle and my dorm was ahead of me. Gray caught my eye, and with a smirk, he ran in front of me, my own smile forming as I dug my heels in and took off after him. We raced to the stairs, and I finished just behind him.

"You cheated," I said as I bent over with my hands resting on my knees while I caught my breath.

"You were slow," Gray countered with a grin as he pulled his leg up behind him to stretch it out.

Straightening, I watched him as he switched legs, making sure to pull them close and ease the tension in his muscles. "You heading to the house or back to the stadium?"

"Stadium." Gray looked at my arm to my watch. "Time?"

"You have a half hour before your first class."

"Plenty of time." As he dropped his leg, he stretched his arm across his chest. "I'll even have time just to walk back."

"Okay." My eyes ran over him, taking in the damp shirt, the strong legs, the muscular forearms. He had to be exhausted. I pitied the fact he had to walk back to the stadium just for a shower. The words were out before I even thought about them. "You should have taken your stuff and showered here." With more willpower than I knew I possessed, I kept my face blank as I cringed internally at my thoughtless offer.

"You been thinking about me in your shower?"

With reddening cheeks, I looked away from his piercing blue eyes and down at my feet. My feet were safer, they didn't see through my defences and strip my soul bare. "No, you know what I meant," I mumbled as I smoothed my T-shirt over my hips.

Gray stepped closer to me, and I had to stop myself from being a complete cliché and holding my breath. I watched his gaze roam lazily over my body, slowly, torturously dragging his eyes up to meet my frozen stare.

"I'm not sure I did know what you mean, why don't you explain it to me?" Gray's voice was low and husky, and dear God, did he know he was looking at me like that? It seemed that I was a cliché after all as I felt my pulse racing, and my lips parted as I saw the heat in his stare.

"Gray." I swallowed past the hoarseness of my own voice. He took another step, and now he was almost pressed against me. I quickly looked around to make sure there was no audience.

"Nervous?"

"No," I breathed as he dipped his head down. The smell of him, a mix of sweat, spice and smoke, combined with his raw sensuality was playing havoc with my senses.

His lips skimmed my jaw as he breathed one word into my ear. *"Liar."*

It was as if he had thrown a cold bucket of water over me. I jerked back from him as my hands flew up and pushed him back. Anger replaced anticipation as I watched him step back, his cocky smirk wide as he laughed at me.

"God, you're a complete asshole," I growled at him as I shoved past him, and angrily I climbed my stairs to my apartment. "I hope you get a cramp!" I called over my shoulder before I slammed my apartment door closed behind me.

My shower was cooler than normal, and well it should be. What was I thinking? I knew better how much of a bastard Gray Santo was. Tipping my head under the spray to wash out my shampoo, I let my temper cool, and despite myself, I gave out a low chuckle at his complete assholeness. And yes, it was a word. It was a word that was in the dictionary, and beside it for a definition was a picture of Gray Santo.

As my fingers combed my conditioner through my hair, I remembered the last time he had touched me. Really touched me. The way only he could. Maybe I needed a mindless hookup to get me to move on. It had been a while after all. Rubbing my exfoliating shower gel across my skin, I thought about it. The Saints were playing at home this week, so there would be a party somewhere, and I needed to be there.

I lost my virginity when I was sixteen. I had hooked up with a number of guys since then. Some were good, some were terrible, only one made my body sing for him, and only two I had ever actually cared about. Maybe that's where I was going wrong, maybe I needed to feel something for the guy. Or maybe I just needed one hot hookup that blew my mind while rocking my world.

After twisting my hair to get out the excess water, I dried myself hurriedly. I had spent too much time in the shower, and now I was going to be late if I didn't hurry. Blasting my hair with the dryer until it was half dry and wild, I quickly ran it into two French braids.

I got dressed quickly and grabbed my book bag and a protein bar as I rushed out of the door. My first class was at one of the sports buildings beside the stadium, and it wasn't lost on me the irony of the fact that I should have gone with Gray instead of getting dressed here.

Power walking as I ate my breakfast, I cursed myself for forgetting my water, internally seething that it was all Gray's fault while also knowing it wasn't his fault. Not really. My phone started ringing, and I answered it with a smile.

"Hey there."

"You heading to class?" Jett asked me, and I could hear students and knew he was already at his first class of the day.

"Yeah, heading there now, I took too long in the shower," I replied as I took another bite of my breakfast.

"You seen my brother?"

I paused chewing, hesitant about what I should say. "Yeah, he joined me on my run this morning."

"Of course he did." Jett sounded frustrated but amused.

"What's going on?"

"What time are you free?" Jett asked me instead.

"Two-hour practical this morning and then I have an hour before my next class."

"I can't make that, after?"

"Nope, my afternoon is full; Tuesday is my busy day. I don't finish until six." I was at the sports building now. "I'm at class, what is it?"

"We have a three-hour practice session today. We'll be done by six, maybe six thirty. Make your way to the stadium when you're finished. Family meeting," Jett instructed me.

"Why?"

"Queeny." I heard the reproach, and I fought the eye roll at the tone. He was younger than me, but I swear to God, sometimes he thought he was my older brother.

"Fine. Ash?"

"You get us all, I said family meeting."

He hung up on me, and I added another Santo prick to my list of people I was going to punch today.

I liked sports. I enjoyed the company of athletes, and even if I didn't, pounding the shit out of people in the form of a "massage" was soothing to me. The deep tissue massage image I had shown Jett a few weeks ago was so amazingly zen...for me. The recipient was sure I hated them, I had no doubt, but I would challenge anyone to tell me the next day that they didn't feel great. As I watched the point guard for the basketball team struggle to get off my table, I amended it to two days. He may still hurt tomorrow, but after that, he would be like a new guy.

"Quinn, you look like you're enjoying yourself," my professor said as he approached me. He was great, I loved his classes. Dimitri had been a trainer for the Olympic gymnastics squad and was so incredibly down to earth. Learning from him was a joy. His experience was unparalleled, and he taught both theory and practical with equal passion.

"It's quite relaxing," I admitted to him. "Although, I'm still hesitant about bending his leg that far back."

"And you'd be right to, because your clients may not be honest with you. They may not tell you that they actually have a strain or a twinge. Something so small to us may be the reason they don't play the next game if the coach thinks they could be injured."

"But to not tell me could hurt them more." I cleaned my hands as I waited for my next victim.

"But you can't stop them from playing."

"I can if I take small muscle discomfort and turn it into inflamed ligaments."

"Exactly!" My professor smiled at me as he looked at the centre for the basketball team waiting for my attention. "You're exceptionally talented, Quinn, there is no denying that, but I am going to have to put an end to the number of 'volunteers' that come to your table for your practical."

I didn't hide my grin as he looked uncomfortable. "You think I'm popular for more than my healing hands?"

Dimitri laughed. "Yes, unfortunately I do. Plus, you don't need the practice that your classmates do. So, for the rest of this lesson, you will supervise their skills and technique and assist. Yes?"

My eyes lit up with delight. "Play teacher?"

Seeing my enthusiasm, Dimitri clasped my shoulder with affection. "Don't make me regret this." With a laugh, he walked away from me, and I called one of the guys in my class over to my table.

"You're up, Dimitri asked me to help."

Instructing my classmates wasn't as satisfying as actually carrying out the work, but the time still passed quickly.

Heading to the coffee shop after class, I spotted Ava sitting under her tree. It wasn't her tree obviously, but she named it as hers, and I was pretty sure even in the dead of winter, I would find her here. Her head was bent over a book, her hair loose, which caught in the wind, but it wasn't distracting her.

"Hi," I said as I approached. Her smile was wide as she looked up at me, and she immediately patted beside her.

"I'm going to get coffee," I told her with a shake of my head, and I saw her face light up. "Want to come?"

"Does a bear shit in the woods?" Ava asked me as she started packing her stuff up.

"Um, sure. What if they're in a zoo?"

Ava hesitated slightly and then shrugged. "Okay, does a bear in its natural habitat shit in the woods?"

"You drive Jett insane, don't you?" I asked knowingly as I grabbed her hand and hauled her to her feet.

"Yes." She was proud of it, and together we headed for coffee. "Were you okay last night, you know, after the bar?"

"Hmm?"

"The guy," Ava clarified.

"Him? Yeah, I forgot about him, to be honest, until Gray saw the bruise and gave me shit."

"He saw you with your sweater off?"

I didn't miss her curious look that she thought I didn't see. I had spoken without thought, but then, what was I hiding? He used my bathroom, it was late, and I was getting ready for bed. "Yeah, he used the bathroom."

"You don't seem to be close to him. Do you get along well?"

I choked back my hysteria and contemplated my answer. "We get by."

"Is it because of Ash?"

Yes, but not why you think it is. "Something like that," I admitted.

"Ugh, I'm prying again!" Ava scolded herself. "I'm so sorry, I seriously am not this gossip girl, but you and them, it just fascinates me."

"Why?" Now I was curious.

"Well, you're Ash's ex, you're Jett's BFF, and I can't help wonder what your history is with Gray." Ava didn't meet my stare, but she carried on. "He intimidates me, to be honest. He and Jett pulled a shit move on me when they thought I was complicit to the water spiking, and he just, he's..."

"Unnerving."

Ava flashed me a grateful smile. "Yes! I mean, he's the other half of Jett, so I should know what he's like."

"They're fraternal twins, not identical," I reminded her as we got to the coffee shop. "He's nothing like Jett, and then sometimes, he's a carbon copy."

"Do you have a favourite?" She asked it innocently enough, and from what I had learned about her, there was no maliciousness in her question. But very few people in my life had asked me which Santo was my favourite.

"They're not ice cream flavours," I chided softly.

Ava laughed. "Oh my gosh, that would be amazing if they were." She quickly ordered a caramel latte and then asked me what I wanted. Giving the barista my order, we waited before she suggested we sit inside, and looking around, I found an empty table.

As she collected the drinks, she came over and grinned at me. "I have it, I couldn't help it. Tell me what you think? Ash, I'm thinking raspberry ripple; Gray, I'm not sure, maybe mint choc chip; and Jett would be...chocolate."

"We're still on ice cream then?" I mocked as I took a sip of my coffee.

"Yeah." Ava flushed red as she continued. "Although maybe I think I just want Jett and chocolate ice cream."

"I actually like chocolate ice cream, so could we not ruin my favourite flavour please?" Ava sat back in her seat as she looked out the window, and I feared I had lost her to her thoughts. "Raspberry ripple?"

"Yeah, Ash is all about fun, I think," she added hastily.

"You don't need to worry all the time, Ava, Ash and I were a long time ago." I sipped my coffee as I watched her and decided just to put her out of her misery. "I cheated on him. He didn't take it well. Who would? I've never had sex, nor do I want to ever have sex, with Jett; he's my best friend."

I watched as her eyes widened at my harsh honesty, and I braced myself for the question she had asked me before and I knew she would ask. But she surprised me by taking it one further.

"Did you cheat on him with Gray?"

Well, what the hell was I supposed to say to that?

CHAPTER 7

Gray

I MAY NEVER STAND AGAIN. LYING ON MY BACK, STARING UP AT THE floodlights, I realised the turf was comfortable. Okay, it wasn't, but my body was broken, I was sure of it.

"You going to get up?" Jett asked me, and I could hear the amusement in his voice.

"No."

"Woods hit too hard?" Ash asked me as he joined my brother.

"No."

"Worked your legs too hard?" Jett said as he leaned over me, blocking out the floodlights.

"Yeah," I groaned. "I need a rub down."

"We're meeting Quinn later. She's got a new textbook, and I'm scared of her," Jett told me as he grabbed my arm, and between him and Ash, they pulled me to my feet.

"I heard from the centre yesterday she almost broke his calf," Ash muttered as he patted me on the shoulder. "Maybe you need Izzy?"

"Yeah, Izzy is better." We had all been test subjects for Quinn at some point, so we were all wary.

"She dug her hands in 'cause he was getting hard," Jett grunted. "We all know she's going to be shit hot at her job."

Ash and I exchanged a look, but neither said anything. However, I hadn't been told the dipshit had overstepped with her, and now I was glad that she hurt him on purpose.

"Of course, if you hadn't trained so hard today, you wouldn't be so fucking sore," Jett scolded as we walked—well, I limped—to the locker room.

"I did what you did," I defended myself.

"You ran with Quinn this morning," he said, and I caught Ash's quick look of surprise.

"And we said she needed to be watched."

"Why are we watching Quinn?" Ash asked us quietly as we all naturally paused at the twenty-five.

Quickly Jett told him about the guy in the bar, and I filled in the missing pieces about what he had said to her, about the Devils and calling her Queen.

"You think they're watching her?" Ash asked with a scowl. "They touch her, they die."

"Agreed."

Jett watched us both, his look calculating before he looked around. "We need to be careful, and we need to make sure she is safe."

"We never had any reason to think she was at risk." Ash sighed as his hand ran through his hair. "I mean, what we've seen on the memory sticks, that didn't happen to her, not all of it."

"You sure?" My voice was so low and quiet, but it caught both their attention. "She lies. She only told Jett what happened because she needed him to get her out of that hospital. If she had been able to get hold of her stepmom, Anne, would we ever know what happened to her on her summer break?"

We stood in silence, each in our own thoughts before Jett clapped us both on the back. "This gets us nowhere."

"I think we need to press her."

I looked at Ash in surprise. "Serious?"

"Yeah." He hadn't looked sure, but as his attention flicked between me and my brother, I saw his resolve hardening. "We need to know it all. She knows we got involved, she knows she can't stop us, and I say we ask her to sit the fuck down and tell us exactly what we need to know."

"I already said this," Jett reminded him. "I said she needed to know."

"Her needing to know and us asking her what we need to know, is not the same thing," I warned them both.

"Then it's full disclosure," Jett snapped. "If, and I appreciate it's a big *if*, they are looking at her to see who she tells or told, then we need to know what they have on her. Or what they would do to her to keep her quiet."

"They will know she said nothing," Ash argued. "She didn't report it."

"And thank fuck she never did, else where would we be now?" I grunted out a laugh. "Jail. Goodbye, college."

"You want to back out?" Ash looked at me in surprise.

"Never." I just knew it wasn't going to be an easy conversation. Some wounds were better left to heal on their own without picking at the scabs.

"Maybe we should get her drunk," Ash mused as we resumed walking to the showers.

"She's meeting us outside." Jett told us both.

Even I glared at him as I heard Ash curse. "Seriously? No warning?"

"I'm telling you now," he said as he shrugged carelessly. "What more do you want, a written invitation?"

"God, you're a dick." Pushing past my brother, I headed into the locker room. When I got into the shower, I used my tired body for the reason I stood there longer than necessary. Not the fact that we were about to force her to tell us her worst nightmare. No, not a nightmare for Quinn, to her it was real. Maybe *I* needed a drink for this.

It was with a small measure of appreciation that I noted that Ash was as reluctant to leave the locker room as I was. However, as usual, my brother wasn't one for waiting when he got an idea in his head.

Finally, when we left the locker room, she was standing outside the stadium, laughing at something Ava was saying.

Ava.

Well, that complicated things. Or did it? I saw the smile she gave us all in greeting, and I saw the small triumph in her eyes as she met Jett's enquiring look.

Well played, Queeny. She knew Jett wanted to push, and this was her fuck you, telling him she would open up when she was ready. I hid my smile behind my hand as I pretended to scratch my jaw.

"Hey, this is a nice surprise," Jett greeted Ava, pulling her into a hug as his hard stare met Quinn's. She held her hands up in supplication as if she were innocent.

"Mia had practice until late, Quinn thought you would all be tired, so I thought we may want to grab some food?" Ava looked around at the three of us expectantly.

"What about our meal plans for your assignment," I asked, watching in satisfaction as Quinn's look of smugness was replaced by one of irritation.

"Yeah, thought you had our food all planned out?" Jett slung his arm around Ava's shoulders as he watched Quinn falter for a response.

"Oh, we thought of that," Ava told him cheerfully as she tilted her head back to look at him. "Quinn can tell you what to order and what to leave off." Ava smiled up at him, and I looked at Quinn, who was failing to hide her victory. "It can be our first real dinner date," Ava added softly to him.

And for the winner of most conniving bitch of the year, ladies and gentlemen, I present Quinn Lawrence.

"You okay with all of us being on your first dinner date with my brother?" I asked Ava sceptically.

She always looked nervous when she spoke to me, and I still remembered her punching me on the jaw. "You're Jett's family; it would be nice to eat together."

My eyes flew to Quinn as she pretended to look at her nails.

"Wow," I muttered as I shook my head and saw Quinn's small triumphant smile.

"Don't you want to?" Ava looked confused as she finally picked up on the tension, and my response was about to shatter her illusions until I saw my brother's glare at me over her head.

"Sounds like a great idea, I'm starving," I growled as I walked past them and hooked my favourite trainer's arm as I passed. "Want to talk to you about a deep tissue massage." Looking over my shoulder, I saw Ash and Ava engaged in conversation and met my brother's curious look. Ignoring him, I turned back around. "What are you playing at?" I asked her as she walked beside me, head held high and back straight.

"I thought you may be hungry after a hard day of training."

"You used to be more convincing when you lied," I grunted.

"You used to be gentler when you touched me," she countered quietly.

I almost let her go, but instead, my grip tightened on her arm. "Really? I didn't hear any complaints when my hand was wrapped around your throat and your pussy was sucking my dick dry."

"You're such an asshole."

"Never pretended otherwise."

"Hey, you two, slow down!" Ava called out behind us. "Not everyone has your long legs!"

With a deep breath, I let go of Quinn as we waited for the others to catch up. I was not looking forward to this.

WE'D TAKEN TWO CARS TO GET TO CARDINAL. QUINN HAD OPTED for an Italian restaurant. Smallish in size, it had a handful of booths and then a mix of small tables with red and white gingham tablecloths, with half-used candles in empty dark green wine bottles for authenticity, or something. I'd been to Italy many times, and I had yet to see a half-used, heavily waxed, empty wine bottle as a candle holder, but hey, who was I to raise questions about authenticity?

The atmosphere between us was, to say the least, awkward. Ash refused to acknowledge Quinn, Jett was whispering sweet nothings into Ava's ear, and I was seriously considering faking an illness. Anything that would let me walk out of here without having to endure an hour of this.

Ava, through no fault of her own, managed to catch my attention, and I saw her happy smile fade as she read the tension in my eyes, and with a quick glance, she looked at the other occupants of the table.

"Have you been here before?" she asked us all, and I wanted to pat her on the head for her feeble attempt at trying to make conversation.

"You know, Ava," Ash told her with a grin, "this is the first time you've probably ever sat with four other people who are all as crazy about football as you."

Ava beamed. There was no other word for it; she looked positively giddy with glee. "Oh my God, you are so right. You can talk routes and drives all night long, and I won't even feel ignored," she said to Jett with a smile.

"Or we can talk about other things," Jett said to her as he kissed the side of her head, his hard stare on Quinn.

I saw her moisten her lips as she reached for a glass of water. "What else could we possibly have to discuss?" Her answering look was equally as hard, and I loved my brother, I did, but he deserved that virtual slap she just delivered him. This was not the time, and it was not the place. More importantly, he may be in love with his girl or whatever, but this was not a conversation for Ava to be party to.

Not now and possibly never.

"Who did you get to practice on today?" Ava asked her as she again quickly picked up on the tension and changed the subject.

"Basketball team." Quinn smiled at her, and studying her, I saw it was genuine. That was interesting. I turned my attention back to Ava, my head tilting as I studied her. I just didn't see this fascination they all had with her. What was she offering to make them all like her? She didn't appeal to me at all, and honestly, I found her kind of irritating. For Quinn to willingly spend time with her, she had to have something to keep the ice queen interested in being her friend.

"Ooh, who did you get?" Ava leaned forward with a breadstick, eager for the details.

"You like basketball too?" I asked her. Maybe she was a sports "fan," or maybe she was a stage five clinger.

"Yeah, don't you?" Ava asked me curiously.

"Doesn't really interest me," I answered as I met my brother's look. He arched an eyebrow, and I mimicked him. Snorting, he looked away with a small shake of his head.

"You don't like me," Ava blurted out. "I get it, we got off on the wrong foot, you know, the whole 'you did nothing to stop Jett from almost decapitating me, then you had octopus hands, and I punched you.' I get it, we're not going to be besties and, dude, I am more than okay with that...trust me. But you are going to have to accept that I'm with Jett, he's with me, and you're his twin, so we can't really avoid each other." She took a bite of her breadstick and chewed as she waited for my response.

"Is that right?" Leaning back in the booth, I looked her over. Blonde hair in a high ponytail. Her blue T-shirt annoyed me on principle due to which school it represented. Her shoulders set waiting for my reply, but her face was open, her words genuine. She had nerve; I'd give her that. "What do you propose we do about it?"

I watched her chew the inside of her cheek as she thought

about it. I could feel Ash tense beside me, waiting for my reaction. Quinn had leaned forward, her hand cupping her chin as her elbow rested on the table. Jett's glare...well, I knew when to ignore my brother.

"I propose we do nothing," Ava told me calmly as she broke another piece of her breadstick off.

"Nothing? You think that's the best option?" I was testing her, and she knew it. With narrowed eyes, she looked me over as I did her.

"Actually, I would suggest something else, but I'm not sure if you aren't a sensitive soul under all that outward testosterone."

Ash's cough covered his laugh, which broke the stare off, and Quinn was openly grinning at me, enjoying Ava's spunk.

"I think I can take it," I murmured as I waited. "Take your best shot."

"I thought I did that when I decked you."

Jett pressed his lips to the side of her head, and I saw his shoulders shaking. So, she amused him. Interesting.

"It's nice that you have something else to latch onto." Raising my water glass, I gave her a mock salute. Jett stopped laughing, Quinn lost her smile, and I felt my cousin press his leg against mine in warning.

"What do you mean?" Ava asked as she looked around the table, picking up on the shift in atmosphere.

"I agree, we do nothing. I don't really know you to like or dislike you," I told her bluntly but politely. He couldn't give me shit for this. "And I don't really want to get to know you to find out what the answer is, so I agree, we do nothing."

"That isn't the best option," Jett said softly. "I think you both just need to spend more time with each other."

"I have football to concentrate on and other things that are more important. The three of us should be focusing on these more important matters. If your girlfriend is still around by the end of the season, I'll see what I can do."

"Isn't it cold in here?" Quinn suddenly announced. "I left my jacket in the car. I'll be right back." She stood abruptly and held her hand out to me. "I need the key."

"I'll get it." Slipping out of the booth, I welcomed the break. What the fuck was with Jett? It was not time to play happy families; we weren't the fucking Waltons for fuck's sake. Wrenching open the car door, I snatched Quinn's jacket from the back seat, and as I closed the door, I took a moment to take a deep breath. I was too highly strung for this. I shouldn't have come, but I didn't have a good enough excuse to get out of it. Tiredly I rubbed my forehead. I'd had zero sleep, two training sessions, and a run with Quinn. I was ready to pass out.

"You're tired," Quinn said from behind me.

Turning, I looked at her as she held her hand out for her jacket. "Yeah, I am."

"You should have said no to this, got some rest."

"I can make my own decisions." Handing the jacket to her, I walked past her, back to the restaurant.

"You're just going to piss him off."

"Ship sailed."

"Gray!" Quinn called, and I turned to look at her. Her dark eyes held a plea, and I inhaled deeply, trying to stave the words that were ready to spill in frustration.

"I'll be better."

She took a small step towards me. "You're doing too much, you're pushing too hard. Ava shouldn't be the one you break."

"That isn't what this is." Looking around the street, I noticed how few people were out and about. Halloween decorations were everywhere, and I studied them with an interest I didn't have. Halloween was Quinn's thing. She'd always tried to make the four of us dress up and then do stupid party games. When we got older, it was high school parties, and by then we weren't that averse to seeing our fellow students in their costumes—the less clothing the better.

"I know you're still doing whatever it is you're doing."

"Do you hear yourself?"

"Yes, don't be a dick to *me*. I'm not Ava, I will slap you in front of everyone."

"Wouldn't be the first time," I reminded her. I headed back into the restaurant, not caring if she followed, knowing I should.

"You took your time," Ash grumbled as he flicked his eyes to Jett and Ava, who had obviously forgotten they were in public.

"I was hoping the food would be here," I confessed as I sat. "Although, I'm really glad I'm not eating at this precise moment in time."

Ash grinned as he reached for a breadstick and then pulled his hand back. "I'm starving."

"Me too," I agreed as I looked over my shoulder, hoping the food would be coming.

"Did you get your assignment in?" Ash asked me as he turned slightly in the booth so he didn't have a direct line of sight to the giggling, whispering couple.

"I did. Think it may be a B, maybe a B plus." Shrugging, I looked over my shoulder again. "Seriously, where the fuck is my food?"

"Do you get hangry?"

Fuck, but this girl was annoying. "What?"

"It's someone who gets irritable when they're hungry. My friend Mia is horrific for it. Honestly, you need to take cover when she's hangry." She gave me a smile. I thought we'd just discussed we weren't going to do this.

"No, I don't get hangry. Maybe I'm just always angry," I added quickly before she gave me a smartass comment.

"I think I could get hangry," Quinn piped up.

If I wasn't so good at schooling my emotions, my mouth would have dropped in shock. Was this really Quinn, being...nice? What actual hell was I in?

"Nah," Ash spoke up as he looked at her. "You're just a bitch."

"Will you all quit it?" Jett looked at us all. "Fuck me, we all agreed to come to this, can we all remember we're not fucking animals and be civil. I'd actually like to enjoy my food when it comes."

The table fell into another silence, but thankfully my brother stopped groping his girlfriend long enough for the silence to be at least comfortable. I watched Ava out of the corner of my eye. She shifted in her seat as her hand tugged her hair. She looked at Quinn, she looked at Ash, and then her eyes met mine. Very slightly, I shook my head, the message clear: *don't ask*. And I didn't lift my stare until she dropped her head in acknowledgment.

"What did you think of Atticus Dawn?" Ava asked Quinn, and I tuned them out as they spoke about music.

When the food finally arrived, Ash and I attacked ours like the starving men we were. I heard Quinn sigh, and I ignored her silent reprimand about the speed with which I ate my food. Mushroom ravioli in a garlic and herb sauce, with a side of roast chicken displayed artfully across the top. The portion size was lacking.

When we were finished, we watched Ava and Quinn take forever as they made small talk and ate their lasagne at a rate that made snails look speedy. In this, we all agreed, as I noticed Jett was also finished and his fork was idly twirling in his hand. He looked ready to dig into Ava's plate at the merest hint that he could.

"Is that it?" Ash asked me as he looked at both our plates. "We got food at home?"

"Yeah, we'll sub out some of what we were supposed to eat tonight for this and fill up on the rest," I said to him quietly.

"Thank fuck." My cousin tilted his head back to look at the ceiling as I waited patiently for the girls to finish their food.

Eventually they put their forks down. Jett finished Ava's, and

Quinn wordlessly handed her plate to Ash, who finished her food in two bites.

"We done?" I asked impatiently as I felt tiredness roll over me.

"Yeah—"

"Ash, let's go." I got out of the booth quickly, my cousin eagerly following behind me. "See you later." We left without a backwards glance. Outside, we exchanged a look and headed to my car.

"He's gonna be pissed."

"Yeah? Or maybe he's just *hangry*."

Ash's laughter was infectious, and grinning, we headed home to eat some actual food.

CHAPTER 8

Quinn

I SWAM MY LAPS, ENJOYING THE RHYTHMIC MOTION OF THE WATER AS my body sliced through it. Swimming always soothed me, which, considering how I was introduced to the water, should surprise me. However, I think it was the fact all three of them had, at that time, made me feel safe and secure, so much so that swimming had become a regular exercise for me. A run every morning and four times a week, I did my laps.

My hand touched the poolside, and I lifted my head out of the water. Hard blue eyes stared into mine, and I jerked back in surprise.

"Gray?" Looking around, I realised there was only one other person in the pool, and I was, as they say, shit out of luck. He was crouched down at the poolside, like he was ready to pounce.

"We need to talk."

"About?"

"*Queeny,* why you being awkward?" His head tilted to the side as he baited me. "You know as well as anyone that your stunt last night was a delaying tactic. It doesn't wash with me, and it won't wash with Jett either. He's determined. You know what he's like when he decides something."

Placing my goggles on top of my swimming cap, I stared up at him as I treaded water. "What if I say no?"

"Do you think it's an option?"

"What about it all being my choice?"

"I'm on your side in this," he told me quietly. "You seem to forget that."

"You make it easy to forget when you're a massive dick all the time," I snapped back. This whole thing with him looking down on me like this was pissing me off. "Ambushing me in the pool is a cheap shot, Gray." Placing my hands on the tile, I pushed myself up. Strong hands took hold of my upper arms, and effortlessly he lifted me out of the water. Without breaking eye contact, Gray handed me my towel before he dropped my flip-flops beside me.

"How long do you need?"

"More than you plan to give me," I snarled as I brushed past him and headed to the locker rooms.

The locker room was open plan, and I genuinely hated that. There were three stalls only, and they were usually occupied, but today I was in luck as one was free. Grabbing my stuff from my locker, I headed to one of the stalls. With a quick squirm and a tug, my suit was off, and wrapping my towel around me, I headed to the showers. I didn't need to wash my hair, as the cap had protected it, but I strongly wished I'd had that to my advantage. I didn't want to talk to him, Jett or any of them. Not about this.

They knew enough. The rest? They seemed to be filling in the blanks, and I was not okay with that. But I also knew they had found out more, and they wanted to ask questions of me that I didn't have the answer to. To do that, they were going to tell me what they had found out, and I knew I didn't want to know. What could I do, and more importantly, what good would knowing do me?

As I finished my shower, I slowly made my way back to my stall. Another girl was in the locker room, and she gave me a courteous reflexive smile before I was in my stall and locking the door behind me.

With a heavy heart, I sat on the small bench and stared at the floor as I considered what they were going to say to me. Or ask me. Could I do this again? Jett and I had been through this when he collected me from the hospital.

"Where am I?" I asked as I looked around the sparse white-walled room. Looking down the length of my body, I realised I was in a single

bed, with a really bad blanket and only one chair in the corner of the room. A nurse was at the bottom of the bed.

Why was there a nurse at the bottom of the bed?

"Am I in...the hospital?"

"Hey there, you're awake, been waiting for you." Her smile was kind, and she looked gentle and calm. Soothing.

"Who are you? Where am I?"

"My name's Susan, you're at Nashville Memorial Hospital," she told me as she walked around the side of the bed to stand beside me.

Pushing myself up the bed into a sitting position, I watched her warily. "Are you with them?"

"Them?" She had wide eyes, slightly set too far apart. They were light brown in colour and...kind. Everything about her screamed kindness. It was weird and unnerving.

Looking back down at me, I saw the horrible hospital gown, and a feeling of dread overcame me. With a trembling hand, I placed it over my stomach, above the covers. With closed eyes, I asked the question.

"I lost the baby?"

"You did."

Tears slid down my cheeks as my fingers tightened on the blanket that covered me. Covered my loss. "How?"

"We don't know a lot." Susan sat gently down at the side of the bed. "I was hoping you could tell me?"

Shaking my head, I kept my eyes tightly closed. "I don't remember."

"You took a fall." Her voice was soft and even. "You have a cut to the side of your head, which we think is the cause of your unconsciousness."

"It happened because I bumped my head?"

"You were found at the bottom of some steps; do you remember falling?" Susan asked me.

Did I? No...wait. Yes, I was running. My head snapped up as my eyes looked around the room wildly. "Are they here? Did they get me?"

Susan grabbed my hand, her gentle squeeze soothed me. "Shh, no one's here. You were taken in because a lady found you at the bottom of the steps. You were unconscious, your head was bleeding, and you had bleeding elsewhere."

"The fall caused it?" I asked as I tried to keep my voice calm, even, soft, like Susan.

"I think so, do you have someone we can call for you...?"

"Quinn, my name's Quinn."

She gave me a warm smile as her other hand stroked over the hand she was holding. "You're going to be okay, Quinn." I felt her hesitate. "You still have to pass the baby."

"What?" I could feel the sobs building, and I fought them back; this was no time to cry.

"You're about sixteen weeks, yes?"

I nodded, and she watched me. "We've administered the drugs while you were unconscious so you can complete the miscarriage. I'll need you to take another two tablets soon if nothing happens. You need to deliver. It won't be long now. The baby will be very small, so some slight discomfort may occur as we wait until everything passes naturally. Do you have someone to call, someone who can be here with you?"

"Is my purse here?"

"No, honey, we didn't have any way to contact your family." She paused. "Do you have family?"

"Yeah." No. Shit, I couldn't phone my dad. He still didn't know I was pregnant. No one knew. Fuck. What did she mean I had to deliver?

"I can get you a phone? Or you can write it down, and I can call them?" Susan stood and pulled out a notepad and pen from her pocket.

"No, um, a phone. Please."

"Okay. I'll be right back."

She was as good as her word; she came back with a phone and a clipboard of admission papers. Ignoring them, I took the phone and then waited for her to give me some privacy.

When she was gone, I threw the covers back, and with a gasp, I fell awkwardly out of bed. My head was swimming, did I have a concussion? The pain in my back was dull and aching, and I didn't know why. I felt something move and cried out as a feeling of wetness coated my thighs, and looking down, I saw the blood run down my legs. Susan must have been right outside the door, because she was beside me within moments. Her hands caught me, and together, we made it to the adjacent bathroom where she hastily put a bowl over the toilet and urged me to sit down. As I did, she pulled up my gown and started to clean my legs as best as she could. I was aware of the passing, and with care and gentleness, Susan helped me stand as she turned me away from the bowl and handed me wipes to clean myself while she covered the bowl and removed it from the bathroom. She came back almost immediately, and when I had a pair of underwear that were not mine and a pad for my bleeding, I was taken back to bed.

Numbly, I let her put me back into the bed and cover me up.

"That was quicker than I thought," she said quietly. "Why were you out of bed?"

"I wanted to use the bathroom," I lied easily. I wasn't telling her I was trying to get to the window so I could check I was really in Nashville. My trust limits were very, very low at the moment, and my heart was breaking from everything that was happening since I woke up.

"You should have called for me," she reprimanded gently as she handed me a cup with water. "Drink this."

"What is it?"

"Quinn, it's just water. I'm not going to hurt you."

That's what they said. I remembered why I was running, and I remembered falling. I remembered screaming as I fell and then nothing.

"Sorry, I'm just disoriented and"—my breath caught—"heartbroken."

"I know, honey, I know." She patted my hand and then handed me the phone. "I'll let you make that call. I won't lie, I'll feel better when your fella turns up."

Well, that would be a trick.

She left me again, but I saw the concerned look in her eyes, and I felt bad for doubting her. I stared at the black handset for too long.

I knew five phone numbers off the top of my head. My dad's cell, my home number, and three Santos. A tear fell over as I realised I'd been absently rubbing my hand over my abdomen. Hesitantly, I lifted the phone and dialled my house. Anne, my stepmom, would come, but could I trust her not to tell my dad? I hung up and called the safer option.

"Jett?" The tears flowed heavier. I heard his concern, and I was scared I wouldn't be able to speak. "I need you, just you. Don't tell anyone else."

"Where are you?"

"Nashville Memorial."

"Why?" He was already moving; I could hear him jogging down the stairs.

"Just come, Jett. I need you." My voice was choked with tears.

I heard a thud and then the engine of his car starting. "Where are you, emergency?"

Squeezing my eyes tight, I said the word he wasn't expecting. "Maternity."

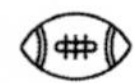

I SAT ON THE COUCH IN JETT'S ROOM AS HE WATCHED ME, AS GRAY perched on the corner of his brother's bed. When they were thinking or scowling, they looked so alike it made me smile. Well, sometimes it made me smile. Not at the moment.

"Is there anything more you need to tell us, that we need to know?" Jett asked me as he looked at me so intently I felt like I was under a microscope.

"You know everything I do, probably more."

"You know that we continued to look into the fuckers who did this to you," Jett said with no embarrassment or shame.

"You did, even though I asked you not to."

"We found out more than we thought we would," he continued as if he hadn't heard me.

"You said." I moved on the couch; it was too soft for my liking.

"Quinn, can you listen?" His voice was quiet and sounded tired, which was fucking hypocritical if you asked me. I wasn't the one hounding him to declare his darkest secrets.

"What if I don't want to, Jett? What if I'm really truly sorry for whatever or whoever you've found, but what if I really don't need to know because I've had enough? I've lost..." I shook my head in anger at myself for almost saying too much and in anger at him—he needed to back off.

"You've lost a lot, I know that, but don't you want to know what they planned?"

"No." Dropping my head into my hands, I pressed the heels of my hands into my eyes to stop the tears. I couldn't cry anymore. I was so tired of crying.

"But, Quinn, if you knew—"

"That's enough."

My head snapped up as I looked at Gray, and his eyes met mine as he spoke to Jett. "She isn't ready. It's not your place to force this on her."

"Gray, she needs to know, if—"

"I said no." Gray cut his brother off again. "Back off and shut the fuck up," he warned him quietly. "Look at her. See past your own self-righteousness and *look at her*."

Jett glanced at me and looked away, and then I saw his head and shoulders droop. "I'm a dick."

"You are." Gray walked over to me and held out his hand. "Come on, I'll take you home."

Slowly I reached out my hand, and his fingers wrapped around mine, pulling me to my feet. Bending his knees slightly, he looked into my eyes and nodded in question, asking me if I was okay. My head dipped quickly, breaking the stare. He saw too much sometimes.

Jett mumbled something and then was wrapping his arms around me, and I heard him whisper sorry as he crushed me to him. Reluctantly, I let go of Gray's hand to return the hug.

"I'm angry, Quinn," Jett said as he pulled back and looked down at me. "I'm angry this happened, I'm angry they got away with it, *are* getting away with it and worse."

Cupping the side of his face, I reached up and kissed his cheek. "I know, and I'm sorry I can't help you, but I can't, Jett. I don't know anything else."

His hand pressed against mine that still cupped his cheek. "Okay, I'm sorry for pushing."

"No, you're not," I teased him gently. "You're just sorry Gray was in the room before the interrogation began."

Jett closed his eyes at my attempt at humour before he opened them and embraced me again. "I'm scared you may be right," he whispered before he let me go.

"Come on," Gray said gruffly as he opened the door.

Silently he walked me home, our thoughts both elsewhere. At the foot of my stairs, he looked at me.

"I'm not Jett."

"Thank God you cleared that up; that fraternal twin thing was confusing me."

"Don't be a smartass," he reprimanded me. "I'm not my brother, I won't push like he is, and I actually told the stupid dick not to do this."

"But Jett thinks he has right on his side," I spoke quietly as I looked away from him, watching my fellow students go about their evening with their own worries on their shoulders.

"He does. And he *does* have right on his side, and I do think you probably do need to know."

Turning back to him, I could feel my frown. "Then why did you tell him to back off?"

"Because I think I should be told first, don't you?"

"What?" Stepping back, I looked him over. I could feel my defences rising, rushing to protect me from the verbal blow that was coming. "What difference is there in me telling you and Jett versus me just telling you?"

"You know why, don't insult us both."

Clutching my book bag strap over my shoulder, I gave him a tight smile. "I thought you were being kind, I thought you understood. I didn't know you were playing bad cop, worse cop."

"I'm not playing, Quinn."

With a derogatory laugh, I walked away from him. "You're always fucking playing," I snarled as I climbed my stairs. "Thanks for walking me home."

As I unlocked my door, I felt him behind me, his body pressing into mine as his breath tickled my ear.

"You can tell me what happened, all of it, today or next year or in ten years, I'll never push. But what I won't allow, and you will *not* do, is disregard my right to know."

Gripping the handle, I pushed the door open. "You know everything you need. I have nothing else to tell you. Today, tomorrow or in ten years."

His hand pulled me back into his chest as his arm wrapped around me, holding me tight. "You're a heartless bitch."

His words hurt more than a physical blow ever could. "Then let me go."

His warmth was gone as quickly as it had come. Taking a few steps into my apartment, I turned to look at him and faltered when I saw the pain radiating from his eyes.

"Gray..."

"You can't even tell me to my fucking face? You were always nothing but a coward." His mouth twisted in a sneer as he looked at me.

"I'm not a coward."

"Then tell me to my face, look me in the eye, and fucking say it," Gray demanded as he took a step closer.

"Say *what*? What else do you think I need to tell you?" I cried.

Swiftly he was in front of me, his hand curled around the nape of my neck as he drew me close to him, his mouth hovered over mine. "Tell me that it was mine."

"Gra—"

"Do *not* lie to me." His arm was shaking, his whole body was shaking with rage or adrenaline as he watched me. "So help me, Quinn, if you lie to me right now, I won't be responsible."

"Please, Gray," I pleaded even as my heart was breaking. I could feel it happening all over again. "Don't do this."

I felt his hand tighten as he pulled me closer. "*Tell me*." His voice was a tortured whisper. "Tell me that you were going to give away our baby."

The tears were falling rapidly now, I couldn't stop them, and I wasn't sure if I would ever be able to stop them as he looked at me. I could see every ounce of pain that he carried, pain that I had hidden and tried so hard to hide, but he wasn't hiding his right now.

"I wasn't," I gasped when his hold got even tighter. "I *wasn't*, I changed my mind, I couldn't do it."

"Swear." Gray's head dropped to my shoulder before his head sought the crook of my neck. "*Swear* it."

Hesitantly, I wrapped my arms around him as I felt his lips pressed to the side of my throat as his head burrowed into me, as if he too couldn't bear to see the pain he felt reflected in my eyes. "I swear, I swear to all that is holy, I told them no."

"Which is why they chased you?" he asked, his voice muffled against my skin.

"Yes." My whisper was so quiet I didn't know if he heard me until I felt his body stiffen, and I knew the words that I had never been asked directly were coming.

"It was mine?"

My eyes squeezed shut, blocking out the low autumn night, blocking out the world. "Yes."

He held me to him for a moment. For a few seconds, he held me so close to him like he was afraid to let go. When he pulled back, his face was a cold mask.

"You should have told me." He didn't move except to run his eyes up and down over me. His look was so sharp I could almost feel the cut. "I don't think I can ever forgive you."

My breath left my body with a sharp huff as I shook my head in disgust. "Don't worry, Gray, I wasn't looking for your forgiveness." I moved away from him. "You got what you needed; you can go."

"Who do you need to forgive you? Jett?" he asked me, his words laced with scorn.

"You're an idiot." I slammed the door in his face before I locked it, shutting him and the world away outside.

Why didn't he understand? I didn't need Gray's pardon. To receive anyone's forgiveness, first, I had to forgive myself.

CHAPTER 9

Gray

It had been a few days since the disaster that was dinner. I had stayed away from her, not that easy to do when she was fucking everywhere, but I'd managed it. I couldn't help it, and I knew I was being a dick, just as I knew we needed to sit down and discuss it, and I knew I had to, at some point, tell my cousin that I'd fucked his ex. Not once, not twice, but three times.

And I couldn't tell him.

I couldn't tell him how much I hated myself for loving her. From the moment she jumped into the pool just to prove me wrong, she'd owned my heart. I didn't recognise it for what it was when I was ten. Didn't really understand it when I was twelve and we made the pact not to date her.

A pact. A fucking pact.

We were all stupid. She was captivating, even with braces and hair that looked like it had never seen a brush, she was all I saw. I went out of my way to make her laugh, make her happy. All I ever wanted was for her to see me. Not as Jett's twin or Ash's cousin, but *me*.

I still don't think she ever did.

She saw Ash flirt with girls, she never noticed that I didn't. I watched her eyes follow Ash in the cafeteria when he flirted with the other girls, and I saw her frown. My only reassurance was that she never ever looked at Jett that way. They were so firmly friend-zoned; it was laughable that neither Ash nor I were good enough.

Well. Ash was good enough. I grunted as I ran. Coach had given me grief about my focus, and I had talked back to him. So I was running laps as punishment, because Coach was a giant dick. But also because he was my coach, I respected him, and I shouldn't have been a smart-ass.

My mind went back to her as I ran. I knew as soon as Ash told me he had kissed her that I was in danger of killing them both. How fucking *dare* he touch what was mine, how fucking dare *she* let him touch what was mine.

But what had I done? Nothing. I pretended it didn't matter. It was just a kiss, big deal. She'd been kissed before. And like before, I would tell her to stop it and she would. Because she knew that she belonged to me.

But no, she let him kiss her again, and she opened her legs and let him finger fuck her in a closet at a party, like a fucking cliché. He had boasted to me that he'd had his fingers inside her, and my rage had known no bounds. I'd beat up three guys that night until I felt nothing. Jett had been furious, even more so when I wouldn't tell him what was wrong with me. Our older brother, Onyx, had found me sitting in the dark at the end of the pool, a towel wrapped around my hand to soothe the sting of the cuts.

"You're being reckless," he warned me.

"I know."

"She isn't worth it." Onyx looked over at me, and I stubbornly refused to meet his gaze.

"She is."

"No, brother, she isn't. She doesn't care, you're making yourself weak."

"I'm not *weak," I growled at him as he stood and looked down at me.*

"Then stop being a fucking pussy. Tell her what you want, let her slap you down, and then get over it."

But I wasn't Jett, I never had been. My twin knew what to say to people, say to girls, I didn't. However, I'd told her. I'd asked her to put a stop to it. I had kissed her to show her what she meant to me. And she had kissed me back, just as eager, just as desperate to be mine.

It had been done. I was sure of it. Then Ash told Jett and me he was dating her. Thank fuck I'd been training on the punchbag at the time, or else my fists would have connected with his face.

Why would she do that? I had made it clear. *She was mine.*

Was Onyx right? Was she truly not worth it? Five months they went out for, and it was as painful to watch as it was amusing. Ash was content as he had a prize. She was known to be an ice queen in school, and he had snagged himself *the* Queen. Made even more true because she acted like he wasn't there. He would hold her hand, and she would let him, but she would give her cheek when he went in for a kiss. She never let him kiss her on the lips when I was there. Every single time he tried or put an arm around her, she would look at me with guilt as she shook him off.

She should be fucking guilty. Anger and hurt had continued to build in my chest until I didn't know how to let it out.

Onyx took me to a college party. We didn't tell anyone. He was in his junior year, and he took me to the football house, keeping me pretty much out of sight. I was sixteen, I was a walking fucking hormone. In a room in the basement, he pushed me inside, and then ten minutes later, he came back with a dark-haired girl. She didn't even tell me her name, she just dropped to her knees, undid my jeans and swallowed my dick. When she was finished, she stood, undressed and lay on the bed with her legs spread. I hesitated for one moment, and with a smile, she turned over and raised herself on her hands and knees. She told me it was easier sometimes not to put a face to the body under you.

She was right.

With her hair wrapped around my fist, I fucked her while I thought of whose hair should have been around my fist, whose body should have been under mine, whose pussy should have been clutching at my dick.

When we were finished, Onyx drove me home and asked me if I felt better. I had no words, and thankfully my brother didn't seem to need any, because how did I tell him I thought of *her* the entire time?

Then one night at a party, Ash was flirting too much with too many girls. It pissed me off. Why was he out here, with us, fucking about when she was at home? Some dick commented on the very same thing, only Ash never heard him. I did though. When the dick suggested it was because the ice queen was too frigid, I nailed his ass to the ground. Jett got pissed at me and suggested I call it a night.

Why I went to her house, I didn't know.

When she undressed in front of me, it took every ounce of control not to grab her and make her mine. But I couldn't, because I had convinced myself she *wasn't* mine. She had never been mine, and I was trying hard to accept it, and just when I thought I had it under control, she climbed into my lap and said *touch me*. I told her to end it with Ash; it was clear to us both now he wasn't who she wanted.

Two weeks. It took *two weeks* for her to fucking end it with Ash, and then when she did, she lied. Again. Telling him someone else had fucked her. No one had been near her. I don't even think Ash had been close to her.

She couldn't tell him the truth, always lying, always deceitful, always hiding.

I watched her as she waited for Ash to calm down. I watched her as my brother tried—and failed—to remain neutral. I watched her run out of the door, away from them, like the coward she was.

When Jett told me to check on her, I almost refused.

Finding her in the bathroom, crying, I watched her. The cowardice and guilt were gone. Her anger at me, for pushing her, rose to the surface, and she lashed out, her temper wild, her pain obvious, and she was breathtaking.

Even as she glared at me, all I wanted to do was make her feel what I felt. I never meant to kiss her. I never meant to touch her, and I sure as fuck didn't mean to screw her on the bathroom sink. But she was so willing, so open, so fucking intoxicating, I needed to be inside her. Own her.

No one made me crazy like she did.

Then we froze her out. How could I not? What was I to do, tell Ash I fucked his ex ten minutes after she ripped his heart out? Not happening.

And it *was* better. She wasn't constantly there. She wasn't constantly close to me, tempting me, taunting me.

We caused mayhem a few months later at a rival's party. I spotted her on the balcony, half hidden in shadows, looking down on the party like the queen she was.

As Jett and Ash caused mayhem downstairs, I quickly climbed the stairs and found her in the bedroom. I gave her the in to come back into the fold. The can of spray paint I gave her was her way in, and the moment she looked at me, I knew I would never be free of her.

Later that night, I'd found her again. She was on the lounge chair beside the pool, her legs bare, her jean shorts covering her ass and not much else. A black hoodie, mine I noticed, was wrapped around her as she slept. The pool was in darkness, and I found her because she hadn't been at home when I checked. I knew there was only one other place she could be.

I woke her from her sleep, and she looked up at me, not surprised to see me at all. Holding out my hand, I offered to walk her the short distance to her house, which sat beside ours.

In the dark of the path that led around the side of my house to the drive, she grabbed my hand and, like she did the time before, placed my hand on her chest. Nothing held me back that time. I already knew what it felt like to be inside her, and I had been craving to feel it again.

I fucked her hard against the wall on the side of my house. My hand over her mouth to stop her cries, my other hand strumming her clit as I thrust into her again and again, needing her to come so I could.

She was more than a drug. She was more than a craving. She consumed me, and if I wasn't careful, she would burn me.

Afterwards, I confessed what I had done to my brother, Onyx. He hadn't been impressed I had fallen under her spell again. He told me what I needed to hear. What would Ash do? How could I tell him? It didn't matter that I had never touched her when she was with him; what mattered was that I had touched her at all. He was family. Blood. She was...

I closed my eyes as I ran my laps, memories of the past crowding my head rather than clearing it. Quinn Lawrence was the girl I wanted but couldn't have. I knew it. She knew it.

It didn't fucking matter.

I had to walk away. I had to put the distance back. Until I was free of her spell, I needed to stay away. After the other night and what she had told me, I knew I couldn't be near her without demanding she tell me everything. As much as I knew it was all her choice, her body, her decision, it burned inside me that she had made that decision without me. She knew how much I'd care. She knew just how fucking much it would hurt.

I hated her. I'd loved her for so long it was no longer love I felt for her. How could I love a woman who ripped my heart to shreds, not once, but twice?

I heard Coach blow his whistle and knew I could stop running. Easing my run gradually, looking over to the benches where the others were cooling down. I saw my brother and Ash still out on the field. Jett was throwing, and Ash was running and catching. They wouldn't go in until I was with them. They didn't even realise they were waiting for me.

Slowly I made my way towards them, watching Ash laugh at whatever my brother had said to him. Jett turned to me with a grin.

"You looked in the zone," he said with a casual flick of the ball my way.

I caught it and tossed it back and forth between my hands. "Yeah, I think I needed it."

"Lot on your mind?" Ash asked curiously.

"Got a paper due," I answered easily.

"You need to get laid," he said to me as he took the ball off me. "I don't remember the last time you hooked up with anyone."

My smile was tight, but I kept my tone light. "Just don't feel the need to brag about my hookups like you do," I joked.

Jett snorted in agreement as we headed to the locker room, and I tried to ignore my cousin's speculative stare.

"Seriously, when did you last hook up?" Ash asked me as he pulled his jersey off. "Maybe you need to stop being so picky and hook up with one of the Elises."

Fuck no. "Never," I drawled as I took off my cleats. "Anyway, think One's off the market now," I added with a nod over to Jamie, who was rubbing his right shoulder and couldn't hear us.

Ash watched him and then turned back to us both. "Didn't realise it was a thing."

"Pretty sure he doesn't either," Jett said with a grin as he stripped off his uniform.

"But he isn't stupid," Ash said as he considered our defensive lineman again. "I mean, he has to know she has an agenda...right?"

"Not our business," I answered as I headed to the shower.

After we got showered and dressed, the three of us headed to the front of the building.

She sat on the steps leading up to the stadium, a textbook on her knee, and her shoulders hunched like she was cold from the chill of the air. It wasn't even cold; she was such a drama queen.

Opening the door, Jett called out a greeting, and I watched her turn towards us, a ready smile on her face as she looked at Jett.

"Hi, so, I need to talk to you about nutrition." As she rose elegantly to her feet, Jett picked up her books, and even Ash helped her with her stuff. I hung back, watching her, like the spider she was, snaring them in her web.

I remembered Onyx's warnings in my head as I approached them, my walls already up, my emotions already shutting down.

"I'm out," I told them as I moved alongside them.

"You are?" Jett asked me in surprise as his eyes flicked between her and me.

"Yeah, got shit to do."

"You going to get laid?" Ash asked with a wide grin, giving me his full attention and not seeing her face pale in displeasure.

"Maybe I will." I winked at him before I turned and headed in the opposite direction.

He'd slept with every eligible female in high school when she broke up with him. I hadn't questioned his actions and neither had Jett. He'd been hurt. Well, his pride had been hurt, I think his heart was just fine. However, it wasn't for me to criticise him; I was in no position to be casting judgment, on him or anyone. The girls had not been kind to Quinn when they told her, going out of their way to shove it in her face that they'd either fucked or sucked him.

The only ones she'd reacted to were the Elises. I don't know what was said between them, but it had taken me and Jett to get Quinn off of Elise. The she-cat had scratched my arms up badly as she practically hissed with fury as Jett picked Elise off the floor while Quinn fought to get to her. Jett had already been with Elise and one of the other ones, Ash had done all of them, and I had never touched any of them. When we finally had Quinn calmed down, Jett had asked her what the fuck had happened.

She'd said nothing, just glared at me like it was *my* fault she was brawling in the school corridor like a third grader. Jett had picked up on it and turned to me with an eyebrow raised in question.

Confused, he'd asked me what I'd done. Not having a clue how I factored into a fight with Elise, I'd answered honestly and said,

"Nothing." She'd laughed, called me a dick and then stormed out of there like we were in the wrong.

My phone vibrated in my hoodie pocket, bringing me back to the present, and I pulled it out.

Quinn: **You didn't need to leave**

I shoved it back in my pocket. I didn't need to reply. Of course I had to leave, how could I sit there, looking at her, knowing that she had been giving away *my* baby. My fucking baby. She was going to give it to strangers and what, never tell me? Anger boiled in my blood as I walked and fought the memories, my older brother's words once more resonating through my head.

"He is your family, he is your blood, what is she?"

"Everything," I whispered in reply.

"Then you'll never be free of her," was his sad reply.

Yes, I would. I needed to cut all ties to her, every single one of them. We would find the bastards who hurt her, and then I would be free, and I would never look back.

The agency she went to was bogus, a front for something I hoped and prayed she didn't know about. Stopping in the cool October air, I looked to the darkening sky. There was one other person who knew everything, who knew about the "adoption," one sick fucker who we had on camera.

With grim resolution, I turned and started towards the dorm house. It was time for that house call.

CHAPTER 10

Quinn

I LISTENED TO JETT AND ASH TALK ABOUT THEIR PRACTICE SESSION as my fingers tightened around my cell. He wouldn't text me back; he hardly ever did, even when we were on good terms. Gray wasn't big on communication.

You would think that with him being so quiet, text would be his thing—he didn't need to actually speak to anyone and he could remain his reclusive self. But no, he just didn't text people.

Jett slung his arm over my shoulders, and I felt his kiss to the side of my head. He had done it since we were twelve, ever since my mom died. It was his way of giving me comfort.

"I'm sorry I pushed," he told me as we walked to their dorm.

"I know," I answered him, and I saw Ash look at us both and look away.

"Gray said you were quiet on the walk home the other night," Jett told me, and I fought the eye roll. He would never give up. It wasn't who he was, and suddenly I needed Gray here more than I realised.

"Lot on my mind." I shrugged off his shoulder and fixed the strap of my book bag.

"You need to help us," Ash blurted. I looked at him with wide eyes. He never spoke about it. Not to me. I understood his reluctance, I did. I'd hurt him, and he'd hurt me, which meant the gulf between us was wide, no matter how tentative our truce.

"I told them already, I really don't."

He stopped walking and glared down at me. "How the hell can you be so cold?" Ash shook his head as he looked away from us both, his jaw clenched. "I know you, Quinn, I know you push your feelings down, and I know you think it makes you strong, but right now, it's making you weak."

My anger flared. "What the hell did you just say to me?"

"You're hiding." Ash gave me his full attention. "You're hiding behind your fear, and it's pathetic."

I would have been less shocked if he'd slapped me. *Fuck him and fuck this.* "Hiding? I'm not *hiding*, I have nothing *to* hide. You know everything, and everything you didn't know, you ignorant bastards went snooping in and tried to find out anyway. Despite me telling you not to. Despite me begging my friends to leave it alone, you had zero consideration for what I felt, what I was going through or what I wanted!"

Ash took a step back at my fury, and I saw him pale. "Queeny—"

"*No!*" I snapped at him and took a few steps away from them both. "No. You don't get to do this to me, it was *my* loss. It's *my* heartache, it has absolutely nothing to do with you."

I strode away from them, my anger fuelling my steps, and I'd walked halfway home when I realised that I wasn't alone. Turning my head, I looked at Jett, who gave me his usual smirk, and I fought the sigh.

"I stormed off," I muttered at him, and I heard his snort of amusement.

"It was very dramatic, had real flair," he answered easily as he stepped beside me.

"You're such a dick," I told him. "You can't even let me walk away in peace."

"A random dude bruised you the other night. He knew who you were. I'm not letting you out of any of our sights until we either find him or his friends."

My steps slowed as I looked around us. It was true that the nights were getting darker, but I had never felt unsafe on campus. "You think it's them?"

"I don't know, it's unlikely. More likely it's a pissed off rival team's fan. Or some douche who's into women who are far out of his league."

My hands tightened in my pockets. "Not making me feel at ease here."

"I don't want you to be complacent."

"I can look after myself," I argued as we reached my dorm.

"Course you can." Jett strode past me and waited at the door. "What?" he asked as he looked down at me. "You wanted to talk nutrition, I'm all yours."

Reminding myself repeatedly that he was my best friend—and it was wrong to stab him—I climbed the stairs and opened my door.

We spoke for thirty minutes or so about the things I needed for my class assignment. My professor had looked over my work earlier, and realising I had been more or less looking after the boys since I was serious enough to know what I wanted to do with my life, she decided to throw me a curve ball for extra credit. I had to introduce new food to them, new high fat food, and make it balance with their exercise, training and other food intake.

I was very lucky in that all of the boys on the football team were serious about their game. Most were hopeful for the draft, and those who weren't, well, they weren't letting their teammates down with living off pizza and chips.

Jett was looking between the list and me with furtive glances. "If you make me eat it, I'll die."

"I thought I was the drama queen?" I goaded him as I nudged his shoulder.

"Queeny, I can't, I'll throw up."

"It's because it's green, isn't it?" I asked him shrewdly. "What if I blend it into a drink? Like a protein shake."

"I'm going to barf."

Sighing, I leaned back into my sofa. "Well, I need one of you to eat it."

"Make Gray do it," Jett said instantly.

"That's cheating, he already eats it on toast with a boiled egg." I pointed at my spreadsheets. "See, three days a week."

Jett peered at the screen and then back to me. "He's so fucking weird," he said to me.

"It's just avocado," I muttered. "It's not like it's chicken feet."

"Gray eats them anyway," Jett mused. "If it's got chicken in the title, he's munching on down."

I giggled despite myself. "Fine, you can skip avocado, but I'm putting it in your food diary, and you will lie and say you ate it."

"Why can't Ash eat it?" Jett read over the list of foods.

"I could, but I need him to eat the raw eggs."

"He's never going to do it." He leaned back beside me, his voice strong with confidence. "He knows they build muscle. He doesn't want to tip over his weight."

"I know. Ugh, at this rate, I'm tempted to make you all smoothies and not tell you what's in them."

"You should have gone with that plan." Jett nodded as he grinned at me. "But now you can't, because I know it's raw eggs and avocado." He stuck his fingers down his throat, and I laughed along with him.

We sat in comfortable silence for a few minutes before he ruined it.

"What's going on with you and my brother?"

"Which one?" I teased him, hoping my voice didn't give away my nerves.

"You know which one."

"Nothing. Why would you say there was?" I moved forward, ready to stand, ready to walk away from him. His hand clasped around my wrist as he pulled me back.

"I will never hate you. I will never leave you. I will never judge you."

The words caused my throat to close and my eyes to fill with tears. Blinking rapidly, I turned my head away from him. "Jett..."

"You need to tell me. He's off, more off than normal, and I know it's more than he has a paper due. I can't help him if I don't know how," Jett spoke quietly.

"You should speak to your twin."

"I'm speaking to you," he countered. "We both know Gray won't tell me shit unless he thinks I already know." Turning on my light cream sofa, he faced me, even though I wasn't facing him. "You're not a coward, never have been. You jumped into that water the first day we met, completely fearless. You've been fearless ever since." He reached out and pulled my hair gently. "You're my family, Quinn. He's my brother, my *twin*. Don't shut me out like he is."

"I'm not shutting you out."

"Then be honest with me. Do it like when we were kids and we played question and answer. Don't think about it, just tell me the truth."

I hated that game when we were younger, and I knew I would hate it now. Turning in my seat, I faced him like he was facing me. His eyes were full of concern as he watched me cautiously, probably scared I was either going to break down or run. To be honest, I wasn't sure which one I was going with either.

"We're too old for games, no?" I asked him as I plucked the sleeve of my sweater.

"Nah, I play hide the sausage with Ava every chance I get."

The sheer ridiculousness of his statement made me laugh, and then we were both laughing. It eased the tension and weirdly made me feel calmer. Clearing my throat, I ran my hands through my hair as I moved in my seat, getting comfy, crossing my legs in preparation.

"You tell me, I'll tell them. Deal?" Jett asked me as he sat up straighter. "Like we used to do."

"You mean when I told you in secret I thought Dustin was cute, and you told Gray and Ash, and Gray punched him three days later?" I asked him with a smile. "Or the time I told you, in secret, that Gina wanted to make out with me, and Ash asked her in class if it was true and could he watch?"

"Okay, we're dicks, but you already know this." Jett gave a shoulder shrug. "And Ash ended up screwing Gina at the summer fair. He was always her end goal, not you. He knew it, everyone knew it, just not you."

"Wow. My one and only female admirer, and you take that illusion from me too?" I asked him in mock outrage.

"I genuinely thought you knew, fuck, I thought everyone knew."

"Ugh, I hate you all." I pulled a cushion into my face and yelled. Firm hands tugged the cushion from me, and I looked up into his unwavering stare.

"Fine. What do you want to know?"

"Was it abortion or adoption?"

I swallowed as I met his steady look. My throat was tight, and I was a little unprepared for how he just came right out with it. "Adoption. I would never…I wouldn't."

"Did you change your mind?"

"Yes."

"How far along were you?" Jett's face was set, and I couldn't read him. His foot nudged mine, and I rubbed my nose.

"Sixteen weeks."

"Four months?"

"Yes."

He nodded. "When did you decide to go to an adoption agency?"

"About ten or eleven weeks, I think."

"When did you find out you were pregnant?"

"Seven weeks."

"You dealt with it alone for four weeks before you decided to give it up?" His tone was slightly harder, and I shifted uncomfortably in my seat.

"Yes."

"Why?"

"You wouldn't understand." I broke the stare off, and I heard him snort.

"When did you tell my brother that you were giving away his baby?"

The world stopped turning. I froze in my seat, my eyes glued to the far wall, my chest tightened, and I realised it was because I wasn't breathing.

"Breathe, Quinn," Jett spoke, but his voice sounded far away.

My lungs rebelled, and I let out a loud cough before I started wheezing, and Jett handed me a glass of water. Standing up, I paced the room, avoiding his knowing stare, too chickenshit to meet his eyes.

"Ball's still in play," Jett said to me quietly from his spot on the couch.

"When did you know?"

"For real? Now. I suspected it for a while."

"Did he tell you?" I asked.

"No, like I said, you confirmed it tonight. Gray, my twin, has never mentioned it to me." Jett looked pissed off at that, and I wasn't really in the mood to rub his shoulders over being excluded from his brother's life. "When did you tell him?" Jett asked.

"Last night." I sank onto the only chair in my living room and put my head in my hands.

Jett stood as I sat. I knew he was angry. "Jesus Christ, Quinn! It's been over a year."

"I'm well aware of how much time it's been, Jett." My voice was dry, my tone scathing, but I didn't care.

"How could you keep this from him? From me?"

"What was I supposed to do?" I yelled at him. "We hooked up, we screwed, he went and fucked someone else three days later. I went skiing with dad and Anne. When I came back, he was in a fucking relationship."

"You tell him, and he ends the relationship!" Jett snapped at me. He stood looking at me, his fingers laced together at the back of his neck, his head tilted slightly back as he watched me. "What relationship? I can't think of one girl my brother's ever been in a relationship with. He had something with some girl from Onyx's class, but it wasn't a relationship."

Onyx, the bastard. "Well, he looked pretty involved when I saw him fucking her in Dustin's pool house."

"Jesus, Quinn, if it was, it was sex. Nothing else. You were pregnant with his kid, *my* niece or nephew. Did you feel nothing for us?"

"I thought you weren't going to judge?" I asked him angrily. "I thought I was in a *safe place* telling you?"

"You are." Jett swore some more as he resumed his pacing, and then he was in front of me, hauling me to my feet. His arms wrapped around me, and I welcomed the crushing embrace. "You are," he repeated softly. "It just hurts that you couldn't come to us."

"I was scared," I whispered into his shoulder. "I was eighteen years old and pregnant by my childhood best friend, who was cousin to my ex. It's freaking complicated."

I heard his huff of laughter as he hugged me close. "I would have helped you. I would have talked through your options. Jesus, Quinn, you shouldn't have been alone." Pulling back, Jett took my hand and led me to the couch. "Okay, I'm sorry I overreacted. Tell me it all."

"Can I get a drink?" I asked him as I stood again. He nodded and I pulled a bottle of bourbon down from the top shelf in my closet. Pouring two shots, I handed him his as I sat back down, wincing as I drank the room temperature bourbon. "Needs ice."

"It'll do." Jett downed his and placed his glass on the table.

So we weren't wasting time then? Right.

"I found out when I was seven weeks. I never even thought I could be, but see what thought did? I knew I couldn't tell him." I held my hand up to stave off Jett's interruptions. "I say it all now, because I'll never be this brave to do it again." At his nod, I continued. "I never at any time wanted to take care of it by the way you mentioned earlier. However, I knew I couldn't keep it. I was eighteen, my dad would have killed Gray and put me in a nunnery. I had my whole life ahead of me." I turned my head and looked at the wall. I could still feel the weight of his stare, but it was easier this way. "I don't even know how it happened. I was at the doctors, confirmed pregnancy, and I left without picking up any of the leaflets he had given me. I had a note of what vitamins I needed, and the woman came from nowhere."

"What woman?" Jett asked me.

"She was in a nurse's uniform, and she looked like she was heading into the clinic. The note was loose in my hand, the wind caught it, and I dropped it." I remembered it like it was a bad dream, everything seemed in slow motion. "She read my note and asked me if I was okay. I started to cry. I never cry." I paused as I sipped my drink. "She asked me if I needed help, I said no. Then she said she had something that could help me. And she gave me a leaflet. It was an adoption agency."

"They work outside the clinics?" Jett mused as I took another drink.

"I don't know." I shifted in my chair and closed my eyes. "I phoned them a couple of weeks later, they made an appointment, and I went in. They checked me over and showed me a binder full of people waiting."

"Waiting?"

"To adopt." Wrapping my arms around myself, I pulled my knees to my chest. "I went through all the paperwork, but I didn't sign. I think I was pissing them off, and I dunno, I felt wrong. So I left. They phoned me twice every day for the next few weeks." I felt the tear slip over, and I hastily brushed it away. "He knew something was wrong, he's like a freaking bloodhound, that brother of yours." I sat still even though I heard Jett murmur his agreement. "He came to me, and he asked me what was wrong, but I couldn't tell him. I didn't know how to say the words." I felt another tear slide down my cheek, and again I angrily swiped it away. "He was so gentle. He was almost pleading, and he—" I cut myself off. I didn't need to tell Jett that he told me he loved me, and I told him to go home. How could I have accepted his love when I was giving away his baby? And that night, I knew I couldn't do it. No matter what happened, I couldn't do it.

"I couldn't do it, I knew I couldn't do it. Dad would have to deal, and Gray would, well, I wasn't sure what, but he would have to accept it. Ash too." Sitting up abruptly, I startled Jett, but he didn't speak. "I answered their call the next day, told them I changed my mind. They asked to meet. I refused. They said they had paperwork that they had started that I needed to sign to make the claim go away."

"What claim?" Jett asked me.

"I don't know, something about starter's fee or something. I don't remember. They asked me to come to them, I refused. They said they would come to the house. To school."

"Bastards."

"So I went to Nashville to meet them." I turned my head to look at Jett. "I didn't even make it to the office door. I knew that the building was, I don't know, *wrong*. I turned and left because I was coming home to tell dad everything. I heard someone shout for me. I don't even know why I did it, but I started to run. I was so scared."

"I'm sorry." Jett reached over and rubbed my back, and I sat up as he pulled me into a hug. "You fell?"

"Yes, I was running, and I didn't want to lead them to the car.

I'm so stupid," I cursed myself. "I didn't see the stairs, I fell. Then I woke up in the hospital. I didn't believe the nurse when she told me I was in the hospital, and then I had to, you know, deliver, and it was all so surreal, and I don't think I really believed anything until you walked through the door."

"Never been so scared in my life as I was, seeing you lying in that bed."

"I'm sorry."

"You have no reason to be."

We sat curled up, my head on his shoulder as he gave me the comfort I needed a year ago but had never sought from him.

"Does he know all of it?" Jett asked me softly.

"No, he asked me last night to tell him it was his, and I told him. I told him that I changed my mind, I was never giving it up, and he said he would never forgive me and walked away."

"He's a stubborn bastard," Jett mumbled, but I could hear his disappointment.

"He has a right to be angry." I stared at the opposite wall. "I mean, it happened, I stayed with you at the cabin for a few days, and then I took off for a few months to get away from everything. I never told him anything."

We sat in silence for a while longer until Jett's phone rang. Then it rang again. A beep told us he had a message. With a curse, he stood and snatched his phone up. His face went white as he read the message.

"What is it?" I asked as I stood, my legs suddenly shaking.

"It's Onyx."

That didn't make me feel better. Jett was already grabbing his stuff as he phoned his brother back.

"Jett?" I asked.

"Get your stuff, I need you," Jett told me as he headed to the door. He looked at me over his shoulder. "*Now,* Quinn, it's Gray. He's in trouble."

CHAPTER 11

Gray

THE HOUSE WAS EMPTY WHEN I GOT THERE. NO SIGN OF HARRY OR his wife, and the For Sale sign pissed me off. He had moved? Why? Had it been the fact we took his memory stick, or was it merely coincidence? I didn't believe in coincidences.

The fucker moved, and I needed to know where. I wasn't a hacker like Ash was, and Ash was good, but I didn't want to tell him where I was. I called the only other hacker I knew.

"To what do I owe the pleasure?" Onyx asked me as he answered the phone.

"Need a favour," I told him as I watched the empty house. Was that movement?

"For my little brother, anything."

His tone caught my attention, and I stared at my cell. "You okay?"

"Dandy."

"Oh fuck, what have you done?" I asked cautiously.

"I blocked all her personal credit cards."

"Whose?" But I knew whose. I knew because I wasn't the only Santo with a woman in his life who drove them insane. "Angel's? Tell me you didn't."

"I could, but…it would be a lie." I heard his smirk.

"She's going to kill you."

"Pft." I heard his humour. "She needs to prove it first."

"Dude..." I had no words. They had a *strained* relationship. They were business rivals, and yet it seemed that they were both as intent as the other to destroy each other rather than compete in the boardroom.

"Now, what can I do for you?"

"I need to know about a house listing."

"Why?" I heard him lose some of his humour. "You moving out of the frat house?"

"It's not a frat house," I reminded him for the hundredth time. "You were in the same house."

"Pure frat house."

"We're not in a fraternity!"

"Whatever, which house?" I gave him the address, and I heard the silence. I waited. "Why? Is this because of *her*?"

"No."

"Lie."

"Fuck, Onyx, just fucking tell me where the fucker's gone."

And then I saw movement. Definitely movement in the house. "Forget it." I hung up and put my phone on silent and off of vibrate as I shoved it in the glove compartment. Checking my surroundings, I made my way to the house. Hesitantly, I tried the back patio door handle. It opened, and I made my way inside, pulling my bandana up over my face.

I listened.

Shuffling overhead made me move to the stairs. The study was on the ground floor, and I quickly looked in, seeing the hole in the wall where the safe used to be. It could be painters in here, making good the redecoration for selling.

Or it could be Harry the happy cameraman.

Slowly I made my way up the stairs. I ducked at the last minute as the punch came swinging for me, almost losing my balance as I blocked the follow up, and then with only defence on my mind, I punched the hitter back. Confusion cleared, and I saw I had hit Harry. Rage made me hit him again, and then I hit him one more time. With feeling.

As he lay on the floor in his hallway, I looked around, making sure he was alone.

"There's nothing left to steal," he told me as he raised his hands in supplication. His nose was broken by the looks of it, but it didn't stop me from wanting to stomp on his face. "There's nothing here of value to you."

Well, he was wrong about that, because he was here, and he was very valuable to me.

"My wife is going to be home any moment," he said as he tried to stem the blood from his nose. I knew my snort conveyed my disgust.

Did I look stupid? There was nothing in the house, what the hell was she coming home to? No, Harry was alone and was exactly where I needed him to be.

At my mercy.

Basements are always the last thing people pack. Because the likelihood is that, last time you packed, half that shit was still in your basement or your garage. Harry didn't disappoint me. His basement looked like a packrat had moved in and had never moved out.

One hideous wooden chair and a handy length of rope later, and I had him tied to the chair.

My hood was low, and my bandana covered most of my face, but I still knew to disguise my voice. "What are you here for?" I asked him.

"This is my house," he told me as he looked around.

It struck me as odd that he didn't seem nervous, and I wondered who was really coming for him. Colleagues? Business partners? More men whose kids he tried to take?

"What do you do with the kids?" I asked him, and I saw his demeanour change. He wasn't as confident now.

"I don't know what you—"

My punch shut him up.

"I'll ask you again, and I advise that you don't lie. What…do you do…with the *kids*?"

"They're adopted into good homes."

My next punch made him lose a tooth. I rolled my head on my

shoulders as I looked at him, flexing my fist, glad I had the foresight to put gloves on, but pissed his stupid teeth had nicked the latex.

"You like to make films, Harry?" It gave me great satisfaction to see him whiten so much I was sure he was going to faint. "You like to watch girls give birth and watch their kids get taken away without them even seeing which fucker you give them to." I leaned on his knees as I stared into his eyes. "You like to watch them bleed out and die on your table?"

He swallowed loudly. "That doesn't happen often," he whispered.

"*Once* is too often, because you have them in a room with no doctors, no medicine. You like to hear them scream?" I punched him again.

I hit him too hard. I heard a crack, and as I stood back, I took in his slumped form. With a curse, I felt for a pulse. Shit.

Had I just killed Harry?

A creak above me had me still, listening. Was this the company he was waiting for? Looking around the basement, I searched for an exit. Shit. My only way out was up the stairs, and with a small measure of relief, I heard Harry groan.

The footsteps moved closer, and I had no choice but to duck behind a pile of fuck knows what and hide. I needed to know how many there were before I either fought my way out or was busted.

A guy came down the stairs, and I recognised him from the third house we did. Squinting, I watched him as he looked at Harry and then looked around the room. The fact he wasn't rushing to his aid told me its own story.

"We seem to have company," he yelled from his position on the stairs.

I waited—how many were coming? If I kept the element of surprise, I could maybe manage two.

Heavy footsteps sounded on the wooden stairs, and then

another bulky guy was in the basement. Him, I didn't recognise, but I wouldn't forget him. The scar on the side of his face was memorable.

"What the fuck happened?" he asked as he strode over to Harry, who was, thankfully for me, alive, but definitely unconscious.

"Mugger?" the other one suggested.

"The house is empty, what was left to take?"

"You think they're gone?"

Scar Guy looked around the basement. "Well, there's nothing upstairs. They could be down here, or they could have split when they heard us arrive."

Were they stupid or lazy? I mean, if they were both, I would thank the angels, but there was no way they weren't checking the basement. I almost laughed with relief when they did exactly that and both turned and climbed the stairs. My sense of good fortune lasted right up until I heard the bolt slide home.

Fuck, they locked me in.

No, they locked me *and* Harry in.

I looked at him.

This wasn't good. Now I knew why Harry swung first. He was ready to defend himself.

Quickly, I searched the basement again, and then I saw the small window, hidden behind a pile of boxes that reeked of damp. It was too high—and small. I wouldn't fit through there.

Shit.

I heard them moving around upstairs. They seemed almost methodical in their movements. What were they doing? It hit me at the same time as the smell of the smoke.

They set the house on fire.

Frantically, I ran up the stairs and tried the door. I didn't care who was on the other side, I would fight my way out. It didn't budge.

Turning, and almost falling down the stairs in my haste, I made my way to the window. The only thing to stand on was the fucking chair I tied Harry to. Cursing myself at my adeptness at knots, I finally managed to untie him and pushed him out of the chair. He landed with a thud and a groan, but he was alive, and that's all that mattered.

The window didn't open. The smoke was now making its way into the basement, and I knew I couldn't be in here longer than I had to. I needed out.

Drawing my hand back, I punched the window and cried out in pain as it held and I heard a crack in my hand. I punched again and broke through the pane of glass, slicing my hand in the process. Still, I had it open. Taking off my hoodie and wrapping it around my hand, I punched out the rest of the window, ignoring the pain, and then gripping the frame, I pulled myself up. It didn't matter how hard I tried, I was never going to fit.

Hands grabbed me, and I fought them off, but my brother's voice calmed me down.

"You won't fit," Onyx growled at me, and I dropped back into the basement. "Hurry, he's in the basement!" he yelled to someone, and then I heard the door opening and footsteps coming down the stairs. Jumping off the seat, I ran and stopped dead the same time as Jett saw me.

My brother grabbed me and started to haul me upwards.

"No!" I shouted as I wrenched free. "I need help."

I ran back down the few stairs and picked up the still unconscious Harry off the floor.

"What the fuck?" Jett yelled at me as he hastily covered his face.

"I need him to talk," I said as I started back up the stairs. The smoke was thick now, and I could feel the heat of the flames.

"I'm not fucking dying for Harry," Jett growled as he helped me.

"We need him."

The house was an inferno; my brother was insane to run into this house for me. Battling our way to the kitchen, where Onyx was pacing outside the door impatiently, I could hear the sirens, and I knew we had little time.

"We need to move," I coughed as I struggled to stand upright. "We can't be caught, our chance will be gone."

"What the fuck were you thinking?" Jett grunted as he took Harry off me and put him over his shoulder.

"Let's move," Onyx ordered us tersely as more and more lights came on in the street.

"We need to split up," Jett said as he watched the yard and the surroundings. "We're fucked if we get caught."

"My car...it's a street over."

"You go there, we'll go this way—"

"I'll make it to my own," Onyx cut him off, grabbing Harry off Jett. "You know where to meet," he instructed with a pointed look at Harry, who was coming around. I quickly punched him again to knock him out, and Onyx glared at me in frustration. "Jesus! Fuck, just *run*."

I hesitated before Jett pushed me into movement, and he took off with Onyx following closely behind him. I turned and ran back to my car, keeping to the cover of the darkness, wincing as the sirens raced nearer.

Pulling my bandana off my face, I pulled my hood over my eyes, keeping my head low, hoping I looked like a guy out for a walk rather than a guy running from a crime scene.

Knowing I was nearing my car, I glanced up to make sure there was no one around. I was in the car when I saw her emerging from the shadows, hoodie pulled low, blending with the night like we'd taught her. She walked swiftly to the passenger side door and then was slipping in beside me.

"Drive," Quinn ordered. "Get us out of here, and then you can tell me why you're trying to get yourself arrested...or killed."

We kept our heads low as I drove away, both of us watching for anyone watching us. We were a few miles from the house when she reached over and took my hand, looking at the damage.

"You're *so* reckless."

Without a word, I laced her fingers with mine and she didn't pull away, and I didn't care that it hurt my damaged hand.

We drove in silence as I headed to my brother's office, preparing myself for the fireworks that were coming.

But I had Harry, which meant I was close to the answers that had eluded me for so long. If I couldn't make him talk, I had no doubt that Onyx would.

Lifting her hand to my mouth, I brushed my lips across her knuckles and held them there for the rest of the journey. She brought me peace, even when she drove me wild and made me reckless, peace came when she was near.

After all, she was my sanctuary.

CHAPTER 12

Quinn

His lips never lifted from my skin. I didn't care that it was uncomfortable, and after I had managed to stem the bleeding a little from his hand, we drove in silence. My heart was still racing, and the drive wasn't calming me down. When Jett told me he needed me, I didn't hesitate. Very few people could calm Gray down when he lost it, and for Jett to say he was in trouble...I knew it was bad.

I didn't ask where Jett was taking me, I didn't query why he circled a row of houses before he spotted Gray's car and then made sure he parked nowhere near it.

I didn't question when he told me to go wait by Gray's car and be ready. Ready for what, he never told me. He pulled his bandana over his face, his hood low, and he was gone.

I didn't have a bandana, but I had the sense to grab a hoodie on the way out with Jett, and I pulled my hood low, covering my hair completely as I walked the opposite direction of the car in case anyone was watching. They taught me a long time ago to blend into my surroundings, never hurry, always walk with purpose, and never under any circumstances, look like you were lost or checking out your surroundings.

When I approached Gray's car, I passed it and kept on walking.

I saw the smoke from the house and the low flames.

He set a house on fire?

No. He wouldn't. Gray was reckless sometimes, but he wasn't stupid. He had never been stupid or careless. He took great efforts to make sure everything he did was thought out and planned. He was meticulous to the point of unreasonable sometimes. When I saw him approach the car, I felt relief, but I had hung back to make sure there was no one else coming, or following, and when I knew it was safe, I let him see me. I had so many questions, but I knew, when he was like this, not to ask. He would tell me when he was ready. As we drove, I realised how very similar we were.

Slowly we approached Onyx's building. Not just the building he worked in, the building he *owned*. It was sometimes easy to forget they were so wealthy they didn't need to work hard at school or train hard; they could be privileged trust fund kids and do nothing. But they were too clever, too ambitious, and they had been raised to be exceptional.

Kerr, their father, had been successful in the draft but had never played pro. Kage did until his knee had one too many operations and they told him he couldn't play anymore. Kage was often a "celebrity" commentator, but it wasn't his main income. When he was playing and earning good money, he and Kerr had invested it, and then they were advising Kage's teammates on investments. Until they had their own agency of financial advisors.

Onyx had taken it a step further, and now he represented some of the biggest names in sports. His fee percentage was steep, but if asked, he would tell you that to be the best, you paid for the best. Gray was very close to his older brother, and I was not in the least bit surprised that it was Onyx who knew Gray had been reckless tonight.

As we parked in the underground parking reserved for the Santos, Gray let go of my hand and turned to look at me. His face was unreadable, but when he reached out to stroke my cheek with his hand, his touch was gentle.

"You okay?" he asked me in the quiet of the car.

"Yes." I nodded to confirm as he watched me. "What did you do?"

"You need to stay outside," he said instead of answering me. His finger on my lips cut off my protest. "You don't need to hear it, not tonight."

Swallowing my complaint, I nodded again.

Smoothly, he exited the car, and I followed nervously. Making our way to the elevator, the doors opened automatically, and I said nothing when he pressed the lower-level button. Glancing at him with concern, I saw he was watching me. With a quick movement, he hit the stop button, and then his mouth was on mine, as demanding as it was dominating. I opened my mouth when he licked the seam of my lips, and then he was really kissing me. His hands tangled in my hair, and somewhere my brain registered he had blood on his hands, but I didn't stop him. He tasted of smoke from the fire, heightening the fact that he tasted of danger and ruthlessness.

Wild and raw.

I was helpless in his arms, and when he drew back, with only a breath between us, his lips were gentle when he kissed me again.

Lazily, he reached out and hit the button, and we finished the descent into the basement in silence. I followed him to a far room where he opened the door, pointed at the coffee machine in the corner, and with a hooded look, he closed the door behind him.

Resigned to the fact that I was to wait, I made my way around the large table, guessing this was a conference room or maybe a training room. I didn't really care, my focus was the coffee machine. I had no idea what time it was, but coffee was never a bad choice. I was trying to figure out how to work the machine when I realised out of all of them, *I* was the one who should be in the room while they discussed *me*. No matter how bad it was or what they thought I needed to hear, it was *my* choice.

With grim determination, I opened the door and went to find them.

I didn't expect to find Onyx with his black shirt sleeves rolled up as he struck a guy in a chair. I didn't expect to find Jett holding Gray back from attacking the guy, and it seemed from the look on his face, he looked like he would kill him.

I didn't expect to recognise the guy in the chair, especially as he seemed to have already been beaten, or to register that each of them still had their faces half covered. Even Onyx had a bandana around his face. All I could do was stare at the man who had tried to convince me that adoption was the best thing for me and my baby.

"Dr Newton?"

Onyx whirled around as Jett's and Gray's heads snapped to look at me.

"Get her out of here," Onyx growled as he looked at me with his usual loathing.

Gray was in front of me, and he half carried me out of the room and back to where I had been.

We stood several feet apart, but I felt that there was a gulf between us as deep and wide as the Grand Canyon. He pulled his bandana down as he pushed his hood back. He always looked softer than Jett, but right now, his face was all hard lines and tight with anger.

Anger at me? I wasn't sure, nor did I care. "You need to explain."

"Do I?" He walked over to the machine and started to make himself a coffee.

Cold. Detached. Despite my earlier observation in the car, sometimes he was like a stranger to me. Even after he'd just kissed me like I was the only thing that mattered, he could turn it all off and just be...nothing.

Unemotional. Callous. Bordering on cruel.

"Why is he here? Who did that to him?" My voice was steady, low, and I was proud of myself for keeping it together. "Did you set fire to his *house?*"

Cold blue eyes watched me as he added creamer to the coffee that he effortlessly made from a machine that had given me nothing. "No."

"No? What are you answering no to? No, you didn't set fire to it?"

"Why would I set fire to it?"

If I had asked him what time it was, he would have answered with the same casualness. "He's in a chair, half beaten, in a basement, where your crazy brother is torturing him!"

"He deserves it." Gray took a drink of his coffee as he watched me, grimaced and placed the cup down. "He deserves to swing from a fucking rope."

"Gray…"

"You *don't* know," he suddenly shouted at me as his hands hit the table in fury. "You haven't *seen* what they do, what *he* lets happen!"

"And you do?" I asked in confusion. "How?"

"Because the sick fucker in that room *records* it."

I saw his fury as he looked at me, I saw it as clearly as if he had spoken the words to me, accusing me, that I was going to be the same as the girls on the film. Was his anger at me or Dr Newton?

"Tell me." I moved closer to him, and the pain that rushed through me as he stepped out of my reach was sharp.

"How do you know him?" Gray asked me.

"He was the doctor who talked me through the adoption process." We stood apart, and I wanted to close the distance almost as much as he wanted to widen it.

"How did you find them?" His voice was low, toneless, and I watched him reach for the cup and drink his coffee. I noticed the shake in his hand, and I knew it was adrenaline.

Shit, his hand.

"Gray, let me fix your hand." I walked towards him, my hands raised as if he were a wounded animal. "I'll answer all your questions. Just like I did with Jett earlier."

I flinched when he threw the coffee cup across the room, realising my mistake as soon as the words had left my mouth.

"Of course you told *him* everything," Gray sneered at me as he walked past me, his shoulder knocking me out of the way. "I can look after my own hand."

Wildly, I grabbed for him, my arms hooking around his forearm as I pulled him back. "No! *Stop* walking away from me," I growled as I physically tried to restrain him. "Gray, talk to *me*."

He whirled on me, but I stood firm as he glared down at me, the heat of his rage radiating from his body. "Like you talk to me? Okay, Queeny." He grabbed a seat and pulled it back from the table, waiting for me to take it. "Sit. Let's talk."

I hesitated. I knew him. I knew with him this heated, things would go badly. Still, I sat. I had kept the truth from him for a year, and whatever they had found had made him reckless, and because I was part of this, whether I accepted it or not, I could sit and I could talk.

Lowering myself into the chair, I watched him as if he were a caged animal while he regarded me almost warily as though he expected me to bolt. When I was seated, he yanked a chair out and dropped into it, his hard stare never leaving mine.

"Tell me everything."

Carefully, slowly, I told him what I had told Jett. I watched him as he sat rigid in his chair, his gaze never wavering, his attention wholly on me, and while I spoke, I waited for the eruption. Gray would never harm me, not physically. Emotionally…well, we had no problems taking those blows from each other.

"You changed your mind?" he asked me, the tone in which he asked me almost daring me to say no.

"I changed my mind. I couldn't do that to him, her, I don't know, it?" I sniffed as I finally broke his stare. "I couldn't do it to us."

"There is no us."

The unforgiving words caused more pain than he knew, and I'd be damned if I showed him. Instead, I sat in front of him, the mask firmly in place as he assessed me, equally as closed off to me as I was to him.

"And now you know it all." Leaning back in my seat, I looked at his hand. "Coach is going to kick your ass."

Gray grunted but said nothing as he looked at his hand. "I fell."

"I can see teeth marks."

"I fell against someone's face."

My eyebrows rose as I turned away from him. "He films the births?" I asked quietly.

"Yes."

"You watched them?" Why? What else was there on the film?

"Yes."

"Why are you so angry about them?"

Tiredly, he rubbed his eyes. "I stink."

"Your personality could be better, I agree," I murmured as he stood, and I caught the quick flash of a smile.

"There's showers down here, I'm going to clean up." He didn't look at me, but he turned his head towards me, and I was already agreeing before he spoke.

"I won't leave the room again."

"I won't be long." The door closed softly behind him, and I was once again alone.

Sitting in the chair, I realised neither of us had cleaned the mess of the coffee-stained wall and the broken cup. I sat for longer than I should have before I moved and started cleaning up. There was a large pile of napkins that I used to clean the wall, and then crouching, I gingerly started picking up the broken shards of the cup.

It was inevitable that I would cut my finger; it was my luck, I suppose. Hissing at the cut, I stood with my finger in my mouth as I dropped some more napkins onto the floor, pressing my foot on them to soak up the spilled coffee.

Reaching over for another napkin for my finger, I opened the cupboard to see if Onyx had a first aid kit. He didn't. Wrapping a napkin around my finger, I watched the blood soak through the white paper.

Strong hands unwrapped the napkin, and then Gray was investigating my small cut. Compared to his hand, it was nothing, but the care with which he held my hand? You would have thought I had a serious injury. Blood oozed out from the cut and trickled slowly down my index finger.

There was something fundamentally wrong with me, because when Gray's tongue licked the blood from my finger, my insides clenched with desire. Slowly his tongue traced the length of my finger again before his lips covered the soft pad, and I felt my body heat when he sucked slightly. Hooded eyes met mine as he looked at me, and I didn't resist when his other hand reached out and grabbed my hip, pulling me into him.

His hand lowered to cup my ass, and then I was flush against him, feeling the hard length of him pressing into me as he pulled my finger slowly from his mouth, dragging it over his bottom lip before his tongue flicked out one final time, as if he were sorry that it was leaving the warmth of his mouth.

I felt his fingers dig into the softness of my ass as he dropped my hand to curl around the back of my neck and pull me to his lips.

"I'm angry." His words were low, quiet, full of emotion. "I want to kill him. I want to kill them all. I want to rip them apart with my bare hands."

"Gray—"

His lips pressed against mine, not in a kiss but as a way to stop me talking. With wide eyes, I watched him as his eyelids fluttered closed before they opened again and he stared right past all my defences and into my darkest depths.

"I want to rip *you* apart with my bare hands." He spoke against my mouth, but I heard every word, felt every word. "But I can't."

"Why?"

"Because as much as I may want to, it's not my desire to hurt you." Again, he cut my words off by pressing his lips to mine, but this time it was as a kiss. And like the helpless fool I was when it came to this man, I returned his kiss. It was slow and sensual and brought all my defences crashing down around me. My hands curled into the front of his hoodie, pulling him closer to me. Gray gave a low growl, and his fingers dug into my ass as he pulled me into him, deepening the kiss as his tongue brushed against mine, swallowing my moans as his hand on my neck tilted my head to give him better access to my mouth.

To my soul.

His hand on my ass slipped up over the curve of my hip and then was dipping under my hoodie and caressing gently over my breast. His thumb ran over the pebbled nipple, causing me to moan louder against him. I felt him hard against me.

I winced when his teeth bit my bottom lip, but it only made me ache to be closer to him. Slowly he pulled away, my blood staining his lower lip. His hand dropped from my neck and untangled itself from under my hoodie. Never breaking my gaze, with slow measured steps, he moved away from me.

"I can't be around you."

"Gray—"

"I can't," he cut me off again. "Knowing what I know, what I always suspected, and seeing the film..." He hesitated. "You need to stay away."

What could I say? No? I had no right to do that. I had no hold over Gray. What was between us really? Nothing. Nothing but heartache and hurt that we may never be able to move past.

How in the world could I deny him anything after the last few days? Days? After the last year.

"Okay."

"I have..." He hesitated before he gestured to the door. "I have to see this through. I need to do this, and I have...I have football. And I..." He shook his head.

"I know." I wrapped my arms around myself as I watched him while I prayed that I could keep it together long enough so he wouldn't see me break. "I know, Gray, it's okay. I understand."

He took another step back, his hands running over his hair and grabbing behind his head as his eyes searched mine. He stood there like that for a moment, beautiful, pained, broken.

I did this. I caused this. The urge to reach out to him and give him the comfort he didn't want or probably need, at least not from me, was strong.

"It's okay," I repeated softly. "Go."

He looked almost as if he wouldn't, and I closed down my emotions as I felt a brief flare of hope in my chest, but he turned and, with purposeful strides, left the room.

Bending over, I clasped my arms around myself as I allowed myself to feel the pain. It rose from the pit of my soul and engulfed me, threatened to consume me, but I had to fight it. As I squeezed my eyes shut as if I could shut out his tortured words, I straightened. With my hands trembling slightly, I finished cleaning the mess. Realising that my finger had stopped bleeding, I gave it an accusatory glare.

As I finished with the coffee cup and the numerous napkins I had probably wasted, I straightened my hoodie, pulled my hair over my shoulder, and sat back down again to wait for Jett or Onyx to come.

My life was in tatters around me, but I was not broken. I was not beaten. I had overcome so much; this pain too, I would endure.

However, when Onyx opened the door later and looked at me with his usual scorn, I knew I shouldn't have been surprised even though my stomach plummeted with dread. Rising to my feet, silently I followed him to his car without a word spoken between us. He drove me back to college in total silence. I noted his damaged hand, and he noted the one tear that spilled over, but neither of us acknowledged the other's hurt.

This relationship, I had always understood.

It didn't surprise me he knew exactly where my dorm room was. He always knew too much.

Reaching for the handle, I made to leave the car when his words stopped me.

"I told you years ago...you would ruin him. I won't let you destroy him again."

Focusing on my hand on the door handle, I spoke to him with the same coldness he gave me. "You know *nothing,* but I'll tell you what I told him, I'll keep my distance."

"Make sure you do, from *all* of them. Your reign is over, *Queeny*."

Turning my head, I met his black stare brimming with cold hatred, and it was exactly what I needed, because it hardened me further. "Fuck you."

I got out of the car and made it into my apartment, closing the door behind me as the weariness washed over me. Heading straight to my room, kicking off my boots as I walked, I didn't bother undressing as I collapsed onto the bed. Lying face down on my pillows, I finally let the tears fall as I wept for what I had lost.

CHAPTER 13

Gray

Driving in silence, my head was a jumble of words and confusion, and twice I had to straighten the car as I drove on autopilot and didn't pay the right attention to my surroundings. I knew Jett was behind me, keeping his distance but close if I needed him, and I didn't know if I needed him or needed *her*.

God, she tasted like I remembered, of sin and temptation. Her soft curves were mine to claim, and I knew how soft she was. She bruised so easily; she'd have marks on her skin tomorrow from where my fingers dug into her flesh tonight.

Two of the times that we had been together before were both hard and fast. The third time… I exhaled as I thought about the night we spent together where I'd stripped her bare and fucked her all night, her cries of pleasure fuelling me on. My intent to leave my mark on her backfired in the worst way possible.

I had more than left my mark, I had gotten her pregnant.

And she never fucking told me.

I had no explanation as to why she never told me, and as I drove, I realised I had never asked. Too angry, too consumed with revenge on the people who had hurt her, I hadn't asked her why she never told me.

Is that why? Did she think I wouldn't care? Or was the thought of *my* baby so abhorrent to her that her only logical solution was to give it away?

Didn't I have a right to have an opinion? Didn't I have the right to have a say? I knew all the arguments, and I agreed it was her body, her choice, but didn't I too get a chance to be heard? She would never have been alone in this, whatever she decided. Didn't she know that? As I drove through the blackness of the night, I realised maybe she didn't.

Maybe she really thought she had been alone.

Alone and scared.

A small snort escaped me as I thought about how much we had in common. Which is why she pissed me off whenever it came to us. She had chosen wrongly so many times, and the consequences of her actions affected us both.

Now look at us. Too jaded and wounded to be anything more than what we were.

Broken.

My head tilted back against the leather headrest as I stared at the road in front of me, my brother's headlights a distance behind me. Always there, always ready for when I may need him.

With a sharp turn of the wheel, I pulled onto the shoulder and got out of the car, resting against the hood as I looked up at the night sky. Moments later, Jett's stupid, flashy car was pulling in behind mine. He left his lights on low behind my car as he got out and joined me.

"I told her she needs to stay away."

Jett was silent for a long time before he nodded. "Okay, do you think that's for the best?" he asked quietly.

"Yes," I answered sharply.

"Okay." We stood there, and I knew he was giving me the space I needed. If I wanted to talk, he would listen.

"She never told me."

"I know."

"She never told me she was pregnant, and she never told me she was giving it away."

"I know."

I heard the heaviness in his own voice, and I knew he was having his own struggles with her decision.

"She called *you* that day. Not me."

Jett straightened slightly beside me as I remained with my stare on the stars. "She did. I'm not defending her, but given what we now know, she must have thought I would be the easiest one to tell."

Shaking my head, I turned to look at him. "It's always you she goes to first."

Jett met my stare, and I didn't need to see the challenge in his eyes, daring me to argue with him. "She's my best friend, I tell her everything, and until that day in the hospital, I would have said the same about her."

"I'm your brother."

"I'm aware." His voice was dry, and even though I couldn't see him clearly, I knew the eyebrow would be raised.

"She didn't tell me."

"What are you angrier about?" he asked me, and I looked at him, not understanding. "Is it because she told me tonight, are you pissed that she called me from the hospital, are you angry she was pregnant in the first place, or are you mad she never told you until she had no choice but to tell us both?"

I thought about it. "All of it."

I heard his quiet scoff. "Or should you be angry that the girls we've seen on those delivery beds could have been her? That she was so scared of our reaction, she panicked and thought she couldn't tell anyone, not even me."

"We let her down?" I asked sceptically.

"We failed her, and I think we should remember that. We failed her in every way possible, and I don't think it's *you* who should be telling Quinn to stay away from us," he finished quietly, noticing my wince when he said her name.

"Maybe you're right." I shrugged. "But that doesn't change that I feel like this and that I could still happily wrap my hands around her throat and squeeze."

Jett gave a humourless laugh. "I don't need to know your kinks, little brother," he said quietly as he nudged me with his shoulder.

"Did she tell you why she never told me?"

"Yes."

"Don't make me fuck up my other hand, Jett," I warned.

"She said she saw you in Dustin's pool house with someone else, she left and had the family skiing weekend, and when she came back, you were in a relationship."

"What the fuck is she talking about?" I asked in confusion. "Who?"

Jett looked at his boots. "I think it was one of Onyx's friends."

And I remembered. Closing my eyes in resignation, I let out a long sigh.

"I didn't fuck her," I growled, pushing myself off the car angrily. "I told her to get out, I was trying to sleep. I was drunk."

We'd all been at Dustin's end-of-school party that he held before graduation. Quinn and I had been with each other a few days before, but she had been more aloof and distant than usual after it, and I'd given her the space she seemed to want. I'd gotten wasted at the party, relieved school was over, and I had a few weeks to enjoy summer before training started for college football.

After graduation, Quinn was so scarce, I hardly saw her at all, and then Jett came home one day and told Ash and me that he'd spent the day with her in the hospital and was taking her to the cabin. Quinn had miscarried, and he said she was acting off. On top of everything, he said she was too jumpy, as if she was scared of someone.

Quinn Lawrence had never been scared in her life, no matter what names I called her.

I'd waited until Ash had asked his questions and Jett had told him what he knew. He looked devastated as did Ash. But I kept it all inside. Ash asked how many weeks she had been pregnant, but Jett didn't know—she hadn't answered him when he had asked her.

I thought she'd fucked someone else.

I thought it was someone else's kid.

And she let me think it.

I didn't begin to suspect it was mine until I saw her on her first day of school at college. Her hair was longer, she'd lost weight, her skin lacked colour, and she couldn't look at me when she spoke to me.

I watched her for a week, and so did Jett. By the end of the week, Jett had been busy. He was sure there was something else. He thought she was scared of the guy who had gotten her pregnant. She answered a few questions from him in the beginning, and then she clammed up.

We never expected to uncover what we did.

The more we dug, the more we found. Progress was slow though, and it had only really been the last few months where we were getting anywhere.

The first time we saw that film, I remember how sick I felt. That could have been her. That could have been her bleeding out on the table as they ripped her baby, *my* baby, out of her. It was horrific. Then they walked out of the room and left the girl dead on the table.

Forgotten.

I couldn't forget.

It consumed me. I saw Quinn on that table every time I closed my eyes. The need to know if it was mine ate at my insides. And she didn't see it, she didn't see the damage she was doing by keeping her silence.

Or she didn't care.

The night Jett texted me to say she needed me, I'd held her as she cried, and as she clung to me, I knew with no more doubts that it was mine.

And *still* she didn't tell me.

When she stopped crying, she pulled that fucking mask she wore so well on, thanked me for the comfort, and then held the door open and asked me to leave.

I could have challenged her, to be fair. I could've quite happily shaken her until she told me everything, but instead, I had walked out and left her. At her request.

I didn't know who was right, but I knew we needed distance from each other now.

"Are you okay?"

His question brought me back to the side of the road, both of us standing in the dark cool Tennessee night.

"No."

Jett reached out and clasped my shoulder. "I'm truly sorry."

My head hung low as I bowed my head, and I felt an emotion other than rage. Sorrow. My eyes squeezed closed as I fought it back. If I let myself feel it, it would consume me.

"I know," I told him as I raised my head and looked at him. "It's good she has you." I hated it. I had always been jealous of their relationship, but in this moment, I was glad she had someone, even though it wasn't me.

"You can't do this anymore." Jett's hand dropped away from me. "This recklessness. Onyx is involved now, and we both know that's dangerous."

"He's on my side."

"We're all on your side," Jett snapped. "But we're in the middle of something huge, and we would be stupid to think this is for us to fix." At my glare, he held his hands up in acceptance. "I know. I know, I thought we could do this, but whoever came for Harry tonight, they aren't fucking about. They were happy to leave him for dead in his basement."

"Maybe we should have left him," I grunted. Rubbing my head, I looked over at my brother. "What else did he say? Did he recognise her?"

"I don't think so," Jett answered carefully. "He didn't tell us any other names, but you think you know one of the guys who came tonight?"

I nodded as I looked over the low wooded area we were parked beside. "He was film three, I'm sure of it. The second guy, him I don't know."

"Onyx is going to want to know everything."

"Then we tell him everything," I said easily.

"And Ash?" Jett spoke softly beside me.

I wet my lips and realised I was fucking cold, standing in the cold night air with only jeans and a hoodie on. "Not yet."

Out of the corner of my eye, I saw my brother nod. "I agree."

I barked out a cynical laugh. "How the fuck do I have that conversation?" Rubbing my hands through my hair, I hissed as I cracked the cuts on my hand open again.

"We need to take it one day at a time." Jett straightened and eyed his car. "You can't keep holding it in. Tonight has to show you how dangerous it is, how reckless you are. It is not our future to be in a jail cell, Gray."

"She wouldn't talk, and I needed answers."

"And now we have something, and she talked, but now, now I need you to let it out and work on moving forward."

He moved towards his car, the lights illuminating him in the dark. I couldn't see his face anymore, but he would see me, and I knew he would see the scepticism because I wasn't hiding it.

"I need more than a heart-to-heart on the side of the road and a kumbaya session."

"Mom can hook you up with a therapist."

The dryness of my brother's tone made me chuckle, and then I was properly laughing. I heard his low laughter join mine before he got back into his car and waited for me to get into mine.

With the heat on high, I drove the rest of the way back to the dorm.

In silence, we both climbed the stairs. He didn't go to Ava, and I was surprised but grateful he was going to be close tonight.

Pushing my door to my bedroom open, I reached out and grabbed his arm to stop him from going into his.

Onyx sat on my couch, dark eyes fixed on me, and he remained quiet as I pulled my twin into my room and closed the door behind us.

"Hey," I greeted him. "She okay?"

Our brother was six years older than us and had a wildness in him that our father swore he got from our grandfather.

"I didn't ask." His eyes flicked to Jett, and I knew he would be waiting for Jett to jump to her defence. "I did see a tear, but there was only one. It could have been the light. With her? It was probably the light."

Clenching my jaw, I crossed to my desk chair and sat. "Don't be a dick, she's had a hard time."

"I have no doubt. I also don't care." Onyx watched Jett sit on the edge of my bed and shifted so he could see us both without having to turn his head. "Why would you do this without coming to me?"

"We had it handled," I cut Jett off as I met my brother's hard stare.

"If I hadn't tracked your phone, you would be nothing but a burnt-out husk. Tell me at what point were you *handling* tonight?"

"Situation got away from me."

"The situation?" Onyx crossed his legs casually as if we were discussing the weather. "Humour me, *Devils*, a piss poor example at that." He glared at me. "Tell me what the fuck you were thinking before I kick your ass so badly you won't play the rest of this season. Either of you."

"You don't—"

"Don't!" He was on his feet, and I could feel his rage as he strode towards me. "Make me understand. Make me understand why you would throw everything away for that little tramp." Grabbing my chin, Onyx forced me to look up at him. "Tell me why you would risk it all for her."

"Because it was his baby."

Three heads swivelled to the door where Ash stood in the open doorway. With a single step, he was in the room and closing the door behind him.

Onyx looked down at me and squeezed tighter. "Is it true?"

I couldn't take my eyes off Ash, who held my stare with a shuttered one of his own.

"It was." Jett rose from the bed and looked at Ash.

Onyx flung my head away from him as he gave a disgruntled growl and started to pace the room, ignoring the tension between us all. "Why do you three boys fall over yourself for this fucking girl? What hold does she have on you that makes you behave like mindless fucking fools?"

"I know you don't like her," I said to him as I rubbed my jaw, "but you don't need to speak about her like that."

"Why? She's poison."

"Stop it," Ash murmured as he sat on the armrest of the couch. He was still watching me, and I was watching him. "She's been a part of us since we were ten. She's as close as family."

"She cheated on you," Onyx reminded him as he turned his glare onto him.

"Did she?" Ash gave me a considering look. "I think she lied."

Onyx snorted and threw his hands in the air in disbelief. "And how long have you thought this?" he snarked at Ash.

"About five seconds ago." Ash tilted his head in question as he looked at me. "I think she was told to break it off, am I right?"

I nodded once, and with a slight shake of his head, he looked away from me.

"You're both fucking clowns." Onyx looked between us both. "Fix this shit later. For tonight, tell me what I need to know about the house, the fire and the doctor I knocked unconscious in my basement."

"What?" Ash was on his feet, looking at Jett and me.

Quickly Jett retold the night, and I filled in the bits none of them knew.

"Why the hell would you take Quinn?" Ash asked Jett when he was finished.

"Because I knew if I needed to bring him back from the edge, she was the only one who would be able to," Jett replied with a heavy sigh.

"Seriously, has she got a fucking diamond-encrusted pussy?" Onyx spat, and for the third time that night, I bust my hand open when I smashed my fist into my brother's jaw.

CHAPTER 14

Quinn

HALLOWEEN WAS MY FAVOURITE TIME OF YEAR, AND I DIDN'T HIDE IT. It had been a week since the night of the fire, and all three of them were avoiding me. I'd received a couple of texts from Jett and only one from Gray. Which had come the night he told me he couldn't be near me.

I stared at it now, as I sat in the coffee shop with a pumpkin spice latte.

Gray: **Ash knows**

That was it. No how did he know or what he knew or how he reacted. Just *Ash knows*.

And if I were honest, I was glad that he did. Yes, I'm a horrible, terrible person, and I will burn in hell no doubt, but it was one more weight off my shoulders, and truthfully, I was grateful I didn't need to be the one to tell him.

Ash wouldn't need to be told to keep his distance; he would gladly avoid me.

Looking down at my laptop, I looked at the food plans. I needed to go to the house and check in with the football players for my assignment, but I knew I couldn't right now.

I knew they would fuck up this assignment for me.

Tapping my pen off the side of the table, I jerked in surprise when a large hand stilled my pen. Looking up, I met Gray's stare and sat in silence as he pulled out a chair and dropped into it.

He pulled his book bag onto his lap and started rifling through it. His hand was still strapped up, and he had missed a game and was due to miss Saturday's away game too.

He handed me several sheets of paper, and I hesitated before I took them from him.

"I don't have it all—they're fucking useless at paying attention—but it's the best I could do."

Shuffling through the sheets, I realised they were food diaries, and as I began to scrutinise them more closely, I saw he had even guesstimated at the portion size.

"You didn't need to do this."

"Well, you weren't coming for them, and you didn't set up a shared document for them to input stuff, so I improvised."

"A shared document would have made sense," I muttered as I continued to flick through the papers. "This is great," I told him seriously as I looked up and saw him watching me. "Thank you."

His casual shrug told me more than his words did.

"I mean it. Thank you."

"Ava's roommate does computer science. Get her to help you set up shared documents, that way you have a better record."

"Yeah, I will." I nodded as I carefully put the papers in my tote. "I know how to do it in Sheets, I just thought I would be more hands on." He grunted as he looked out the window to the cool grey afternoon. "Speaking of hand..."

Gray glanced at his hand and gave a half shrug. "Car accident."

"I heard," I spoke softly. "Whose car did you sacrifice?"

Gray's mouth twisted in displeasure. "Onyx took great pleasure in smashing mine up."

I hadn't been expecting that. "Why?"

"I broke a few bones when I punched him."

I definitely hadn't been expecting that. "What? Why?"

Gray looked at me and then started to stand. My hand reached out and grabbed him, halting his movement. "Me?"

"Don't worry about it." He gave me a tight smile, and then picking his stuff, he left me at the window of the coffee shop. I watched him walk outside, and then I watched as he crossed campus. I watched until I could no longer see him.

Twisting my phone in my hand for a moment, I made the decision and texted Ava.

Me: **Hi, do you know anything about shared documents and how to set them up?**

Ava: **A little, but Mia is your girl. She's with me, hang on**

The phone rang about two minutes later.

"Hey, where are you?" Ava's cheery voice was much needed, I realised.

"Coffee shop."

"We'll see you in ten," she told me before she hung up, and I sat back smiling at the thought of her. Both girls came through the door not ten minutes later, and I pointed to the mugs in front of me I had already ordered for them.

Ava bounded over to me with enthusiasm, and Mia followed with a ready smile.

"You've been hiding?" Ava greeted as she leaned over to give me a brief hug, which I returned as Mia gave me a wave and sat down.

"Just busy," I replied easily.

"Surprised you haven't been to check on the guys," Ava said as she took her jacket off before reaching for her latte.

"We're not in each other's pockets," I reminded her a little too sharply.

Ava hesitated, her mug halfway to her mouth before she continued and took a drink. Swallowing, she looked at me with a glance to Mia. "I didn't mean that you were," she spoke softly, keeping her voice low. "I meant because Gray was in an accident."

Of course she did, and I cursed myself for a fool. "I've seen him today." I pulled out the sheets. "He brought me these. Mia, can you help me?" I turned my laptop around to her and showed her my data collecting screen. "I use this for each of the players, and I had them recording it for me, but Gray's right, I should have it as a sharing document. But I need one for each of them, and I don't want all the data seen by them."

Mia was staring at my spreadsheet and tabs and the papers. "Easy, tell me what you want and let's do it."

"It's easy?" I mean, I knew I could do it, but I wouldn't have classed it as easy.

"Sure, you just need a hyperlink, share capacity, and we can even link the cells to feed into your master spreadsheet." She was already reaching for the laptop. "And see here?" She pointed to a column I was totalling everything to. "Let's make that a pie chart for easiness, and we can replicate that in each sheet so the players can see it too. Pictures mean more to some people than numbers." She took a drink of her coffee and pushed her red hair behind her ears. "You have their email addresses?"

"Um, yes, I have all their details on"—I leaned over and scrolled to the first tab—"here."

"Super." She then quite effectively cut me off and started to get to work.

I looked at Ava, who smiled at me. "We've basically lost her for —" She poked Mia on the arm. "How long will it take?"

"Thirty maybe thirty-five minutes," Mia said absently as she clicked like a maniac on the mousepad. With a grumble, she was in her purse, and then a wireless mouse was on the table as she set up on the table adjacent to Ava and me.

"How are you?" Ava asked me as I watched Mia lose herself in my spreadsheets.

"I feel like I'm cheating," I confessed to Ava as I turned my attention to her.

"For class?" Ava laughed. "Why struggle for hours when she enjoys this and can do it in a fraction of the time?"

"It's true," Mia told us as she carried on working. "This is like freshman year all over again."

"You're only a sophomore now," I laughed.

"Yeah, but I'm wiser, more knowledgeable."

"Well, it's appreciated," I told her honestly.

"Ash could have done this for you," Mia said, not realising what she said, and I saw Ava stiffen.

"I only thought of it today," I replied, which wasn't a lie. Turning to Ava, I forced the smile. "How have you been?"

"Good." Her eyes were sad as she looked at me, but whatever she saw in my face made her reach out and pat my hand. "You look like you need a party," she said with a wide grin.

"Do I?" I replied dryly as I heard Mia snort beside me.

"Yes, the basketball team is having a huge Halloween party, and before it, we're going into Cardinal to the bar where Atticus Dawn is singing, and then we're going to do the Halloween maze in the fields behind the grocery store."

"Sounds exhausting," I teased her as she playfully swiped at my arm.

"No, it's going to be *so* good!" Ava leaned forward eagerly. "You're coming with us," she declared.

I felt my smile falter. "Who's us?"

"Mia and me. The team's away as you'll know, so they won't be there until the party later."

Running my teeth over my bottom lip, I thought about it. They were away this weekend, and because Gray was injured, he wasn't like Jett, he would be with the team. That meant the bar and the maze I could go to and not see any of them, *and* Halloween was my favourite holiday.

"Done," I agreed as Ava beamed with happiness.

"I already have the theme of our costumes," she exclaimed.

"Let me guess," I said with a look to Mia. "You went Charlie's Angels, didn't you?" Ava clapped her hands with delight as I shook my head in resignation. "Because we have different coloured hair?" I asked her in despair.

"Yes!" She was practically bouncing in her seat, and I noticed even Mia had raised her head and was shaking it in mutual despair.

"No." Mia rolled her eyes and returned to the screen.

"Ghostbusters?" Ava suggested as she looked between the two of us. "The female one."

"No," Mia and I spoke at once.

"But I could be the green slimy one," Ava protested, and I started to laugh.

"No."

"You both suck," Ava mumbled as she slunk back in her chair.

"She was never this active; I used to have to beg to get her to go anywhere," Mia told me offhandedly as she continued to work. "Then she falls in love with a footballer, and now she's all about the social events."

"Why?" I asked Ava curiously. "To be seen with Jett?"

"Huh?" Ava blinked at me in confusion. "No, I just enjoy being with him," she said as she once again lost her smile. "I'm not using him, Quinn."

I couldn't deny I had thought it before, and I thought it now, and I felt bad. "It's my instinct to protect them."

"I know, but not from me," Ava said and waited for me to believe her.

"So, I have an idea," I told them as I shared a look with Mia.

"Tell me," Ava urged, and I did and chuckled when she moaned in protest even as Mia said *yes* enthusiastically.

We were all in my apartment, and I had to give Mia credit: the girl had skills with a makeup brush.

"Is there anything you can't do?" I murmured as I inspected my eyes.

"Cook," Mia told me immediately, and I laughed as I looked her over.

"I don't think your future guy is going to mind," I said honestly.

Mia was smoking hot, even painted blue. She was wearing a blue skintight jumpsuit that Ava's friend Bea had altered for her.

Mia combed her hair back again and looked at me, her cat eye contacts believable in her blue face.

"You are seriously hot, Mystique," I told her.

"You're looking good too." Mia smiled at me and looked over my own jumpsuit.

"I think an assassin suits me," I mused as I looked at the black band of face paint across my eyes.

"A man killer, you mean?" Mia teased me as she fixed her lipstick. With a grin at me, we looked at the bedroom and waited. "She might chicken out."

"She can't, she needs to complete our supervillain trio."

The door opened and Ava stood there, looking at us uncertainly. "I don't care how many times you tell me that this jacket hides me, I'm still showing more skin than either of you."

"It's what the character wears in the comics," I told her again. "White jumpsuit, diamond cutout on her stomach, and a white fur-trimmed cloak, which we altered to make a cute fur-trimmed coat."

"Why did I have to be Frost?" she complained again.

"Because you're blonde," I reminded her. "I'm dark-haired, therefore Black Widow. Mia is a redhead, therefore Mystique, and you, my dear blonde, are Emma Frost."

"I could have worn a wig," she muttered.

"Mia is wearing less than you are; she just looks covered because she's painted."

Ava looked at her best friend, and her jaw literally dropped. "Shit, Mee, you are hot as shit." Ava looked at us both. "Okay, you both look drop-dead gorgeous."

"We *all* look drop-dead gorgeous," I said to her. "I'm genuinely excited. I never got to do this with the guys," I told them as I looked at my cell and my purse and started to narrow the things I needed down to the bare essentials that I could hide in my costume.

"They don't do fancy dress?" Mia asked curiously.

"Nope, their idea of dress up is their football uniforms. Has been every year since I've known them."

"That's so lazy." Ava shook her head as she picked up her lipstick. Which was white, and I had no idea where Mia had gotten it from, but it was perfect.

"So, you what?" Mia asked as she handed her bank card to Ava, who zipped it into her pocket. "Didn't dress up?"

"Oh I did, I just always looked stupid beside, you know, three fully dressed footballers."

"Which outfit was most popular?" Ava asked as we left my apartment after I decided a bank card, key, lipstick and cell phone were all I could feasibly "hide" on my person.

"Slutty cheerleader." I laughed as we got into the cab. "Even Jett made me wear a coat that year before we got to the party. Until we got there, and half the girls were dressed as *Malibu Barbie,* and suddenly I was overdressed."

"It's a shame you never had anyone to theme it with," Ava said as she looked at Mia again. "We always match."

"I suppose I kind of matched them," I mused. "Cheerleader, nurse, stalker, zombie." Seeing their looks, I clarified, "They were zombie footballers that year."

We made small talk until we arrived, and then we headed into the bar to a chorus of catcalls and whistles, which thankfully were from fellow students and not the normal patrons of the bar.

The band was dressed up as vampires, which in my opinion suited the lead singer anyway.

Ava snapped a selfie with the three of us and sent it to Jett before she made Wade take one of the three of us together. Jett's reply made her blush scarlet, and I looked away to give her a moment.

My phone vibrated in my bra, and I turned slightly from the crowd to pull it out and then laughed at my best friend's message.

Jett: **Were all the nun costumes sold out?**

Me: **We're covered from top to bottom**

Jett: **Keep that coat on my girl.**

Me: **Yes boss**

I went to put my phone back when it vibrated again.

Gray: **Be alert, remember the prick last time**

Me: **I'll be careful**

Gray: **Wearing what you're wearing...I think that ship sailed**

Staring at the phone, I chewed my inner cheek.

"Send it," Mia said quietly from beside me.

I looked at her and my phone. "I haven't written a text."

"I know, but you're thinking about it." She shrugged as she smoothed her hair back. "Whatever you're thinking, send it."

"You don't even know who I'm texting."

Her hazel eyes stood out in her blue makeup. "It's a guy, I know that much, and the way you were smiling when you read his text, you like him. Send it." Her eyebrow arched as she looked at me. "I thought you were a *Devil?*"

Touché.

Me: **You like it?**

Completely inappropriate, considering everything, but Mia was right. I *was* a Devil, and why were they the only ones who got to be reckless?

I burst out laughing when I received the eggplant emoji with the water drops emoji beside it.

I was still smiling when the music started, and I danced all afternoon to country rock with my girlfriends.

CHAPTER 15

Gray

Sitting on the bus, I glanced around before opening the text message again. The three of them looked hot, but I only had eyes for the dark-haired assassin. Her black costume moulded to her figure. The zip stopped just under her breasts, showing too much cleavage in a black push-up bra.

Her hair was in a braid, and she had black face paint over her eyes, making her dark chocolate eyes stand out even more. Her lips were painted a deep red, and just looking at her made me hard.

Checking the time, I worked out how long it would be before we were back on campus. Jett was already dozing in his seat with Ash fast asleep beside him. Things with my cousin had been strained, but we were still talking. He hadn't asked for details, and I hadn't offered.

That wasn't who we were. But I caught him watching me, assessing me, and I returned his look, waiting, but he didn't say anything.

But he would.

I knew him, and he would let it build, and he would think of it from every angle, and then he would eventually ask me when he already thought he knew the answers.

If I were a better man, I would approach him and explain.

But I wasn't a better man, and even on a good day, I couldn't explain me and her without sounding like a crazy person.

Her.

My eyes went back to the screen, my eyes drinking in the sight of her.

I hated her.

I loved her.

I had to stay away from her.

I needed to be closer to her.

Fuck.

It was the same push and pull pattern that had been between us ever since we were younger.

I closed the phone down and stared out at the passing scenery before I closed my eyes. I hadn't played today. My hand wouldn't heal fully for weeks, but there was no way I was missing out on the last few games. I'd agreed to sit two games out. I had no choice for those two, and Coach really had almost killed me when he saw my hand strapped, but then Jett showed him my car, and he relented.

Just.

Because my car *was* wrecked, not due to a car accident, but due to my crazy fucking brother having taken a baseball bat to my Mercedes after I punched him. Twice. And I broke two bones in my hand when I bust his jaw, and then he went out and bust up my car.

He also wasn't talking to me. The list of people currently on the outs with me was growing.

However, Onyx was still talking to Jett, who had told me the next day that Onyx had fixed our "medical" problems, and with a shake of his head telling me he didn't know, it stopped me asking *how* he had fixed it. Did I actually want to know? Probably not. Which was chickenshit of me because it was my fault.

All because I couldn't cut her out of my life.

All because I didn't *want* to cut her out of my life.

Thumping my head repeatedly off of the headrest, I thought about her. Again.

I thought of the kiss in the basement of Onyx's building. I thought of the way she clung to me when I held her. With little encouragement, I thought back to the last night that we were together. A Valentine's party that I hadn't wanted to go to, and one she should never have been at…especially with a date.

But she was, and she had been in full bitch mode. Her hair had been loose down her back, and her black dress had been short. Her legs had been on display, and the killer heels had made her taller than my six one height.

Ash had taken one look at her and promptly ignored her, and Jett was already preoccupied with some random girl he'd already planned to hook up with. Honestly, the change in my brother since dating Ava was nothing short of miraculous, and if I hadn't witnessed it myself, I would have been demanding they run tests for body possession.

Staying on the outskirts of the party, I had watched her dance with her date, some douchebag who had wandering hands. I had seen her subtly move out of his reach once or twice but not every time, and it was pissing me off the longer she spent with him.

The date had gone to get her a drink, and she had taken the opportunity to go to the bathroom. I was following her with no conscious decision to do so. I waited for her to come out, and when she did, I pushed her back in.

"Gray?"

"Queeny," I greeted her as my eyes ran over her. "You trying to impress someone?"

"I have a date," she replied with sarcasm.

"Is that what we call fuck buddies now?" I sneered at her as I leaned against the door.

"You tell me...fuck buddy."

I had her turned and pressed up against the door with my hand on her ass as she stared at me in challenge.

"That what I am?" My nose trailed along her jawline as my other hand flexed on the plump cheek of her ass. "A fuck buddy? That all?"

"No," her soft whisper caused my dick to harden more.

"You wet for your date? You've let him touch you all night."

"No." Her tone was sharper as if I had insulted her.

"You fuck him yet?"

"No!" Her glare was full of venom, and I grinned at the outrage in her eyes as my hand flexed on her ass and my other hand traced along her collarbone.

"You wet for me?" I whispered in her ear as I moved my hand between her legs. "If I put my hand here"—I cupped her pussy, and my dick strained against my jeans as her little gasp excited me further—"will you be wet?"

I didn't wait for an answer as I pushed her panties aside. My fingers found her pooling wetness, and when I looked at her, she was pissed at her body's reaction to me.

"This for me?" I asked again. I slid a finger inside her as I watched her eyelids flutter closed and her tongue wet her lips. "I asked you a question." I pushed another finger inside her as I began to move them slowly in and out of her.

"Yes," she answered.

"It better be," I growled as I dropped to my knees, hitching her leg over my shoulder. "It better fucking be," I told her before my tongue slid inside her as her hands gripped my hair.

I made her come twice on my tongue, and then I bent her over the sink and fucked her, my hands gripping onto her hips, knowing I would bruise her. My teeth bit her neck as I sucked her sweet flesh, marking her so her date would know she didn't belong to him.

She belonged to me.

When we were done, Quinn cleaned herself up and then turned to me where I waited by the door...watching her try to contain her fury at what had happened between us, again.

"You have a kink for bathrooms?" Her scorn at me and herself was strong, and I shrugged, knowing it would piss her off more.

"I don't really care where I fuck you. Want me to take you outside and fuck you in the hallway?"

"I'd rather you didn't fuck me at all," she snarled as she pushed me aside and walked out of the bathroom, leaving me grinning behind her. She was so full of shit.

Of course, I followed her out, and I saw her hesitate on the edge of the room as she saw her date, standing alone at a high school party. I saw her hand go to her neck where I had marked her, and then I saw her shoulders slump, and my fearless queen slipped out of the front door and left.

I should have felt victorious, but I didn't. I felt like a bastard, and with a groan, I followed her out the door.

I picked her up in my car as she walked along the side of the road. She stopped walking when she saw it was me, and with a resigned sigh she got in the car, and I drove her home in silence. Her house was in darkness when we got there, and even though her folks were the type to go to bed early, her dad always left a light on for her.

"They're not here," she told me as she saw me checking the house out. "Romantic break to New York."

I heard her bitterness, and I knew not to ask. Quinn loved her step-mom, Anne, but she just got pissed off sometimes when her dad showed such open affection to Anne, which I don't think he ever showed her mom.

"I'll walk you in."

In her hallway, we looked at each other, and then I turned to leave her. Her hand on my arm stopped me.

"Gray, can we just forget?"

"Forget what?" I asked her as I watched her hesitate.

"That you hate me for dating Ash." Her eyes were wide as she looked at me, vulnerable. "I made the wrong choice, I know."

"You think I hate you for that?" I shrugged out of her hold. "I love my cousin."

"You hate that I hurt him."

"Of course."

"I hurt you too," Quinn said as she stepped closer. "I was confused."

"You were confused? So...what...you fell on the wrong dick?"

"Ugh!" Quinn threw her hands in the air and turned away from me. "I'm done, I've said sorry. I'm hurting too, you know."

"Good."

"Good? Seriously? Get the fuck out of my house." She stormed towards the stairs, thinking I would go like she ordered.

She thought wrong.

I caught her on the stairs and effortlessly lifted her as I climbed the stairs and strode towards her bedroom. Slamming the door closed behind me, I dropped her on the bed as I ripped my T-shirt off over my head.

"What are you doing?"

"What the fuck does it look like?" I unbuckled my belt and quickly pushed my jeans down my legs as I kicked my boots off. "You drive me crazy. All I can think about is fucking you. Ever since the first time, knowing what you feel like wrapped around my dick, I'm going crazy."

Picking her leg up, I unsnapped her shoe, tossing it behind me without a care. Swiftly I did the other one.

"And your suggestion is what?" Quinn got off the bed, back to her normal height without the shoes. She looked up at me. "Fuck it out of your system?"

Bending slightly, I grabbed the hem of her dress and pulled it roughly over her head as she lifted her arms, helping me undress her.

"No, but I'm going to fuck you *out of my system." I kissed her to shut her up before I pushed her back onto her bed. "Do you have any objections?"*

Quinn lay on her back as she ran her eyes over my naked body before she propped herself up on her elbows with a grin. "I say give it your best shot."

We'd been insatiable. I hadn't been able to get enough of her, and she'd been as equally demanding as I was. When the morning broke through the blinds in her room, we'd been lying side by side, exhausted.

Groaning, I sat up and swung my legs over the side of the bed.

"Where you going?"

"Practice starts in an hour," I told her as I looked for my jeans.

"You haven't slept."

Looking at her as she lay in the bed with her hair spread around her and her sheet barely covering her, I smirked. "Whose fault is that?"

When I was dressed, I turned back to look at her. She was still watching me, and I really just wanted to climb back into bed and sleep beside her. But I had practice, and in the cold light of day, I was wondering what the consequences of my actions would be.

"I gotta go," I said as I headed to the door.

"Gray?"

I turned back.

"Am I out of your system?"

No. *Instead, I walked out without answering, because I didn't trust myself not to tell her that she was everything.*

I'd been worried what the consequences would be when I told my cousin I had slept with her, when what I should have been worried about was getting her pregnant. I had never used a condom with Quinn. I used one with other girls, but Quinn…no.

The first time because I had been crazy with anger and lust, I hadn't even thought about it. The second time had been just as spontaneous. The night I spent with her, I had asked her and she said no, I'd already been inside her bare that night, and she was on the pill. Selfishly, the thought of anything between us was loathsome, and I was relieved when she said no.

Practice had been brutal, as I had been clumsy, lethargic, half asleep. I'd been given the "I thought you were serious about football" talk from my coach, my twin and my dad. Which sucked because football season was over, and practice was just for "fun" now, and I was getting grilled for being tired.

They were right though. Quinn distracted me. Football was my focus.

So after a night where we had finally been together, with no barriers, exactly as it always should have been, I'd stepped back. Because my whole entire future was football, and Quinn knew that. She would understand. I was sure of it.

I knew that I'd confused her, and she withdrew from me, but a handful of text messages should have been enough to see us through. Only it wasn't. She was pissed I took a step back, and because of that, I was pissed she decided it was a one-time thing.

Maybe she didn't feel like that, but she sure acted like it. The following weekend, she was on a date with someone else. She saw all three of us arrive at the party, and she had turned her back on us.

Literally turned her back as if we were nothing. I saw Ash turn his head and go straight for the drinks, but my brother's face was what I remembered the clearest. Jett had been hurt at her shun. I knew he was still in contact with her, not as much as before, but they were still talking. They were still friends, and she was willing to hurt him because I had hurt her.

Her cold shoulder that night reminded me of what I had to lose if we were ever together.

I didn't just risk messing up me and Quinn but the relationship with my brother and my cousin as well. Was she worth it?

Were we actually destined to work, or were we two stupid teenagers with too many hormones and nothing other than a strong attraction for each other?

Over the next few weeks, I convinced myself it was the latter. But she was everywhere. My whole entire body was attuned to hers, and I knew whenever she was in the same room long before I saw or heard her.

To be with her was crazy. I would risk everything.

To be away from her was making me miserable, and I made the decision she was worth the risk. A few months after we spent the night together, I snuck into her bedroom, ready to tell her everything.

"How did you get in?"

"Back door, I could pick that lock in my sleep," I said with a grin as I moved towards where she sat on the edge of her bed.

Her room was creams and naturals, tones that didn't suit her in my opinion. She should have colours of black and neon pink or something similar. That would suit her more because there was nothing soothing or neutral about Quinn.

"Why are you here?"

"Would you believe me if I told you that I missed you?" My voice was low, my nerves were high. This was stupid; I knew her, this shouldn't be so hard.

"No." Quinn's look was heavy with scorn, and I couldn't help but smile at her tone.

"Well, I have." I reached out to touch her, but she moved out of my grasp.

Quinn rose from the bed and walked towards her adjacent bathroom before she turned back to me. Her loose T-shirt and PJ bottoms made her look younger, softer. She looked tired, and I knew it was late, but she was a night owl. Like me.

"You okay?" I asked as I got up from the bed and walked towards her. Reaching out, I caught her arms and pulled her into me. My surprise at the ferocity with which she pulled away from me was obvious.

"Don't touch me," Quinn barked as she pulled away. "It's too late."

"Too late for what?" I asked. When she said nothing, I decided to carry on, as my nerves weren't going to last. "Are you going to listen to what I came here to say?"

Tiredly she looked at me, her shoulders slumped, and I noted the dark circles under her eyes. Quinn wet her lips as she gave a small shake of her head. "And what can you possibly say to me that I need to hear?"

"Why are you so fucking pissed?" I demanded, my own temper rising. "What the fuck is the 'tude for?"

Her hands flew in the air in frustration. "I don't know, Gray, why don't you guess?"

"Guess?" I looked her over and couldn't understand what the hostility was for. "Can you talk to me?" I tried to reason with her.

"What? Like you talk *to me? Or did you just come over to fuck me again?" The hard accusation in her tone pissed me off.*

"Never heard you complaining," I snapped back.

"Well, I'm complaining now."

This wasn't going the way I wanted it to. She was angry, but I didn't know why, but Quinn had a bad temper, so maybe I just needed another tactic?

"Let me try again," I started, but her sneer stopped my words.

"I'm not interested."

"You don't even know what it is," I countered quietly as I watched her.

"I don't need to. I'm not interested in anything you have to say now or ever. It's the same worthless bullshit I've been listening to for years. Please leave."

"Fine." Shutting my own emotions down, I took a few steps to the door. "Knew I was being an idiot."

Whether it was my tone or the look on my face, she called out to me to stop. "Tell me."

"No point, like you said, I'm full of shit. You're probably right."

We stared at each other in silence, the hurt and anger between us heavy in the air.

"Just say it," Quinn said with a heavy sigh as she rubbed her hand over her eyes and stared out the window. "Get it over with."

"I love you."

Her head whipped around to look at me, her eyes searching, her face mirroring her shock. "What?"

"That's what I came to tell you, but you're right, I'm full of shit and it doesn't make any fucking difference."

She stared at me, and then I watched her turn away from me. She didn't say anything until I'd had enough and turned to walk out.

"It's too late," she whispered behind me.

"Yeah? I just got the fucking memo. See you around, Queeny."

If only she had been honest with me that night, if only I had pushed her more, maybe all of this could have been prevented. As I sat on the bus heading back to Cardinal, I knew one thing for certain, hindsight was one of the few luxuries I couldn't afford.

CHAPTER 16

Quinn

I HADN'T LAUGHED LIKE I DID THAT AFTERNOON FOR A LONG TIME. Because Mia had embraced her inner mutant and had painted herself blue, it was impossible to hide in the maze, and we spent so much time running and laughing and basically losing the competition of who could get out in the fastest time.

Plus, every ghoul, zombie and vampire "scarer" within the maze took great delight in hunting us down, sometimes even in packs. As we ate candied apples on hay bales, we burst out laughing every time we heard other students complain that there had been hardly any scarers this year. There were plenty of them, they had just been intent on catching *us*.

Ava was the proud carrier of the wooden apple. We had come in dead last due to the amount of time we had spent trying to get out and how many times we got caught. We were awarded a carved wooden apple with the phrase "dead losers" etched into it.

We were carrying it with pride.

"It's getting dark, should we be heading to the party?" Mia asked as she ate her cotton candy delicately.

"I kinda want to stay here," Ava said as she looked around the field. "It was fun."

"It was," I agreed. "But, you know, the party has warmth, music, dancing and bathrooms."

The girls laughed as they stood, and we agreed being warmer would be a benefit.

"Jett's almost back at the house," Ava told us as she pulled her coat around her shoulders. "He said they won't be long."

"So I only have you for a short time then," Mia said to her with a pout. "I better make the most of it."

"Hey, that's harsh." Ava swatted her as she stood. "I'm not that girl."

"What girl?" I asked as we started to make our way to Main Street for a cab.

"The girl that ditches her best friend when she gets a boyfriend," Ava explained, and I looked at her before I met Mia's flat look, and I started to laugh.

"You are totally that girl." I chuckled. "I mean, really?" I gave her a fond smile. "You're delusional if you think you aren't."

"Thank you!" Mia beamed at me as she handed me her cotton candy. "You may share my sugar."

"Well, that's an offer I just can't refuse."

"Am I really that girl?" Ava asked as she leaned over for some of the spun sugar and protested as Mia lifted it out of her reach.

"Yes!" we both shouted and giggled together.

Ava bit her lip as she looked between us, and then I saw the slow smile across her face. "Is it bad that I don't care?"

I started laughing at her honesty as Mia squealed and threw her arms around her friend.

"No! You need to tell him though." Mia handed Ava the cotton candy.

"Tell him what?" I asked curiously as I checked my phone. There were no messages for me. Not that I expected them, but sometimes he surprised me.

"That she's in *lurve* with him," Mia said confidently.

"I think he knows," I replied dryly as I looked up at them both.

"But I haven't said it," Ava confessed.

This was making me uncomfortable. I didn't do well with my own feelings, never mind other people's, especially not my best friend's girlfriend. "Well, did he tell you?"

"Not yet. I think he's waiting," Ava admitted as she looked at me hopefully.

"Nope, not getting involved, you can take those puppy dog eyes somewhere else, Missy," I berated her.

"You have to tell her," Mia encouraged me. "It's girl code."

"I don't have girl code," I said with a snort. "I have friendship code and"—I cut her off before she could interrupt me—"the code is to *my* best friend."

Mia wrinkled her nose at me as she assessed me. "Ugh, fine!"

Ava grinned at me. "You're right, sorry. I'm just nervous."

"Why?" I asked as I looked up the street for the cab.

"What if I tell him and he says nothing?" Ava exclaimed as she looked at me with wide eyes.

"Or worse, what if she says it and he turns his back on her!" Mia added with a look of horror. "Can you imagine? Pouring your heart out to someone and them turning away from you? I'd die. Legit, I would die."

I felt my smile die as I remembered the night something very similar happened to me. "Jett would never be that cruel." I heard my own voice and forced the smile on when I saw Ava's eyes narrow in concern. "So, enough of this, what are we drinking at the party?"

"I want cocktails, but you can never trust the punch bowl," Mia said as the cab arrived.

As we all got in, I glared at the driver, who had checked us all out, and then I realised we were three young women wearing costumes that left pretty much nothing to the imagination. Still, he didn't need to be so pervy.

"I know the captain of the team. He has a clean stash. I'll talk him into sharing it, so we can make our own," I told them.

"Seriously?" Mia asked me with appreciation.

"Sure, I'll make us a pitcher of margaritas." I looked between the two of them. "That cool?"

"Yes," Ava said eagerly. "Is it weird I'm now more cautious of the soft drinks?"

"No," I told her as I reached out and rubbed her knee. "Guys are scum, it's simple."

Mia high-fived me, and I caught the eye of the cab driver and raised an eyebrow in challenge. The fact his eyes dipped to my chest before he looked away confirmed my earlier statement.

The party was already in full swing. The last few weeks had been fun watching people decorate their dorms and things, and I had my own mini-Halloween theme going on in my own dorm, but the basketball team had gone all out.

I jumped when the skeleton appeared out from behind the giant pumpkin, and Mia screamed when the guy with the papier-mâché chainsaw grabbed her ankle from under the entrance steps.

Inside, there was no furniture, and I was a regular visitor here, so I knew they had a shit ton of stuff, but it was all gone.

I saw Denzel at the makeshift bar, and grabbing Ava, who grabbed Mia, I led the way through the partygoers. Denzel saw me at the same time and gave a long whistle of appreciation.

"Quinn, you look incredible!" He looked past me, his eyes taking in Ava and Mia, and he lingered on Mia the longest. "I think I just got hot for blue," he said to her with a wink.

Denzel was dressed as a Roman centurion. Honestly, sports guys needed imagination. I knew with certainty my Devils would walk in with their football gear on.

"Don't be a dick," I chided Denzel. "I need your booze," I told him with a look at the bar.

He stood back as his arm swept out and gestured to it all. "What's mine is yours," he told me with a slow lingering look over my costume.

"Good," I replied as I reached out and tilted his head up to meet my eyes. "Now give me the clean stuff."

"It's all clean." Denzel lost a little bit of his flirtatiousness. "We all heard about the douchebags spiking water. I swear I have three guys, all sober, on the drinks all night."

I met his stare and then looked behind him to the three freshmen. With a grimace, I shook my head. "Gimme access to your stash, and don't make me ask again." I felt Ava squeeze my hand in appreciation. "I'm making margaritas for me and my girls," I added with a smile. "If you're extra nice to me, Denzel, I'll even make you one."

"You're gonna make me a drink with *my* booze and my ice?" he asked with a laugh. Denzel hooked his arm over my shoulders. "It's a good thing you rub me down so good," he said as he led the three of us to the kitchen.

As he sorted out the bottles from his hidden stash and I got the blender, Ava and Mia talked to Denzel easily. He was a good-looking guy, tall obviously. He was the centre for the team. His skin was a warm chestnut, and he wore his hair in a groomed afro. He was so incredibly laid-back; it was always a pleasure when the professor let me practice on him.

"So how come you got the football house again?" Denzel asked me as he leaned against the counter, watching me mix the drinks. "Do they request you or something?"

"For my assignment?" I asked him as I prepared the plastic tumblers he had given me.

"Yeah, we all got asked if we would be willing to volunteer for your class, and then we got Chas, and she's good, but she's not you," he told me as he looked me over again, and I realised he was flirting with me.

"Well, no one's *me*," I drawled as I looked for salt.

"I know, that's why I'm sad we got Chas."

I caught Ava's grin as she listened, and I saw Mia watching us both too. "Well, it would probably have been easier if I got the basketball house," I said to him with a smile as I put the blender on. When it was finished, I looked at them all as I raised the jug victoriously. "At least you guys would eat what I tell you to," I added, hoping my casual conversation would be a hint.

"Baby, I'd eat whatever you were offering," Denzel said as he leaned into me.

Ava's mouth dropped open in surprise at his brazenness as Mia hid her smile behind her hand, and I knew I blushed as I looked away and met Gray's stormy gaze across the room.

Shit.

"Drinks are up," I announced as I poured our drinks. Turning, I dismantled the mixer and shoved the dirty jug into the dishwasher. "Thanks," I said to Denzel with a hasty smile. "We're going to mingle." I grabbed Ava's hand, and the three of us left him behind. My attempts to shush them both were wasted, and I stopped midway between the kitchen and the door where the football team had arrived.

"Ooh, Jett's here!" Ava saw and Mia turned to look too, quickly grabbing Ava and pulling her back to us.

"No, you must make him come to you," she admonished her gently. "You're with us. If he wants you, he can come *to* you," she finished.

I saw Ava roll her eyes, but she clinked her tumbler against Mia's and then mine. "Fine. Cheers!"

We all took a drink, and I studiously avoided looking at the three men walking towards us. I knew what Mia was doing, but I wanted to tell her it wouldn't make a difference. The two of them were like magnets: either Ava went to Jett or he to her. He didn't see it as a power play; he was as eager as Ava was to be in each other's space.

"You look fucking incredible," Jett told Ava as he wrapped his arms around her. Ava smiled and then we lost the two of them as he kissed her in greeting.

"You had a good game," I said to Ash, and he nodded, although he avoided looking at me. "You'll be playing for the conference championship if you keep this up."

"Should be," he answered, and I watched him look at Mia. "I have no idea what you're supposed to be," he told her.

"You didn't read comics?" Mia asked him with surprise. "I'm Mystique."

Ash's eyes flicked to mine, and I helped him out. "X-Men, she's the shapeshifter."

"She's blue?" Ash asked me as he looked at Mia. "If she's a shapeshifter, why is she blue?"

"Superheroes aren't their jam," I explained to Mia. "Which is why I never got to do this before."

"They really did come as football players." Mia shook her head in sympathy at me. "They must have sucked so bad when you were younger."

"*We* are standing right here." Gray's dry tone didn't bother Mia at all.

"You didn't even wear the tight pants," she protested as she obviously checked out Ash's ass. "I mean, the jeans are nice, don't get me wrong, but the pants...ya know."

"You want to see my ass?" Ash asked her with a grin.

"Well, not yours," Mia answered as she looked around the room. Her sights landed on Ben Kowoski, the backup quarterback. "His? Absolutely. Mama's hungry," Mia said with a gleam in her eyes.

"You're such a horndog," Ava said as she slapped her arm. "Plus, Ben has a girlfriend."

Mia pouted and then stretched on her tiptoes to see over the crowd as Ben turned. She gave a low whistle. "Girl can still look," she said as she settled back down and took a drink of her cocktail. "And I have no problems looking."

"You having fun?" Jett asked me, and I turned to give him my attention.

"We are," I said with a quick nod. "The maze in Cardinal was so much fun. We came in last."

"That's…good?" His look was quizzical as if he couldn't understand me being pleased at the result despite my nodding. "So, superheroes?" he guessed.

"Super*villains*," Mia corrected him. "We're the hot bad guys… well, girls."

I heard the snort beside me and chose to ignore it. Jett turned his attention back to Ava. "I think I like it," he said to her as he pulled her in closer.

"You're not the only one. Quinn just got hit on, like completely, *blatantly* hit on," Ava told him. "My jaw was hanging open and everything, and she just brushed him off, with style. It was epically smooth."

Jett's eyes flicked to the dark presence standing beside me and back to me. "Denzel?"

"It was harmless," I told him as I hid behind my drink. Gray reached over and took it off me before lifting it to his mouth and downing my margarita. Mia opened her mouth to protest, but I saw Ava nudge her to be quiet.

"Thirsty," Gray growled when he finished. "Need another, be right back. *Jett!*"

Jett hesitated and then followed his brother to the kitchen, and the four of us stood in silence for a moment before I heard Ash grunt out a laugh.

"How the fuck didn't I see it before?"

I knew he was talking to me, and I turned to face him, bracing myself for whatever was coming.

"I'll catch you all later," he told us instead, and I watched him walk over to Ben and the rest of his teammates, and I was selfishly relieved that I had yet again managed to avoid this conversation. I looked away from him.

"What was that?" Mia asked as she looked between me and Ava.

"Maybe he likes Ben's ass too," Ava blurted, and despite myself, I started to laugh. Mia joined in, and the tension was eased again. Ava handed me her cup, and I took a much welcome drink.

"Ooh, there's Bea, be right back." Mia was already halfway across the room before Ava could reply.

"It's nice to have you," Ava said as she watched her friend. "I don't mind really, but wearing this, I'm glad everyone's looking at you."

Glancing down at myself, I looked at her. "Not everyone," I said as I looked over to the kitchen, and with a heavy sigh, I watched Gray talking to Denzel.

"You need to talk about that?" Ava asked me quietly.

"No, it's nothing."

"Okay." I felt her arm slip through mine. "If you ever want to, I'm here."

Ava was smaller than me, and I looked down at her. "Why? You hardly know me."

"I'm a great judge of character," she said as she took a sip of her drink before handing it to me. "I mean, I completely knew Jett would be awesome and Gray would be a dick."

"You told me Ash was the nice one," I reminded her dryly.

"He is…to *me*," she countered as her eyes searched the crowd for him. "He's the most open, I think."

That was true, the twins played it tight to their chests. Ash was a little more relaxed about things.

"They each have their positives and negatives."

Jett and Gray were walking back to us, and I shifted nervously where I stood. "Ava, I hate to do this..."

"Go," she said as she took her cup back. "You're having fun, go mingle with Mia."

I didn't need to be told twice. When I reached Mia, the music that had been playing as background music got turned up, and she grabbed my hand and yelled *dance* to which I agreed.

I spent the next while on the dance floor. Mia drifted in and out, but I liked dancing and was never alone. Two guys approached me, and I danced with them, always stepping out of their reach when they tried to get closer.

Mia was back on the dance floor, and we were both dancing to Thirty Seconds to Mars's "Closer to the Edge," and I was having fun. The lights dimmed, and my feet faltered when I saw six of the football team had all pulled up black bandanas. Wildly, I looked at the door and saw it was closed, and then as I looked back, I saw Gray watching me. He gave a wink, and just like that, the lights went out.

The screams were instant as the music cut off, and I got shoved as people on the dance floor moved.

"Mia?" I called, and I felt a hand take mine. "Mia?"

"It's me," she said as she stepped closer to me. "Mayhem?"

"Yeah." I turned slowly in the darkness. They hadn't told me. They always told me when it was mayhem.

I startled when I heard a loud scream pierce through the speakers, and then low eerie laughter followed. Suddenly, a spooky voice screamed *run,* and it echoed all through the house as people panicked and screamed.

"Don't run," I warned Mia as I felt her pull away. "Never run, they can't do anything if they can't catch you."

Reaching out my hand, I guided us to the wall and pushed us both up against it.

"You knew this was happening?" Mia whispered over the noise of people running, falling into each other, and the horrible creepy laughter.

"No." We stayed there as we felt and heard people laughing or crying out around us. I'd always been clued in on mayhem before, but being on the other end of it was pretty unnerving.

"Oh look!" Mia tugged my hand, and I looked around and saw the neon glow sticks moving through the darkness. "Is that new?"

"No, that's not the Devils."

I heard a crash and a scream, and I had a sudden bad feeling. Holding on tight to Mia, I made my way towards the kitchen. Bumping into the drinks table, I grabbed onto the edge and felt along the side, trying to remember the way.

Suddenly the lights and music came back on, and I jumped at the brightness, blinking in surprise. Looking around, I saw a number of people entwined, a few people shoving each other, ready to throw down, and I saw the captain of the basketball team putting ice on his busted lip as people fussed around him.

Searching the crowd, I found him, right where he had been standing, Jett beside him, talking to him with his head turned away so no one could lip read. I knew from the set of Jett's shoulders he was angry.

Gray wasn't listening. He was staring at me as his good hand checked his strapped hand. I turned to look at Denzel and back to Gray, the question in my face clear.

His answer was a smirk as he watched me put it together.

Jealous possessive dickhead. I hoped he'd broken more of his bones. He deserved it.

"Why do they do this?" Mia asked me in bemusement as she watched the party get wilder as a result of mayhem.

"Because they can."

CHAPTER 17

Quinn

THE ROOM WAS STUFFY, AND I KNEW BETTER THAN TO LEAVE. HE would find me. He always found me, and tonight, well, tonight I wasn't interested in his mood swings. *He* was the one who said he needed to stay away, and that's what I intended to do. Mia had drifted off with Bea, Ava was completely wrapped up in Jett, and Ash was… I looked around the room. Okay, Ash was busy.

Fine.

Denzel was leaning against a wall, and I knew he kept looking over at me. Did he know it was Gray who hit him? Probably, Gray was hardly subtle.

"Hey, Quinn, how are you?" Jada asked me as she approached. She was dressed as a cheerleader, which I found amusing since she was the volleyball captain.

"Hey, decided to try life on the other side?" I asked with a grin at her costume.

"Yeah." She looked down at the short skirt. "The cheerleaders are in our clothes, and we're in theirs. At the time, I thought it was hilarious." She looked at me with a sigh. "Now…I'm going to punch the next guy who pats my ass."

"You think you're getting hit on because you're a cheerleader?"

"Why else?"

"'Cause you're crazy hot. The outfit isn't the reason." I laughed at her expression.

"I'm telling you, Quinn, it's the uniform. It makes guys complete jerks." She shook her head. "They've all got these stupid fantasies."

"Hmmm," I pretended to think. "Maybe I picked the wrong choice." I looked down at my jumpsuit. "It's like a onesie though, I'm so comfy," I confessed.

"It's a great costume. You and the other two girls look badass. Melly keeps drooling over Mystique."

We both looked in Mia's direction, and I remembered she got stage fright, which was odd because she had no issue being the centre of attention. Maybe she needed to go up on stage wearing blue body paint. "She looks good," I said to Jada.

"Yeah, um, you know who else looks good tonight?"

It was the hesitation in her voice that caused my spine to stiffen. "Tell me," I said, and I knew what she was going to say before the words left her mouth.

"A certain Cardinal Saint. Number twenty-two to be exact."

"Gray," I murmured as I wished I had a drink. "Thought you'd already been there?"

Jada flushed and shook her head, her ponytail swishing around her shoulders. "Um, no, that was Jett."

"Oh." I knew that, but still my inner bitch wanted to watch her squirm. "It's hard to keep up sometimes." I gave a light laugh and she smiled. She either didn't pick up on my falseness or didn't care.

"Do you think you could see if he would be interested?"

No. "You're nineteen?" I asked her with a cool look. "Can't you find out yourself?"

Jada squirmed some more, and I didn't care that I was sounding pissed off. "He's kind of intimidating."

My head fell back as I let out a loud laugh. "And you want to fuck him?" Her face was beet red, and I didn't care.

"*Quinn!*" Jada hissed as she stepped forward. "Shh! I just want to know if he's interested."

Shaking my head in pity, I looked at her hopeful gaze, and with exasperation I turned to look for him. He was easy to spot, deep in conversation with two of the defence for the team. He was leaning against the wall, a beer in his hand, his face tight with concentration as the three of them discussed who knows what. Football most likely. I would bet my life it was football. His eyes flicked to mine and held. An eyebrow was raised as he looked at me, and completely pissed off with the whole situation, I made my way over to him.

I noticed the other two guys looked me over the same way Gray did, but the heat of *their* stares meant nothing to me.

"What is it?" he asked as I reached them.

"Jada wants to know if you're interested in her," I said to him and ignored the two other guys' laughs and whistles.

Light blue eyes held mine, and I glared back at him. *You're pissed,* his look said. *Yes, I'm fucking pissed,* my stare said back. I saw his mouth curl in a smirk, and I broke the stare as I looked over the crowd.

"Why she sending you?" Gray asked as his grin stretched.

"Because she thinks you're scary," I sneered at him, my tone telling him exactly what I thought of that.

Gray laughed. He so rarely laughed freely my eyes snapped back to him in surprise. "Why's that funny?"

Gray stepped up beside me and looked over at Jada, his eyes running over her. "Because I am."

He took another step, and my hand caught his wrist as I turned my back to the crowd and looked at the wall behind him. "Don't." My head dipped down, but I still felt his stare as he turned his head to look at me.

"*Don't?*" His tone was low, angry. "Why should I listen to *you*? You never listened to me."

"Gray...please."

"I wouldn't." His breath tickled my ear, and I felt the knot in my stomach unravel as I turned my head slightly to look at him. "Any girl who can't tell *me* she wants *me* herself, I've no fucking time for."

We stared at each other for a heartbeat more, and then he stepped away from me, my hand dropping from his wrist, and as I turned back to look at the crowd, I caught Ash watching me. I didn't see where Gray walked to, all I saw was Ash, and I saw his hurt.

God, this was messed up.

With a tilt of my head, I gestured to the door, and I saw his small nod in acceptance. I really needed another drink, but I walked towards the front door anyway. Turning to look over my shoulder, I saw Jett watching me. Ava was held close to him, her back to his chest with his arms wrapped around her as they watched the party. He gave me a small encouraging nod, and it gave me a boost as I reached the front door and headed outside to have a long overdue conversation with my ex, but more importantly, my friend.

Several people were still outside. The scarers were still doing their jobs, and I was startled as a skeleton jumped out at me. With a laugh, I carried on walking until I spotted a bench a little way down the street from the house, and feeling a bit self-conscious, I sat down as I zipped my costume over my chest.

I watched him walk down to meet me. His hair falling loose over his forehead, he needed a trim. Ash walked with his shoulders straight, which meant he wasn't comfortable, but he was still coming, so that was a positive…right? With no hesitation, he sat down beside me, his manspread taking up half the bench.

"Still hogging the seat," I murmured with a small smile, and I heard a huff of laughter as Ash sat up straighter, his legs closing a little.

"Habit."

"I know," I replied as I crossed my hands on my lap.

"Strange to do it now, isn't it?" he began as we watched people pass us by. "Is this too open?"

"Probably," I admitted. "I wasn't thinking."

"Want me to walk you home?" he asked, and I could hear the hesitation in his voice, which is why I said yes. I shot a quick text to Jett to tell him to tell Ava I was heading home, and I put my phone back in my bra. Ash noticed my "pocket" and grinned as I shrugged.

Slowly we walked to my apartment and neither of us spoke. The silence was actually companionable, and despite the chill in the air, I enjoyed it. At the foot of my stairs to my door, he looked at me for the first time since we started walking and then the door.

"I don't know if my cousin would let me survive the night if I go in," Ash told me gruffly.

"Don't be stupid," I murmured as I walked past him and up the stairs. "This isn't a conversation for outside."

I heard his answering grunt, and then he closed the door behind him.

Inside, he looked around, taking in the pale walls with only one shelf, the neutral-toned couch and chair. Ash hadn't been inside my dorm room since I got here, and I saw him note the size even as he leaned forward to look at the few framed photos I had.

"Communal kitchen?"

"Yes," I answered as I unzipped my boots and dumped them inside my bedroom at the door. When I went back to the living room, we sat and stared at each other in silence for a moment. "How do you want to do this?"

Ash sat on my chair and leaned forward. "I don't know," he told me as he stared at the floor. "I've been pissed off for so long I don't know where to start."

"You want me to start?"

"You didn't actually cheat, did you?" he said instead as he raised his head to look at me.

I needed to be honest. "The intent was there," I spoke softly.

"But nothing happened? Which is why when I was screaming at you and kicking the shit out of furniture, you wouldn't answer who you slept with." He leaned back and crossed his arms. "Because there was no one to name."

"It would have made no difference. The damage was done. I

wanted to have sex with someone who wasn't my boyfriend, so it's moot."

"When did you first hook up? With Gray."

Swallowing, I held his stare. "Not long after we broke up."

Ash nodded like he was expecting it. "How many times?"

"A few." My voice was quiet, but I saw his answering nod again.

"He didn't know you were pregnant?"

"No."

Ash was looking everywhere but at me as his head nodded, like he was having a conversation with himself. "I didn't think so, he would have killed someone." Ash grunted. "He may *still* kill someone."

"I know." My whisper was barely audible.

"You ripped my heart out," he told me.

"I didn't mean to." I was scared to move as Ash looked at me with his emotions open. "I didn't know how you felt. We'd never really been serious."

"Now I know why." Ash's voice was dry as he stood, not to leave but to pace. My apartment was a decent size, but Ash was six four; he was making me feel claustrophobic. "When you told me that day in the classroom that either you or I would have cheated first, it really stunned me." Walking over to my shelf, he picked the photo up of the four of us. Jett and I were standing together, his arm over my shoulders. Gray stood beside me, his arms crossed against his chest, and Ash to the right of him. I loved this picture. Jett and I were laughing, Ash was grinning, and Gray stood stoic in the middle, a slight smirk on his face. "You want to know something?" he continued without waiting for an answer. "At first, I thought it was Jett."

That shocked me. "Really?" I pulled my legs up onto the seat, and my chin rested on my knees. "I guess most people would since they don't understand our friendship."

Ash grunted as he sat back down. "He's so protective of you, but after my own paranoia calmed down, I realised Jett and you together wouldn't work." Dark blue eyes met mine. "But Gray…" He bit the side of his thumb as he looked back to the photos. "Gray was always possessive of you. I just didn't see it, I guess."

"It's not your fault," I said as I watched him struggle with what had happened.

"I can't help but feel that it is though," Ash admitted as he looked my way. "I mean, I got the girl, or thought I did, and Jett warned me not to mess it up. Did he know?"

"No." My reply was immediate. "He only found out last week."

"Nah." Ash shook his head in denial. "There's no way he didn't know before then."

"I think he suspected," I whispered as I leaned back slightly. "But he never asked me outright until last week."

"Why didn't you tell him?"

"Who? Jett?"

"No, Quinn, why didn't you tell Gray you were pregnant?" Ash's heavy stare met mine, and I forced myself to hold it.

"When I found out, I'd seen him a few weeks before with another girl, and I was pissed. We were never anything really, a few stupid hook-ups that meant little." I felt the burden of truth weighing heavily on me. After all, what were we? Two hot and heavy make-outs and one night together. That was it.

"Another girl?" Ash looked at me curiously. "Who?"

I shrugged. "I don't know, I didn't ask."

Ash couldn't hide his grin. "Sucks, doesn't it?"

I gave a rueful laugh. "Yes, it really does." We sat in silence for a while longer, both lost in our own thoughts before he spoke again.

"You hurt me. I was so pissed at you. We hurt each other, and I genuinely wished you ill." He didn't look apologetic when I glanced at him, my surprise showing at his harshness. "But what you went through? I'm truly sorry, Quinn, I'm sorry you felt that you had no choice and that you were alone."

The lump in my throat was sudden, and I looked away. "It's over," I mumbled. "It's best to move on. Everything happens for a reason, isn't that what they say?"

"I don't give a fuck what anyone says," Ash said as he reached over and grabbed my hand. "I may not be the Devil you wanted, but I still know you. I know that you need to talk about this."

"With you?" I countered as I pulled my hand away.

"If it helps?" He scratched his jaw. "I won't lie, it's going to be uncomfortable as fuck, but if you think it would help, telling me, then I can do that."

I didn't deserve that; I didn't deserve this level of friendship. "I'm sorry I hurt you," I said instead. "I'm sorry we've been fighting ever since."

"Meh." Ash grinned. "You were always a bitch." He winked at me, and I laughed.

"We should maybe have had this talk sooner." I curled my legs under me as I shifted on the couch.

"I don't think I would have been ready," Ash admitted as he stretched his legs out in front of him. "Still not sure I'm ready to forgive and forget, and I still *really* want to punch Gray."

"You should totally do that anyway," I told him eagerly.

Ash gave a low rumble of laughter as he tipped his head back and stared at the ceiling. "I always thought Onyx was on my side, but he wasn't, was he? He was on Gray's."

I scraped my teeth over my lip as I took in Ash's profile. "I can't answer that. I think Onyx is always on *Onyx's* side, to be honest."

"That's true." Ash grinned as he spoke. "He's wrecked the Merc."

"I know, how?"

"Took a baseball bat to it after Gray punched him."

I sat silent for a nanosecond before I exclaimed. "What really happened?"

"Ran his mouth, Gray took offence, punched him, bust his lip, so Onyx bust his car."

Covering my face with my hands, I groaned. "Why are they both so stupid?"

"Can't answer that. Dodgy DNA, I think."

I snorted as my shoulders shook with laughter. "Hmm, definitely the genetics to blame," I agreed.

"So." Ash looked everywhere but at me. "How do you feel knowing what we found?"

"Um, I don't know..."

"What kind of people were they? That they could fool you? I mean, you're...*you*."

I'd asked myself the same thing a thousand times. "I was desperate, I think."

"No one's that desperate, are they?" Ash looked at me with accusation. "I mean, okay, you changed your mind, but what would you even need the money for?"

"Money?" I asked him. "I wasn't getting *paid*."

Ash's face paled as he closed his eyes, and I heard him curse under his breath.

I suddenly felt sick. "Ash, tell me. Tell me right now," I demanded as I stood on shaky legs.

"Quinn, I thought you knew," he whispered, his eyes full of anguish.

"Knew what?"

"The people who take the babies, they don't adopt them, they sell them."

CHAPTER 18

Gray

I WAS IN THE BACKYARD WHEN MY BROTHER FOUND ME, MY STANCE wide, my arms across my chest, shaking my head as I watched two guys beat the shit out of each other. Or try to. A result of mayhem. One of them kissed the other one's girl just as the lights came back on. Apparently, they had laughed it off, but now they were drunk, and their insecurities were showing, so they decided, with some help, that they needed to fight it out.

I was officiating.

Technically.

"You need to come with me," Jett said as he joined me.

I didn't pay him much attention. "Why? One of these losers is bound to actually land a decent punch soon," I said as I watched them both trip over their feet as they swung their arms wildly.

"Gray, you need to come with me," Jett repeated as he placed his hand on my arm.

His tone made me turn my head to look at him. "What's happened?"

"Ash told Quinn." Jett took a deep breath. "She isn't handling it well."

I stared at my brother in silence, my brain refusing to accept what he had just said. Seeing the truth and the worry in his eyes, I dipped my head. "*Fuck!*"

Together, we left the party. I didn't ask what he had said to Ava. It took all of my control not to run to her dorm room.

"Why the *fuck* would he tell her?" I demanded as we made our way there.

"He thought she knew, he thought we had told her," Jett explained.

At her apartment, I bounded up the steps and opened the door.

Ash was on his feet pacing, and when he saw me come in, he immediately held his hands up. "Man, I swear I thought she knew."

Looking inside her bedroom, I saw it empty. "Where the fuck is she?" I growled at the same time as I saw the bathroom door closed. Pushing past him, I tried the handle. It was locked, and I could hear her crying.

"Open the door," I insisted as I knocked it.

"Fuck off!"

Rolling my head on my shoulders, I took a deep breath. "Quinn, open the door. Let us see you're alright."

"No! I hate you!"

I felt a hand on my shoulder, pulling me back, which I shook off irritably as I placed my hand on the door. "You hate me? Fine. You're no fucking picnic either," I snapped through the door. I heard Jett mutter that I wasn't helping. I took a deep breath to calm down. "Open the door."

"Go *away*!"

"Queeny, open the fucking door, or I'll kick it down."

"Fuck you!"

"Fuck me? Fuck *you*!" I yelled back at her.

"Let me try," Jett said from behind me. "Please."

Shoving off the door, I glared at him. "Be my fucking guest."

"Queeny, it's Jett. Open the door for me."

"No." I heard her crying get louder. "Just leave me alone. All of you. *Please*."

Jett sighed and stood back. "Maybe we would be better leaving her? Until she's calmed down."

Idiot.

Pushing past him, I pounded on the door. "Open the fucking door, or I swear to Christ, I'm coming through it."

"You wouldn't dare!" I heard her screech.

Watch me.

Stepping back, I heard either my brother or cousin shout out, and then I kicked her bathroom door open. She was on the floor, her legs pulled up to her chest, her face wet with tears. When she saw me, she started to cry harder, and I didn't fucking care that she hated me. Reaching down, I grabbed her by her upper arms, ignoring the pain in my hand as I hauled her to her feet. She had no choice but to stand, but she didn't come easily. Her hands slapped and punched me as I pulled her up, and then my hands gripped her thighs as I lifted her up. Quinn's fight was gone as quickly as it had come, and she wrapped her arms around me as she buried her head into my shoulder and sobbed uncontrollably.

"I know, baby, I know," I told her as I rubbed her back. "It's okay. I'm here." I kissed the side of her head as I walked out of the bathroom. I could see Jett and Ash standing to the side, but I ignored them both as I headed to her bedroom.

"I didn't know," she cried, her voice muted as she tried to speak through her tears. Her fingers dug into my shoulders, twisting my jersey. "I swear I didn't know, Gray."

"I know," I said as my hand stroked her hair. "I know." I sat on the edge of her bed, with her still holding onto me. Jett hovered in the doorway uncertainly. "Can you make her a cup of tea?" I asked him quietly.

"Of course." He disappeared from the doorway, and I pulled her closer to me as her crying continued, but it was softer now. My hand smoothed over her hair as she clung to me, and I tilted my head slightly so her head could rest against my neck as I soothed her.

"Shh, it's okay," I whispered as I rocked her gently. "It's okay."

It wasn't okay, it may never be okay, but as she cried out her heartache, it was all I could say to comfort her. Ash filled the doorway, and I met his look, and I don't know what he saw when he looked at me. His face was blank, his emotions closed off, and I was relieved when he moved away. Then I heard the front door close, and I knew he was gone.

"You okay?" I asked as I heard her tears lessen.

"No," came the muffled reply.

"Jett's making you tea," I told her.

"I want bourbon," Quinn replied.

"Yeah? Well, you're getting tea." I heard a soft laugh as she pressed closer to me, and my arms automatically tightened.

"Bastard."

"Bitch," I countered with a small smile as I felt her body relax a little.

"I freaked out," she said as she moved her head to lie against my shoulder.

"Really? Didn't notice," I said, trying to put her at ease. "I did too when I found out," I admitted when she said nothing.

"I didn't know," Quinn said as she straightened and looked at me. "Gray, I would never—"

My kiss wasn't gentle. It wasn't soft. It was as hard and demanding as I was, and Quinn readily accepted it. With a moan, her hands were in my hair, pulling me closer. Standing with her still wrapped around me, I kicked her bedroom door closed. I didn't care if Jett was out there, I wanted him gone.

Lowering us both to the bed, I settled in between her thighs as I rocked my hips against her. Quinn was already pulling at my jersey, and with a quick jerk, I pulled it over my head and flung it on the floor. She was still in her costume, the one piece tight against her body. Kneeling between her legs, I slowly pulled the zip down, uncovering her chest, all the way past her belly button. With care, I pushed the open sides aside, uncovering more of her. My hands cupped her bra, and I winced at the pain in my hand before I brought my hand to my mouth and tugged the strapping off with my teeth.

"Gray," Quinn started to protest, but she stopped when I slipped my other hand inside her jumpsuit and moved it down lower. Finally free of the strapping, I encouraged her to sit up as I pushed the jumpsuit off of her shoulders.

"Lie back," I said as I pushed her back down. With a quick rise of her hips, I had the costume pulled down her legs and then on the floor. She was in a black satin bra and matching panties. Even with her eyes red from crying, she looked amazing. Her body was toned and smooth, and I watched as my fingers trailed slowly over her abdomen as she sucked in a breath at my touch. With a sharp tug at her hips, she lifted her hips once more as I pulled her underwear off her. I heard her gasp when I lifted the small piece of fabric to my nose before I tucked them in my back pocket.

"You're perfect," I told her as I dipped my head between her open thighs and took a slow lick of her pussy. She tasted so sweet I had to stop myself from lurching forward. "You taste good," I whispered as my tongue traced over her. I was aware of the pain in my hand, so I adapted, using my other hand to slip my fingers inside her. My tongue lapped at her entrance as I moved two fingers in and out. "So fucking wet, is this all for me?"

"Yes." Her whisper was almost inaudible as she arched her hips to meet my mouth, urging me to taste more of her. "Gray, please," she moaned as I curled my fingers inside her.

"Please what?" I asked her as my teeth grazed over her clit.

"Make me come."

I licked and sucked her slowly, ignoring her urges to go faster, and I lifted my head away when she tried to thrust her pussy into my face. I took my time until she was screaming her release, her walls clenching around my fingers as she begged me not to stop. As I took her to another orgasm, I unfastened my jeans and pulled my dick out, stroking it in time as my mouth moved over her.

"Gray, I need you," Quinn groaned as I kept fucking her with my tongue. "Please, I need more."

Unhurriedly, I pulled away and sat back on my heels as I looked down at her, savouring the sight of her spread out under me.

"I won't be gentle," I warned her as I stood and kicked off my boots and jeans. After a moment's hesitation, I pulled my wallet out and then opened the foil packet before I rolled on a condom.

"I don't want gentle," Quinn told me as she watched.

Kneeling between her legs, I pulled her towards me. "Good," I growled as I entered her in one thrust, ignoring the wince of protest in my hand and her cry of surprise.

How the fuck did she feel so fucking good? Her pussy was snug as I moved in and out of her slick heat. Quinn's legs wrapped around my hips, pulling me in closer, and I pulled the cup of her bra down with my teeth before I was sucking her nipple as I drove my hips into her.

"Harder," she demanded as her hands dug into my forearms and her back arched for more.

"Look at me."

Dark brown eyes met mine, and I increased my pace. "Don't stop looking," I ordered as I pulled myself up from her, my good hand wrapping around the column of her throat. "Wider," I commanded, and her legs dropped from my hips as she opened them wider for me. "That's it," I encouraged her as I picked up my pace. "You better be fucking close," I warned as I gritted my teeth, feeling my balls tighten.

"Don't stop," Quinn moaned as her hand clutched at my hand around her throat.

Letting her go, I pulled her up suddenly until she was almost in my lap as I pushed my body harder into her. I felt her teeth bite into my shoulder, and pushing my hand between us, I pinched her clit as she cried out her release. I felt her nails rake over my back as her pussy clamped down on me, squeezing me until I had no choice but to let go, thrusting into her a few more times before we both fell to the bed, spent.

"Shit," I groaned as I reached down for the condom, pulling it off and knotting it.

"Tell me they left," Quinn whispered as she lay beside me, her breathing still heavy.

"Fuck, I hope so." I draped my arm over my eyes as I tried to control my own breathing.

"I can't believe you kicked the door down," she muttered.

"Next time, just open it," I said as I yawned widely.

"We need to talk."

"Yeah, we probably do." I felt her move closer to me, and I lifted my arm, letting her slip under it as I curled my arm around her.

"In the morning?" she asked softly.

"Sure."

I FELL ONTO MY BACK AS I CAUGHT MY BREATH. I HEARD HER panting beside me, and I felt the smile creep onto my face.

"That was intense," Quinn murmured as she moved on the bed, and I felt her fingertips run lightly over my arm.

"Hmm, I didn't know you were that flexible," I said as I tried to flex my hand. "Fuck, it's never going to work right," I muttered as I felt the stabbing pain in the back of my hand.

"You should be more careful," Quinn chided as she reached out to touch it.

"You want to stop?" I asked as I turned my head to look at her and saw her already flushed face burn deeper.

"We maybe do need to get out of bed," she said self-consciously. "It's dark again outside."

We hadn't made it out of bed yet. I had ignored the calls and texts as had Quinn. I had also ignored the conversation we had said we would have, but then Quinn hadn't been pushing for it either.

"Never fucked you in the shower before," I said as I turned onto my side and looked at her.

Quinn rolled her eyes and looked at me. "Hmm, I wonder why when you say it so sweetly?" she snarked as she turned her head away.

"What? You saying you don't like the idea of me and you in the shower?"

"Stop it," she said as she sat up. "*I'm* going to shower, you stay here. Or maybe let Jett know you haven't killed me. Or me you."

She stood from the bed and walked out of the bedroom, and after watching her ass before it disappeared, I lay back down. I wasn't entirely sure that us having sex all day was the best solution, but it beat talking about our shit, and since Quinn was as eager as I to avoid the conversation, sex was a welcome distraction.

I thought back to last night and Ash's face when he looked at me from her bedroom door. I don't know what my expression had told him, but he hadn't looked like he was going to accept me and Quinn anytime soon. Rubbing my hand over my eyes, I sat up and looked for my jeans. When I located them, I fished my phone out of my pocket and read Jett's messages.

There weren't many. One asking if she was okay, one asking if we thought this was the best way to handle it. One telling me that Ash hadn't come home and wasn't answering his phone either, and a few more after that, all about Ash.

I had no texts from my cousin, and my thumb hovered over his name before I chickened out and dropped the phone beside me.

Was sleeping with her and having sex with her all day the best solution? I would say *who were we hurting,* but I was afraid the answer was ourselves and our family.

It had been a long time since she and Ash were a couple, but a lot of the hurt to him was new. Pushing myself up, I groaned at the sharp jab of pain in my hand, and I studied it as I swung my legs over the side of the bed.

I'd definitely made it worse. When I punched Denzel last night,

I had felt it move, and when I was with her last night and today, I had been content to ignore the warning pains in my hand.

Coach was going to kill me. The team was going to kill me.

Standing, I winced as I stretched, and I felt the burn in my thighs as I headed to the bathroom, a grin spreading across my face when I saw the full mug of tea on her coffee table and then the broken door to the bathroom.

Her back was to me as she showered, she was lathering shampoo into her hair, and as I leaned against the doorframe, I watched in fascination as soap suds ran down her smooth back, the curve of her spine accentuating her perfectly shaped ass.

She turned and faced me, her eyes closed as she tipped her head back to let the hot water wash away the shampoo. Her arms raised above her head as her chest arched out which was enough to encourage me to open the shower door. Quinn's eyes flew open as I pushed her backwards, letting the water hit us both.

"You're hijacking my shower," Quinn accused me.

"I am," I told her as I grabbed her hand and wrapped it around my dick. "What's my reward?" I asked as I encouraged her to pump it.

"We'll eventually get fed up with having sex and not talking," Quinn warned me as she looked down at her hand and what it was now doing with no assistance from me.

"Okay," I nodded as I enjoyed her ministrations, and my eyes closed in pleasure. They flew open seconds later when she wrapped her lips around me and looked up at me as she got comfy on her knees.

"Don't get used to this," she warned before she took me back into her mouth.

I did my best to remind myself this was a false sense of safety. We weren't solving anything or healing from our past as I thrust eagerly into her mouth. This was a temporary bandage on a fucked-up situation. I knew that. I accepted it.

Her tongue flicked over the head of my dick, and I grabbed her wet hair into my fist as I brought her closer to me, encouraging her to take more as I kept moving between her lips. It was only temporary, I reminded myself as I felt the stirring at the base of my dick. Quinn looked up at me, her eyes wide as she sucked me down and I hit the back of her throat. Quickly she drew off of me, and then she was sucking me back in.

Yeah, it was temporary, I knew that. I accepted it. This wasn't the answer to my problems. Quinn's hand wrapped around the base of my dick, and I was unravelling in the sensation of her mouth, her wrist action, and those chocolate brown eyes staring up at me.

With a hard thrust and a groan, I was emptying my balls into her willing mouth.

Fuck me, she was exquisite.

My head tipped back as I enjoyed the sensation of my release. I could still feel her tongue stroking slowly over me as she drew back, and then she let me go.

Reaching down, I helped her to her feet, and then she was in my arms, my head in the crook of her neck.

It was temporary, I reminded myself. I knew this. What I didn't know was if I would be able to let her go.

CHAPTER 19

Quinn

I MADE A POT OF COFFEE IN THE SHARED KITCHEN AND THEN TOOK the cups back to the apartment. After the second shower of the day, Gray had finally agreed we had to face reality. I think it helped, knowing that the others knew that we had been together before and had spent the night together.

Not in a couple way.

I understood the basic need to heal from last night and the past.

Ash hadn't been malicious when he told me, I knew that. He hadn't done it to hurt me, and Gray hadn't even considered that as a possibility, which emphasised to me that they would be okay. Eventually.

When I went back into the apartment, Gray was frowning at his hand as he flexed it, and I put the coffee cups down as I watched him.

"Hurt?"

"Yeah," he said with a wry smile. "Tried to fix your door." He jerked his head to the side, and I looked at the bathroom door.

"Why?" I exclaimed as I hurried over. "You idiot, you're going to damage yourself, permanently!"

"It's just a few breaks and a sprain. It's fine."

"You need to play the last few games," I admonished him as I gingerly took his hand. "What if you've damaged it even more? It isn't worth it."

Gray pulled me to him with his other hand. "And if I disagree?"

"Yeah, well, tell your brother, your *captain,* that you fucked your hand because you were..." I flushed and looked away from his knowing look.

"Fucking you?" he finished. "I think he knows."

Turning away from him, I went to sit on the couch. "Have you heard from Ash?"

"No." Gray's playful tone was gone, and he picked up his coffee. "I'll speak to him face to face, not over the phone or over a text."

"I should be with you."

"No point," he said as he pulled his phone out, and I saw his thumb race over the screen. "He may feel inclined to rate you higher if you're listening."

My jaw dropped, and I stared at him incredulously. "Rate me? How? Do you mean in *bed*?"

Gray looked up and then burst out laughing. "Your face!" He laughed again, and I watched him lose it as I felt my temper rise. "Fuck," he said as he wiped his eyes. "That was classic, I can't even tell anyone."

"It wasn't funny."

"It really was." He chuckled as he drank his coffee. "Your face." He snickered again, and I was sure I was going to smash my coffee cup off *his* face.

"Who did you text?"

"Jett, who else? Told him to meet me here."

"We're doing this now?" I asked cautiously as I reached for my coffee.

"Yeah, may as well. He's bringing food." Gray sat back and looked at me appraisingly. "The sex was good, better than good." His eyes ran over me slowly. "But it's time to stop hiding."

"I agree," I said simply, "about the hiding. I'm reserving judgment on the quality of the sex."

I smirked as his eyes narrowed on mine, and then he grinned. "I need to sleep," he said as he leaned back on the chair, tipping his head back as he closed his eyes.

"You don't sleep much anymore?" I asked as I studied his beautiful face.

"Had a lot on my mind," he answered honestly as he remained in the position.

"Gray, don't sleep," I warned him as I drank my coffee, my feet tucked under my body. "Jett will be here soon."

"I know, baby."

I sighed in despair. He was already half-asleep. He hardly ever called me *baby;* it was a term both he and Jett rolled their eyes at when they heard it used. Leaning over, I took the mug out of his hand and placed it on the coffee table. Last night when I woke up during the night, dying of heat exhaustion because Gray Santo was spooning me in his sleep, I had slipped out of his embrace and gone to the bathroom. On the way there, I had seen the full cup of tea, and I had burned red knowing that Jett had come back when Gray and I were having sex.

I prayed it was only Jett who may have heard us. Ash didn't need us to rub it in his face.

Ash.

He had handled it well. I mean, I know I wouldn't have, which made me even more deplorable in my actions towards him, I knew.

I watched Gray doze in the chair, and I thought about what Ash had said. The agency wasn't an adoption agency. They *sold* the babies. They were going to sell my baby. Our baby.

No wonder they wanted me back to change my mind. Had they already sold my baby and would have to what? Refund the money? Did babies get sent back for a refund if the parents didn't like them? I felt a bubble of hysteria rise at the thought, and I clamped my hands over my mouth to stop it from bursting free.

How long had the guys known about the fact the babies were for sale? To think they thought—that *he* thought—that I had signed up to that, made me sick.

"It's such a mess," I whispered in the quiet of the room.

"What is?" Gray's low voice in the stillness of the room made me jump.

"I thought you were asleep," I said as he brought his head forward and opened his eyes.

"The wheels turning in your brain were enough to keep me awake," he joked as he sat up straighter. "I'm starving. If Jett comes in here with anything other than pizza, I swear I'll kill him."

"You're not allowed pizza," I reminded him.

"I'm starving. I've worked a ton of calories off. I need and I deserve pepperoni pizza."

Sighing, I shook my head in despair. "No one deserves pepperoni pizza." I shuddered.

"You're right, double pepperoni, extra cheese."

"Gray!"

"Quinn!" he mocked back as he finished his coffee and stood, striding to the window to look out. His smile faded. "Well, we have pizza coming our way," he told me as he turned back to me.

"Okay?" I looked at him and then the window. "But?"

"More than one delivery boy," he said as he headed to my front door.

Sounded like Jett had found Ash.

I heard the murmur of voices as Gray let them in, and then they all walked into my living room.

"Hi," Jett greeted me as he leaned over and kissed the side of my head. "Never seen you like that before," he said as he hugged me with one arm.

"I know, I'm sorry."

"Nothing to be sorry for," he told me as he kissed me again. Drawing back, he looked at me, and I saw the question in his eyes.

"I'm okay," I assured him.

"Okay." He stepped back and then looked at the bathroom door. "We'll get that fixed," he promised me.

"Okay."

I looked at Ash, and he looked back. "Brought food." He held up three pizza boxes, and I gave a small smile.

"Thanks."

Gray said nothing to them, only lifted the first box off of the pile and opened it. His lip curled in distaste. "This is yours." He handed it to me without making eye contact.

Curiously I opened it and beamed. Hawaiian pizza. Ham, pineapple, cheese on pizza dough—who could hate it? "Yum!"

Jett gagged as he handed a pizza box to his brother. "This is ours," he said as he sat on the floor easily.

Picking up a slice, I realised I was ravenous, and I took a hearty bite. I saw Gray watching me with abhorrence, and Ash gave a small laugh.

"What?" I demanded.

"It's pineapple...on *pizza*." Gray took the slice his brother handed him. "How could you?" he demanded of Jett.

"Ash ordered it," Jett said to him around a mouthful of pepperoni pizza.

Looking at Ash in surprise, I swallowed my mouth of food. "Thanks."

He shrugged as he ate his own slice. "Thought you may need it," he mumbled as he avoided eye contact. His glance flicked to Gray, who was still in last night's clothes. "So you stayed?"

Gray was many things, some good, more bad, and a few diabolical...but what he was and always would be, is brutally honest. "I did. In her bed, before you try to skirt around it."

Ash said nothing, just bit into his pizza as he looked away, and Jett cleared his throat. "So, we know you two have hooked up before. I don't know the details"—he looked at Ash who shook his head slightly—"and I don't think we need to know."

I took a bite of pizza to disguise the fact I had been holding my breath.

"You were pregnant, and you didn't tell us, any of us," Jett said as he ate his food. I nodded. "Well, that was the first mistake." His tone was hard as I knew it would be. "You were giving the baby up for adoption?" I nodded again, and I saw him place his hand on his brother's knee to stop the shaking. "And you changed your mind?"

"Yes." I closed my pizza box, my appetite diminished. "I knew I was doing the wrong thing, and I knew no matter what it took, I would make it work."

Jett nodded and kept on eating, passing a slice back to his brother, who I thought was eating mechanically now, so focused on me.

"And when you told them you'd changed your mind?"

"They started to call me all the time. I didn't answer until I finally did, and they asked me to go to them and discuss it."

"Who's they?" Ash asked me.

"Dr Newton," I said as I looked at Jett and saw him nod. "He said if I didn't meet with them, they would come to the school or my house. Or both."

"Fuckers," Gray bit out as he tossed his slice onto the open box in Jett's lap.

"And you went to meet with them?" Jett encouraged me.

"Yes, but even when I got to the building, I knew it was wrong, and I was walking away when I heard someone call for me. Then I heard feet, like they were running."

"What did you do?" Ash asked me.

"I ran." I rubbed my nose before I picked up the pizza again. "I ran and I never saw the stairs, and I fell."

"And you lost consciousness?" Jett pressed.

"That's what the hospital said." I tapped my hand off my head. "You saw the stitches."

"I did." He looked at me with sadness as we both remembered the hospital. He had stayed with me all day before they let me out. They made sure I'd passed everything naturally before giving me a final scan.

"And you took her to the cabin," Gray spoke as he looked away from us all.

"I did. She needed to heal."

"And you told him nothing?" Gray demanded.

"I'd just lost my baby, I needed time."

"You lost *our* baby," Gray snapped. "Didn't I have the right to have time to heal?"

"I think it's safe to say we all made mistakes," Jett cut in smoothly.

Gray snorted and Ash grunted, and I shared a look with Jett as they both focused on looking at anything but me or him.

"You need to show us where they wanted you to go," Gray said suddenly. "We need to know when you met them, who you met with, what names you remember, all of it."

"Gray...I—"

Fierce blue eyes met mine and held. "This isn't just about you, we all lost something. We need to make it right."

"Revenge?" I demanded.

"These people *sell* babies," Ash reminded me. "It's not some legitimate agency trying to give parentless couples a family. They sell innocent babies to the highest bidder; they're *monsters*."

"Are you sure?" I asked them as I looked down at my hands.

"We are." Jett's voice was quiet but firm.

"How?" I asked wildly, my heart racing. "How do you know?"

"Because we found a paper with your name and three names beside it, and beside each name was a price." Gray's voice was cold. "I knew what it was as soon as I saw it."

"Numbers?" I questioned, averting my eyes from his glare to look at Jett.

"Their bid, Quinn," Jett supplied. "It was the bidding sheet for your child."

"And we have film," Ash added, "of the girls giving birth." He too dropped his food back into the box. "One of them died."

I could feel the tears at the back of my throat. “Why haven’t you gone to the police?”

“We needed to know more,” Jett answered. “We needed to make sure that we had enough to give them.”

“And do you?” I asked them. Jett shook his head in sadness. “What else could you possibly need? You have Dr Newton and you have the films.”

Gray caught my eye and held it. “Isn’t it obvious? We need you.”

CHAPTER 20

Gray

SHE STARED AT ME BUT SAID NOTHING. MY BROTHER WENT TO SPEAK, but I nudged him with my knee. He needed to be quiet; she needed to realise that this had to happen. This is what we needed. What she needed.

They needed to be exposed, brought down so they could never do this to someone else again.

In a way, it was a good thing I hadn't had my suspicions confirmed earlier about whose baby she was carrying. I would have destroyed something. I wasn't such a dick that I wouldn't admit it would most likely have been her. I heard Ash move uncomfortably in his seat, but he didn't speak and I was grateful for it.

Quinn finally broke our stare and looked down at her lap. "What do you need?" was her quiet whisper.

"What I asked. Show us where you met with them, if it was different from the place you went to in Nashville, then take us to both. Names, *all* the names, descriptions, how many times you met, what they asked, what you signed?"

Her head rose sharply. "I signed *nothing*. I had my initial meeting, and I told them I would think about it." She looked at all three of us.

"Did they know whose baby it was?" Ash asked quietly.

She hesitated. "No."

Jett was watching her, and I felt him lean into my leg in warning. "You hesitated," he spoke softly. "Did you tell them it was Gray's?"

Quinn shook her head as she met my look. "No, I didn't. But..."

"But?" I asked as I felt my brother tense beside me.

"My phone rang when I was with them. One of them recognised the caller."

"Me?" Jett asked. He was the only one she had an actual picture of attached to his caller ID. Ash's was a football helmet, and I had the angry dude from some animated film who went up in flames when it was angry, which she thought was funny.

"Yes," Quinn answered as she held my stare. "Do you think that's why they kept harassing me?"

"Because you had one of the state's star footballers on your phone? Yeah, I'd say it was a good guess," I bit out angrily.

"I didn't do it intentionally!" Quinn yelled back at me.

"Did I say you did?" I snarked back, and my brother got to his feet.

"Okay, you both need to take a step back," he said as he put the pizza box on the table. "Arguing won't help anything."

Ash grunted and I turned to look at him. "What?" I asked.

"If they recognised Jett and thought they hit payday with the kid of a Santo, then we may have been reckless doing the houses," he said carefully.

"You were reckless irrespective of who they saw on my phone," Quinn bitched.

"And if we hadn't, we wouldn't have known what we do now." My teeth hurt from clenching my jaw too hard.

"I think I would be okay with that," Quinn muttered as she straightened in her seat.

"What?" I looked at her in amazement. "You would be okay never knowing what they had intended to do had you gone through with it?"

"I mean I would be okay with you three not breaking the law and doing stupid reckless shit that may get you caught and put in jail."

"Fuck jail," I snarled as I stood. "And fuck you."

"Gray..." Jett groaned.

"How can you say that?" Quinn snapped angrily at the same time. "After..." Her eyes flicked to Ash guiltily.

"What? After I fucked you all night, you mean?"

"*Gray!*" Quinn shouted in protest.

"What?" My temper was rising. "You think it would be easier if we didn't know? You think it would be easier if we knew you'd lost a baby and that you were scared, and we did nothing? You think it would be better if we ignored that it happened, like you are? You would prefer to keep us all in the dark and let this happen again and again to other girls who are as clueless as you?" Leaning over her, I glared at her. "That what you mean?"

"No," her quiet, furious whisper pissed me off even more.

"Well, it doesn't fucking sound like it." I scowled as I straightened. "Stop being a selfish coward, stop fucking hiding, and help us fix it."

"You can't fix this!" Quinn screamed in anger suddenly. Soon she was on her feet, and the two of us were staring at each other, equally angry. Jett and Ash may as well have not been in the room. "You can't make this better for me! Nothing you're doing helps me, helps me get past it; all you're doing is making me feel bad and cruel and like shit."

"Good."

"Good?" She blinked at me in shock.

"Yes, good." I folded my arms across my chest. "You fucked up, you know it and I know it. That's okay. In time, I'll accept that you lied to me for eighteen months, I'll get past the fact you looked me in the eye almost every day and didn't tell me that you miscarried my baby or that you were going to *give it* to fucking strangers."

"Brother—" Jett began, but I wasn't listening.

"I hope it keeps you awake at night, the lies you told me." I looked her over, and I saw the rigid way she held herself. "You changed your mind, and I thank fuck that you did because, Quinn, if you had carried my baby to term and handed it over to those bastards, I would be in jail because I would have killed you."

"Easy, Gray," Ash warned me.

"And all that means nothing," I continued, ignoring them all. "It means fuck all because what happened, happened. You weren't the only person who lost something, Quinn. And we're telling you, *begging* you, to help us so these fuckers never do this to anyone else. That they don't prey on confused, helpless girls and take advantage of them. Do you know none of us sleep at night, seeing those films? Thinking that could have been you? Do you know that it consumes us, that the very thought of you being on that table makes all of us sick?" I ignored the tears that were streaming down her face. "And we're asking for your help. We're asking you to help those who may have just been as uncertain and scared as you, and you tell us what? We're preventing you from moving on? Are you fucking kidding me right now?"

"Get out."

I stared at her as she met my fierce glare and raised her chin in defiance. "No."

"Get the fuck out of my apartment. I don't want to look at you." Angrily she wiped her eyes and pointed to the door. "I said leave."

"C'mon." Ash nudged me with his shoulder as he passed. "You need your hand looked at."

The randomness of his statement made me look at my hand, and I saw it was swelling again, the cuts from the basement angry and red.

"Jett gets to stay?" I asked her quietly as I tried to flex my hand before I looked up at her. She nodded once, and I barked out a laugh. "Maybe you'll have better luck this time and finally fuck the Santo you want to."

"Gray—" Jett protested, but I walked past them both to meet Ash at the door.

Quickly we both left and headed outside. We walked in silence as my demons raced through my head, and my temper rose higher and higher. "I need to fuck shit up," I declared suddenly as I came to an abrupt stop.

Ash turned to look at me, and I was aware I had a lot to answer to my cousin, but right now, I needed to pummel something.

"Think you fucked that up back there spectacularly," Ash said dryly.

I snorted as I looked at my hand again. "She pisses me off," I muttered.

"Really?" His sarcasm didn't go unnoticed. "Your hand's fucked. You know that, don't you?" Ash reached out and looked at it. "You're not gonna get to play."

I winced at the truth of it and looked at my cousin. "What the hell do I do now?"

Ash stood a few feet away from me. "Was it always like this? Between you two? The...desire?"

"You mean the rage?" I asked, and he gave a small snort at my terminology as he half shrugged. "Yeah, I think it was."

"I must have been so blind." He ran a hand over his jaw as he assessed me. "Why did you never say anything?"

"Because I was fifteen and stupid," I snapped. "I never even considered she would go out with you," I admitted and then saw his affronted glare. "No offence, I thought she knew she was mine," I added as I looked over my shoulder to her apartment.

"'She was mine?'" Ash asked me with a raised eyebrow. "You sound like a possessive dick," he told me.

"I am." I resumed walking, and I heard him follow. "Look, I don't need to tell you that I'm not Jett. We're all family, you know me. I'm not going to fall over myself for forgiveness, I'm not that guy, and you would hate me if I was. You've seen me at my worst, and you've seen me at my best. I'm not going to sugarcoat shit: I fucked up. She's mine, I should have told you to back off, and I didn't. That's on me. Everything that happened before and after is for me and her to fix." I groaned. "If it can ever be fixed, but when she was with you, she was with *you*. She didn't cheat," I added.

"I know. She told me."

"Okay, good. I'm a bastard, I get it. But I'm not a fucking bastard," I muttered as we walked.

"You're a shit cousin," Ash said as we passed the rows of the dorms, and I grinned. "Worse friend."

"I probably am."

"Not the best brother either," he added as he scuffed his foot off the sidewalk. "You know it's never been like that between them."

"I know." Rubbing the back of my neck, I did regret saying that to her. "She knows what I'm like when I'm pissed. Maybe even more than Jett."

"You think you two will work?"

"Fuck knows," I told him honestly.

"I don't think I can take it," he admitted, "seeing you two together."

I cast a quick glance at him and ran my tongue over my teeth. "If you make me choose," I started.

"You choose her, I get it," he cut me off.

Stopping, I stared up at the sky and the cloud cover. "I'm sorry." I turned to look at him. "This is a shit way to find out, it's a shit situation, and I know a thousand times I made the wrong choices, but the choices I made were for her. She's mine, she was *always* mine."

"I'm going to lie to myself and pretend that she didn't get the memo either," Ash said with a rueful laugh. "My ego needs to believe the lie."

"She's ruthless, I agree, but she isn't callous," I told him quietly. "She didn't play you."

"I hope not." Ash resumed walking, and I followed him. My desire to hit something was dissipating until I realised he wasn't walking to the house.

"Where we headed?"

"Going to get Izzy to check your hand, so when we tell Coach tomorrow that you fucked up royally, he won't kill you if he knows first how long it will take to heal."

I nodded in agreement as I jogged to catch up with him. "That's actually a great idea."

"You're a shit cousin and a bad friend, but you're still the best running back on the team."

I laughed out loud at his honesty. "Still family too, cousin," I said as I nudged him with my shoulder.

"Yeah, well, you're a dick. I hope you're out all season."

"No, you don't."

He grunted and then nudged me back a little more forcefully than he needed. "No, I don't, but I sure as hell hope it hurts like a motherfucker."

"If it's any consolation, it really does."

Ash grinned maliciously as we headed to the team's doctor's house, and I couldn't help but feel a flicker of hope we would be okay.

"Tell me again how you messed your hand up worse when you haven't been doing anything?" Coach Bowers glared at me, and I met his stare.

"It must have been worse than we originally thought," I lied blithely.

"You're out for the rest of the regular season."

That did suck, and I was pissed, but I couldn't do anything about it. "Yeah, Izzy said that."

"You punch the centre for the basketball team?" Coach asked me shrewdly.

"What? Denzel? Nah, why would I?" *Who the hell told him?*

Coach looked at me for a long moment, and I didn't give him anything. "Out." I didn't argue but stood and headed to the door. "Santo," he called, and I turned back. "You do nothing for these last few weeks. I am not ruling you out for the conference championship. If we get there. You're not going on the reserved list. You hear me? You fuck this up, boy, and I will gut you myself."

"And if we don't make it to the conference championship?" I asked.

"Then your brother and your teammates know who to blame."

"Good talk," I said sarcastically as I pulled the door open. "Real motivational."

Jett was sitting on the benches, waiting for me. "You're still breathing."

"He may be slightly pissed off," I told him as I grabbed my backpack. "You'd think I'd done it intentionally, just to fuck up his Monday."

"Your hands are important," Jett said as he stood.

"I know," I growled as I headed out.

"Why are you self-destructing?" Jett asked me quietly.

"Didn't know I was."

"Course you are," my brother scoffed. "You're so full of shit."

"So I keep getting told," I mumbled as I pulled my phone out of my back pocket.

"She's skipping today."

"Why?" I asked him as I looked up from the phone.

"I dunno, Gray, maybe because you fucking destroyed her yesterday," he bit out angrily.

"Hardly."

"Don't be a prick. You were cruel, and she didn't need that."

"She needs to pull her head out of her ass and face the facts," I reminded him. "She can help us. Tell me you told her that." I saw him hesitate, and I groaned. "You had *one* fucking job," I scolded as I passed him and headed to her apartment.

"Where you going?" Jett yelled from behind me.

"Where the hell do you think I'm going?" I grumbled as I flicked him the finger with my good hand while walking away.

When I got there, the door was locked, and she didn't open it when I knocked. I knocked louder.

"Dude, get the hint, she isn't in." Some blonde said as she walked out of the lower apartment, and I ignored her as I pulled my phone out.

Me: **I have no problem knocking this door in either**

Quinn: **I'm not talking to you**

Me: **Okay. Open the door**

Quinn: **Go to class**

I pounded on the door harder. It worked, because she threw the door open in fury, her eyes wild with anger and her temper riding high.

"What the fuck is wrong with you?" she demanded as she glared at me.

Pushing past her, I walked inside and grinned when I heard her hesitate before she slammed the door shut behind me. Turning, I looked her over, black yoga pants, bright pink T-shirt, her hair in two braids.

"Working out?" I guessed as I noted her coffee table pushed to the side.

"Trying to," she sassed back at me. "What do you want?"

"Thought that was obvious," I said as I took a seat.

"Well, consider me dumb and spell it out for me." Her arms were folded across her chest as she stared at me.

"You."

I watched as the temper was knocked out of her. "Wh-what?"

"You asked what I wanted. It's what I always wanted. You."

"Gray?"

Rolling my eyes, I stood and pulled her into me. "I'm a dick, I have a bad temper, you piss me off, those fuckers make me want to do time for what you went through, but all I ever wanted was you."

Quinn looked up at me, the uncertainty and confusion clear in her eyes. "You're insane."

"I know." Dipping my head, I caught her lips in a soft kiss. "Doesn't change the facts."

Quinn's teeth scraped over her bottom lip as she watched me, and then with almost hesitation, she reached up and traced her fingers over the side of my face. "I thought you hated me," she whispered.

"Sometimes I do."

"Really?" She drew her hand back and tried to step away, but I pulled her closer.

"There's a thin line, they say, between love and hate. Some days, I'm on one side; some days, on the other, but every day, it doesn't fucking matter which side I'm on, all that matters is you."

"You were horrible yesterday."

"I'm not going to apologise, don't expect me to. You need to hear things. You're not weak, stop hiding."

"What if I'm just scared?" she asked.

"We're all scared, Quinn. I'm scared I never stop them and they keep doing this shit to others."

Her head dropped onto my chest as she embraced me. "I'll tell you everything I know."

Kissing the top of her head, I held her close. "Thank you."

We stayed like that for a while before Quinn pulled back and looked up at me. "You love me?"

"What, you think I'm this much of a dick just because we're friends?"

She smiled and I marvelled at how beautiful she was. "You *are* a dick," she teased as she reached up to brush her lips against mine.

"Yeah, well, I never claimed to be anything else." I kissed her before she could say anything further.

CHAPTER 21

Quinn

Sitting in the cafeteria, I was reading my textbook when I heard the chair scrape back, and looking up, I smiled in greeting at Ava. "Hi."

"Hey." She lowered to her seat and placed her tray in front of her. I looked at the plate of fries and the bowl of grated cheese, which she unceremoniously tipped over her fries. She looked up and saw my nose wrinkled in distaste. "What?"

"How are you so slim?" I asked her as I looked her over. Her loose grey sweater over black leggings emphasised her curves, but she wasn't plump in any way. "You eat terrible food, you don't exercise, and you still look good."

Ava shrugged as she started to eat. "I eat better at home. Mia's always on a diet of some kind, so at home, I make nice healthy food. Here's my place to gorge on the not so good stuff," she said with a grin as she held a fry out to me. "Want some?"

"No." I shuddered as she shrugged and popped it in her mouth.

"What did you bring?" Ava asked as she nodded towards my containers.

"Chicken breast, salad and a few crackers."

"Dull," Ava commented as she ate more of her lunch.

"I enjoy it," I countered wryly. "Where's Mia? I wanted to thank her again for the help with the spreadsheets. The guys have been sending me regular updates."

"Oooh, I'm glad it worked," Ava said enthusiastically. "I know you've been busy, and I was wondering."

Shifting in my seat, I avoided her look. I knew she was curious—she had every right to be—and I knew that Jett would have told her nothing. I liked Ava, I did, but this wasn't something she needed to know. "Yeah, the sheets were a hit."

"It sucks so bad Gray's out for the month," Ava said as she scrolled through her phone. I knew she wasn't digging, but I was still uncomfortable.

"Broke more bones than he thought." I told her the lie that the Devils were telling.

"Well, he shouldn't have punched Denzel," Ava muttered as she ate. Her shoulders were hunched over as she ate and scrolled; she looked like a teenager. Okay, she *was* a teenager, but her posture was that of a teenage boy.

"You should sit up straight," I chided her quietly. "Your posture is terrible; your back will ache."

Ava straightened automatically and then frowned at me. "Mom?"

"You'll thank me later," I assured her. "Back straight, feet on the floor, elbows *off* the table," I finished.

"I just want to eat my fries," Ava complained.

"I know you've been invited to Sunday lunch with the parents. You can't slouch at Sable's table." Ava squinted as she looked at me, trying to decide if I was joking—I wasn't.

"I have no idea what to wear. They're like…rich."

"They are," I agreed as I sat back and assessed her. "You've met them though, and you were wearing jeans and a jersey."

"At a *game*. This is Sunday lunch. With my boyfriend's parents, his *rich* parents. Who have staff in the house to cook and clean."

"That's because Sable can't cook." I grinned. "It'll be fine."

"Are you coming?" Ava asked, and I saw the desperate hope in her eyes.

When I met Ava, I never thought I would be on her wish list of people she needed for support. "I've been invited as have my dad and stepmom, so yeah, I'll be there too."

"Oh, is your mom nice?"

"My mom was wonderful," I answered as I looked over the cafeteria. "Anne, my stepmom, is nice."

"Oh, sorry." Ava waited a nanosecond before she asked. "Are they divorced?"

"My mom died when I was twelve."

"Oh," Ava automatically reached over the table and squeezed my hand. "I didn't know, sorry."

"Why would you?" I smiled at her as she sat back. "She had cancer, everywhere. By the time they realised there was something wrong, it was too late."

"How do you miss cancer?" Ava asked with confusion in her voice.

"Dad was away a lot. I'm a navy brat. Dad is—*was*—an admiral, not a lot of home time. Mom thought it was fatigue from looking after me."

"Which is why you're older than us."

"Yes," I answered as I reached forward for my soda.

"I'm sorry, I'm prying, you're just really mysterious."

I snorted out a laugh. "I'm really not."

"You are!" Ava leaned forward as she looked around. "You're like the glue to the Santo guys. I mean, before, I just thought you were a friend, but the more I see you all together, you're another Devil."

"I told you that."

"I know, but I thought you were simply insane." She swirled her fries in the melting cheese. "But you really are."

"Really what? Insane?" I teased as she laughed.

"Yeah." Pushing her plate away, she sat back in her seat. "You have to help me, I don't know what to wear."

"Wear what you're comfortable in," I said easily and then thought about it. "But maybe not jeans."

"A dress?" Ava's nose wrinkled as she grimaced. "Will you be wearing a dress?"

"I haven't thought about it," I told her honestly. "I usually just grab something," I added with a shrug. "But for Sunday lunch...yeah, it wouldn't be pants."

"Drat."

"Drat?" I laughed at her terminology. "You have a black skirt, I've seen it. Wear that with a top you like. It's simple."

"Okay." She nodded thoughtfully. "So, who else will be there?"

"Us, Jett's parents, Ash's parents, my dad and Anne."

"The other brother?"

I clenched my jaw. "Only if we're very unlucky."

"You don't like him?"

"We have a mutual agreement to detest each other." There was no point denying it. "But you *will* get to meet Tilly, Ash's little sister. She's adorable."

"I'm not really good with kids." Ava shrugged awkwardly.

"It's impossible not to love Tilly, she's awesome."

"I'm so nervous," she said again.

"You'll be fine. You've met them already. Jett will be there and so will the others and me. You're going to be fine." She nodded before she picked her phone up.

I returned to my textbook while Ava spent time on her phone. I heard them approach before I looked up and saw them. The calls and commiseration that Gray was injured had been pretty consistent for the last few days.

They all stopped at the table we were at, and I looked up. "What?"

"Come sit with us." Jett gestured to the football table, and I shook my head.

"No."

"Queeny," he started.

"I'm not on the football team, I'm no longer in high school, and I don't need to be sitting beside you all at lunch time."

Gray was grinning openly as Ash huffed out a laugh as he carried on to their usual table.

"I thought you would want to, now that..." He glanced at Gray, who raised an eyebrow at his brother.

"Now what?" Ava demanded as she looked between us all. She was half turned in her seat as she tried to figure out what Jett was saying.

"You thought wrong," I told him as I packed my books away. "Anyway, I'm heading to the library." I saw his look of disappointment before he reached out to Ava's discarded plate. I pulled it sharply out of his way. "Don't even think about it," I scolded him. "You *know* what's on your food plan for today, and it better be in that backpack."

"Have fun at the library," he said dryly as he pulled Ava to her feet, and they headed to the back table.

Gray tilted his head to the side as he waited for me to walk around the side of the table.

"What?" I asked him as he crossed his arms across his chest.

"Nothing, have fun." He winked as he walked past. I jumped a foot in the air when his hand slapped my ass, and the cafeteria hooted and hollered.

Bastard.

With my face on fire, I walked quickly out of the cafeteria and detoured to the coffee shop.

Me: **Was that necessary?**

Gray: **Yup**

Me: **Why?**

Gray: **Why not?**

I didn't bother fighting the smile as I entered the coffee shop and placed my order. There was still so much for us to sort out. There was a lot of hurt to heal and things to talk about. I still needed to know who he had been with in the pool house, and I was reluctant to ask. Did it matter? Hadn't too much happened since?

No. I still needed to know who she was. Call me irritational, call me jealous, call me insane. The need to know was as strong today as it was then. Maybe just less violent...maybe.

Gray wasn't like Jett, who genuinely had never cared who he was hooking up with. Ash had made sure I knew who every one of his hookups were after we broke up. After they locked me out, I hadn't been much better. I hadn't slept around, but I hadn't been a nun either.

Until Gray, until that night when he spent the night with me.

Afterwards, I was hurt he hadn't made a big deal out of it. Then I was furious he shunned me. Then he was with someone else, and then none of it mattered because I was pregnant. After the miscarriage, I'd pretty much shut up shop and hadn't been with anyone.

Until Gray. Again.

Always Gray.

Gray, who was the complete opposite of Jett. Gray never shared who he was with. He never bragged, and whoever his hookups were, they never boasted. Jett had once let slip that Onyx took Gray to his college parties now and then, and it was then that I realised he was sleeping with college girls.

Why would they want him? I'd wondered. Until the day in the bathroom when I realised I'd asked myself the wrong question. Why *wouldn't* they want him?

Was that who she was? A college girl?

I needed to know.

Me: **Who was she? That day, the girl in the pool house?**

He didn't immediately answer, and I wished I could take it back even as I rationalised that he would be eating his lunch. Finally, three dots appeared.

Gray: **Audrey. She was a casual fuck nothing else.**

Me: **Charming**

Gray: **The day you thought you saw her with me, I wasn't. I was drunk and sleeping, she woke me up and I told her to get out.**

I read the message a few times. I needed this to be true so much it scared me.

Me: **Promise?**

Gray: **I've never lied to you before, not going to start now**

Was there something wrong with me that reading that message gave me butterflies?

Putting the phone down, I looked up and saw him watching me before he walked towards me. Bending down, he caught my lips and kissed me soundly. In the coffee shop. In front of everyone.

"I'm telling the truth," he said to me huskily.

"Okay."

"Believe me?" Gray asked as his eyes searched mine.

"You don't lie."

"No, I don't." His lips claimed mine again, and I didn't give a damn he had just outed us to the student population of Cardinal Saint College.

SMOOTHING DOWN THE SKIRT OF MY DRESS, I ASSESSED MYSELF IN the mirror. My dress was simple and casual. A cute, deep pink, floral, ditsy dress with three-quarter-length sleeves, stopping mid-thigh. It was as girly as I got, and I wasn't sure why I was suddenly embracing my inner cute girl, but I wanted to be pretty for this afternoon. Jett had already warned me that Onyx was home, and tensions between him and Gray were already high.

I should probably have changed the choice of dress—maybe a slim-fitting shift dress would have given me armour—but I was stubbornly clinging to the belief that Gray would stop his brother from being too much himself. Plus, dad and Anne would be there. Onyx usually reined it in when dad was in the vicinity, because my dad literally knew people who would kill you with their thumb.

I snorted out a very unladylike laugh as I thought of the first time that I had told the three of them that my dad could kill them with only his thumb. Gray, being Gray, had of course asked my dad, and he told them no, he could not. Three pairs of eyes had glared at me in accusation until my dad finished by saying *he* couldn't, but he had plenty of Seals who could.

"Quinn, we're leaving," my dad called up from the bottom of the stairs.

"Ready!" I yelled back as I grabbed a small purse, which had lip balm and my phone in it.

"Why aren't you wearing a jacket?" dad asked me as he frowned in disapproval.

"Because they live literally next door," I answered as I kissed his cheek while passing him at the foot of the stairs.

"Anne?" my dad called to my stepmom, and I saw her smile at how predictable he was.

"Quinn's right, it's just across the path." She smiled at me, and I gave her a thumbs-up behind his back. "I can smell lunch, come on," she urged dad.

He grumbled the whole way across, which even though it was next door, our house was humble in size compared to the Santo house. Ash's house was beside theirs, and I often wondered why our house was smaller in size. Not that we needed the sprawling estate the Santos did, it just looked odd.

Or maybe I was being sizeist?

I suppressed the shiver I felt in the autumn air, and I relished the warmth as my dad wrapped his arm around me. He didn't say "I told you so," and I didn't comment, but I did lean into him in thanks.

Sable opened the front door as we were halfway up the path. "I'm so glad you're here," she greeted us warmly. I got a huge hug, which I returned wholeheartedly.

"Quinn, you look beautiful as always." She kissed my cheek, and I beamed as we followed her into the drawing room.

Ava was already here, talking to Kerr, and from how animated she was, I knew it was about football. Jett had his arm wrapped around her waist as he listened, the small smile on his face a broadcast to the whole room how enamoured he was with her.

Gray was talking to Kage, Ash's dad, while Tilly was deep in conversation with her brother, Ash. He was crouched down listening to her, and I smiled at the familiar sight. My smile froze when Onyx walked into the room, a casual sweep of the room before dark eyes glittering with hatred focused on me.

"Oh good, the Queen is here," he sneered as he looked me over. "What are you wearing?"

"It's called a dress, Onyx," I said, trying to keep my voice neutral.

"It's *girly*. It doesn't suit you," he snarled as he walked to his seat at the table, and I felt Anne stroke my arm in comfort.

"If you're going to act like a viper, then we'll leave." My dad's voice was firm and his glare hard. Onyx raised his glass in apology to dad.

"What can I say, she brings the worst out in me," he gibed.

"Don't worry, dad," I said to dad with a wide smile. "You know I'll only stab him in the eye with my fork if he's sitting beside me." I turned to Sable. "He isn't, is he?"

"No, sweetheart," she assured me. Sable turned to look at Onyx. "And he knows he can sit in the kitchen if he continues his nonsense."

Onyx grunted but merely took another drink of his whisky.

Everyone greeted each other properly, and while they were doing so, Gray made his way to my side. I noted that Onyx's eyes followed every step, and I almost wanted to tell Gray to move away, but I was selfish, and I wanted him beside me.

When we were all seated and served roast beef, I watched with quiet amusement as Ava tried to keep up with all the questions Jett's parents were bombarding her with. When they skirted around the topic of her drink being spiked, she handled it well and assured Sable she didn't need the therapy they had offered to send her to.

"Quinn, dear, Jett tells me your assignment for class is to work out food plans," Sable asked me and carried on with no hesitation. "I told Cook to write down everything, everything's been weighed and proportioned. Do you need anything else?"

"No, thank you, I'm sure what Maureen has done is more than enough," I replied.

"You know we're not getting chocolate fudge cake because of you?" Ash grumbled as he ate his lunch.

"I didn't do anything," I reminded him with a laugh. "It was your cousin who blabbed." I pointed at Jett, who winced at Ash's glare.

"I wasn't thinking about dessert," he admitted as he scratched his jaw. "Sorry, man."

"I'll eat yours," Gray told Jett with a grin as he held his hand up. "It won't hurt me."

"Tell me again how you broke your hand?" Kerr asked Gray, and I saw all three of them sit straighter. If I saw it, so did their dads. "What did you do?" Kerr asked with a heavy sigh.

"I had an accident with my car." Gray didn't flinch under his dad's stare, and I saw his Uncle Kage look between the three of them. Onyx snorted, and both Kerr and Kage turned as one to look at the oldest.

"What did you do?" Kerr asked with a groan.

"I took a baseball bat to his car."

"Why?" Charlotte, Ash's mom, asked in alarm.

"He broke his hand on my face."

"Gray!" Sable turned to Gray with a question.

"He shouldn't speak shit he knows nothing about," Gray said simply with a casual shrug even as his mom chided him for his language.

"It's all Quinn's fault," Tilly grumbled from the middle of the table, and I looked at her in surprise, but she turned her head away from me.

"Tilly? Why would you say that?" I asked her curiously.

"Because you kill babies."

CHAPTER 22

Gray

THE SHOCKED SILENCE WAS DEAFENING, AND I SAW HER FREEZE IN her chair before the rumble of my brother's laughter broke the stunned stupor.

"You bastard," Quinn seethed. Pushing her chair back, she stood in one smooth motion. "Are you happy now?" she asked him as she looked at him, and as if in a daze, I turned to look at Onyx.

"Makes no difference to me." He lifted his fork and resumed eating.

"Quinn?" Her dad, George, was sitting rigid, his back ramrod straight.

"I'm going home," Quinn said to the room. She looked at Ash, who was white with shock, and then she looked at Jett. "I can't..."

Jett was on his feet and moving around the table as I sat there, frozen. When I saw his hand land on her arm, I was on my feet, pulling her to me.

"I'll take you." My voice sounded far away, and I heard a clamour of voices as Quinn shook beside me.

"Sit down," George commanded. His voice was hard and authoritative, and I felt Quinn wince at the tone. "Now."

On autopilot, she sat, her hands clasped together in her lap as I hovered beside her.

"Gray, I suggest you sit," he directed me, and my brain registered that this was still my house, even as I sat.

"Sable, Charlotte, perhaps Tilly should be removed?" It was more of an order than a request, and Aunt Charlotte quickly ushered Tilly, who was now crying, from the room.

Ava looked uncomfortable, and I saw her raise her hand. George's attention snapped to her, and she flinched. "I think I should be removed too. This isn't for me... It's private, I don't think I should be here."

"Stay." The whisper was Quinn's.

Aunt Charlotte came back in, closing the doors firmly behind her. She sat beside Sable, who was staring fixedly at the tablecloth.

I watched George look at Onyx, who had put his fork down, and then he turned to look at Quinn.

"From your reaction, I think there may be something you need to tell me?"

I heard Quinn take a deep breath, and then she squared her shoulders and looked up at her dad. "I had a miscarriage last year." Her voice was steady, matter-of-fact, her face a blank mask. "I fell down some stairs and knocked myself out. When I came to, I was in the hospital, and I had lost the ba— it."

"Quinn." My mom reached out to her, but Quinn was fully focused on her dad.

"I didn't tell you because there was nothing to tell." She wet her lips quickly. "I was going to tell you, and had it not occurred, I was coming home to tell you." Her eyes flicked to Anne, who had a hand pressed to her mouth. "Both of you."

"Pregnant?" her dad asked. His face was stern, but I saw his confusion as if he had mistaken what she said.

"Yes."

"By whom?"

Quinn flicked her hand dismissively. "It doesn't matter, does it?"

"Answer me."

"It was mine." I met and held his angry glare. "The baby was mine."

I heard my mom gasp, my dad curse, and I heard *him* chuckle. I was off my feet and launching myself at my brother much to the horror of my family. As the two of us punched the shit out of each other, I felt hands pulling at us, trying to separate us.

"Enough!"

Startled at the scream, both Onyx and I stopped to look at Anne, who stood over us and a broken dish at her feet.

"You're not helping," she shouted angrily. "Now get up, shut up, and sit the fuck down."

The whole room stared at her in shock. Anne was one of the timidest women I had ever met.

Slowly I picked myself up off the floor, wincing at the pain in my hand. I may as well have chopped the fucker off. My eyes searched the room, and I saw Ava standing by the door.

"She's gone."

I hurried to the door, but George grabbed my arm, stopping me. "No. Not you."

"With all due respect, sir, you either knock me out now or get the hell out of my way. I'm not leaving her alone. Jett and Ash can tell you what you need to know." He moved forward, and I shoved past him. "I'll let you beat the crap out of me later," I said as I ran out of the room, leaving chaos behind me.

Running to her house, I climbed the stairs two at a time. She was curled up on her bed, her eyes fixed on the wall as silent tears ran down her face. Kicking off my boots, I climbed onto the bed behind her and pulled her close. She didn't resist.

"I'm so sorry," I whispered in her ear as I wrapped my arms around her.

"Tilly hates me," she whispered.

"She's eight, she doesn't know what she's saying," I assured her.

"Why would he tell her?"

"I'm so pissed at him, I am, but even Onyx wouldn't tell Tilly this. She must have heard him talking to someone."

"Who?"

"I don't know," I answered honestly.

We both heard the front door slam open, and I felt her stiffen. "I can't do this," she admitted quietly.

"Course you can." I kissed the back of her head. "I'm here, we'll do it together."

I looked up when the bedroom door slammed against the wall, and her dad was standing there, rigid with anger.

"If you could both come downstairs, I would like to speak with you."

Quinn sat up and I followed. As we headed down to the living room, she reached out for me, and I took her hand.

Anne was sitting in a chair, and George was at the window. He half turned when we walked in, and Quinn led us to the couch.

"How long have you two been a thing?" he asked with scorn.

"Since I was ten and she was eleven," I answered, and I saw Quinn dip her head and the small smile that broke free.

"I'm not in the mood for games," her dad snapped.

"I'm not playing a game," I answered him as I pulled Quinn closer. "Your daughter miscarried our baby. She's not at fault here. She was eighteen when she was pregnant, an adult. Which is why the hospital didn't notify you and why she never told you."

"Gray," Quinn murmured softly. "It's okay, he deserves to know." Quinn stood and approached her dad. "I'm sorry I didn't tell you. I was scared, I was really scared, and I know you would have been disappointed in me, but I also know I should have told you."

"What happened?"

"I was giving the baby up for adoption," she told him honestly, ignoring Anne's gasp behind her. "But I couldn't do it, and I changed my mind. I fell down some stairs—it was an accident—I tripped and fell. I woke up in Nashville Memorial, I had a concussion, a few stitches, and I…I wasn't pregnant anymore."

I saw her dad close his eyes before his head dipped to his chest. "I'm sorry," he said to her when he looked back at her.

Quinn sniffled and then I heard her hiccup. She wiped her eyes as she nodded. "Me too, daddy."

Her dad pulled her into his arms, and I heard her crying as he rocked her. Turning away, I met Anne's sad look, and she held her hand out to me, which I gratefully accepted.

"I'm sorry," she whispered.

"Yeah."

"Come, let's make some tea." She pulled me to my feet, and we left Quinn and her dad alone.

The two of us were in the kitchen when my mom came running through the back door. I placed my cup down on the counter as I took a step towards her.

"I need you," she told me urgently. "Jett's going to kill him."

We ran out of the kitchen, and I heard the raised voices coming from the pool. Running past my mom, I skated around the side of the house before I stopped in astonishment at the sight before me.

Jett was on top of Onyx and was literally banging his head off the concrete paving.

"Fuck!" I ran towards them and threw myself at Jett, knocking him off Onyx.

Jett growled as he got to his feet, and Onyx staggered to his. "What the fuck are you doing?" Jett screamed at me.

"Are you crazy?" I shouted back. "You're going to kill him!"

"He's a piece of shit," Jett seethed.

"Yes, well, he's our piece of shit."

"You're defending him?" Jett looked stunned, which was good as it calmed his temper down.

"No, he's a dick. But he's our brother, and if anyone is going to kill *our* brother, it will be me." I thought about it as Onyx staggered slightly. "Or Quinn."

"How is she?" Jett asked as he spat blood on the grass.

"She'll be okay, she's strong." I watched Onyx shake his head as if to clear it. "You okay?" I asked him begrudgingly.

He looked up at me and nodded before his eyes rolled backwards in his head and he passed out, falling right into the pool, which was covered with a mesh net for the autumn leaves.

He and the covering disappeared, and I yelled as I dived after him, vaguely aware that Jett had jumped in too. The panicked thought that my mom was going to lose all her sons today raced through my head while I struggled to grab my brother as my feet tangled in the mesh covering. All three of us were tangled, and I was losing my grip on my unconscious brother as I fought to free us both.

Another pair of arms grabbed me, and I was being hauled upward. Jett was suddenly in front of me in the water, helping to move Onyx, who was still unconscious.

Strong arms pushed us to the side of the pool, and I remembered the time Quinn jumped in and we had pulled her to the shallow end.

Gasping, I pushed my hair out of my eyes and looked at my dad, who was pulling Onyx out of the water.

"He needs a doctor."

George stood in front of me and held his hand out, and with a slight hesitation, I took it and he pulled me out of the pool. My foot snagged on the mesh, and I kicked it free before I was on my back, beside the pool, trying to catch my breath. Turning, I helped Jett out of the water, and then we were both lying side by side, taking a moment before we had to face reality again.

"He okay?" I asked anyone.

"Taking him to the ER," my dad replied. "Both of you better be here when I get back."

"I don't need the hospital," Onyx protested.

"I suggest you go," George spoke to him, "before I drown you." He looked down at me. "I think we all need to talk."

"Yes, sir." Jett sat up, and I heard him curse.

"Dad!" I called from my prone position. "You better take Jett too."

"Kerr," my mom spoke up. "Take them all. Gray's no doubt done more damage to that hand."

Which is how all three of us ended up in the ER on a Sunday afternoon. Neither of us spoke, and each of us was given a very curious look by the doctor who treated us, who clearly knew there was more than "we tripped and fell into the pool," but we weren't questioned.

When we were discharged, dad drove us home, and in single file we headed to the kitchen where my mom and George were waiting. Quinn was there too, and when I went in, she flew across the room and flung her arms around me. Burrowing my face into her neck, I didn't care that we were in front of our parents, all I needed was to know she was all right.

"You okay?" I asked as I pulled back, stroking her hair as she nodded.

"Where's Ava?" Jett asked tiredly. "And Ash?"

"We sent her to sit with Anne," mom told him. "Kage took them home. Tilly's quite upset."

"You sent Ava away? Bullshit," Jett grumbled as he searched the kitchen for his phone and ended up opening the back door to leave before he hesitated. "Quinn?"

"Yes, both of them."

"Will do."

He was back minutes later with Anne and Ava as the rest of us settled around the table.

When we were all seated, my dad fixed his sights on me, and I met his stare. "Tell us everything"—his hand shot up as I went to speak—"everything."

My eyes flicked to George, who was waiting for it. "Quinn thinks she's clever, but she isn't; she forgets I'm her father. Tell me it all."

I didn't. *Obviously*. Despite today's actions, I wasn't a complete idiot. I told them what they needed to hear. Onyx was silent, Jett nodded when he needed to, and Quinn sat beside me, with her head on my shoulder, saying nothing.

"Did they hurt you?" Anne asked Quinn directly when I was done.

"No, they never hurt me. I got a call after I met with them to make sure I wasn't going to change my mind, but I never heard from them again."

"Who told Tilly?" I asked as I forced myself to look at Onyx.

My brother met my accusatory stare before he looked away in disgust. "I'm a bastard, it's true, but I'm not a cunt."

"Onyx!" mom chastised him. "Language!"

"She's eight; someone must have said something," I insisted.

Jett suddenly looked at me. "Does Ash still keep a journal?"

Fuck.

I saw Jett glance at our brother guiltily before he turned to Quinn. "I didn't even think of it."

"I forgive you," Onyx grunted.

"Shut up," Jett and I snapped at the same time.

"His hand?" mom asked my dad.

"He isn't playing for the rest of the year," dad said with a sigh.

Quinn turned to look up at me, and I rubbed my nose against hers. "It's okay."

"So this is happening?" George asked us both sternly. "After everything you've been through, *this* is your idea of a good idea? You two, together."

"I love her," I told him simply. "I've been apart from her for too long. She is and always has been mine." It was the truth, and I didn't care who knew it. I was done hiding my feelings for Quinn.

"And Ash?" my mom asked us both.

"Will learn to accept it," I told her firmly.

George stood and held his hand out to Anne. "I'm going home. I'm sorry the lunch was ruined. I need...time. Quinn, you're coming home with us."

"Yes, dad." She stood and bent down, dropping a brief kiss on my lips. "I'll see you tomorrow."

I watched her apologise to my mom and my dad for the chaos of this afternoon, and then she surprised me when she turned to Ava. "I could use a friend, you ready for that talk?"

Ava rose swiftly, and with a hug of Jett's shoulders, she dutifully followed. My mom stood too and sighed.

"I need a long soak in the bath. Will you all behave if I leave?"

She filled a large glass of wine before she left with a kiss to each of our heads. "I love you all, please try to heal from this."

We waited until we heard the upstairs bedroom close, and then dad rose and closed the kitchen door to the hallway just as the back patio doors opened and Uncle Kage and Ash walked in.

"Right, now tell us what the fuck you're all involved in. Don't bullshit me." Dad's hard stare met each of ours. "I will do more than send you for a visit to the ER if I hear one more lie tonight."

CHAPTER 23

Quinn

My dad looked at me in the kitchen, and I waited quietly before he gave me a curt nod and went to his study. I wasn't offended, as dad kept things tight to his chest, a bit like the other man in my life.

"Can I make you anything to eat?" Anne asked me as she stood to the side, and I recognised that I had hurt her too by not telling her. Embracing her, I felt myself relax a little in the tight hold she held me in. "I'm so sorry, Quinn, I'm so sorry you went through this alone."

And I had gone through it alone, and I had foolishly thought that I had to. I had support, I had a family that loved me, and I had chosen to keep them all out and keep my pain to myself.

"I think I was numb," I admitted as I drew back a little. "I didn't know what to do, and my options seemed so limited, but now, when I realise what I could have had, they weren't. Gray would have accepted me and the baby with no hesitation. Dad, well, he wouldn't have been delighted being a grandfather so early, but he would never have cast me aside, nor would you. It wasn't the best situation, but I would have and *could* have made it work. I was just too blind to all of that because all I had was my fear."

"Adoption is a big step," Anne said carefully. "I mean, it's not like you would have been able to hide the fact you were pregnant."

"I know." I gave a rueful shake of my head. "And I never really thought about how I was going to discuss this with...anyone really."

"Did Gray know?" Ava asked from where she was standing in the kitchen. She was leaning against the counter worktop, and there was no judgment in her face or her tone.

"No." I took a deep breath. "I never told any of them. All they knew was that it happened."

"He's so incredibly protective of you," Anne murmured as she walked to the fridge. "I didn't think he would have supported your decision for adoption. I mean, I know he would have, because of how he feels about you, but he wouldn't have been happy."

The laugh that burst out of me had too much emotion. I could feel the pain and the hurt and also the genuine humour at the fact Anne was so incredibly right. "I made such a mess of everything, I don't know why he loves me."

It was Anne's turn to chuckle. "Because you're amazing," she said. "I don't care if I'm biased and you don't listen, you are. That boy's loved you for years."

"I dated Ash," I said as I stared at the floor.

"You were seventeen. You're allowed to make the wrong choices." Anne poured herself a glass of wine and then looked at us both before she pulled two more glasses from the shelf. She poured us each a glass and handed them to us. "I think we all need this."

Ava murmured her thanks and took a sip.

"I guess you girls want to be alone." Anne gestured to the door and sighed. "I need to check in on your father. He doesn't show it, but this will have rocked his foundation a little."

"He's disappointed," I said sorrowfully as I placed my glass on the counter.

"I think he's hurt that you went through this on your own. He won't understand why you didn't tell him, and honestly? I think he's going to blame himself that you couldn't tell him."

"It wasn't, I didn't mean..."

"I know," she said as she reached over and squeezed my arm. "I know, Quinn. I'll go explain to him and let him come to terms with it all." She walked to the door and then turned back to look at me. "I'm sorry you couldn't come to me with this. I feel like I failed you as a parent, and I know I'm not your mom, but I should have never allowed you to think I wasn't here for you. I love you very much, Quinn."

The tears I had been holding at bay spilled over, and I nodded at her as my capacity for words had left me. When she was gone, I looked at Ava, who wordlessly closed the distance and pulled me tight into her arms and held me while I cried.

Cried for the loss of my baby and for the hurt I had caused my family because I didn't think about them and how my actions hurt them too. It wasn't intentional, and I think I knew that when I made my mind up to keep my baby, that they would have supported me. I just didn't give them the choice to help me heal from my loss. I kept it all inside, and all I had done was hurt myself more and the people I loved.

"I love Gray," I whispered into Ava's shoulder.

Her snort of derision was loud in my ear. "Duh, really? I never would have guessed."

"He loves me," I said to her as I stood straighter.

Ava squinted at me as she looked me over. "Is this a newsflash to you?" she asked me curiously. "'Cause the whole damn world can see that the guy adores you. I mean, he doesn't hide it."

"But Ash..."

Ava nodded thoughtfully before she looked at me and the wine glasses. "I think he knew. I never understood the animosity towards you, and it felt off. It was more like a disgruntled friend than an ex, if you know what I mean?"

"I didn't physically cheat on him," I blurted out. I needed her to know that. "But I would have had Gray said yes. And I know that makes me a horrible bitch, and I understand if you judge me. I judge myself every day."

Ava picked up the two wine glasses before she placed them down again and, opening the fridge, pulled out a bottle of wine, which she handed to me. "Snacks?"

"Top cupboard."

As I watched her stretch for the chips, I stepped up behind her and took them off the shelf for her.

"Thanks." She grinned, and then picking up the chips and the two glasses, she looked at me. "Lead the way," she said with a smile. "We have the wine, the snacks, and you need to purge your soul."

"Purge my soul?" I asked as I started to leave the kitchen.

"Yup, get it all out. Every bit of angst and drama and Devils needs to come out. I'm here for it. I think we may need more wine, but fuck it, I can always make Jett run out and get some."

She was so refreshingly honest and uncensored that despite the awful day, I laughed. "I've never purged my soul before," I told her as we headed to my bedroom. "It sounds painful."

"Oh, it totally is. I hope you have tissues; we're going to cry a shitload of tears."

Pausing, I looked back at her, and she half shrugged. "I'm just being honest. If you don't cry it out, you're not doing it right."

As I climbed the stairs, I thought about it. "You're odd," I told her offhandedly.

"Says the girl who only eats things in twos and hates green Skittles," Ava mocked behind me, and the ridiculousness of her statement had me chuckling as I entered my bedroom.

We spent the next few hours just talking, crying and drinking wine. A lot of wine. Anne made us sandwiches and sat with us for a while as we talked. Well, I talked. It was nice, and Ava was right, I felt lighter after it.

I didn't tell them what the guys had been doing for the past year. I trusted Ava, but I thought the fewer who knew about their revenge plan, the better for everyone. Selfishly, I think I would have preferred not knowing. I can't say I blamed them, and the more I mused on it, the more the burning rage within me began to grow.

Gray was right. They were all right. The agency couldn't get away with this. I had been lucky in my escape, and just that thought alone made me realise how fucked up everything was that I considered myself lucky to have escaped them, considering what it had cost me to do so.

Jumping to my feet, I staggered slightly. Ava was dozing on my bed, and Anne had long since left us. I hadn't a clue what time it was, but I needed to see him. I needed to tell them I was all in.

Running down the stairs, I ran to their house, my desire to let them know I was no longer hiding burning within me. Seeing the back lights still on, I headed to the kitchen and burst through the patio doors like a woman possessed. Gray was on his feet instantly, and I didn't even register the full table of occupants.

"Jett!" I called out, and Jett was suddenly beside his brother. "You're right—you're absolutely right—I need to tell you everything. We have to stop them."

"We will," Jett said as he walked around the table to meet me. "You okay?"

"Yes. I've plurged my soul."

I saw him glance to his side, and then I saw him fully. *Gray*. He was grinning at me as he walked towards me. Lord, he was hot. "Are you drunk, Queeny?" he teased me as I reached out to him eagerly, stumbling a little as I did so.

"I think I am." I nodded emphatically. "We have to stop them, Gray." I wrapped my arms around him and looked up at him, my eyes wide.

"I know." He dropped a kiss on my nose and then turned to the others in the room. "I think I may need to take her home."

Looking around, I saw them all. Kerr, Kage, Jett, Ash, and Onyx.

Onyx.

"Why do you hate me so much?" I blurted to him, and I saw him assess me before he dismissed me. "No." Pushing away from Gray, I marched to the table and poked him in the chest. "You're always such a prick to me, why? I did nothing to you, ever."

"I don't like you, it's that simple." Onyx leaned back out of my touch, and I wasn't having it.

"But why?" I staggered a little as I stood straighter, but I wasn't willing to let it go. "You have no reason to be such a complete dick to me."

"Okay." He shrugged, and I narrowed my eyes at him, or at least I think I did.

"You're a dick."

"You're a bitch."

"I am a bitch," I agreed as I nodded. "But that's no reason to hate me."

I heard the muffled snickers, and I looked around the room. Kerr and Kage were watching me, both trying to hide their amusement. "Oh, I forgot you were here."

"Thanks," Kerr said dryly.

A warm hand tugged at mine, and I turned to look at Gray. He was so beautiful, my hand reached out to touch his face. "Hey," I said quietly.

"Hey." He tucked my hair behind my ear and pulled me closer. "Do you know you're in your jammies?"

Looking down, I saw my sleep shorts and camisole top. Oh. "Um...no." Looking up at him, I bit my lip. "We had wine."

"You don't say," he laughed. "C'mon, little lush, let's take you home."

"Jett!" I called out, my hand reaching out for him. "You have to let me help."

He nodded, but even in my confused state, I saw him glance at his dad. "Oh shit, um, I mean with an English paper."

Ash snorted, and I looked at him as he rubbed his forehead. "Good thing they already know."

"Oh." That wasn't good, was it? "Oh...um."

"Please stop talking," Gray urged me as he pulled me to the patio doors.

"Okay," I mumbled as he led me outside. When we were around the side of his house, I pulled him to a stop. "Hey, do you remember the night we had sex here?"

He turned back to look at me, and I saw the sudden hunger in his eyes. "I do, you scratched the fuck out of my back."

Pulling him towards me, I leaned against the wall, the stone hard on my bare back. "You held your hand over my mouth the whole time to stop me from screaming." I tried to sound sexy and husky, but I wasn't sure it worked, because Gray was grinning widely at me.

"Queeny, are you trying to seduce me?" he teased.

Was I? Damn right I was. "Is it working?"

"No, babe." He chuckled as he took my hand and pulled me off the wall.

"Why not?" I heard the whine in my voice and flinched at how needy I sounded.

"Because you're wearing your PJ's, you're freezing, you have no shoes on, and most importantly, you're shitfaced drunk."

I considered his words as I followed him back to my house. "Which one is the turnoff?"

Gray laughed in the dark, a loud unrestrained burst of laughter. "It's a toss-up between you turning blue and being too drunk to know what you're doing. I prefer you sober."

"Huh, not many people can say that," I muttered as I entered my kitchen. I went willingly into his arms when he pulled me close.

"Are you okay?" he asked me as he wrapped his arms around me.

"No," I answered as I looked up at him. "But I think I will be."

"I'm here with you. I'm going nowhere."

"You've always been here." It was true; I may have had more wine than I intended, but it was true, and I knew he could hear the truth in my words.

"I really wish you were sober right now," Gray groaned as he pulled me into his embrace quickly before pushing me away. With no effort, he picked me up bridal style and carried me to my bedroom.

Ava was sound asleep on one side of my bed, and I heard Gray's huff of amusement as he took in the disarray in my bedroom. The empty wine bottles, the glasses and the dirty plates.

"Jesus, you girls don't mess around," he commented as he dropped me gently onto my bed. "Go to sleep, I'll see you in the morning."

"Stay?"

"Your dad's already close to killing me; let's not sign my death warrant."

"Daddy will be fine. He knows how much I love you."

Gray's breath caught, and then he looked at me so fiercely I thought I had said the wrong thing. "You don't get to say that to me drunk. Tell me tomorrow when you're sober."

"It won't change," I promised.

"It better not."

He kissed me swiftly, and then he was gone.

Sighing, I turned onto my side and faced Ava, who was looking back at me. "You did the drunk emotional feelings thing," she said with a heavy sigh.

"I did." I nodded as I placed my hands under my head.

"You're not so scary after all," she muttered.

"Not even a little bit," I agreed.

"Still weird."

"You're weirder."

We fell asleep grinning at each other like idiots.

CHAPTER 24

Quinn

Why did I drink all the wine? Wine was evil. Wine took up residence in your head and plagued you for days.

Nursing my coffee, I glared at Ava, who was bright-eyed, bushy-freaking-tailed, and full of the joys of life. Did Jett really love her, or would he forgive me if I accidentally stabbed her cheery little face?

"You thinking about stabbing me?" Ava asked me shrewdly.

"How did you guess?" I asked her, a little startled I had been so transparent.

"Mia looks at me the same way," she told me with a grin. "I can't help it, I don't get hangovers. Well, I've only ever had *one* hangover."

"Pretend," I groused as I stood and made my way to the coffee pot. "Good friends pretend."

"Okay," she groaned theatrically, and it was so loud I reconsidered strangling her.

"Go away, go find Jett, distract him," I ordered her as I took my mug and opened the back door. I needed fresh air.

"Will I send Gray over?" Ava asked as she happily bounded past me.

"No, he's probably still sleeping."

Ava hesitated and then was happily rushing off to the Santo house to see Jett. I welcomed the peace as I closed my eyes and tilted my head up to the cloudy sky. I think I dozed, because I startled when a cool hand removed the coffee mug from my hand. Opening my eyes, I stared into light blue ones, and I smiled as I reached out for him.

"Hey," I greeted.

"Hangover?"

"So bad," I admitted as Gray lifted me out of my seat and then sat down with me in his lap.

"Your hand's never going to heal," I told him as I curled up into his chest.

"The splint works wonders, and I think I'm resigned to knowing we won't win the championship, so I have the time to heal."

"You've written the team off because you can't play?" I asked him incredulously.

"Nah, not just me. Ash and Jett missed practice, Jett's hurt his shoulder, Coach is going to have to play Kowoski, we have 'Bama again soon. Our focus has slipped."

"That's my fault."

He tightened his grip on me, and I took the comfort he offered. "No, it isn't. We were already distracted, but it was our choice to find who did this to you."

"But to miss the games..." I protested.

"My hand is my fault. I went after Harry, I did this to myself. Not you."

"But Jett."

"Hit Onyx all on his own. Jett knocked him out, Onyx went for a swim unconscious, and we all have bruises from yesterday."

I lifted my head off his chest to look at him. "These are flimsy excuses," I told him.

"Doesn't make them any less true." He kissed the top of my nose, and I smiled at him. "You have something to say to me, Queeny?"

My smile grew wider, and I shook my head. "Nope, don't think so." I settled against his chest, and I felt his rumble of disapproval.

"Quinn," Gray warned.

"Gray," I mocked him as I ran my fingers over his splint.

"Tell me," he ordered as he pushed me away from his chest to sit upright.

Shifting in his lap, I was now higher than him, and looking down on him made me feel bold. "Would you prefer I was taller?"

Gray blinked and then frowned. "Are you still drunk?"

"No," I laughed, but my stomach churned and my laugh turned into a groan. "I wanted so bad when I was younger to be at least six feet so I could be the same height as you, but I stopped growing at five ten and got boobs and an ass instead."

Gray squeezed my ass as he grinned. "I for one am very grateful for your boobs and ass," he teased. "Plus, I'm six one—that extra inch is very important." His good hand caught the back of my neck as he pulled me to his lips. "You like my inches," he murmured against my lips.

"I love your inches, all of them," I whispered as I watched his eyes widen. "I love you."

He kissed me slowly. His mouth moving over mine with unhurried urgency, yet I still felt his wild need barely contained within his kiss. His tongue stroked mine as he claimed my mouth, branding me forever with the slow, steady kiss that left my knees weak, my heart racing and me utterly compliant in his arms.

My knees adjusted, and I was straddling him on the patio chair, my ass rocking gently into his hard length that lay solid between us.

"Shit, we need to stop," Gray said as he pulled away. "The Admiral sees this, he'll cut my balls off."

Dipping my head to his neck, I lightly nibbled on his ear. "The Admiral and Anne left this morning to go to the store. It's just you and me."

Gray tugged my head back with his fist wrapped in my hair. "Serious?"

"Deadly."

I cried out in alarm when he rose, lifting me with his good arm, and carried me into the house. I contented myself with nuzzling on his neck as he took me to my bedroom and dropped me to my feet as he turned and locked the door.

Pulling his clothes off, he nodded towards the bed. "Strip."

I was only too happy to do so, my sweater and leggings coming off quickly, and I squealed when I felt his hand smack my ass before he pulled my panties down.

"On your back," Gray ordered as he pushed me lightly backwards. I did as he instructed, and then his strong forearms were holding him up before he crawled up the bed to meet me. Dipping his head, he looked down at my breasts before his head dropped and he captured a swollen peak in his mouth.

He licked and sucked my breasts until I was squirming for more. My hand trailed down to the apex of my thighs, and I slowly rubbed myself.

"No," Gray growled. "Mine." His hand pushed mine up the bed, and then he had both my wrists in one hand as he kneeled over me and glared at his splint.

"Don't!" I warned as I guessed he was going to take it off. "You'll make it worse."

"Promise you'll leave both hands here," Gray asked me.

"Why?"

"Say it."

His words were so heavy with desire and his eyes clouded with lust, he was simply too gorgeous to deny. I nodded silently, and he closed his eyes briefly before he trailed his hand over my body, playing with my breasts until he sat back and watched his hand slip between my thighs. Deft fingers stroked me, and I closed my eyes in pleasure.

"You're soaked," Gray murmured as he brought his fingers to his lips, sucking my wetness from them. "So fucking sweet," he muttered as he bent down and pushed my legs apart wider before he took a long slow lick of my pussy. "How long they away for?"

My mind stuttered on the question until I realised he meant dad and Anne. "Um, an hour, maybe."

"I don't have the time I need," he told me as he licked again. "I want to eat this pussy for a lot longer," he said as he licked again. "All fucking day." His mouth moved over me urgently, and I cried out as his tongue centred on the small bundle of nerves, my back arching in pleasure as he sucked lightly. I felt his fingers enter me, and my hands curled into his hair as I urged him on.

His mouth was incredible. He had always excelled at this skill, but this morning, he was making my body sing for him. Parting my legs further, I forced his head in deeper; I needed everything. I was so close I was going to explode. My hips were moving in frantic rhythm with his tongue, and I thanked the heavens we were alone because the noises coming from my mouth were almost inhuman.

"Jesus fucking Christ, Gray, don't stop, please God, don't stop," I begged him as his teeth grazed over me, and I lost it. My entire core detonated, and I was smothered by the tsunami of pleasure that washed over me. As awareness trickled back, I felt fingers trailing over my clit gently, and I moaned at the touch before I felt him press against my entrance.

Steadily he slid inside me, and I moaned again as he stretched me, pushing his way inside as my quivering oversensitive body yielded to him.

"You feel so good," Gray mumbled as he started to thrust into me.

"You feel amazing," I groaned as my hands blindly reached for him. "I can't think, you feel so fucking *good*." My hips rolled in rhythm with his, and all I could focus on was the euphoria coursing through me as he moved inside me. His lips were everywhere, covering my body with kisses, as his good hand cupped my ass.

"Roll over," he ordered as he withdrew, and I whimpered at the loss of him filling me as I eagerly flipped onto my stomach, lifting my ass into the air.

His tongue and lips were back at my core, and my head was on the bedspread as my hands curled into fists on either side of my head. As his tongue flicked over my clit, I almost sobbed with need when his fingers started thrusting in and out of me. Soon I was screaming my release into the pillow, and then he was inside me again, his hips slamming against my ass, his hand between my shoulder blades, holding me flat.

I felt the coarse texture of his splint as it rested on the small of my back.

"More," Gray growled as his hand moved and tangled in my hair, pulling me back, my back arching with need as he continued to move relentlessly inside me.

I came again, and I heard his rumble of approval before he picked up his speed.

"I'm gonna come," Gray announced tightly. "Fuck, baby, I'm gonna come." I felt him leave me, and then I felt him empty himself on my ass, rubbing the head of his dick against me as he groaned his release.

Slumping down onto the bed, I moaned in exhaustion. Jesus, that had been intense. My eyes opened when I felt him leave the bed, but he was back moments later with a warm cloth as he cleaned my back.

"Thanks," I mumbled tiredly.

"I didn't have a rubber, sorry." I felt the soft kiss between my shoulders, and then Gray was lying beside me. I opened my eyes and took in his dishevelled hair, the light sheen of sweat on his body, and I met his gaze with a smile.

"I love you," I told him simply. "That was amazing."

"Hangover gone?" he asked as he grabbed my hand and kissed my fingertips.

"I had a hangover?" I answered back with a small grin.

"This splint needs to go so I can fuck you properly."

My eyes widened slightly in alarm. "I think you're doing fine, better than fine."

Gray grinned, but I still saw his frown as he looked at his hand.

"Being out for the season sucks," I told him quietly. "Don't put on a brave front. I know this is my fault, and I'm sorry. I know you're not blaming me, but you need to. I did this, and I'm sorry."

"I would break every bone in my body if it meant protecting you, Quinn."

I felt the tears well up, and I was pissed at myself. I missed the days when I didn't cry; this slushy, squishy girl wasn't me. "I think that's the most amazing thing anyone's ever said to me, and also the most profoundly terrifying, because I believe you."

Gray shrugged as he closed his eyes. "I love you. I've always loved you. You were mine the day you jumped into that pool, you were mine when I kissed you in the kitchen for the first time, you were mine when you gave my cousin your virginity, you were mine when you begged me to touch you, you were mine the night I told you I loved you and you turned me away. Now that I know why you did it, it hurts less, but even that…it doesn't change the simple fact that you belong to me, and I'm yours. Even when you chose others over me, I am and always have been yours. Just as you are mine."

"Gray..."

"It's okay. I knew you would come to your senses eventually."

Rising up on my elbows, I looked at him as I wiped away the tears. "I don't deserve you."

Gray huffed out a laugh as he opened one eye to look at me. "I know, I'm a moody, angry bastard. I won't apologise." His hand tugged me to him, and I fell ungracefully onto his chest as his good arm wrapped around me. "Football, you, family. That's all that matters."

"In that order?" I teased.

He kissed my forehead as he looked at the ceiling. "No, you first."

Football was everything to Gray, more so probably than it was to Jett, and I didn't think people realised that. "Football first," I corrected.

"Football is going to be a few years of my life, Quinn," Gray corrected. "You're forever."

I was going to burst into tears—he couldn't say this to me without me bawling my eyes out. Knowing that, I hid my face in his shoulder as he stroked my back softly. "I don't deserve that," I mumbled into his skin. "But I promise that I will."

I felt him kiss my hair, and we lay like that for a while longer.

"Quinn, you here? We're home," Anne called up the stairs.

"Shit!" Diving off the bed, I scrambled for my clothes as Gray lay naked on my bed, laughing at me.

"Do you want him to kill you for definite?" I whispered furiously as I pulled on my leggings and then shoved them off as I searched for my panties. "Where's my panties?"

Gray guffawed loudly as he swung his legs over the bed. "I'm going for a shower," he said casually as I paused to watch his naked ass as he headed to the shower. "Coming?" he asked me over his shoulder.

"My dad is downstairs!"

"That a no?"

"You're impossible," I hissed at him as I pulled my sweater on. "He's going to *know*, Gray."

"I never, ever thought he was stupid." With a cocky grin, he closed the bathroom door, and I heard the water running. The door popped open again, and Gray looked me over. "Your sweater's on backwards," he told me calmly, and I stared at him wordlessly. My bedroom door was knocked, and I jumped at the sound.

"Quinn, we're making lunch. Does Gray want anything?" Anne asked me from the other side of the door.

Gray winked as he laughed at me and closed the door again.

Well, this wasn't going to be awkward at all.

CHAPTER 25

Gray

Heading back to school, I kept my hand tightly wrapped in Quinn's. She was staring out the window as Jett drove us back, Ava in the front seat talking to Jett about something. I wasn't paying attention to what she was saying. Even as I faced forward, my awareness was all on Quinn beside me.

My feelings towards Ava had softened slightly, as she had been welcome support for Quinn these last few days. When she had offered to leave the room so we could all talk, my regard for her had risen as she openly showed respect for my family. For Quinn. She wasn't eager to stay and learn the gory details; she had offered to give us, my family, privacy.

I had no doubt my girl was going to be including Ava in all her plans from now on. Yeah, Quinn was cool towards most people because she was loyal to us and, as a result, she showed more wariness of outsiders than the rest of us. She knew people had an agenda, and she made it perfectly clear she was not their way in. But Ava? Ava had gotten past her walls, and I guessed she had a strong permanence in Quinn's life now.

Which was nice. I guess.

Or until Jett dumped her. Or she dumped him. But until then, it worked, and maybe they would surprise me and stick—stranger things had happened.

My brother's stare caught mine in the rearview, and I saw the eyebrow lift in question. We were twins, but sometimes I forgot how in tune we were. He knew exactly what I had been thinking about his girl. I gave him an eye roll in return, and he snorted out a laugh, which caused Ava to pause in her one-sided conversation and stare at him in question.

"What did I say that was funny?" she asked self-consciously.

"It was me," I jumped in before Jett had to think on his feet. "I was pulling faces at him."

Ava had turned to look at me when I spoke, and I saw her expression change as I told her. "Oh, okay." She turned back to face forward, and once again my brother's demanding glare in the rearview had me biting back a sigh.

"It wasn't about you," I told her. "I was thinking about this weekend, and because my brother is my twin, he knew where my thoughts were."

"Were you thinking about me?" Quinn teased as she suddenly focused back in the car.

"No, don't flatter yourself," I chided her as I squeezed her hand to show I was joking. "I was thinking about Ash."

Which was partly true. I had been thinking about my cousin, but Ava's incessant chatter had interrupted me.

"Ash?" Jett's glance flicked to Quinn and then back to me.

"He'll be playing this weekend, without me and you on the team. Coach is going to move him to a more defensive role to protect Kowoski in the pocket. He isn't going to be happy."

Jett nodded in agreement, and I saw Quinn's head dip in guilt.

"Why did you think jumping into a netted pool was a good idea?" Ava chastised Jett. "Gray was already in there. Why did everyone have to potentially drown?"

"Because both my brothers drowning wasn't an option," Jett replied with a sideways glance at her.

"Pft, I don't think anyone would have minded if Onyx drowned," Ava muttered as she turned to look at Quinn. "Am I wrong?"

Quinn smirked as she looked first at Ava and then Jett. "I'm not sure I can argue with that," she said with a fist bump to Ava.

So Ava was also loyal, to Quinn. I liked that.

"He's just protective," Jett muttered as he drove. "He sees you as a threat. He eliminates threats."

Turning my head, I looked out at the passing scenery. That was true, Onyx was fiercely protective. He made me look sloppy in comparison. He had always known how I felt, and he had known how much it pissed me off when Quinn went out with Ash. His fear that she would be the cause of disharmony between the three of us may have been correct, if I wasn't who I was and Ash wasn't who he was.

I knew Quinn and Ash would be temporary. I knew because watching them for five months was like watching them for five years, and I knew I wouldn't have lasted any longer had she not undressed that night and asked me to touch her. The moment I knew for certain that I was who she actually wanted, I had acted.

Yes, I could have done it better. Our first time together shouldn't have been in a bathroom on a sink. We both had made mistakes. We weren't perfect.

My cousin was a big boy, he could look after himself. His hands may not have wandered when they were together, but his eyes had. He had flirted and teased, and I'd caught him more than once whispering to a girl who was pressed far too close up against him.

The fact he had fucked almost the entire senior year hadn't surprised me. She hurt his ego more than his heart. As long as Ash had pussy, he would be fine. If he were honest with himself, and us, he would have admitted he wasn't heartbroken over Quinn. Which is why Onyx's fears had always been unfounded.

Ash didn't love Quinn the way I did, and we both knew it.

However, that didn't mean he would be wanting to go on group dates and hug it out by the campfire. He would need a little bit of time. I was happy to give it to him.

"You're deep in thought," Quinn murmured to me, drawing my attention back to her.

"Thinking," I said as I reached over to tug her closer.

Dad had given us mom's SUV to drive in while my hand was in

a splint. Onyx had wrecked my car, even though he was replacing it, and Jett's pointless R8 was a two-seater only.

Quinn slipped out of her seat belt and moved over beside me. Ignoring Jett's warning to put a seat belt on, she curled up at my side. "What are you thinking about?" she asked as she looked up at me.

As she tilted her head, my lips brushed her ear. "You naked on my dick as I fuck you senseless." My tongue flicked out to lick the soft spot under her ear, and I heard her moan as she shifted in the seat.

"Gray," Quinn protested as she looked quickly to the front where Ava was still talking, and Jett laughed at something she said.

"Do you think they'd notice if I fuck you back here?" I asked as I nuzzled her neck. "If we're really quiet."

"Yes," Quinn gasped as my hand slipped under her ass. It was awkward, but I managed to put my hand right under and cup her pussy as she hastily pulled her sweater down to hide my fingers as I slowly began to rub over her leggings. "You can't do this," Quinn whispered to me as she pulled at my fingertips.

"Already doing it, baby," I said in triumph. Quinn turned her head into my neck, and I raised my head briefly and met Jett's knowing stare in the mirror. Leaning forward, he turned the music up slightly, telling Ava he liked the song playing when she asked him why.

I would have given him a hundred dollars if he knew who was playing right then, but he was doing me a solid, so I let him off. Jett gave me a meaningful look, and I pretended to close my eyes, watching as he reached over and grabbed Ava's hand, placing it on his leg. She turned hurriedly to look back at us, but the way Quinn was hiding her face and I was pretending to be sleeping, she assumed we were both going to sleep and gave him a wicked grin.

I locked eyes with my brother once more, and he gave a slight nod.

With a smile, I closed my eyes properly as my hand moved. I slipped it down the back of Quinn's leggings, under her panties, and then my fingers were stroking through the wetness as she squirmed beside me.

Quinn's lips were on my neck, hidden by her hair, and I continued to finger fuck her as my brother and I pretended that he wasn't getting a hand job from Ava, and I wasn't pleasuring my girl.

When the car jerked to the side a while later, I fought the grin as I opened my eyes a little to see Ava sit back up straight and hurriedly wipe at her mouth.

Lucky bastard, I grumbled internally as I eased my fingers out of Quinn. She was panting into my neck and was red in the face from trying to keep her orgasm quiet.

Straightening my dick in my pants, I sucked my fingers when I noticed Ava staring at me.

"Missed a bit," she said sarcastically.

"You too," I quipped back and laughed out loud when her hand shot to the corner of her mouth to wipe at it.

Yeah, I was liking Ava more. This time when I closed my eyes, it really was to sleep.

"How you doing?" I asked Ash the next morning as we both got breakfast ready in the kitchen.

"I think I slept funny," he grumbled as he rolled his head from side to side.

"You sleep here?" I asked him as I waited for my egg to boil.

"Yeah, eventually." He stretched and his hands touched the ceiling. "Took a detour on the way home," he said with a shrug.

"That what caused the crick in your neck?"

"Nah, she was fine. I think I passed out when I got here." He rubbed his eyes as he pulled his white T-shirt down with his other hand. "It's been a crazy few days."

"It has." I checked the timer and sighed—I had another two minutes. "I should have done this last night," I told him as I walked over to get the avocado.

"I can't believe you eat that." Ash shook his head. "It makes me want to vomit."

"Good thing you aren't eating it then," I said with a laugh. Three times a week, I was to eat crushed avocado on a slice of toasted rye with a boiled egg. I liked it. Jett had almost passed out when I offered it to him, and Ash had backed away as if I had told him eating it would cause leprosy. "What are you making?"

"I get some weird smoothie thing she makes me drink." He shrugged as he pulled it out of the fridge. "She makes it up for me and leaves me it in here. Jett tried it once, barfed, and refuses to drink it."

I had a sneaky suspicion it was because my brother knew what was in it and had never actually tasted it. I said nothing as Ash poured a tumbler of the green gloop. It genuinely couldn't be called anything else.

"When does she make it?" I had been with her all night, inside her for most of it. I had been fucking horny after that car ride. Quinn hadn't left my side once, and I had left her fast asleep around five this morning.

"She made it back at home," Ash said as he took a swig. "I took it with me," he told me.

That made sense. "You okay with, you know, you two?"

"No?" He frowned. "Maybe?" I watched him take another gulp and grimace. "I think she hates me, which is why I have to drink this when you get food, actual food."

Should I have told him he had two thirds of what was on my plate in his drink? Probably not. "She takes her assignments seriously."

"Ha." Ash looked at my plate. "I never thought I'd see the day where I was envious of toast and a boiled egg. Man, I'd kill for a cooked breakfast."

I nodded in agreement as I watched Jett come into the room.

"You can get all the cooked food you want in December," Jett told him as he crossed the living room to the kitchen. "Where is everyone?"

"Practice," I answered as I shelled my egg. "If Jamie was here, he would have poached my egg," I lamented as I scooped up some of the avocado.

"If Jamie were here, he would have made pancakes." Ash tipped his head back and drained his smoothie. "Well, that was disgusting."

Jett grinned as he reached for the cereal.

"You're not supposed to eat that," I warned him.

"Well, I can't cook. And Jamie is the only one who can make the protein pancakes, even if they are revolting and need butter and syrup. It's either this or a breakfast wrap. Which would Quinn rather I have?"

"Cereal," Ash and I said at the same time.

"Exactly." Jett poured too much milk in his bowl. "And if you both agree, how can all three of us be wrong?"

I shared an amused look with my cousin, who lasted a nanosecond before he was pulling the cereal box towards him, while I ate my breakfast and drank my coffee.

"It's a wonder she lets us have caffeine," Ash mumbled around his spoon as he refilled his mug.

"She's ambitious, not suicidal," Jett snorted as he held his mug out for more.

"Speaking of…" I decided to tease Jett. "That was some dodgy driving yesterday."

Jett looked at me with a Cheshire cat grin. "Was it? Didn't hear anyone complaining."

"What happened?" Ash asked curiously as he looked between us.

"Someone got some light hand relief when they were driving," I told him as I bit into my breakfast.

Ash's eyes widened before he grinned. "Ava gave you a hand job? When you were driving?" He turned to look at me. "With you and Queeny in the back?"

"I don't think it was her hand that caught it," I said gleefully as my brother's smile vanished, and he glared at me.

"Fuck off," Ash exclaimed incredulously. "No way!"

"You're a dick," Jett told me as he finished his breakfast. "What are you? Twelve?"

"I can't believe little Ava would be so bold," Ash said as he shook his head in wonder. "I almost want to rib her for it, but she'd more than likely cut my balls off."

I saw my brother beam with pride, and I took another swig of coffee. However, even though Ash and I had been fine, as Ash teased my brother more and Jett had to remain silent on what *I* had been doing—because he was a better brother than I was—I felt Ash and I slowly ease back into our normal relationship.

Later as I was getting ready for class, I didn't appreciate the punch my brother delivered to my kidneys in revenge.

"You asshole," he hissed at me as he looked over his shoulder to ensure he had closed the door. "Low fucking blow, Gray."

"You think?" I groaned as I straightened. "What the fuck?"

"You spoke about Ava like she was some cheap whore," Jett whispered furiously.

"No, I didn't. She isn't, and Ash knows that," I corrected him crossly. "And he also knows had it been someone other than Ava, she'd have been bent over the steering wheel."

"You're unbelievable."

"Thanks, bro." I grinned at him.

When his fist raised to punch me again, I dodged it. "Ava and me in the car *isn't* what you and Ash should be bonding over."

"Ugh, don't be a pussy. It worked, okay? He won't say anything, and neither will she."

He glared at me for several more moments before he shouldered past me and headed into my bathroom. He came back out with a box of condoms.

"You better use these."

"I love you, bro, but guys aren't really my thing, neither is incest."

"With Quinn, you fucking ass."

My smile faded as I regarded him steadily. "You think I don't know the consequences?"

Jett scratched his nose as his feet shifted. "I know, I just don't want her to go through something like this again."

"She won't," I told him firmly. "And if she does, if *we* do, I'll be there every step of the way."

Finally, Jett nodded and tossed the box onto the bed and opened the bedroom door as he turned back to face me. "Just wrap it up, okay? I don't want to be an uncle at twenty." I started to laugh, but it died in my throat as I saw her standing there.

"Seriously?" Quinn's face was pale as she stood there.

"Queeny," Jett gasped as she looked between the two of us before she took a step backwards.

"Fuck you, Jett." Dark chocolate eyes met mine, brimming with accusation. "Fuck you too."

I leapt forward to chase her as she ran down the stairs.

"Quinn!" I yelled as my brother hauled me back. "What?" I snarled at him.

"Shoes." He pointed at my bare feet, and cursing, I pushed past him to grab my sneakers before I was running after her.

CHAPTER 26

Quinn

STRIDING ANGRILY DOWN THE SIDEWALK, I HAD TO STOP MYSELF from running, but there were students out, heading to classes, and I would have brought too much attention to myself.

When I heard his desperate cry behind me, I put power to my pace and speed walked so fast that I probably would have been less noticeable had I run.

A strong hand wrapped around my right arm, and I was being pulled into Gray's embrace. Despite my inner monologue about not wanting to cause a scene, I punched his arm to get away from him. Gray cursed but merely held on tighter, his splint an immovable force on my back pinning me to him.

"Quinn, you need to listen," he began as he ducked the hand that went to slap him. "Baby, calm down. You heard that all out of context, let me explain."

"Fuck you!"

"That can be later. Right now, calm down." His voice was soothing as he walked me backwards, and I glanced around, realising he had manoeuvred us behind a tree. We could still be seen, but we weren't right in front of everyone.

"Fine. Explain." If he gave me room, I would have been able to cross my arms, but he didn't. Gray pressed into me, his splint still at my back, his other hand cupping my face.

"Look at me," he ordered, his voice low and gentle. I refused and kept my eyes trained on the point of his shoulder, focusing on his black T-shirt and hoodie, his standard attire when he wasn't in his jersey. "Babe, look at me." His nose trailed along my jawline, and I felt the press of a soft kiss below my ear.

Gray pulled back to look at me, and my eyes involuntarily darted to his. "What?" I demanded.

"Eyes, Quinn, on me." His hand slid to cup the back of my neck as he tilted my head to look at him. "You know I like to look into your eyes," he whispered as he dropped a chaste kiss on the corner of my mouth.

"I thought that was only when you were physically fucking me, not verbally."

Gray whistled through his teeth as his fingers tightened minutely on the back of my neck. "I love your fire," he breathed into my ear. "Don't fight me, listen to me. Jett was being a dick. I embarrassed him in front of Ash this morning over Ava blowing him on the drive home yesterday. Jett thought he was being smart, reminding me to use a condom with you." He felt me stiffen, and he continued as he looked at me because I had jerked my head in surprise when he said Ava gave Jett a blow job in the car. "He actually was thinking of you. He reminded me about my box and told me he didn't ever want you to go through what you went through again. That last remark that you heard was just shit, he's a shit, we're both shits. He was messing around."

"I don't think it's a laughing matter," I snipped at him as I tried once again to push free of him.

"It isn't, and if you'd heard all of it, we weren't laughing. We lost something too. Fuck, baby, I almost lost you. Don't do this. You know Jett would never let anyone, especially himself, hurt you."

I did know that, but it wasn't that easy. The words had hurt, and yes, maybe I was overly sensitive or maybe I was overly defensive, but either way, I wasn't ready to kiss and make up. "Let me go."

"Quinn." Gray's hand tightened on my neck, and his lips hovered over mine. "No. Not like this."

"Let me go. I'm going to be late for class, and I don't want to be the girl that gets manhandled by a Devil up against a tree on a Tuesday morning," I snarked at him.

His eyes narrowed slightly before he took a step back. "Better?"

"It will be." Without another word, I resumed my walk at a slower pace and ignored the fact I could see Jett in my peripheral as I walked away.

I headed straight for the sports building. I didn't look behind me to see if they followed; I suspected they would, and it pissed me off even more. I was not a fragile damsel in distress.

Okay, I had maybe acted like a fragile damsel in distress, but that didn't mean that I was one.

Dumping my stuff in the locker beside the gyms, I shrugged off my coat and changed my shoes. Retying my ponytail, I took a deep calming breath, picked up my book bag, and headed into class.

There were several tables laid out throughout the room, and I groaned inwardly when I saw Denzel talking to Jada.

Shit. Two people I didn't want to see.

My professor saw me before they did, and I turned to Dimitri. "Morning."

"You look tired," he said immediately. "Are you okay?"

"I'm fine, thanks." I tried for a smile and knew I failed. "Spent too much time on the nutrition spreadsheets."

"It's a good assignment," Dimitri said enthusiastically. "Difficult because the serious athletes already treat their bodies like temples." He jerked his head back to indicate Denzel. "And then others think vegetables on pizza count as your five a day."

My laugh burst out of me before I could stop it, and Dimitri beamed. "That's better," he said fondly. "I thought pop quiz physical-style today."

My laughter turned into a groan. "Why would you lull me into a false sense of security like that? Thinking you were a nice professor?"

"Because I'm evil," he said with a grin. More of my classmates were behind me now, and I turned to share a look of commiseration with a guy in my class. "Did you all hear? Pair up, pick an athlete, we start in five minutes."

"Me and you?" the guy suggested, and I nodded. I didn't mind who I got. "Who we taking?" It was a mix of volleyball and basketball players, and I knew who I didn't want. "The point guard took a fall on Saturday. He's been hiding it, but his ankle's giving him issues."

"Really?" I asked as I started to walk to the poor victim of my morning.

"Yeah, saw it happen, been watching him ever since," my partner said, then hesitated. "I'm not saying I have been, but if someone said *stalker*, I may not be as innocent as I would like to claim."

I grinned at him as we stood in front of the athlete in front of us: six eight and a bad ankle? I flexed my fingers; this was exactly what I needed.

Two hours later, and I was happily finishing a mocha caramel latte as I strolled leisurely to the library. Class had been exactly what my inner peace required. My mind had cleared as I worked on the physio of the Saint this morning. My partner had been knowledgeable, and Dimitri had been completely underwhelmed when we aced his pop quiz.

Now I needed some alone time with my spreadsheets to get my assignment back on track. It's why I had gone to the house this morning. Waking up to find Gray gone and a note telling me he would see me later, reminded me that I hadn't checked their fridges. I'd been away from my project for a few days, and Dimitri's quip about Denzel eating pizza had been my same fear when I woke up this morning.

I hadn't expected to overhear my boyfriend and best friend joking about pregnancies. Gray and I had been careful since we got together. I had condoms at my apartment, and when I was back at home, he had pulled out each time we'd been together. Not ideal, and he had laughed that when the time came for him to reach his orgasm, his body was screaming at him to dig in deep, not pull the other way.

I'd changed from the pill to the shot after the miscarriage, but still, it made me nervous, Gray coming inside me. I hadn't been ill —I hadn't even had a sniff of a cold—but the thought of him being let loose in there made me squirmy.

As I tossed my empty coffee cup into the recycling and entered the library, I realised the idea of it wasn't as abhorrent to me as I thought. Selecting a seat in a reclusive part of the library, I set up, but my mind had one track, and it was the track that led to me and Gray, naked in the bedroom with him coming inside me.

I dropped my head into my hands. *Oh my God, did I have a fetish?*

Gray liked to wrap his hand around my throat; it really got him off. Was my kink him getting off inside me? My other partners had worn condoms, Ash included, but it felt fundamentally wrong for Gray to be covered when he was inside me. I wanted him flesh to flesh, I wanted to feel him spill either inside me or on me.

"Hey, you."

I jerked up in surprise as Ava grinned at me with Mia beside her. Mia snorted at whatever my face said.

"Three guesses for what you were thinking right now!" she teased.

I was so flustered I couldn't even lie. "Um..." Licking my lips, I decided to just own it and gave a half-hearted shrug.

"Nice." Mia high-fived me, and I thought it was slightly odd, but I went with it.

"We saw you come in, but you looked lost in thought," Ava said as she crouched at my one-person table. "You want to be alone, or do you want to sit with us?"

"Alone." Wow, major bitch issues, I chided myself.

"Cool." Ava stood easily and dived into her purse, producing an apple and a protein bar. "I never see you snack, not really. And I know, you're like the guys, your body's a temple, but you need fuel too, okay?"

She was adorably sweet. "Thank you," I told her, and her happy smile was enough to know she knew I meant it.

"We'll be here for about another half hour, then we're going for coffee," Mia said. "Text us if you're coming; otherwise, catch you later?"

"Yeah, I'll catch up after," I assured her.

The two girls said their goodbyes, and I watched them go. Even with the no food policy, I surreptitiously opened the wrapper of the protein bar. My phone vibrated, and I pulled it out of my bag as I chewed.

Gray: **Okay?**

Me: **I guess.**

I thought back to what I had been thinking of before Ava and Mia interrupted my thoughts. Immediately I was squirming again. Is this what animals felt like when they were in heat? This was ridiculous.

Gray: **He never meant it the way you took it, we wouldn't. Ever**

I remembered the way he held me and the sure confident touch of his fingers as he took ownership of me.

Ownership of me? The startling realisation that I wanted to be dominated by Gray was almost as alarming as the fetish thought. Maybe I'd drunk something weird? Maybe I was having an allergic reaction to something. One that made you hot and horny and think delirious thoughts.

Gray: **Why are you so quiet?**

If only you knew. I couldn't possibly answer him. He'd either run very fast away or, knowing Gray, would spread me wide on the library table and fuck me. I groaned when my pulse raced at the thought. On what planet, in what universe, do you decide on a Tuesday morning that you're so deliciously wicked?

Gray: **Quinn?**

I stared at the phone for a long time, drawing my bottom lip between my teeth. I pulled my teeth over it time and again as I stared at my messages.

Me: **I think I'm due my period**

Random, but then I realised that's what was wrong with me. I should have known as soon as my brain said *animal* and *heat*.

Gray: **Aren't you on the shot? Do you need painkillers?**

Good grief. Not only was he listening, he was sensitive too. Could he be any more perfect?

I didn't answer, and then he was phoning me. Looking around, I saw no one and slipped the phone to my ear.

"I'm in the library," I whispered.

"Oh. You okay? Do you need anything?"

"No," I said as I swallowed, and the itch that I needed scratching ramped up as he spoke to me, his voice low. My sigh of want was too loud.

"You sure you don't need anything?"

"I need *something*." My eyes squeezed shut at saying that out loud. I heard Gray's sharp intake of breath.

"Quinn?"

To hell with it. "Yesterday, you said I couldn't. Can I...can I do it now?" My foot was tapping off the floor as I waited for the answer, praying he would know what I was talking about.

I heard movement, and then I heard his voice, low and tight. "Baby? Are you asking for permission?"

"I might be," I said as I tilted my head back to look at the ceiling tiles, my whole body strumming with anticipation.

"Ask me."

My stomach flipped as I chewed my bottom lip like a crack addict jonesing for their next fix. "Gray," I whispered.

"Say it."

"Can I?"

"Can you what?" His voice sounded strained, thick with lust.

I looked around me. There was no one there. "Can I touch myself?" I asked him, my voice almost inaudible.

His breath caught, and I knew exactly how he would look, eyes heavy with desire, his cheeks would be sucked in as he looked at me, making him look angry, fierce, *masterful.*

"No."

My whole body deflated at the word; I could feel the gnawing in my gut intensify. "*Why?*" I actually flinched at the neediness in my voice.

"Only *I* get to touch you."

I wanted to hang up on him. I wanted to shove my hand down my pants and find my release while he listened. I realised in a certain foggy part of my brain I was acting irrationally; the rest of my brain didn't care.

Packing my stuff, I kept him on the phone. "Fine, I'm on the third floor of the library, and I'm heading to the disabled bathroom. If you're not here within ten minutes, I don't care what you say, I'm doing it whether you say I can or not."

He was there in seven minutes.

CHAPTER 27
Gray

WE WERE PARKED UP FROM THE HOUSE, IN A BLACK SEDAN THAT JETT had borrowed from one of our teammates. We'd put fake plates on the back of it, more paranoid than ever that we were going to fuck up.

When my dad had grilled us all at the house after the fighting and the craziness, dad had quite vehemently demanded we stop looking into the agency.

I wanted to say that our fathers knew better than to expect us to listen. Because not only did they have us to parent, but Onyx was also now involved too. Despite Jett trying to break his head open earlier and me having punched him several times, again, our older brother was still very much as committed to finding the bastards as we were.

Dad had asked Onyx what he had done with Harry. Onyx had merely drunk his whisky and returned dad's glare. He was twenty-five, he had his trust fund, and more importantly, he didn't need it. Onyx had his own money. There was little my dad could actually threaten Onyx with to make him stay in line.

For which I was very grateful.

When my brother left later that night, he had asked me to walk out with him. Surprised at the request, since my fist was the reason that his jaw was bruised and his eye was black, I had gone with him as he waited for his car.

"I got as much as I could out of your doctor," he told me quietly as he lit up his smoke in the dark of the night. "I'm making enquiries." He took a drag as he held his hand up to shut me up. "I really don't like your little queen, but you all seem to love her. You genuinely seem to be besotted with her, and it annoys me."

"Why?"

"I thought once you had her, you would move on. If anything, it's made you worse."

"Because I love her," I told him.

"Yes, seems to be. Pity." Onyx blew a smoke circle. "Anyway, the people I handed your good doctor over to were a tad careless with his well-being."

I had snorted in disgust at the word good, *but my breath faltered. "Dead?"*

"Yeah, as I said, careless really." Onyx shrugged. "What he gave me, I'm looking into. Anything I find, I'll share, but, Gray"—my brother's dark gaze met mine as his car approached, illuminating his face—"you do nothing more. I will keep you informed. Dad and Kage will try to do it legally, but that's too much red tape for me. You do nothing, my little brothers, my football stars, who have their whole future ahead of them, you do nothing. *Do you understand?"*

I wet my lips as I assessed my older brother. I nodded once to say I understood what he was saying. Satisfied, Onyx hugged me briefly, and then his car was taking him back to Nashville.

When I turned, Jett was in the shadows. "You understood, but you didn't agree."

"Glad you understand the importance of technicalities, brother." I fist bumped him as we headed back into the house.

Now we were back at house number three. The guy who liked to sleep around with men in his wife's absence. Unfortunately for us, she was at home. We weren't sure if he was.

"You sure it was him in the basement?" Ash asked as he sat in the back seat.

"Yeah, would recognise him anywhere."

"What else is there to find?" Ash asked quietly. "We can't jump him. His wife is there. We can't kidnap him; we already have one on our hands. We have the memory stick."

Jett and I exchanged a look. "We're not looking for more on Quinn, we're looking for more on *him*," Jett explained. "We need to know who the guy in the bed was. He may be another one of them."

"Or he's some John who gets paid to be fucked in the ass," Ash said crudely.

"He didn't sound like a professional," Jett murmured. "He sounded like they had a relationship."

"Yeah." I nodded in agreement.

"We're not breaking in," Jett reminded him. "Just watching."

"I know," Ash grumbled from his position. "The Mrs is in. It's unlikely we see anything tonight."

"That's true," I said, turning to Jett. "What do you want to do?"

"I want to be clever enough to know how to track people's cars." Jett turned to look at Ash. "How do you know all your geek stuff but don't know this?"

"I do know, I just don't want to go to prison," he snapped back.

"Bet Onyx knows," I said wistfully.

"Your brother is probably glued to the underside of the car like a stuntman in a *Mission Impossible* film as we speak," Ash joked, and Jett grinned.

"You're right, this is pointless, and we look suspicious. Let's go." He started the car, and we drove off. As we left, I noticed the car coming towards us, and I instinctively pulled my bandana up. "Cover now," I demanded as the car approaching slowed down. I kept my face averted so they couldn't see me, but as they passed, I yelled at Ash to take the plate.

"Speed up, slowly," I demanded of Jett. "Don't make it look suspicious."

Jett did as he was told until we were back on the interstate, and I told him to floor it. "You get the plate?" I asked Ash, and he held up his phone to show me.

"Who was it?" Jett asked me as he drove.

"I'm not sure. It just felt wrong."

He glanced at me before he turned to face the road again. "Okay, we'll check it out."

The drive home was quiet, and we cleaned the car, changed the plate back, and climbed the stairs to our rooms all in silence. Jamie, the team's defensive end, opened his door.

"Where you been?" he asked as he leaned casually against it.

"Out," Jett told him curtly.

"Mayhem?"

Ash and I exchanged a look but said nothing. We hadn't done mayhem in a while; were people now requesting it?

"Maybe," Jett answered as he measured Jamie. "Why?"

"I'm a footballer, I've got your back, and when you cause mayhem, you pull extra guys in with you." Jamie stared at us.

"You want to be a Devil?" Ash asked him, and I knew his tone mirrored my own shock.

"Yeah, why not?"

"Because you're...you," I blurted. "You're so...straightlaced."

"Nothing you do is illegal though," Jamie countered.

If he had seen what we'd been doing earlier, he wouldn't be so quick to think that.

"You just cause mischief," he added lamely.

"Is he quoting the wizard prick?" Ash asked in a low voice.

"Dude, did you just compare us to Potter?" Jett asked with a wide grin. "Think we got a chocolate frog for you?"

"You guys are dicks." Jamie shut his door in our faces as we headed up the stairs to our rooms, our moods considerably lighter.

We gathered in Jett's room because it was always the cleanest. He was obsessive. I had a tidy room, but not like Jett's, and Ash...well, if you were looking for tumblers or plates, they'd be in Ash's room.

"He's right," Ash mused as he flopped onto Jett's made bed. "We haven't done proper mayhem for months."

"True," I agreed as I kicked off my boots. "Two parties and the parking lot was dull. We need to juice it up."

"What do you suggest?" Jett asked as he sat on his couch, his phone already in his hand no doubt texting Ava.

"Lift and drop."

I looked appreciatively at Ash, who was propped up on his elbows. "Cars?"

"Yeah." Ash grinned. "At least six."

"Six needs more than us," Jett reminded him.

"We have Queeny."

"Not on a lift and drop," I said firmly. "We'll get her to tag the library." I smiled at the thought of earlier this week when she had asked me if she could touch herself. I'd never been so hard so quick. The disabled bathroom wouldn't have been my choice, but we did seem to have a thing for explosive sex in bathrooms.

When she whispered her need to me, I had almost unloaded in my pants. I looked at my cousin. She wouldn't have been like this with him. It really fucking bothered me sometimes that he had been her first, taking that from me. But I had to remind myself that I was her forever.

Her newfound confidence for dirty talk may be my undoing, but I was willing to power through, for her.

"Ben?" Jett suggested.

"Yeah, he's handy." I nodded in agreement. "We need something else. Something…memorable."

Ash grinned at me, and I shook my head in rejection. "Dude, really? In November?"

"It's my favourite time of year," he said as he lay back down again. "All those databases wiped clean... I'm channelling my favourite film."

Jett threw his head back and laughed as he bounced to his feet. "I know whose car I'm doing, you?"

I didn't like the way a certain professor was so "friendly" to my girl. "Yeah, I have mine."

Quickly we made a list of the professors' cars we would take. It was simple. You lifted the car from where they had parked it and dropped it off somewhere else. It was an inconvenience to them, our classmates got free classes, and no harm was done. Ash was going to wipe the school records for the semester. That was perhaps more harmful, but it was mayhem.

He'd been wanting to do it since high school, and we had told him to save it. Now it seemed like sophomore year was the year to let him loose. He would back the records up, and after the initial hysteria had settled, he would re-wipe everything and put it back the way it was…with some alterations, but they would be so minute, they wouldn't be detected.

"I'm going to bed," Ash told us after we had hatched our plan.

"I'm going to phone Ava," Jett said as he stood with a yawn.

I said goodnight and headed to bed myself. Staring at the empty bed, I hesitated. I wanted my girl.

After a light tap on my brother's door, he opened it, in his boxers and the phone to his ear. He merely grunted when he saw me still dressed, and I headed down the stairs and out of the house as I made my way to Quinn's.

She was still up, because her light was still on, and I texted her to let her know I was outside. She answered the door with her hair in a pile on her head, looking like a bird's nest. Her tank top was tight and displayed her braless breasts. Her PJ bottoms were a soft grey and hung loose. The strip of skin between her tank and her PJ bottoms had my entire focus while she backed into her living room as I closed and locked the door behind me.

"You look good."

"I look like I've been studying all night and haven't showered since this morning," Quinn objected as she resumed her position on the couch, her textbooks around her.

"How long you need?" I asked, looking at her books.

"Ten, maybe fifteen?" she answered as she looked up at me. "You staying?"

"Yeah, I thought I would." I leaned over and kissed her upturned face. "That okay?"

Quinn smiled against my lips. "Yeah, but you need to let me finish."

"I always let you finish," I said as I pushed off her.

"That's such a dick thing to say," she laughed as she turned her attention back to her books. "And don't even make a dick joke," she warned.

"I never joke about my dick," I replied as I headed to her bedroom. "I'll be in here."

After a minute, I heard her groan in frustration. "I can't concentrate knowing you're in my bed, naked!" she called through to me.

"Okay, pretend I'm fully clothed," I called back as I got into bed.

"Are you naked?"

"No."

"Honest?"

"Never."

"Gray!"

"Quinn!"

"I hate you," she mumbled grumpily.

"Liar," I teased back and heard her happy chuckle as she went back to studying.

Closing my eyes, I smiled to myself as I listened to her make her notes and then pack her stuff away.

She climbed into bed beside me after she'd been to the bathroom and done her nightly routine. "Don't freak out," she said as she tucked herself under my arm.

"Okay." I opened one eye and looked at her waiting.

"I bought you a toothbrush." Quinn looked nervous. "It's not that big a deal."

"Why are you being defensive?" I said as I moved my head to look at her. "It's a toothbrush, thanks. I was fed up using yours."

"You can't use mine!" Quinn pushed off my chest in shock. "Were you using mine?"

"Why is this a big deal?" I asked her with a laugh.

"Because it's gross," she protested.

"Quinn, I've had my mouth on every part of your body, and I've swapped enough body fluids with you until you've practically dehydrated me. I've had worse in my mouth than your toothbrush."

"Eeew, *no*." Quinn sat up and glared at me. "No, you cannot say that…just no." She shook her head in denial.

"We shared a spoon last night when we ate the frozen yogurt."

"It's different."

"You sucked my lollipop last week."

Quinn squinted at me. "Is that a euphemism?"

I barked out a laugh. "No, babe, an actual lollipop. Tilly gave it to me, remember?"

Quinn's sad smile at the mention of Tilly had me cursing myself until she looked up at me with a frown. "It's not the same."

"How?" I asked her.

"Because the bristles are dislodging plaque and things. And mouths are disgusting."

"Uh-huh, and when I kiss you? Is that disgusting?"

"It's not the same," Quinn insisted as she folded her arms stubbornly. "Use the toothbrush I bought you."

"Okay." I couldn't hide my grin.

"I mean it."

"Why would I use yours when there's now one for me?" I reasoned.

She went to lie back down again but stopped to shoot me

another warning glare, and I suppressed the urge to laugh out loud. As I shook with laughter, her punch in my ribs only caused me to laugh more.

"It's not funny!" she hissed at me.

"Okay." I forced myself to stop laughing, and she swatted me again. "Okay, I'm stopping."

She asked me to switch the light off as she curled into my side, and I closed my eyes, my grin still wide in the dark.

"Did we just have our first domestic?" Quinn whispered in the dark.

"I dunno, I got hit several times and bullied...maybe?" I baited her as my hand cupped her ass.

"Not domestic abuse, you moron," she whispered fiercely. "I meant domestic dispute."

"You have to stop watching reality TV." I pulled her closer to me. "But if you're asking if we just had a fight, no, baby, we didn't."

"I could take your ass in a fight," she mumbled as she stretched her arm across my waist.

"Probably."

"Don't be patronising."

"Okay."

"Gray!"

"Quinn!" I echoed back and heard her huff. "Shut up and go to sleep."

"Bossy."

"You want me to shut you up?" I teased her as I pulled her hand over the front of my boxers. Her fingers automatically flexed around me before she groaned. With a wiggle and a shuffle, she was under the blanket, her hands reaching inside my boxers.

"I was joking," I said half-heartedly as she licked along my dick. I felt her teeth graze me in warning, and I grinned as she set about shutting us *both* up.

CHAPTER 28

Quinn

WAS IT POSSIBLE TO LOVE HIM EVEN MORE THAN I THOUGHT I already did? Or were we simply focusing on the physical attraction and not the circumstances that brought us together...this time?

Gray watched me when no one else was watching, he saw things no one else saw, and he understood what I needed and wanted before I did. Had he always been this attuned with me? Had I simply ignored it before, or had he never been this open?

I watched him with others, and he was exactly as he had always been, but then he would look at me, and the softness would be there, the tenderness. Maybe I was the only one who saw it?

We'd had the horror that was Sunday lunch, and I hadn't asked what they had done to Dr Newton. I knew Onyx had him, and my heart hoped they never told me, because I knew the chances of Dr Newton speaking to the authorities wasn't a good one. The fact he wasn't at a police station and no one had come asking questions told me all I needed to know.

Gray confessed they had to tell Kage and Kerr everything. But because he was who he was, he told them everything but *not* everything. Which I surmised meant they knew everything except Gray and the house and therefore Dr Newton.

The team had an away game, and they were travelling by bus. All three of them were gone. Even though Jett couldn't play this week and Gray was out completely, they weren't sitting back and waiting. The team was their team, and Jett would coach Ben, and Gray would scare the shit out of the rest of the team not to lose. Plus, they would be there for Ash. Both twins were exceptional team players.

Which left me alone. I hadn't been alone since the night of the Halloween party when I had freaked out and Gray had taken me to bed. However, Ava was also alone, and she had called me in to help her with a Mia problem.

I was to meet them in an hour at the theatre, and I'd been spending time making motivational packs for Mia. The girl had stage fright. Ava had tried everything to help her but had never succeeded. So, I had drinks, snacks, and a portable karaoke machine.

It was probably dumb, but in my head, I thought it was going to work. I had borrowed it from the swim team. I loved their parties. No mayhem ever happened, they were so laid back and cool. Plenty of board games, outside activities and responsible drinking. The swim team were responsible students, and I admired them for it.

I reached for my phone when it dinged as I got ready for tonight.

Gray: **We're here. You okay?**

Me: **Yeah, getting ready to meet Ava and Mia.**

Gary: **You really seem to be liking Ava...**

Me: **She's nice. Genuine. Funny.**

Gray: **I'll take your word for it.**

Me: **Don't be mean, your twin LOVES her**

Gray: **I'll take your word for it...**

Shaking my head in despair at his stubbornness, I sent him the grimacing face emoji and then studied my appearance. I had kept my dark hair down and blow dried it with a slight curl to it. I hadn't put much makeup on, a light brush of eye shadow and some mascara, and I had a tinted lip balm in my purse.

Jeans, a sweater, a jacket and my boots were all I needed. I knew there were no possible parties later. Tonight was all about Mia and her fear. Ava had convinced the janitors of the theatre to leave it open, and one of them was coming later to close up.

It wasn't unheard of for the facilities team to do students favours; it *was* unheard of for them to do the favours for sophomores. Seniors had privileges for their year-end shows and things, but us lowly sophomores hadn't the same urgency to succeed that the seniors did.

Gray: **What are you wearing?**

I rolled my eyes as I giggled.

Me: **Nothing**

I waited and then I burst out laughing at his response.

Gray: **You're so full of shit Lawrence**

Me: **I know, I hate that you know me so well**

He sent back the heart emoji, and I thought that was the most romantic thing Gray Santo would ever have done. He really did love me, and my smile as I held the phone close to my chest was so wide it hurt.

Checking my time, I cursed myself for being eager for the girls night and being ready too early. Could I make my way over now and set up? I contemplated it and then decided to shoot a text to Ava that I was making my way there.

Hefting my bag of supplies over my shoulder, I picked up the karaoke machine and locked up. Friday night on campus was nice. It was dry although cool, and the sparkly lights through the trees for the Christmas decorations kept the sidewalks well-lit. I passed several people, some I knew, some I didn't, and smiled at them anyway.

I didn't recognise myself. I was not this happy outgoing person. Had he really changed me this much? Was Gray randomly smiling at people? The thought caused me to grin wider. No, Gray would probably be glaring at all and sundry as per his normal attitude.

He wasn't saying anything, but I knew he was devastated he was losing out on the rest of the season. Three broken bones and a fracture in his thumb meant he wasn't catching a ball anytime soon. I wanted to reprimand him for his recklessness, but I also knew why he did it, and I couldn't scold him for his actions when they were as a result of keeping me safe.

Of course, if I had been honest, would it have happened? Yes. Probably sooner and he could have been in jail already.

Sighing as I walked, I realised the machine may be portable, but it was freaking heavy. I was only halfway there as well. The theatre was on the opposite end of the campus and was in a lovely enclosed green area that gave it a serene and peaceful feeling. It was a gorgeous campus, I realised as I walked and appreciated it. The rows of dorm houses were kept in streets central to the campus, with the teaching buildings scattered throughout, giving the student a real sense of community and belonging.

The campus was big on its landscaping, and everything just felt very natural. Lots of trees, shrubbery and grass made it pleasing to walk through. I kept that thought up all the way to the turn off for the theatre, and then I was looking at the surrounding trees and woodland with a more critical eye. Where the sidewalks and paths through campus had been populated, the path to the theatre wasn't as well-lit and looked a little bit creepy.

Ava had managed to get the theatre open, but the lights leading up to it were on dim, and not all were fully lit. Glancing back over my shoulder, I checked to see if the girls were heading my way. Maybe I should wait here? What if it wasn't open? My feet slowed, and I put the karaoke machine down as I thought about it.

After another furtive glance over my shoulder, I shook my head at myself. Gray would be calling me chicken, and I would be furious because he was right. With determination, I picked up the machine and made my way towards the theatre.

I told myself I didn't jump at the snap of a twig, which was probably me and not someone lurking in the shrubbery. As if there would be someone in the bushes? I needed to stop watching TV shows on Netflix.

At the side door, I tried the handle, and it opened easily. Again, I hesitated. Which was worse? To stay outside and jump at imaginary sounds, or go inside the empty building where the door had been left open all evening?

Biting my lip, I considered my options. Firing out a quick text to Ava to see how long she was going to be, I then texted Gray.

Me: **Standing outside the theatre, alone, in the semi dark. Do I go into the vacant building or stay out in the dark and wait?**

I waited and was frustrated when he didn't immediately respond. Ugh, I was *that* girl. I looked at the message and then copied it and sent it to Jett—who answered immediately, which just irked me more.

Jett: **Why are you alone?**

Jett: **Does Gray know?**

Me: **Waiting for your girl and I dunno, I texted him the same question as you but he didn't answer**

Bitchy much?

Jett: **Hang on**

I hung. Two seconds later, my phone rang.

"Hey," I greeted him.

"What the fuck you hanging about in the dark for?" Gray asked me, and I rolled my eyes at his temper. "Why wouldn't you wait for Ava?"

"Because I told them I would meet them here and I got bored waiting, but I'm not going to lie, it's kinda creepy in the dark. I mean the door's open, but I dunno...I don't want to go in. I should stop watching horror movies."

"You should stop being so impatient," Gray scolded. "Go in and stay on the phone with me until they get there."

I instantly felt foolish and childish. "You don't need to do that. I can hear the team. You're all together, go be with them. They need motivational Gray to psyche them up for tomorrow."

"I'm staying on the phone with you," he told me firmly, and I heard him move away from the others.

"I'm being silly," I confessed.

"Meh, you were always silly."

"Is this the kind of motivational speeches you give the team?" I teased as I made my way to the auditorium. Pushing the door to the main theatre, I heard him laugh, and the sound made me smile.

"No. I swear a lot, threaten to bust their asses and smash their heads."

"I completely believe this to be true." I laughed as I made my way down towards the stage. "This place is huge," I commented as I looked around. "And really, really creepy."

"Never been in it," Gray replied as I dumped the machine on the stage and looked at the seats.

"I've only been once." I looked up at the lights and back around. "I don't like it."

Gray's soft laughter carried over the phone, and I closed my eyes at hearing it. "I love your laugh," I whispered.

"Why?" I could hear his amused tone, and I knew he would be smiling.

"I don't know, I like knowing you're happy, I guess."

"Ah, a rare thing," he mocked, and I chuckled at his playfulness. My laughter cut off when I heard the thump. "What is it?" Gray asked, instantly alert.

Straining to hear, I pulled the phone away from my ear. "I don't know." I waited. "I think I imagined it."

"Imagined what?" His voice was tight and the tone low.

"Nothing." I forced the cheeriness in my tone, and I knew he wouldn't buy it at all.

"Quinn." His low warning tone actually soothed me.

"I thought I heard a bump. Jesus, I'm a cliché, the things that go bump in the night." My laugh sounded brittle.

"It's only seven thirty. I think you need a few more hours for the bumping to begin," Gray murmured, and I jumped when I heard it again.

"Ask Jett where Ava is," I asked him as I rose to my feet.

"Baby?"

"Ask him." I turned in a circle. I heard the muted conversation, and then Gray was back on the line.

"She's only just left. You're too early," Gray told me tersely. "What is it?"

I heard the thumping more rhythmically now, and I clutched the phone tighter. "Gray? I don't think I'm alone."

"Get out."

My feet stayed frozen to the spot. "It's probably the janitors, I'm overreacting."

"Okay, overreact, but get out." I heard him moving. "*Now*, Quinn. Keep talking and walking."

Spurred into action with the urgency of his voice, I left the karaoke machine, and I started back up the aisle to the doors. "I'm walking," I assured him when he asked me.

The floodlights being turned on for the stage as the theatre was plunged into darkness, made me cry out in alarm. Frozen, I looked back at the stage wildly.

"What the fuck is it?" Gray demanded.

"The lights got dimmed, the stage is lit up," I told him in a low whisper. "I don't care if I'm chicken, I'm running out of here."

I didn't wait for his reply, and I started jogging to the doors. The doors were locked. What the fuck was happening?

"Gray, the doors are locked!"

"Try the next one," he ordered sharply. "It's probably just the janitor. He hasn't got the memo you girls are going to be there and is locking up."

"With the stage lights on?" I hissed fiercely.

"Just get to the other doors. We can be pedantic when you're outside," he snapped.

"Ass," I muttered as I reached the other door. "It's locked."

"You're locked in the auditorium?" His voice was steady and calm, and I knew he was about to explode.

"I think so," I admitted as I looked around again. "Can you ask Jett to call Ava?"

"He's on the phone with her. She's coming, babe."

"Will you stay on the phone with me?" I asked him, my voice almost inaudible.

"I'm going nowhere."

"I'm completely overreacting. I know this." I tried to make light of it. Gray said nothing, and we were merely on the phone, silence between us. I heard the thump again, and I jumped just as the lights went out completely, which caused me to scream in fright. "It's okay, it's okay, the lights are out. I think you're right: it's just the janitor, and he doesn't know I'm in here."

"Ash is on the phone to maintenance," Gray told me. "Just hold tight."

"Now I know how people feel when we do mayhem," I tried to joke, and I heard his sharp inhale. "Gray?"

"I'm here, baby, you okay?"

"What was the gasp?" I demanded as I pressed myself against the wall like a coward.

"Jett elbowed me in the ribs."

"And you say I'm a terrible liar," I mocked him. I glanced at my phone screen quickly. "You cannot kill me for this, I mean it," I warned. "My battery's about to die."

"Tell me you're making a bad joke."

"I thought I had plugged it in," I admitted weakly. "I don't remember switching it on."

"Queeny," he breathed softly, and I heard his despair. "Ava's almost there, okay?"

"Okay." I felt tears threatening, and I cursed myself inwardly at being this oversensitive idiot. I was locked in a building that was supposed to be locked at this time of night. I was fine. I was being hysterical. "I'm completely overreacting," I told him again.

"Who gives a fuck?" Gray replied gruffly, and I had to smile at his complete dedication to me.

"I never used to be so troublesome," I joked weakly.

"Yes, you did," was his quick reply.

"Dick." I heard it go, and I held the phone up as the red flashing battery icon took over the screen and my phone died. "Shit."

What did I do now? Sit and wait for someone to come get me, or try more of the doors? Why hadn't I already tried more of the doors? Carefully, I made my way to the next door, my hands scraping across the wall, keeping me steady. I stumbled over a trash can and yelped spectacularly loudly in the empty theatre, the acoustics echoing back to me. Well, that wasn't fucking creepy at all.

Trying not to be the hysterical girl that panics in every horror movie ever told, I reached the next door and gently tugged. Nothing. Fine. Next one. Sometime later, I was back at the stage, and I knew I didn't have the courage or the energy to try to make my way around the other side. The green glowing sign of the EXIT taunted me, and I cursed myself for a fool as I hastened towards it. I had tried the locked doors, not the emergency exits. Gray was going to kick my ass, and I deserved it.

Pushing on the bar, I almost screamed with frustration as it refused to budge. Weren't they supposed to open? Wasn't that the whole point of them? They opened no matter what and were unobstructed at all times? This college sucked balls at safety, I rambled to myself as I held tightly onto the bar like it was a lifeline. The good thing about the exit was it gave some light to the dark room.

Which was a good thing.

Until I saw the shadow move on the other side of the hall.

Fuck off.

I hadn't seen that. It was my imagination. Please, Lord, let me be alone in here. I stood stock-still hardly breathing for I didn't know how long.

The lights went on at the same time as the doors flung open, and I screamed out loud at the loud bang, and then I heard Ava say, "It's okay, we have her."

Blinking, I looked at her and Mia as I hurried towards them. I didn't care that I looked like a fool. My steps slowed as I saw the janitor.

"You?"

"Well, I didn't know we had royalty in the building," the greasy-haired guy from the bar smirked at me.

"You locked me in?" I could feel my fury overcoming any other emotions, and with a move borne of fear and desperation, I punched him.

CHAPTER 29

Gray

"TELL ME WHAT'S HAPPENING?" I DEMANDED OF JETT, WHO HELD HIS hand up to shut me up. I was going to dislocate his hand soon.

"What, wait. Stop!" Jett said firmly. "Calm down, tell me again." Ash and I stood like spare parts as he listened, and then I saw his eyes widen slightly. "Ah shit."

"Brother," I warned him quietly.

"Okay, hang on, I need to tell Gray, just tell her...tell her to calm down." Jett put his phone down and looked at me. "Quinn's fine."

"But."

"The janitor isn't."

"Why?" Ash asked as he looked between us.

"She punched him. Twice. And may have kicked him in the balls."

"Why?" I asked as I felt my palms itch to hit something in frustration.

"Do not freak out," Jett warned me.

"Too late."

"It's the guy from the bar."

"No!" Ash grabbed me as I launched forward.

"I just need the phone," I demanded of my brother through clenched teeth.

Wordlessly he handed it over. "Ava? Let me talk to her." I heard the phone get passed over. "Baby?"

"I may have overreacted," she said sheepishly.

My eyes closed as I heard her voice, and I gripped my brother's arm tight. "I'm sure you didn't."

"I just was freaked out, and I saw him, and he said something smarmy, and I punched him, and then I hit him again, and then I may have accidentally kicked him…"

"In his balls."

"Possibly."

"Quinn..." My head tilted back as I looked upwards, thanking the heavens. She was okay.

"He's called his boss, who's called his boss, which means he called Dean Porter."

"Fuck," I hissed as I looked at Jett and saw he was on Ash's phone and realised he would be calling Ava from it. I saw Jett nod and Ash looking between the two of us with increasing frustration. Jett saw it too and quickly filled him in, and then I saw him rub the back of his neck as he looked at me, and I shook my head in despair.

"So, what's he called the boss for?" I knew what it was even before she spoke.

"Assault."

"Fuck's sake."

"I'm sorry," Quinn's voice was low and miserable.

"Okay, are you listening?" I told her as I pulled Jett closer to me. "You tell them of the run-in you had previously, tell them he assaulted you then, but you were in Cardinal and didn't know he worked here. Tell them you were scared, tell them you heard movement, *exaggerate* it. Then tell him what he said and that your adrenaline and terror at being trapped caused you to overreact. You believed he was trying to harm you."

"Not all of that is untrue," she said softly.

"I know, babe, I know, but you need to act it up for Dean Prick, he'll love this." I saw Jett nod in agreement, and I looked at Ash, who was focused on me, mouthing my brother's name. "I need to phone Onyx."

"No."

"Quinn, I need to. Dad won't make the drive in time. Onyx is closer than you think, he's had run-ins with Porter before, and he knows about the guy from the bar. Trust me."

"Gray..."

"*Trust* me."

Ash took the phone off me. "Quinn, it's Ash. It's either Onyx fixes it or you get suspended, possibly charged. Is your pride really going to fuck you over?"

I didn't hear her reply, but Ash gave me a wink, and then he was taking his phone off Jett as he handed me back to Quinn.

"You okay?"

"Ash just owned my ass," Quinn muttered.

"Well, I'm going to ignore that," I teased her as I gave my cousin a grateful smile. "Ash is calling Onyx, so give Ava her phone back. Don't say much until Onyx is there. And Quinn, when you get home, charge the fucking phone."

I smiled briefly at her grunt of laughter, and then she was handing the phone back to Ava. I didn't listen as Jett spoke to Ava or as Ash contacted my brother. I felt my legs turn to jelly, and I slumped down the wall as I dropped my head into my hands and breathed deeply in and out while my brother and my cousin took over so I could catch my breath.

Cold hands touched mine, and I looked up at Ash, who was crouched down in front of me. "You got it together?" he asked me quietly.

"She has to stop scaring the shit out of me," I said to him honestly. "The woman's going to be the death of me."

"She's okay," he assured me as he stayed level with me.

"Yeah." Leaning my head against the wall, I looked up at Jett, who was watching me as he spoke to Ava. "What are the chances?" I asked them both.

"Too slim for my liking," Ash answered immediately. "Ava will tell the dean she had the arrangement with one of the janitors, and I guess we can only surmise that douchebag thought he'd scare her when he saw her in there alone." Ash looked at me and then over his shoulder at Jett. "Why was she alone?"

"Because she has zero patience and a stubborn streak that makes me want to strangle her," I growled as I picked at my splint. "This fucking thing needs to come off so I can tan her hide."

Ash burst out laughing. "You're going to spank her?"

"She fucking needs it," I said grimly as I stood, and he followed me up. "Hey, thanks," I told him honestly. "I know it's awkward, but I needed that."

"It's my job to rein you in," Ash said with a grim smile. "Knew you were about to lose it, can't let that happen. Not when they're okay."

"Yeah." I moved my head from side to side as I let out a deep breath. "Onyx no trouble?"

"I think you're going to owe him a sacrifice," Ash said with a grin. "He had a few choice words to say, but he's heading there now."

Jett said goodbye to Ava and then pulled me under his arm for a brief brotherly hug. "I swear to Christ, those girls are trying to kill us," he muttered as he let me go. "Fuck, that was intense." He reached out and gripped Ash's arm, touching base with us both. "You okay?" he asked our cousin, who nodded and gave him a tight smile.

"Well, we missed the pep talk, and Coach is probably going to suspend us all," I said as I looked back at the conference room we had walked out of during the night-before, pre-game meeting.

"Maybe we should injure me too," Ash said as he rotated his shoulder. "Before my teammates do."

We all gave a laugh, but each of our thoughts were back at campus. "How long for Onyx?" I asked Jett.

"He'll be there in about half an hour. Quinn knows how to stall. She'll wait for him."

"It's going to kill her." Ash grinned widely.

"The guy's going to say sue, I just know it," I spoke to Jett, and he nodded in agreement. "Aw, man, her old man's going to blame me." I groaned out loud, and I saw Jett's amused grin.

"Are you three girls done?" Coach barked from the open door to the meeting room. "Were we *boring* you?" he asked snidely.

"Sorry, Coach," the three of us all spoke at once as we headed back into the room.

Once we were settled back in, I returned the hostile stares from some of my teammates and the curious *are you okay* looks from the others. Thankfully, there were more of the latter than the former; however, I saw Ash taking note of the ones who were pissed. Hiding my smile, I nudged Jett, who looked up and noticed too. Ash was always mistaken for the friendliest of us, which is why he caused a bit of a shock to some when he punched them in the face.

Or slept with their girl.

Or both.

Ash wasn't keen on boundaries. I guess I knew that better than anyone, but still, he was a force to be reckoned with when you pissed him off, and some of our teammates had just pissed him off.

Coach went over the game plan for tomorrow, *for the benefit of those in the back,* and I caught Jett's hand before he flipped him off. Ten minutes later, Jett showed me his screen.

Onyx: **I'm here. So's the dean, she's fine as far as I can see. Her victim, not so much.**

I grinned at Jett as he passed the phone to Ash, who snorted out a laugh and failed to cover it as a cough quickly enough.

"Are you three serious?" Coach Bowers barked at us. "Do you want to be back at campus instead of here with your teammates?"

The fact my immediate answer was yes worried me. What the fuck? Football was life. Wasn't it? I'd told Quinn she was more important, and I hadn't lied, but that's because I knew she understood my ambitions as much as anyone.

I tried my best to focus on the game plan, the pep talk, the team spirit.

All I could think of was her. Was she okay? Was Onyx being civil to her? She had been scared. My whole entire being was itching to leave, to drive back and be with her, but I couldn't. I shouldn't. My team needed me here, this is where I had to be if I wanted the NFL. Quinn knew this. Accepted it. *Encouraged* it.

"What's wrong?" Jett asked me quietly, his voice pitched low enough that even Ash couldn't hear.

"I'm slipping," I said honestly. "This? Here? Isn't my focus."

"It is." He cast a sideways look at me and raised an eyebrow. "We'll talk."

Finally, Coach stopped talking, and I refused after-meeting refreshments and headed to my room to check in with Onyx and Quinn. Jett followed me, and Ash, once again, took one for the Devils as he stayed back to chat with our teammates.

Inside the room Jett and I were sharing, I immediately texted Onyx.

Me: **Sorted?**

There was no answer, and I decided he must still be negotiating. That was basically what it was: a negotiation to see how much the dick wanted to shut up and fuck off. He could press charges, and her future was ruined. Even I knew her claims of harassment would be thin. He had a strong case, and I needed the enigmatic persuasion that was my older brother to convince the fucker otherwise.

Plus, Dean Porter had to be dealt with. I hoped he listened to the harassment side more than the authorities would.

"So, what's going on?" Jett asked casually as he took two bottles of water from the mini fridge.

"I don't think I want to be here."

"Tomorrow's game or the team?" Jett queried as he handed me a water and then sat on the other seat in the room.

"Both?"

"Bullshit."

I blinked. "Wow, glad you listened."

"Shut up and *you* listen." He leaned forward, his elbows on his knees as he regarded me solemnly. "You love the game, it's in our blood. The last few weeks have been hard, really fucking hard emotionally. You're reeling. She's your girl, and she's been hurting. You've both been hurting, and I know, you want to be with her now to know she's okay, to see for yourself. And when she's back at her apartment tonight and is FaceTiming you, you'll feel better."

"Yeah." I nodded as if I agreed with him but didn't meet his eyes.

"You have some fucked-up illusion that you have to prove you're better than me," Jett said harshly, ignoring my startled look. "Don't let all the doubters who believe you're second best be right by quitting like a little bitch."

"You saying if this was Ava, you wouldn't be crawling in your skin to be with her?"

"I would probably be halfway back to campus," he said honestly. "But I would be an idiot, and my twin would have kicked my ass before I made it out of the hotel. What can you do?" he asked with a hard stare. "She took care of herself, and our brother is there; he won't let anyone fuck her over, despite his own problems with her. All you would be is a hug and someone to sleep with. Ava and Mia will spend the night with her, she won't be alone."

"Someone to sleep with?"

"You know what I mean. What you would be racing back for is being given to her now. She knows you're committed here. She understands."

"But—"

"There is no but," he cut me off. "This is our dream. Her dream. For us. She will lose it if you rush back to her. She needs to remember she has strength inside her."

"She does," I murmured.

"And she's been hiding, and we're forcing her to face the things she's chosen to ignore. The guy tonight? I think it's a really unlucky coincidence, but Quinn needs to remember she's a Devil not a coward. And you need to remember she came through what happened herself. She needs to remember she's fucking awesome."

I grinned at him and his passion. "She is."

"Do not lose focus on your dream. Quinn is part of it; it's not a 'one or the other.' Not anymore."

Drinking my water, I thought about what he had said to me. He was right, but that didn't make the urge to see her, hold her, any less.

"I just need to speak to her," I told him.

"I know."

"Onyx is going to make us pay for this favour," I said with a heavy groan.

"For years," Jett agreed.

"Ugh, this sucks." Getting up, I lay on my bed. "Thanks."

"Anytime."

"I don't think you're better than me by the way."

"Okay. Neither do I." His look was assessing. "Then who are you trying to prove that to?"

"Everyone else," I said quietly as I closed my eyes even though I could feel his stare.

"Fuck everyone else," Jett snorted as he flopped down on the bed beside me.

"Thought that was Ash's job?" I grinned and we both laughed as we waited for an update from my brother.

CHAPTER 30

Quinn

Sitting in the theatre seats while Onyx directed the dean and the maintenance manager like a well-conducted orchestra was truly something to see. He had insisted that Ava identify the janitor she had made the arrangement with, and he had been hauled in too, to confirm her story and validate that he had told sleaze-ball greaseball that we were using the theatre.

Dean Porter wasn't happy to have Ava's story collaborated, and I remembered she was on probation, and from the fear in Ava's eyes, she was very much aware how thin the ice below her feet was too.

Onyx caught my worried look at Ava as the dean turned to the maintenance manager, and stepped closer to me. "What is it?"

"She's on probation," I told him quietly and winced when his hard stare cut into mine.

"You really are a piece of work," he muttered before he moved over to the dean. "Why are we still here?" he asked in the tone that made me want to punch him most of the time, and from Dean Porter's expression, so did he.

"Because a student committed assault."

"On a guy who's already assaulted her physically and then tonight emotionally, so I'll ask again, why are we still here?"

"Why are you here?" Sleaze-ball asked Onyx. "She's a little too young for you, is she not?"

Onyx snorted in disgust. "Says the guy who tried to pick her up in a bar." He shook his head. "I suggest you keep your words of wisdom to yourself."

Douchebag glared at me before he turned away, and I took a perverse delight in looking at his blackening eye. "I want to press charges," he said as he glanced back at Onyx.

"So do I, but Quinn has already refused to raise the complaint against you, and I think you should show the same courtesy, don't you?" Onyx fixed his cufflink, and I took in the impressive figure he cut. With thick dark hair, slight stubble, broad shoulders and a trim waist, he didn't play the game, but he still kept himself fit. He was stunningly attractive, and I think it was one of the many reasons I disliked him. The guys were all good-looking, and Gray made my tummy flutter, but Onyx was a cruel kind of beauty. He looked stunning until you looked into his soulless eyes and realised a monster was lurking in his depths.

Dean Porter harrumphed, and I switched my attention to him as Onyx took his time to divert his attention from the creepy janitor.

"I think we would be best saying neither party is innocent here and—"

"Water under the bridge?" Onyx clapped once in mock delight. "My thoughts exactly. Quinn, ladies, let's go."

"I wasn't finished," the dean said coldly. He looked at me, and I returned his look with my own impartial mask. "As always, there is little I can do to a Santo." His lip twisted in a sneer when he said their name. "And I knew upon application, Miss Lawrence was just another Santo." He turned his attention to Ava. "But you and I have had a very recent conversation, Miss Bryant, about acceptable behaviour on this campus."

"I didn't do anything wrong," Ava said to him, her outrage making me widen my eyes in warning at her.

"Yes, you did. You approached the janitor, and you offered him money to keep the theatre open. Bribing staff is not acceptable behaviour for our students."

Ava's eyes were wide with fury as she looked between the dean and the janitor. "I didn't!"

"Mr Cairn says you offered him one hundred dollars."

"Mr Cairn is full of bullshit," Ava snapped. "I've never had a hundred dollars to offer him!"

"That may be, but bribing the staff of the college, or implying a bribe"—Dean Porter held his hands up as if he was truly sorry for what he was about to say—"I'm afraid you're in breach of your scholarship."

"What!" Ava clutched Mia's hand as she stared at the dean in shock.

"Bribing the janitor is fine," Onyx spoke up, sounding bored. "Bribing a member of the academia is a punishable offence. Last I checked, the janitor wasn't a member of the staff faculty in that regard. Have I missed an update?"

"He's staff."

"As am I," Onyx drawled with a lazy grin as he looked at the dean. "Or are you forgetting I sit on the Board? And I know the rule book a little more thoroughly than you."

Dean Porter's lips were white with fury, and Onyx turned his attention on Ava. "Scholarship?"

"English Literature," she mumbled as she looked at him with hope shining in her eyes.

"Nice, well done." Onyx dipped his head to her. "You must be very talented and intelligent." He looked her over. "And yet you're with Jett?" His eyes sparkled with laughter, and Ava grinned at him. Onyx turned on his heel to look at the dean. "The girl breached nothing. The janitor? Fire him. This one?" He looked at Dickhead. "Fire him too. Perverts on the staff do give us a shady reputation, Dean." Onyx looked at me, and I steeled myself. "Perhaps a commendation to the young woman, who defended herself when attacked, rather than a judgment would have been better? Pity. Hopefully, we'll keep this debacle from the local news."

Onyx gestured to me. "Ladies, please, I have other places to be," he instructed as he started to walk up the aisle.

"I'll sue!" Sleaze-ball shouted, causing Onyx to stop. He walked back down to him and reached into his inner suit pocket.

"My card, call Monday."

"Why?"

"So I can write you a cheque, and you can fuck off out of my face. My secretary will expect your call. You breathe one word to anyone, no cheque." Onyx looked at Dean Porter as he walked past him and smirked. "*That's* a bribe."

He walked past the three of us with such complete confidence I never knew my mouth was hanging open until Mia nudged me to follow him and I grabbed the karaoke machine. Hastily I caught up with him as he waited at the main doors. Ava and Mia were looking at him with complete awe, which he ignored and focused on me.

"I'll drive you home."

"I can walk," I said as I remembered vividly the last time I was in his car.

"Good for you. Get in the car." He looked between the three of us. "All of you. Now."

Biting my lip, I got into the car with Ava and Mia slipping into the back seat. Onyx drove them to their dorm and exchanged simple pleasantries as they left.

Ava, God bless her, hesitated when I remained in the car. "Quinn?"

"Stays with me." Onyx turned to look at her. "Don't worry, I only bite when she begs for it."

Ava's eyes widened, and I got out of the car and encouraged her to take a few steps back. "I'm fine, he's a dick, he hates me."

"I knew things were tense, but"—she looked back at the car—"I really think he doesn't like you."

"Meh, it is what it is. He helped this evening, so I have to be nice to him." I smiled at her to soften the words. "Plus, he'll want to make sure he can tell Gray he has me."

"Call me," Ava said firmly. "Charge your phone and call me."

"Will do." I reached over and hugged her. "I'm so sorry my drama caused you both a shit night too."

"It's fine, the guy's a creep, and I'm kinda glad he got fired." Ava hugged me quickly again, and then she hesitated before she walked past me and bent down to look at Onyx. "You were awesome tonight. Don't fuck it up by being a dick to Quinn."

I didn't hear his response, but I wish I could've. With a shake of my head at Ava's balls, I slipped into the car and looked at him as he glared at me, while Ava waited on the sidewalk.

"You're like poison. Do you brainwash them?" he asked me casually as he drove away.

"Maybe I'm just a nice person," I badgered.

"Well, it's not your jokes, that's for sure," he murmured as we drove, and I realised he was taking me to the football house.

"Why?"

"Your apartment is shit for security. I can secure the house and know you're inside, and the team is away, so even you can't fuck up in a house alone."

"You're so considerate." Onyx snorted, and I glanced at his cufflink with the Devil insignia. "You're still a Devil," I said softly.

"Always." Onyx grunted as he parked in the drive and got out of the car. I had no choice but to follow him.

"So...you expect me to sleep here, in Gray's room?"

"Or Ash's? Jett's?" Onyx tilted his head as he considered me. "Or have you moved on already?"

"I love your brother, you know this, so why are you so cruel?"

Onyx said nothing as he let himself into the house, and I didn't even ask why he had a key. Why wouldn't he? He was a Santo and a Devil at that. He walked to the kitchen, and I followed slowly. As he considered the contents of the fridge, I sat on a stool at the breakfast bar.

"So you love him?" Onyx asked as he pulled a water out and passed one to me.

"Yes."

"And Ash was what?"

"A relationship that has nothing to do with you."

Onyx sat on the opposite end of the breakfast bar and stared at me. "You see, that's where you're wrong. You know as well as I do, my cousin is very dear to me."

"Well, he's your family."

"He is." Onyx drank from the bottle and placed it in front of him. "You assumed he didn't care, because you clearly didn't care, but he did."

"This is none of your business," I said quietly as I stared at the counter. "This conversation, if it needs to be had at all, should be between me and Ash. I could care less what you think."

"It's *I couldn't care less*."

"Fuck off."

"Charming."

"Just tell me what you want." I opened my own water and took a long drink, wishing it had some kind of alcohol content.

"I want you to break up with my brother. Both of them, and my cousin."

I laughed. When I realised he was serious, I glared at him. "No."

"I'll give you however much you want."

"I don't want your money," I snapped at him angrily. "What the hell is wrong with you?"

"You." Onyx regarded me coolly and then smiled. "You cause disharmony with them. They are my family. One is in love with you, one has always been in love with you, and the other loves you more than his own family sometimes." Onyx leaned forward as if we were having a casual conversation. "You will break them. You have broken them, and you will only continue to keep breaking them."

I stared at him wordlessly. "Ash doesn't love me, not like that. Gray *does*. Jett and I have always been family. You can't twist this into something horrible and sordid. Gray is who I am supposed to be with."

"You will destroy him."

"No"—I pushed away from the counter—"I won't."

"You're so sure," Onyx scoffed.

I nodded as I took a few steps back and turned away from him. Taking a deep breath, I turned back to him. "I am sure, I am one hundred percent positive."

"So fucking confident."

"I am."

"How can you be so sure?" Onyx asked me with an arched brow.

"Because I lost my baby, *his* baby, and he didn't walk away. He didn't run. He fought his own hell while I fought mine, and it made us stronger. I am stronger with Gray in my life, and he is stronger because of me. He loves me, Onyx. He loves me more than you know."

"Which is why you must go."

I blinked rapidly as I shook my head in denial. "Why? Why do you hate me so much?"

"Because when I look at you, I see Sable."

"Your mom?"

"My dad was never injured, not to the extent he says he was. He was drafted, but he walked away. For her. Because she asked him to. She asked him not to chase his dream and be with her instead, and you're just like her. Needy, desperate and afraid."

"Oh my God, that's your *mom*," I said to him in disbelief. "She loves you and does not deserve this disrespect."

"Her love for me doesn't change the facts: she made my dad walk away, and Gray will do the same if you ask him."

"I would never ask him!" I cried in exasperation. "The NFL is all he wants, I know this. It's all he's ever wanted."

"I have scouts interested in Gray. They would have taken him this year, but he got injured. Because of you."

"He's a sophomore."

"I'm aware. It's not unheard of, for them to take them so young, and Gray is exceptional. He can practically write his ticket now, and you're already fucking up his future."

"I didn't ask him to try to kill himself!" I shouted angrily. Scouts wanted Gray, already? He wasn't even twenty. Sure, teams looked at guys in their third year of college sometimes, but in their second? No. His hand being injured ruined that chance? I ruined that chance?

"Stop being selfish."

"I will not hold him back."

"You're already holding him back!" Onyx growled angrily. "He's injured, his head is with you instead of that field. I already know he wanted to come back here tonight rather than stay with his team. You are a distraction he doesn't need, and if you were gone" —Onyx paused to take a calming breath—"he would realise he doesn't want you."

"You're wrong," I whispered as I walked the length of the room. "You're so wrong. He would find me."

"I will give you enough to disappear, Quinn. Please, for my family, take it."

My pacing stopped, and I looked over at him. Cold, distant, so like Gray it hurt to see him look at me with such distaste. Thankfully, his eyes were dark and not the same shade as the twins'. I don't think I could bear it if I saw the same hatred in Gray's eyes when he looked at me. "No."

Onyx rolled his head back on his shoulders as he flexed his hands in agitation. "How much?"

"No."

"Quinn—"

"Onyx! I said no. Gray is a grown man. I can assure you, there is nothing stopping him from his dream of playing in the NFL. He told me the other night, the NFL is a few years of his life." Placing my hands on the counter, I leaned over it and met Onyx dead on. "I am forever."

Onyx's tongue licked over his top teeth in anger at my words. "Idiot."

"He's never been an idiot. None of them have. That's what you forget."

"I forget nothing."

"Neither do I." I met his hateful glare, and I didn't look away. "You need to go. Thank you for your help tonight, I really do appreciate it."

"I did it for my brother."

"I'm well aware," I replied equally as coldly. "I can still say thanks. Unlike you, I'm a decent human being."

"Keep telling yourself that," Onyx snarled over his shoulder as he walked away. I heard the front door slam behind him, and I made sure it was locked as I watched his stupid shiny car drive away.

After going back for my water, I climbed the stairs to Gray's room and then sat awkwardly on the couch. I had never been in here without him. It felt weird. Like I was invading his privacy.

Looking around, I saw his charger and plugged my phone in. After a minute, I was able to turn it on and saw I had messages, all from Gray.

Gray: **Has he fixed it?**

Gray: **Why is no one answering?**

Gray: **Make sure you have an alibi if you've killed him...**

Gray: **Seriously babe, let me know you're okay. I love you**

I hesitated as I read them again. Was Onyx right, was I holding him back? Breaking them?

I read the message again, *I love you*. Taking a deep calming breath, I dialled his number.

"Hey, it's me." I relaxed into his pillows as I heard his voice, and I turned onto my side as I breathed the smell of him in. "I'm on your bed." I gave a light laugh as he asked why. "Because your psycho brother took me to the house so he can lock me in."

"He's keeping you safe," Gray said softly.

Oh my sweet man, if only you knew.

"Tell me about your night," I encouraged him. "Does it suck being there and not playing tomorrow?"

As Gray picked up on my aversion to talk anymore about my evening, I listened to him tell me that Coach was pissed off with the three of them. I smiled as he exaggerated Coach Bowers's temper; he was really a sweet guy.

Knowing I would talk to Gray when they were back about what Onyx had said, calmed my fears. Because we didn't need these secrets between us. Secrets had caused too much damage. As I made my mind up to be honest with him when he came back from the game, I settled back as I listened to his voice. Hearing his laughter made everything ugly that Onyx had said melt away.

I had endured enough ugly and dark; Gray Santo was my light.

CHAPTER 31

Gray

We lost.

Jett and I were still reeling from the loss. This team was easy. We should have won. We should have won, and we should have won well.

Everything had gone against us. Every call, every fumble, every fucking turnover. Kowoski hadn't even played badly. Luck just hadn't been on our side. Ash got tackled more than any other player on the field. The defence even went for him more than Kowoski—and Ben was the goddamn quarterback.

"We can still make the championship game," Jett said to me as we watched our offence come off the field.

"We play 'Bama next after the bye," I reminded him. "I need this splint off."

"Your hand's broken, but my shoulder will be better." Jett turned to me. "Let's go motivate the team. We cannot let this beat us down."

In the locker room, the defence was already stripped and heading for the showers, Coach was yelling at some poor fucker, and we turned to see our cousin coming in with his head down and his shoulders sagging. Looking up, he met our stares before he kicked a bench out of his way.

"What the hell was that?" he asked us angrily. "What a fucking shitshow."

"It was an odd game," Jett said, and we both looked at him incredulously.

"It was a freak of nature, where was the defence?" Ash asked angrily over our heads towards the showers. "What the fuck, Woods, you couldn't even tackle today."

Jamie came out of the shower like a raging bull, regardless of the fact he was stark naked. "You're not blaming my defence. Where the fuck was the offence? Oh that's right, sitting on the fucking bench."

"The offence is not just me and Jett," I snapped back at him. "Look, everyone calm down and, Jamie, for fuck's sake, can you cover it up? I'm sitting right here."

Ash snorted as I made a show of moving away from Jamie's limp dick.

"Everyone get showered and dressed," Jett said to the team. "We can discuss strategy and where we went wrong on the bus. It's a setback, it's not the end of the season."

Grumbles and mutters filled the locker room as we sat side by side. Coach walked down to sit across from us.

"How's the shoulder?" he asked Jett.

"Needs a few more days, but I'll be fine Wednesday, maybe Tuesday."

"Docs will look at you Monday." Coach turned his head towards me. "Pain?"

"No." His eyes narrowed. "Slight discomfort."

"Can you catch a ball?"

I sat back and looked between him and Jett. "Honestly? If he only throws it to my left, maybe. Probably. I do like a one-handed catch. Passing, same. You'll need to move Ash to the right-hand side; I'm more likely to incomplete if I have to run to the right."

"We could work on your wide receiver skills," Coach mused. "You can catch well, move Lopez to the RB for the next game."

"Against 'Bama?" I asked him sceptically. "He isn't me, and I'm not that good a wide receiver. If I were, I wouldn't be your best running back."

"You take too many hits and land on your hand, and it'll be more than a few breaks."

"I could promise not to run and flip?" I said with a sly grin to Jett, who was frowning as the conversation continued.

"Why the hell did you both get injured at the same time?" Coach asked as he pushed up to his feet.

"Bad luck." We both answered at the same time.

"Stop twinning," Coach snapped as he stalked back to the visiting team's office.

"You can't play the next game," Jett said quietly. "You fuck up your hand more, you fuck up your career."

"I know. He knows that too; he's just entertaining insanity," I reasoned as I looked at the floor. "It does suck though."

"You speak to Quinn before the game?" Jett asked as he kicked his feet onto the next bench.

"Yeah, she's fine, back at her own apartment."

"Good. Ava said Onyx was impressive but a complete dick to her."

"Nothing new there," I grunted.

"You going to talk to him about it?"

I looked towards the showers where I could hear the team discuss the game, but there were no loud voices or worse, punches. "I'm thinking he may come around when he realises she's not going anywhere."

"I think you need to spell it out to him," Jett said dryly as the team began to exit the showers. "Drill it home."

"I know."

On the bus home, we discussed the defeat in detail. Jamie, despite being a hothead, was a good captain for the defence, and he wasn't shy about telling people where they failed. He also was honest enough to admit his own bad choices during the game. When the defence had been stripped down and analysed, we moved onto the offence. By the time Jett was finished with Kowoski, I felt bad for him. However, as much as Jett liked to forget, the offence was not purely the quarterback. I picked up on the breakdown of the rest of the offence when Jett finally took a breath. Coach listened to us throughout, he always had. He would hear what the players thought they did wrong, and then on Monday, he would smash our beliefs to pieces as he told the team what they actually did wrong.

When we finally reached the stadium, I was glad to be off the bus, and the nine of us who lived in the football house headed home in silence.

"How's the hand?" Jamie asked as we approached the front door to the house.

"I'm still out for the regular season," I told him.

I heard six despondent sighs and held back my own. "Pity," Jamie said as he unlocked the door.

As one, we walked to the kitchen, and I grinned when I saw the breakfast bar filled with food. Jett walked over and picked the note up.

"Sorry for the loss, you're still the best. Fridge is full, eat up!" He grinned at us all. "Quinn and Ava."

"Your girls are too kind," Ben said eagerly as he walked towards the food. "It's still cold, they must have just left."

And just like that, their spirits were lifted. Ben called some of the other guys, and then they were all eating and drinking together.

Pulling my phone out, I texted Quinn.

Me: **This is really appreciated, it's exactly what the team needs.**

Quinn: **Don't tell them it's all healthy**

Me: **See you at yours later?**

Quinn: **Where else would you be?**

She sent the wink emoji, and I grinned as I shoved my phone in my back pocket.

As I reached for a chicken wrap, I saw Jett put his phone away also as more of the team arrived to share the food.

"It must have taken them a while," Ash said as he ate some chips.

"It's needed," Jett said quietly. "Look at the difference, one defeat and we were ready to roll over."

"Good thing you converted the little lion," Ash said as he nudged Jett with his shoulder.

I said nothing as I ate my wrap. This was Quinn, I knew it, and yeah, she may have had Ava's help, but as I looked over the food, I saw all the things in the food plans, and I said nothing as my teammates ate the healthy food with no complaints. She was so perfectly amazing.

"You guys ditching me?" Ash asked with a groan.

"No," I answered quickly. "I'm going to kick your ass at Madden."

"Yeah," Jett laughed as he flicked Ash's ear. "Teach you how to actually catch the ball."

When the food was gone, and Ash beat me at Madden, I headed upstairs to shower and change. Jett wasn't far behind me on the stairs, and we shared a grin before we went into our rooms to get ready to go meet our girls.

As I was heading back down the stairs, I heard the hollering and cheers from the team and saw Ava blushing furiously under the attention before she curtsied and reminded them all that Quinn deserved the credit.

Passing her, I gave her a smile, and she hesitated before she returned it.

"She's okay," she said to my back.

Glancing back at her, I nodded. "I know. Thanks for helping, last night and today."

"Anytime," Ava said easily, and the tone of her voice made *me* hesitate, and I turned back to her.

"This doesn't make us friends."

"Wouldn't dream of it," she said with a grin.

"We didn't bond."

"Absolutely agree." Her smile was wider.

I closed my eyes in despair. "You're going to make this a thing, aren't you?"

"Definitely."

"And if I ignore it?"

"You can't ignore my awesomeness."

"Your *awesomeness*?"

"You know you like me," she teased. "I grow on you."

"So does fungus."

"And you're a fun guy," she quipped back.

I groaned at her terrible humour. "I'm leaving, this isn't a thing, Ava, we're not friends."

"Night, buddy, I miss you already!"

I couldn't help but grin as I left the house and made my way to Quinn's. She opened the door, and I was finally at ease as I wrapped my arms around her.

"You smell good," I mumbled into her neck as I walked her backwards into the living room.

"You eat?" Quinn asked as she held me close.

"Hmm." My lips moved down her neck along her collarbone as I pushed her shirt down. "You?"

"Yeah, Ava and I had Thai."

Drawing back, I looked at her. "I got healthy and wholesome, and you had take-out?"

"My body isn't a temple," Quinn murmured as she brushed her lips against mine.

"Really?" I ran my eyes over her. "I worship here." My hands cupped her ass, and I grinned. "I need five minutes of this, then you can tell me about last night," I said as I eased her down onto the couch.

"Talk first, sex later?" Quinn's grin was wide, and I rolled my eyes at her.

"Do you know Ash had to talk me out of coming home last

night?" I asked as I raised onto my elbows over her. "Then Jett. So yes, talk first."

Quinn had lost her playfulness as she reached up and brushed my hair back from my forehead. "You were really coming back?"

"Yeah." I dropped my head to her shoulder. "I probably overreacted. I know. But Jett told me I was being an ass. You had it handled, and then we spoke later, and I knew you were okay."

"You can't make impulsive decisions, your career is more important," Quinn admonished me. "Actually, we need to talk."

"We are talking," I said against her throat.

"Serious talk."

"No." I traced the tip of my tongue slowly up her neck to her jaw and smiled when I heard her light moan. "I changed my mind, this first."

"Gray..."

"Shh." I kissed her before she could say anything else. Talking was overrated.

As I slammed my brother's head off the wall, I narrowly missed the punch he threw to my face, but I didn't miss the vicious stab to my kidneys. Onyx shoved me backwards as he straightened.

"I will kick your ass. Back the fuck off," he warned as he rubbed his jaw. "You hit me with the splint? You're a fucking savage."

"You offered to *pay* her?" When Quinn told me last night, I had exploded, and I had left her this morning to make it to Nashville with the sole intent of kicking my brother's ass.

"It was a test," he said as he walked to the coffee maker in the corner of his office. "She failed."

"She didn't accept," I said in confusion as I pulled my shirt up to look at my side.

"No."

"Then how did she fail?"

"She should have taken the money. People tell me she's intelligent." He made a coffee for himself and then one for me. "You have got to stop hitting me with that fucking cast."

"I will when you stop messing with my girlfriend."

"Ugh, it makes my skin crawl when you call her that."

"I don't care," I barked at him as I sat down. "And the shit with the scouts, that was low."

"I didn't lie. I have one interested," he said and gave me a smug smirk when I faltered.

"You're so full of shit." I took a drink of the coffee he had made me. "How much will it cost for Friday?"

"For the janitor?" He saw my nod. "He comes on Monday, I'm giving him one hundred."

"I wish I could be here," I muttered as I glared at the wall.

"Paying off one assault is enough, no?" Onyx said dryly.

Looking around his office, I took in the creams and browns and shuddered. "Who redecorated your office?"

"The Bitch sent in a contractor when I was overseas for two days."

"When were you overseas?" I asked him in surprise. "Angel did this?"

"She's a swear word that starts with a C." Onyx's smile was tight.

"Is the office bugged?" I asked him with a laugh.

"It was. Bitch."

"Maybe you should just bang her and get it over with?"

"More like bang her with a gun in my hand," he snorted as I laughed.

Watching him, I placed my cup down. "You need to lay off Quinn. She's not going anywhere."

"And Ash?"

"Also going nowhere."

"He loves her too."

"No. He loved her. Once. Even then, I have my doubts. He cares for her, and that I don't deny."

Onyx threw his head back and laughed. "Of course you have your doubts, you're blinded by her."

"Believe what you want. I don't need to justify myself to you about Quinn. Tell me what else you found out from the mutual acquaintance we had."

"I got three names." Onyx held his hand up to stop me. "I'm not telling you them, but I can tell you I'm looking into it." He opened a drawer and handed me a file. "As is dad and our uncle," he told me. "Third photo."

I looked at the image of the guy with broad shoulders, buzz cut hair and angled away from the camera. "Who's this?"

"Well, that's the million-dollar question, but from what I can guess, I believe George Lawrence may have recruited his own help."

"Navy?" I asked in surprise.

"Ex SEALs, I would say, but yeah, there are too many players on my board."

Closing the file, I let out a frustrated sigh. "What do we do?"

"*We* do nothing. You? You heal your hand and leave this to the adults."

"So what are you going to do while that's happening?" I snarked at him.

Onyx smirked at my dig. "What I do best. I'm feeling like it's time for some mayhem, my style."

Ah fuck, I was afraid of that.

CHAPTER 32

Quinn

I SAT IN JETT'S BEDROOM ON THE COUCH WITH GRAY BESIDE ME, HIS hand held tightly in mine, and I was grateful for it.

"Okay, so I've edited the fuck out of this. There's nothing that you can see that will cause you distress. We just need you to look at the guys, see if you know them, recognise them?" Ash told me. His voice was low and steady, his look of concern trying to calm me down. I nodded when in reality I wanted to run for the door. The team had a bye week, and this is how they chose to spend their Saturday. I loved how much that they cared, to give up their Saturday on this, but at the same time, a part of me would have preferred not to be here.

Which Gray knew, which is why he was holding onto me, and Jett was perched on the arm of the couch to my side, close but not touching, offering support. I knew I was being chicken, but I really didn't want to look at the laptop Ash was balancing on his knee.

The video played, and I forced myself to watch. I didn't see the table or the girls, and there was no sound, but as I watched, I leaned in closer, trying to identify the men even though their faces were covered.

"Why are their faces covered?" I asked in the silence of the room.

"We don't know," Jett told me.

"We think they may sell the film," Gray spoke up as his fingers flexed against mine.

"Jesus," I breathed out as I kept watching. I tensed slightly as I looked at the larger guy on the screen.

"Who is it?" Ash asked me quietly.

"I think"—I bit my lip—"it could be Dr Campbell." I squinted as

I leaned forward. "The way he stands makes me think it may be him."

"What did he do?" Jett asked as he reached for a pad of paper.

"Well, Mrs Mowberry gave me the leaflet, and it was Dr Campbell I met first. Then, when I was talking to him, Dr Newton came in, and he was the one with the binder."

"Binder?" Ash asked us all.

"With the prospective parents," I told him.

"Pictures?"

"No, they were anonymous." I looked at Gray. "I think he could be Dr Campbell."

Gray raised my hand to his mouth and skimmed his lips across my knuckles. "That's good. Mrs Mowberry? Describe her."

I did and Jett took notes, asking me to remember details I wasn't sure I was remembering or making up. "I don't know," I told him in frustration. "It was a long time ago, and I have spent eighteen months trying to forget."

"I know, sorry." He patted my shoulder and looked past me to look at Gray.

"You don't need to look at Gray," I snapped, and I pushed myself to my feet. "He can't coax it out of me. I'm not holding back, I am doing my best to help you, but forgive me if I didn't notice if her hair was coloured or not!"

"You're a girl," Ash began and flinched at the anger of my stare. "You would notice, you just might not realise it."

"She was in her fifties, late forties maybe." I sucked at guessing ages. "Her hair was dark, and it was, I dunno, mousy."

"What the hell is mousy?" Jett grumbled as he checked his notes.

"Brown," Gray and I spoke at the same time.

I frowned as I thought about it. "It was dull."

Jett looked up at me in confusion. "Huh?"

"It was dull, like it was tired." Screwing my eyes shut, I tried to conjure the image of Mrs Mowberry in my head. "It could have been coloured; natural hair isn't that dull unless it's not cared for, and it was curled, so it was cared for."

Opening my eyes, I saw Ash's smug look to Gray, and I almost kicked him in the shin. "Don't look so fucking smug," I muttered as I resumed my seat, and Gray pulled me into his side with a kiss to my temple.

"Okay, so can we do Dr Campbell?" Jett asked as he scribbled in his notepad. "Describe him." He was completely oblivious to the fact Ash was snickering at his "do Dr Campbell" terminology.

As I ran through what I remembered about the other doctor I had met, I felt the familiar sadness rise from within, and when I finished my interrogation from my friends, my head was on Gray's shoulders, and my eyes were strained from trying to hold the tears back.

"You okay?" Gray asked me softly as Ash took the laptop to the desk, muttering about angles, and Jett followed him with his note-book like a reporter on the tail of a juicy story.

"No," I whispered back. "I don't like this," I admitted as I turned my face into his shoulder.

"I know. You're doing so well." I felt his lips press to my fore-head, and I shifted in the seat to wrap my arm around his torso more.

Ash looked over his shoulder at us, and I saw the frown he failed to hide as he looked at me curled into Gray. "I want to try this," he told me, and I didn't react to the fact his voice was slightly harder. "Then we need to go for a site visit." He turned back to the laptop, and I tilted my head to look up at Gray.

"He seems to be enjoying himself," I murmured quietly.

"He likes a project, you know this."

"I don't like being the project," I replied testily.

"It'll be over soon," Gray said as his nose brushed against mine.

"Will it?"

"I promise."

We sat wrapped in each other while Jett and Ash talked between themselves, and then they were coming back to us. I straightened but Gray didn't loosen his hold, and I welcomed the support as Ash showed the edited films from another angle. I had no idea how he did it, but he did.

"Him." I pointed at the screen. "I didn't see it before, but he has a scar."

Gray lurched forward and studied the guy Ash had paused on. "Down the left-hand side?"

Nodding, I waited for him to continue, but Gray had twisted to look at Jett. "From the basement."

"Okay," Jett said thoughtfully as he looked through his notepad. "I have his description." With a nod to himself as he gathered his evidence, he finally looked at Ash. "Need you to hack," he said matter-of-factly.

"Databases?" Ash asked with a groan.

"Yeah. Can you do it?"

"Yeah, Onyx taught me years ago, but he's better." Ash rubbed the back of his neck. "And I need you out of here in case I fuck up."

"But you'll need Quinn," Gray interjected. "To identify them."

"Searches aren't like the movies, they take days. I've got three people to look for on really basic descriptions." His eyes flicked to mine. "No offence."

"None taken," I told him.

"You'll need to run the search from a different IP address," Jett said as he began to pace.

"We can put it in the basement of Onyx's building." All three of them looked at me in surprise. "Seriously, like he doesn't have a blocker or something to cover his shit," I snorted in derision.

Ash grinned and Jett chuckled. "But if he doesn't have a blocker and the laptop is found, our brother goes to jail," Gray said softly.

The other two sobered, and I kept my opinion about jail being the best place for Onyx to myself. Gray knew my thoughts though, as I flinched from the sharp pinch to my side.

"Sorry," I mumbled as he arched an eyebrow at me.

"I can redirect the redirect," Ash said as he looked at the laptop. "It won't slow someone who really knows what they're doing down, but it will deter run-of-the-mill hackers. And to be fair, you're only going to come across it if you're looking for it."

As they discussed the logistics and pros and cons more, my head slipped back onto Gray's shoulder. He moved his arm automatically to let me under, and I snuggled in. As I drifted in and out of their conversation about their plans, I tried to think back to the day I went to their offices. Mrs Mowberry had met me in the reception area. I thought about the receptionist, and I frowned. I had been so nervous I hadn't really paid attention. She was blonde, I think. Young. I remembered thinking the colour of her dark suit made her pale skin seem washed out.

Mrs Mowberry had taken me to Dr Campbell's room, and he had told me about their agency. About the hope they were able to bring to parentless couples. How I was making someone's dream to be a parent real.

Sitting up, I wiped my eyes as I thought of the lies they had told me, how I had felt slightly appeased that even though I was doing this, someone would benefit. My child would be raised by a family who loved and wanted them.

Unlike me at the time.

Standing up, I heard the lull in the conversation as I walked to the bathroom before Jett started to talk again.

After rinsing my face in the sink, I stood with my head buried in the hand towel until I pushed the tears back and reminded myself, I had thought it was my only choice. The only choice that was right for me and my child.

A gasp escaped me as I said the phrase again. My child.

I felt him close to me before he spoke to me. As he tugged the towel gently out of my hands, I blindly went into his strong embrace as Gray held me and asked me if I was okay. I nodded once, but I didn't want to talk, and I knew he understood as he held me tighter.

I don't know how long he held me for, but eventually a light tap on the door caused me to raise my head from Gray's shoulder.

"You ready for a field trip?" Jett asked me as he looked me over with concern.

"I guess."

Two hours later, we were cruising down the streets of Nashville as Ash drove us past all the tourist spots into the business district. I directed him past it, and then we were on side streets, still very prominent with business occupation but not as high spec as the others.

"There." I pointed to the two-story building. I saw Jett grit his teeth as he looked at the boarded-up windows and the mail choking up the letterbox.

"You sure?" Gray asked me as he peered through the car window to the surrounding occupants.

"Positive." I leaned forward. "I remember the blue trim. They looked weird then and worse now."

Ash grunted his agreement. "Who's going?" he asked as he looked at Jett then Gray.

"I'll go," I said, surprising them all. "You may be recognised. No one noticed me last time when I needed help; they won't notice me now." Hearing my own bitterness and being mad at letting my emotions show, I slipped off the seat belt and then was getting out of the SUV.

"Quinn." Gray grabbed my hand. "I'm right here."

Forcing a smile, I nodded. "I know."

My feet felt like lead as I walked to the front of the building, and I kept my head down when I saw the camera. I knew the building may be abandoned, but I would bet the cameras were still active.

At the door, I reached out to grab some of the mail, checking the dates on some of the fliers. Some were dated a few months ago. Looking around, I kept my back to the surveillance before I picked the building on the left to make my enquiries. A laundrette. Had that been there when I was here last time? I had no idea. I'd had tunnel vision then, and it was taking a lot of willpower now to walk through the door of the building.

There were no customers and no staff. A machine on the wall dispensed quarters, and I noted that a few of the newer machines had card payments. I'd not known that was a thing, but in this day and age, who used money anymore?

Leaving the laundrette, I went to the other business on the other side of the abandoned agency. Lawyers office. Closed.

With a sigh, I turned back to the car where the guys were waiting for me. My feet turned me away, and I walked slowly towards the parking area I had parked in all those months ago. Hesitating at a turn, I took it, and then within a few feet, I was standing at the top of the stairs I had fallen down.

I almost expected there to be some mark or acknowledgement from the hard concrete to note my loss. With slow measured steps, I went down the stairs, and then turning, I looked up them.

They were steep and narrow, the handrail a thin wooden strip that I would never have noticed had I not been looking for it now. I never had a chance to even catch myself, I realised as I looked at the ground at my feet.

The sound of the car pulling up behind me alerted me to the fact that they were here. That *he* was here. Turning, I saw him coming towards me, his hood up and his bandana over his face. He looked intimidating, but I saw the pain in his eyes as he reached for me and folded me into his embrace. Gray bent his knees slightly, and then I was wrapped around him as he carried me back to the car, and I let my silent tears fall.

No one said anything as he placed me gently onto the back seat and closed the door behind me. Moments later, he was on the other side, pulling me tenderly onto his lap, and wordlessly I curled onto him and silently took the comfort he offered so freely.

I knew we were heading back to school, but no one spoke for the entire drive as I stayed wrapped around the man who was slowly piecing the broken parts of me back together.

Helping me.

Healing me.

"I love you so much," I whispered into his neck, and I felt his arms tighten around me in answer. "I'm so sorry."

Pulling back from him, I looked into those blue eyes that saw past all my bullshit. Cupping his face with my hand, I dropped a kiss to his lips.

It wasn't enough, I wanted more. My teeth nipped his lower lip, and he opened for me. My tongue stroked his, and I felt his hand grip my jacket as he kissed me back.

Gray knew my need, but he also had the sense to be more aware of our surroundings, and he finally drew back, his eyes holding a promise that he would finish this later.

A surge of guilt swept over me, and I grimaced when I thought of Ash in the front of the car.

Tucking my head back into the crook of Gray's neck, I pressed my lips to his pulse and smiled when I felt him thicken underneath me.

"You okay?" Jett asked me quietly.

"No, I'm not," I said, refusing to move from the comfort of Gray. "But I will be."

"Yes, you will," Ash spoke up, his tone low, and I knew Gray was as surprised as me. "You're so much fucking stronger than you think, Quinn. Why do you think you've always been the queen?"

Turning, I met his stare in the rearview mirror. "You really think that?"

"Never thought, always knew it," he answered as he flicked his gaze off the road and met my wide-eyed stare once more. "We'll get them, Queeny, I promise."

Jett murmured his agreement, and I turned back to look at Gray.

"And then what?"

"We end them." Gray's look was hard, and I felt fear tingling at my spine as I looked back at him.

"For me?"

"No. For us." He looked over my shoulder to his brother and his cousin before he looked back at me. "For all of them."

CHAPTER 33

Gray

Laying her gently on the bed, I pulled a blanket over her and backed slowly out of her room, closing the door softly behind me. My head rested on it for a moment before I turned to Ash and Jett, both standing in the middle of the room, waiting.

"She's asleep." It was a redundant thing to say, they knew that. She'd fallen asleep on my lap on the way home, and I hadn't wanted to wake her to go into her house. I may have my hand in a splint, but I could still carry my girl.

"What now?" Ash asked as he rocked back on his feet, his hands in his back pockets.

"It's a Saturday night," Jett spoke up. "Getting drunk and fucking shit up sounds like a good idea."

"Mayhem?" Ash perked up and grinned when I pulled my bandana from my neck.

"Well, I'm dressed for it." I looked back at the closed door. "I don't want to leave her though."

"We don't need you for mayhem," Jett said quickly. "Ava's gone to see her mom in Knoxville. She isn't back until the morning." He nudged Ash with his shoulder. "Let's go cause some trouble."

I felt torn. I wanted to go—I could do with a good fight—but my hand hindered me, and as I glanced at the door again, the idea of leaving Quinn to wake up and me not be with her, didn't feel right.

"You are so wifed up," Ash mocked me as he shook his head in disgust.

Jett snorted as he made his way to the bathroom. "Gotta piss, be back in a minute."

Which left me and Ash and no Jett as buffer. "Wifed up?"

"You may as well get down on one knee and get it over with.

Put us all out of our misery." He turned to look at the framed pictures Quinn had, and I knew it was now or never.

"I don't expect you to be okay with this, but you've been over for almost two years. You still telling me that the heartache is there?"

"You never touched her before we broke up?"

"I never touched her when she was your girlfriend." I was making sure he got the distinction. "What I did and didn't do before and after isn't your concern."

His teeth tugged at his bottom lip as he stared at the wall. "Fuck, that's cold."

"Not cold. Honest."

Ash smirked and looked at me. "Honest? Aren't you about two years too late for that?"

"I've never lied to you."

"But you were never very truthful either."

"If you had asked me, I would like to think I would have been straight with you."

"*If* I'd asked you?" Ash's eyes were wide. "On what fucking planet would I even think that this was a thing?"

I shrugged. This was pointless. "This solves nothing. Changes nothing."

"What if it helps *me* understand?" he challenged me, and I tilted my head back to look at the ceiling briefly.

"Okay, you're right. Ask me."

"When did you have sex with her?"

"After you broke up."

"How long after we broke up? The next day, the next week, the next month? When?"

"The same day." I saw his reaction, and I braced myself for his rage.

"Are you shitting me? The same day? The same *fucking* day?"

I nodded. I wasn't ashamed. Okay, I felt guilty, but I wasn't ashamed, and more importantly, I didn't regret it.

"When?"

"Does it matter?"

"Yes! I think it fucking matters, don't you?"

"No. You broke up. I had sex with her. Then I had sex with her again, and then I spent the night with her, then she was pregnant, she miscarried our baby, and now here we are. Nothing for you has changed, Ash."

"You're un-fucking-believable."

"Why, cousin?" My own temper was building. "Tell me why. Because once she and you were over, she never looked back? She never tried for a second chance with you, she didn't regret breaking up, and what you're failing to recognise in your outrage is neither did you. Quinn walked away from you that day, and you were fucking Carlie that night." I shook my head. "Why is that any different?"

"Because Carlie isn't my fucking cousin."

I gave a half shrug. "The point is neither of you were cut up about it. You tried it, it wasn't meant to be. You have remained friends. It's more than most people get."

"Remained *friends*?" Ash's eyes were wide. "Have you been paying attention for the last year and a bit?"

"Yes, and I see a guy who's wounded because his ex didn't sob into her cornflakes or try to get him back. Your pride was hurt. You then made sure her feelings were hurt by making sure every single one of your hookups told her that they'd been with you, and you made fucking sure you let them know how they compared to the Queen of Cardinal Saints High School. They rubbed it in her face, and you did that for a reaction, only she never gave you one. All you did, and all she did, was make eighteen months very fucking awkward for everyone else."

"You're a massive dick," Ash said as he shook his head at me. "A really fucking massive dick."

He barged past me and out her front door, and I looked to the bathroom door where Jett was standing.

"So, it could have gone better," I hedged.

"Why do you have to be so relentlessly brutal?" he asked me as he came into the room more.

"He needed to hear it."

"And you've been dying to tell him since they split up."

"No, I'm not a dick. But he did need to be reminded that neither of them was fighting to get back together."

"Gray, I..."

"I know," I said as I gestured to the front door. "Go. Fuck shit up with him. When he calms down, tell him what I said was true."

"Well, I don't agree with everything you said," Jett muttered as he passed me.

"Okay. Well, bond with him over that. Just don't let him do anything stupid."

Jett grunted as he closed the door behind him, and I stood in her living room alone. With a sigh, I went to the bathroom and opened the cabinet. The blue toothbrush stared back at me beside her purple one. With a grin, I reached for her toothbrush. It made no fucking sense to me why I could put her pussy in my mouth but not her toothbrush.

After I rinsed, I went back to the main room, and then with a sigh, I kicked my boots off and stripped down to my boxers. Making sure the front door was locked, I quietly entered the bedroom and slipped into the bed beside her.

It was ten o'clock on a Saturday night, and it felt right, being in bed with my girl as she slept after a hard day. I was wifed up—the thought made me smile.

"You were harsh," she whispered as she rolled over to face me.

"You heard?"

"Neither of you were exactly quiet," Quinn said as she reached out to trace her fingers over my forehead, pushing my hair back.

"I'm not going to apologise for loving you, ever. He knows me better."

Quinn gave me a sad smile as she leaned towards me and placed a kiss on my lips. "You were wrong, you know," she said quietly.

"Was I?" My hand trailed over her hip. "When?"

"I did react, once."

"Elise?" I guessed. I remembered the fight; I remembered Quinn going absolutely crazy as she fought her.

"Yeah."

"The night of the mix-up?" I was confused, as I had thought that Quinn hadn't cared.

"No, Elise told me she had slept with Ash," Quinn told me. "And then that she slept with you right after. I saw red. The thought of her with you..."

My finger pressed against her lips to stop her words. "I have never slept with Elise, or either of the other two. None of them. They never appealed to me."

"Promise me?"

"Baby, I swear. Yes, I've had sex with other girls—I'm no saint—but them, no."

"I was so jealous," she whispered as she moved closer to me. "The thought of you and her, ugh!"

"Seriously, you never need to have that thought, I haven't. Christ, even Jett's only been there once."

"Once is too many."

I nodded in agreement. "You okay?"

Quinn rolled onto her back. "Yeah, I'm sad for him. You were blunt and unkind."

"I was honest."

"And he was really amazing in the car, and now you've ruined it."

"No, I haven't. He's mad at me, not you." I pulled her back to facing me. "However, you are awake, and you started something in the car, and I don't mind finishing it, if you want?"

Quinn chuckled as she raised herself up on her elbow to look at me. "That your moves?"

"I'm all wifed up," I quipped back, using Ash's term with a grin. "This is what couples do; I say gimme some, you say you have a headache, you slept that off, and I'm still at gimme some."

Quinn laughed out loud. "That is *not* how it works!" She slapped my arm as she laughed again.

Quickly I had her on her back as I pressed my knee in between her thighs, spreading her open. "Tell me how it works," I said as I kissed her neck and moved over her jawline to her mouth. My lips hovered over hers, and my tongue traced her bottom lip softly. "I'm willing to learn." Her hand slipping inside my boxers made me arch an eyebrow at her. "Or we could just get right to it?" I teased.

As her hand started to move with sure confident strokes, I watched her, seeing her pupils dilate in pleasure.

"I want something, and I'll understand if you aren't willing to give it to me." Her hand hesitated, and my hips moving forward encouraged her to keep going.

"Tell me."

"Don't freak out."

"If it's a threesome, it's a no, I refuse to share."

I grinned as she rolled her eyes. "No. Idiot."

"Okay, good." I rolled my hips again to remind her she had a task very much in hand.

"If you freak out, I'll understand," she continued.

"Just tell me, I need to be doing other things than talking," I groaned as she picked up the pace. "Also, so you know, this is an excellent distraction technique. I approve."

Quinn winked at me before she licked her lips nervously. "I want..." She looked away, and I balanced on my elbow to move her head back to facing me. "I want you to come inside me."

I frowned and I saw her reaction. "I usually do that," I said slowly.

"Bare."

I know my eyes widened as I looked at her. "Quinn?"

"I don't know what's wrong with me," she confessed as she closed her eyes so she could say the words. "I think I have a kink or something, but the idea of anything between us, I hate it. I want to feel you."

Surely, she knew I wasn't opposed to this suggestion—my dick was harder than a rock. "But what if it fails, like last time?"

"I was on the pill, then I had a course of antibiotics the week before for an ear infection, and I didn't know they could affect the reliability of the pill."

"And the shot? Does it have weaknesses?" I asked her gently as her hand slowed down.

"Some, I mean nothing is completely one hundred percent, unless you just aren't having sex, I suppose." Quinn looked up at me. "Are you freaked out?"

"No, if you want that, then I'm completely okay with it. I hate the idea of having something between us as much as you seem to," I told her truthfully.

"But what if it happens again?" she asked me, and I saw the residual fear lingering.

"Then we handle it, better than last time." I kissed her slowly. "And I mean both of us. But also this time, we know if you're sick, then we wrap up."

Reaching up, she pulled my lips down to hers and kissed me. Everything she had ever held back was in that kiss. It blew my mind, and I felt myself falling even deeper in love with her. When we pulled apart, her hand was still circling my dick, and her legs were drawn up either side of me.

"I love you," Quinn whispered as she looked up at me. "You know that, don't you?"

"I do."

"Good, now give me what I want."

WALKING INTO THE FOOTBALL HOUSE, I SAID HI TO A FEW OF MY teammates before I made my way upstairs. Rapping against my brother's door, I waited before I tried the handle. His room was empty.

Feeling slightly hesitant, I then knocked on Ash's door. I heard a murmur, and not thinking, I opened the door…to see a girl with long red hair riding his dick as he held onto her ass, his head thrown back in pleasure, his eyes screwed shut.

"Mia?" I couldn't look away even if I wanted to. It was like a bad car crash that held me transfixed.

"Holy moly!" Mia cried as she looked at me in shock before she grabbed the sheet to cover herself.

"What the fuck?" I demanded as I stared at them. And then to my utmost horror, my cousin climaxed in front of me, and Mia's head rolled back as she groaned as Ash pulled her firmly down onto his dick.

Turning my back to them, I knew I would need to bleach my brain and cut off my ears so I never heard or saw that again.

"Fuck, you know how to work that pussy," Ash said, and then I heard a curse. "Gray? What the *fuck*?"

I heard a lot of commotion and grunts and then a firm grip on my shoulder as Ash spun me and glared at me.

"Why the fuck are you fucking *watching* me?" he demanded incredulously.

"Why the fuck are you fucking the best friend?" I exclaimed. "Man, Jett and I both told you not to hit that."

"I can't fuck her, but you can fuck Quinn?"

"What are you even saying right now?" I asked him in astonishment. "It's not even remotely the same thing. And, dude, fucking cover it up!"

"You don't want to see my dick, don't watch me having sex!"

"I wasn't *watching* you. Jesus, that sounds fucking sordid."

We both turned when the bathroom door closed and locked, and Ash turned back to look at me. "Well, thanks for that," he sneered.

My mind was blown. "What are you doing?" I asked him quietly.

"I was enjoying Sunday afternoon, but yet again you fucked up my life."

"Oh quit being a little bitch," I muttered as I pulled out my phone. "And seriously cover your junk up."

Me: **Did you know Ash was screwing the best friend?**

Jett: **Tell me you're joking**

Me: **I literally just walked in as he came**

Jett: **That's nasty, why do I need to know that!?**

Me: **You're my twin—we're supposed to share. Get your ass here, I can't deal with this alone**

Jett: **Fine**

When I looked up, Ash was pulling on his jeans and glaring at me.

"What?" I demanded.

"It's not a big deal."

"It's a huge fucking deal, and you know it. You knew it, and you tapped it anyway."

He flipped me off as he sat back on his bed. I stared at him, and he looked back.

"Are you serious?" I asked him.

"What?"

"She's still in your fucking bathroom," I hissed at him.

He looked over his shoulder and then peered over the side of the bed, coming back up with a top and a bra. "Huh, she's like Ava."

"What?" I had to be in some form of fucking parallel universe, because this was the weirdest shit that'd ever happened to me.

"Naked? In the bathroom?" He looked over at me and rolled his eyes. "Never mind. Fuck off so she can go. I guess you told Jett." When I nodded, he sighed in frustration. "Fine, I'll get rid of her, then you can both chew my ass out."

"Shut the fuck up. I just saw too fucking much already, I don't need your ass added into it." Turning, I headed to my room and paced the floor as I waited.

I heard a murmur, then a crash, and bracing myself, I opened the door. Mia was running down the stairs, and Ash was holding his cheek.

"She hit you?" I asked him curiously.

"Threw a cup at me."

"Savage." I grinned.

"Shut up."

Jett arrived about ten minutes later, and the two of us stood, waiting for Ash to explain himself.

"I have no idea why you're both so hung up on this," he muttered. "She's just a hookup."

"She's Ava's *best friend,*" Jett stressed.

"So?"

"I might hit him," Jett said as he turned to me.

"Ash, this is not cool." I saw him shut down, and I knew no matter what I said, he wasn't listening. So I changed tactics. "Was this the only time?"

Ash shrugged, and I exchanged a look with Jett. "How long?" Jett asked.

"Long? It's just sex."

"With my girlfriend's *best* friend," Jett reminded him.

"It's casual sex. It's nothing. We're in college for fuck's sake."

"If it was nothing, you brainless dick, she wouldn't have thrown a fucking cup at you," I growled.

"What do you want?" Ash demanded. "For me not to have sex with her again? Fine. You happy?"

I was very close to losing my shit. So was Jett. They had the cheek to say *I* self-destructed.

"Look, you stupid little—"

The door swung open, and we turned as one.

Quinn stood in the door, fear in her eyes. "They've come looking for me."

EPILOGUE

Mia

I RAN THE WHOLE WAY HOME. I HAD NEVER BEEN SO HUMILIATED IN my life! Not only was I not supposed to hook up with the sex god that was the Saints tight end, but I also wasn't supposed to get caught while riding him like the stud he was.

Getting to the apartment, I hastily wiped my face and entered, hoping Ava was in her room, screwing her boyfriend and thinking I couldn't hear her through our paper-thin walls.

But today was not my day. She was in the kitchen, singing. Badly.

"Hey," she greeted with a quick look up from what she was doing, and then she looked again. "Are those last night's clothes?"

"Yeah." I started to walk past her, but she moved from behind the counter and caught my arm.

"What is it?" Her look of concern as she checked me over almost made me cry. "Are you hurt? Did someone hurt you?"

Yes. The freaking cousin of your boyfriend. "No. I'm okay. Late night, ya know."

I headed to my room, cursing her dogged persistence as she followed me.

"Mee, talk to me," she said from behind me.

"What do you want me to say? I was out all night, mom, getting a lot of dick, and now I'm tired."

"Mia." Ava's eyes were wide as she looked at me. "You said *dick*."

Her overexaggeration to my using a curse word made me chuckle, and then I was laughing harder. "If I tell you, please don't make this worse."

"Oh fuck...you slept with Ben."

"Ben? Who in darnation is Ben?"

"The backup quarterback. You had him in your Mia Target at Halloween."

"I have a Mia Target?" I asked her. I wasn't sure if I was insulted or not.

"Mia, can we focus?"

"I spent the night with Ash."

Ava's mouth dropped open, and her eyes squeezed shut. "Duu-uude...*awkward*!"

"Yes, I know, apparently it's the worst decision ever."

"Why? Is he bad? In bed?" Ava asked curiously.

"No, he's amazing." I shook my head to clear it. "But it's not good when his cousin walked in just as I, you know, and then he... well, you know."

"You came in front of Gray?" Ava burst out laughing and quickly covered her mouth. "Mee!"

"Shut up." I threw myself on my bed. "And then when I locked myself in his bathroom, naked, I heard them discussing me like I was a common whore."

"I'm getting bad deja vu."

"Don't worry. It's not lost on me how freakishly similar this is to your start with the Devils."

"This sucks."

"Ya think?" I stared at my ceiling. "It's going to be awkward, isn't it? I mean, I'm pretty sure Gray saw my hoo-ha so..."

Ava snorted as she giggled uncontrollably. "MeeMoo, you complete idiot. I thought you knew not to hook up with Ash." Ava slapped my legs. "And he's Quinn's ex. Ugh, it's so many levels of awkward."

We both jumped when the front door was knocked. Ava went to answer it, and being nosy, I went to see who it was.

Jett was in the kitchen, speaking softly to Ava, who was white as a sheet.

"What's going on?" I asked, coming forward.

"We've got an issue."

"Look, I'm sorry I messed up. It won't happen again." It was hardly World War Three. So I had sex with the cousin—seriously, who hadn't?

"I know you don't know everything, and I really can't tell you much, but Ava's coming to stay in the house with me."

"Why?" I hardly saw her as it was. This was terrible.

"And Quinn's going to be there too, with Gray."

"What? Why? What's going on?"

"I really can't tell you. You need to speak to Quinn." Jett looked at me with a smirk, and I knew exactly what he was thinking, like *that* wouldn't be awkward after this afternoon.

"But Mia will be alone," Ava said to him as she turned to look at him. "She can't be alone."

"She isn't involved," Jett spoke quietly to her. "She'll be fine."

"You don't know that…no one does. *I'm* not really involved and you're taking *me*." Ava shook her head. "I'm not going without her."

"Yes. You are." Jett's look hardened, and I watched Ava settle into her stubborn streak and stepped in before there really was war.

"It's fine. I have no idea what's happening. I'll be fine."

"Or..." Ava turned to me, and her grin was impish. "I know how to fix it." She glanced at Jett, and he grinned in return.

"Why am I scared?" I asked them both.

"It would work," Ava said to him, and he nodded.

"Totally would work," he agreed.

"What would work?" I asked them both.

"He'll need persuading." Ava looked at Jett. "Can you do it?"

"Easy. I'll get Gray to do it." Jett's grin was wicked as he looked at me.

"Tell who? Seriously, tell *me*."

"Ash could move in here," Ava said with a gleam in her eye. Jett started laughing as I looked between the two of them with mounting dread.

I shook my head as I backed away from them. Were they crazy? “Absolutely not. No. Not happening. I mean it!” Why were they laughing, why weren’t they taking me seriously? They absolutely could not do this to me.

Could they?

From the Author

Hello! Thank you so much for reading this book and I have to say, I loved this one so much.

Gray and Quinn were woven so tightly together, I felt every emotion of this book. They deserved their second chance, they've been through so much and the way their story unfolded was exactly how it should have been. Yes, Gray may never be your favourite because he is cold and he is brutal, but you cannot deny how much he loves his girl.

There is more to come in Book 3, Ruthless Charm and I am so ready to write it. In fact, I'm diving in right now.

As an author, my hope is always that my readers love my characters as much as I do. The best way to let me know if you did is to leave a review on your favourite retailers site, I do my best to read them all.

Eve x

It may be only me that writes the story (with the aid of the maniacs that live in my head), but it takes so much more than me to present and publish a book.

Firstly, Jay, another fantastic cover, you keep bringing it every time. I really struggled to pick the right image for Gray as you well know, and you were brilliant throughout, thank you.

Speaking of images, Andrey you have the patience of a saint. I don't know how many images from the shoot you held back for me, and then Wander was keeping the best one to himself. Little scamp that he is! But we got there, so thank you for catering to my indecision but helping me find the perfect cover for my book(s).

Thanks to the ladies at the NextStep PR, your help in spreading the word for this book is appreciated. Thanks for the support and the enthusiasm. Colleen, I love your quirkiness and I adore you!

Megan Gatanis, you're a little rockstar and I love how fast you adapted to the 'world of Eve' - I know that I drive you insane with my many many MANY questions, but you always answer and keep me right - even before you've had your coffee most mornings! Now that's dedicated ;) Of course, we won't mention the "aren't you supposed to be writing?" messages you send me...we can't let people know you're actually really bossy under that charming smile. You're a wonderful friend. You are one hundred percent supportive and I'm really glad I have you in my corner so thank you for being you and for all that you've done for me, not only with the release of this series, but everything else. Thank you.

I'd also like to give a huge thank you to Jimmy Gatanis & Nick Wickel; you lovely gents completely stepped up on short notice and explained very quickly, proficiently and simply the intricacies of college football to myself (and Megan) that my brain was just refusing to accept. You both turned my pages and pages of confusing research into bitesized chunks of understanding. Guys seriously, thanks so much for your help (inserts heart emoji). And all the follow up messages of "Ask Jimmy/Nick if..."

And just so you know...my Panthers will beat your teams this season #justsaying A girl can dream...can't she fellas? ;)

To Helayna, thank you for your editing skills.

Ha! I was going to just leave that as it was, but I'm scared you may hunt me down - and tell me in person what a dangling modifier is. I jest (I don't really). You are always the first person to read my full book and I appreciate all your words of encouragement. I don't know how many books we have under our belts together now... I'm going to count them, hang on...nine books (incl this one) and five novellas? Holy crabcakes is that right? Lord above woman, you deserve more than an acknowledgment!! It sounds lame now to say "thanks" - how about... "I could try to recommend a therapist?" You know I love you, we work well together even though after 14 stories, I still don't know where to put a comma, and like to write redundant sentences and still manage to argue with you over Britishisms :) But despite all that, what fun we have! Teamwork makes the dream work. Right? ;)

To my beta readers, Amber, Julie, Katy & Renee - thanks for being on my team and being the awesomeness that you are. I love my girls and I value you all so much. You all have busy lives and the fact that you make me a priority at the drop of a hat is just incredibly overwhelming. I don't deserve you, I can never say thank you enough, but I will keep saying it! Thank you for being my girls x

To the bloggers, reviewers, and bookstagrammers who have supported this launch, thank you so much. I appreciate each and every one of you.

To my readers, thank you always for your support. It means so much to me, and I will never be able to thank you enough.

Mr M, caffeine dealer, hug giver, sanity checker. A few of your many titles and talents. One day, not soon, but one day, I may emerge from the writing cave and make my own coffee. I mean, miracles do happen, don't they? Love you the mostest x

Eve x

About the Author

Eve L. Mitchell is a USA Today Bestselling author who writes contemporary romance and urban fantasy.

Being an avid reader from a young age, Eve still considers herself to be a reader first. She believes there is nothing better than getting that new book either on your e-reader or in your hands, and the fact she may bring that excitement to a fellow reader, fills her with wonder. She writes under a pen name because otherwise her Secret Agent status will be revoked.

Eve lives in the North East of Scotland, with her three coffee machines and her significant other, Mr. M. She enjoys NFL Football, music and having long conversations with the voices in her head, which sometimes turn into the stories she writes.

If you want to keep up to date with all things Eve, to be the first to hear about updates from Eve sign up for her newsletter.

All the books; both fantasy and contemporary:
https://bit.ly/Evesnewsletter
Just contemporary romance book news:
https://bit.ly/Evesromancenewsletter
Just Fantasy books news:
https://bit.ly/Evesfantasynewsletter

Connect with all things Eve: linktr.ee/EveLMitchell

THE BOULDER SERIES

FROM BOOK 1: You'd think the universe would toss me a break after the year I'd had.

I made a plan, one that would give me a fresh start in a new town where no one knew me.
It should have been simple, but nothing is ever as easy as it should be when starting over.
New town, new school, and a new life. It sounded easy enough, or I'd thought it had.

It wasn't.

WWW.EVELMITCHELL.COM

THE DENVER SERIES

FROM BOOK 1: *Be careful what you wish for.* Isn't that what they say? In my defence, what woman *wouldn't* wish for a handsome, intense, and successful man? Aiden is all of these things and more.

He is also a jerk of epic proportions.

He is blunt, closed-off, and secretive. I know there's more to him than just his good looks, but he refuses to open up. So why do I keep going back for more?

THE RUTHLESS DEVILS SERIES

FROM BOOK 1: **She is his enemy. He is her nightmare.**

They say there's a thin line between love and hate, and neither is prepared for the consequences when they cross that line.

Three guys, three girls, one game. Are you ready to meet the Devils?

THE AKRHYN SERIES

Creatures of evil roam the shadows - the Drakhyn. They may look like humans, but their taloned hands and razor-sharp teeth serve one purpose only; killing.
A Sentinel's purpose is to patrol and protect. They are highly trained soldiers with superior skills and abilities. Whether they be Vampyres, Lycan, Castors or gifted Akrhyn, their purpose is the same; hunt the Drakhyn and rid the world of their evil presence.

GET THE SERIES
WWW.EVELMITCHELL.COM

THE WATCHER SERIES

FROM BOOK 1:

One psychic. Six demons. And a whole lot of trouble.

I am a typical, though admittedly anti-social, woman who lives alone in the rural Highlands of Scotland. I also happen to be a clairvoyant who can summon the dead. It's a pity the souls I see didn't give me a heads-up, nor did I glimpse my own future on the night six demons came hunting for me.

GET THE SERIES

WWW.EVELMITCHELL.COM